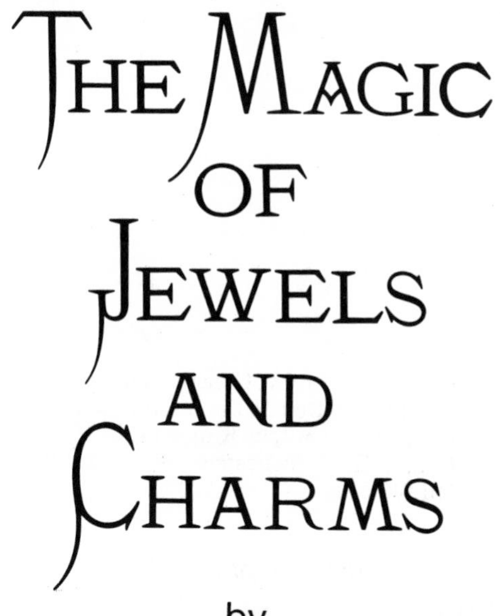

by

George Frederick Kunz

DOVER PUBLICATIONS, INC.

Mineola, New York

Published in Canada by General Publishing Company, Ltd., 30 Lesmill Road, Don Mills, Toronto, Ontario.

Published in the United Kingdom by Constable and Company, Ltd., 3 The Lanchesters, 162–164 Fulham Palace Road, London W6 9ER.

Bibliographical Note

This Dover edition, first published in 1997, is an unabridged reprint of the work originally published by J. B. Lippincott Company, Philadelphia and London, in 1915. Three of the original eight color plates are reproduced herein in black and white; the others are shown in color on the covers of this edition.

Library of Congress Cataloging-in-Publication

Kunz, George Frederick, 1856–1932.

The magic of jewels and charms / George Frederick Kunz.

p. cm.

Originally published: Philadelphia & London : J.B. Lippincott, 1915.

Includes bibliographical references and index.

ISBN 0-486-29671-7 (pbk.)

1. Gems—Folklore. 2. Charms—Folklore. 3. Amulets—Folklore. I. Title.

GR805.K84 1997

398'.365—dc21 97-20117

CIP

Manufactured in the United States of America

Dover Publications, Inc., 31 East 2nd Street, Mineola, N.Y. 11501

To the Memory of

THE LATE

PROFESSOR THOMAS EGLESTON, Ph.D., LL. D.

OFFICIER DE LA LÉGION D'HONNEUR AND FOUNDER OF THE SCHOOL OF MINES, COLUMBIA UNIVERSITY, AN ARDENT LOVER OF MINERALS, KEENLY APPRECIATIVE OF PRECIOUS STONES, AND A KINDLY FRIEND OF THE AUTHOR, THIS VOLUME IS RESPECTFULLY DEDICATED

Preface

JEWELS, gems, stones, superstitions and astrological lore are all so interwoven in history that to treat of either of them alone would mean to break the chain of association linking them one with the other.

Beauty of color or lustre in a stone or some quaint form attracts the eye of the savage, and his choice of material for ornament or adornment is also conditioned by the toughness of some stones as compared with the facility with which others can be chipped or polished.

Whereas a gem might be prized for its beauty by a single individual owner, a stone of curious and suggestive form sometimes claimed the reverence of an entire tribe, since it was thought to be the abode or the chosen instrument of some spirit or genius.

Just as the appeal to higher powers for present help in pressing emergencies preceded the development of a formal religious faith, so this never-failing need of protectors or healers eventually led to the attribution of powers of protection to the spirits of men and women who had led holy lives and about whose history legend had woven a web of pious imaginations at a time when poetic fancy reigned instead of historic record. The writer still holds that true sentiment, the antithesis of superstitious dread, is good for all mankind —sentiment meaning optimism as truly as superstition stands for pessimism—and that even the fancies generated by sentiment are helpful to us and make us happier; and surely happiness often means health, and happiness and health combined aid to evolve that other member of the triumvirate, wealth. Do we not often wish for the union of these three supreme blessings?

At all times and in all periods there have been optimists and pessimists, the former animated by the life-bringing sentiment of hope, and the latter oppressed by the death-dealing sense of fear. Let us always choose a happy medium between a foolish excess of hope and an unreasonable apprehension of future troubles. The world's history and our own experience show us that it is the optimist who has caused the world to progress, and we should trust and believe that the sentiment of hope and faith will always animate humanity.

We know that for centuries it has been believed that amber necklaces protect children from cold. May we not also now add that to pearls the same qualities are attributed? There must be a reason for this. May not this belief be ascribed to the circumstance that in the wearing of either of these gems their virtue consists in the fact that the necklaces do not cover the neck? In other words, they are worn on the bare throat and the opinion prevails that an exposed neck means less liability to cold. For, where the neck is never overheated and then suddenly chilled, a normal temperature being maintained, there should be protection from colds and from the many ills resulting from them. As to pearls, this might serve to illustrate the poetic fancy that these sea-gems are tears by angels shed to bring mortals joy.

Having collected a large mass of material, ethnological, historical and legendary, in the course of personal observations and study, it was decided that the companion volume, the twin sister of "The Curious Lore of Precious Stones," need not treat of gems *alone*.

For courtesies, information and illustrations I am indebted to the following to whom my sincere thanks are due: Prof. T. Wada, of Tokyo, Japan; Dr. G. O. Clerc, President of the Societe Curalienne des Amis des Sciences Naturelles,

Ekaterineburg, Russia; Dr. Charles Braddock, late Medical Inspector to the King of Siam; Sir Charles Hercules Reed, Curator of Archæology, British Museum, London; A. W. Feavearyear, London; Dr. Peter Jessen, Librarian of the Kunstegewerbe Museum of Berlin; Miss Belle DaCosta Green; Dr. Berthold Laufer, Oriental Archæologist, Field Museum of Natural History, Chicago; Dr. Oliver P. Farrington, Field Museum of Natural History, Chicago; Hereward Carrington, Psychist, New York; Dr. W. Hayes Ward, Archæologist and Babylonian Scholar; Mrs. Henry Draper, New York; W. W. Blake, Mexico City, who has done so much to encourage Mexican archæological investigation; Dr. Edward Forrester Sutton, New York; Dr. W. H. Holmes of the United States Bureau of Ethnology, Washington; Mr. McNeil M. Judd, Archæologist, United States National Museum; Dr. Arthur Fairbanks, Director of the Boston Museum of Fine Arts; Tan Sien Ko, Government Archæologist of Burma; Dr. Charles C. Abbott, Archæologist, Trenton, N. J.; Edgar T. Willson, of the Jewelers' Circular Publishing Co.; Dr. Edward H. Thompson, Archæologist, of Progreso, Yucatan, Mexico, and Cambridge, Mass.; Rev. Charles Sadleir of Aurcaria, Chile; Mrs. Nona Lebour of Corbridge-on-Tyne, England; and Dr. Charles P. Fagnani, Union Theological Seminary, New York City.

G. F. K.

September, 1915

Contents

Illustrations

COLOR PLATES

HALFTONES

LINE CUTS IN TEXT

The Magic of Jewels and Charms

I

Magic Stones and Electric Gems

WHILE the precious and semi-precious stones were often worn as amulets or talismans, the belief in the magic quality of mineral substances was not confined to them, but was also held in regard to large stone masses of peculiar form, or having strange markings or indentations; moreover, many small stones, possessing neither worth nor beauty, were thought to exert a certain magical influence upon natural phenomena. An occult power of this sort was also attributed by tradition to some mythical stones, the origin of this fancy being frequently explicable by the quality really inherent in some known mineral bearing a designation closely similar to that bestowed upon the imaginary stone.

To certain stones has been attributed the power to produce musical tones, the most famous example being the so-called "Vocal Memnon" of Thebes. This colossal statue was said to emit a melodious sound when the sun rose, and according to Greek legend this sound was a greeting given by Memnon to his mother, the Dawn. It appears, however, that the statue was a respecter of persons, for when the Emperor Hadrian presented himself before it, he is said to have heard the sound three times, whereas common mortals heard it but once, or at most twice, while occasionally the statue withheld its greeting altogether. A modern traveller relates a personal experience that may cast a side-light upon this matter. His visit to Thebes was made in the evening, but a fellah who was standing near the statue asked him whether he wished to hear the musical sound. Of course the reply was in the affirmative. Thereupon the man climbed up the side of the colossal figure and hid himself behind the elbow. In a moment sharp metallic sounds became audible; not a single sound, but several in succession. Knowing from their quality that they could not proceed from the stone, the traveller asked his donkey-boy for an explanation and was told that the man was striking an iron bar. In ancient times the priests probably performed this or a similar trick in a much more skilful way than did the poor fellah, so that the mystery of the statue was carefully guarded.[1]

The river Hydaspes was said to furnish a "musical stone." When the moon was waxing, this stone gave forth a melodious sound.[2] This should be understood in the sense that when the stone was struck at that season the sound was different from what it was at other times—a fanciful idea based on some supposed sympathy between the stone and the moon. As moonstones are rarely larger than a silver dollar, they would not emit a sound upon being struck, and it is probably a rock known as "chinkstone" (phonolite) that is referred to, an igneous rock, very hard and resonant, that has been found in elongated and flat pebbles of large size; they ring with the resonance of bells when struck. A sonorous stone at Megara is reported by Pausanias [3]; when struck, it emitted the sound of the chord of a lyre. This was explained by the tale that, while helping Alcathous to build

[1] Rosenfeld, "Singing and Speaking Stones"; Scientific American Suppl. No. 1720, p. 395, Dec. 19, 1908.

[2] Johannis Laurentii Philadelpheni Lydi quæ extant excerpta; ed. Hase, etc., Lipsiæ et Darmstadii, 1827, p. 104.

[3] "La Statue vocal de Memnon," by M. Letronne, in Mém. de l'Institut de France, Académie des Inscriptions et Belles Lettres, vol. i, 42, 1.

the walls of his city, the god Apollo had rested his lyre on the stone.

The term sarcophagus is to us so clear and precise in its significance, that we do not stop to think that its etymology reveals it as literally meaning body-devourer. Tradition taught that a stone of this type was to be found near Assos in Lycia, Asia Minor, and also in some parts of the Orient. If attached to the body of a living person it would eat away the flesh. Another type, already noted by Theophrastus in the third century B.C., had the power of petrifying any object placed within receptacles made from it. If a dead person were buried in a "sarcophagus" of this material the body would not be consumed, but would, on the contrary, be turned to stone, even the shoes of the corpse and any utensils buried with it, would undergo a like wonderful change. Possibly actual observations of changes in the bodies of those long buried, their partial disintegration in some cases, and their hardening in others, may have given rise to the fancy that the stone receptacle in which they had reposed was directly the cause of this, whether it implied destruction or petrifaction.[4]

Of the substance named galactite, Pliny gives some details. He states that it came from the Nile, was of the color and had the odor of milk, and when moistened and scraped produced a juice resembling milk. The liquid derived from the galactite when taken as a potion by nurses was said to increase the flow of milk. If a galactite were bound to a child's arm the effect was to promote the secretion of saliva. To these favorable effects must be added an unfavorable one, namely, loss of memory, which was said to befall occasionally those who wore the stone. A kind of "emerald with white veinings" was sometimes called galactite, and

[4] See Theophrasti, " De lapidibus (Peri lithôn), ed. by John Hill, London, 1746, pp. 15–17; cap. 10.

another variety had alternate red and white stripes or veins.[5] Perhaps this "emerald" was a variety of jade, or a banded jasper.

This so-called galactite, which enjoyed such an extraordinary reputation in ancient and medieval times, is not, properly speaking, a stone, but a nitrate of lime. The strange and famous relics of the Virgin preserved in many old churches and called "the Virgin's milk," were merely solutions of this nitrate. Possibly pieces of this so-called galactite were sometimes found by pilgrims in the grotto of Bethlehem, and were supposed to be petrified milk.[6] As everything in this sacred spot was regarded as connected in some way with the miraculous birth of Christ, it is easy to understand why the devout pilgrims came to believe that the milky-hued substance represented the milk of the Virgin, which had been preserved for future ages in this extraordinary way.

A kind of galactite, evidently a finely deposited form of carbonate of lime and perhaps absorbent, is mentioned by Conrad Gesner.[7] This was found on the Pilatus Mountain, Lake Lucerne, and is described by Gesner as being a "fungous and friable" substance, white and exceedingly light in weight. The natives called it *Mondmilch* (moon-milk) and it was sold in the pharmacies of Lucerne. The powder was used by physicians in the treatment of ulcers, and, like all the other galactites, it was supposed to increase the flow of milk and to develop the breasts. Besides this it was credited with somniferous virtues.

An old Mohammedan tradition, cited by Ibn Kadho Shobah in his Tarik al-Jafthi, relates that Noah, after the deluge, on setting out with the members of his family to

[5] Plinii, "Naturalis historia," Lib. xxxvii, cap. 59.
[6] De Mély, in La Grande Encyclopédie; art. pierres précieuses.
[7] Conradi Gesneri, "De rerum fossilium," etc., Tiguri, 1565, fol. 49 verso.

settle and populate the regions to the eastward and northward of Mt. Ararat, confided to their care a miraculous stone known to the Turks as *jiude-tash,* to the Persians as *senkideh* and to the Arabs as *hajer al-mathar,* or the "rain-stone." On it was impressed the word Aadhem or Aazem, the great name of God, by virtue of which whosoever possessed this stone could cause rain to fall whenever he pleased. In the long lapse of time this particular "precious" stone was lost, but some of the Turks were said to have certain stones endowed with a like power, and the more superstitious among these Turks solemnly asseverated that their "rain-stones" could beget progeny by a mysterious kind of generation.[8]

Among the many stones or concretions endowed by medieval belief with wonderful powers, may be reckoned the "rain-making" stones. Some of these were to be found in Karmania, south of Khorassan. The miraculous effect was produced by rubbing one against another. The Arabic author who reports this declares that this rain-making power was a well-known fact. He adds that similar stones might be secured from near Toledo in Spain and also in the "land of Kimar," inhabited by Turkish tribes.[9]

The Oriental rain-stones noted by pseudo-Aristotle and by many other Arabic writers of medieval times, can be paralleled by similar rain-making or rain-inducing stones in many other parts of the world and among many primitive peoples even in modern times. The rain-makers of the African tribe of Wahumas, dwelling in the region bordering on the great Albert Nyanza Lake in Central Africa, use a black stone in the course of their magic rites. This is put

[8] Giovanni B. Rampolli, "Annali Musulmani," vol. ix, Milano, 1825, p. 481, note 75.

[9] "Exposition de ce qu'il y a de plus remarquable et des merveilles," by Abdorrashish, surnamed Yakuti, a geographical work of the fifteenth century, transl. into French and published in Notices et Extraits des Manuscrits de la Bibliothèque du Roi, vol. ii, pp. 452, 520, 534; Paris, 1789.

into a vessel and water poured over it; the pulverized roots of certain herbs and some blood drawn from the veins of a black goat are then mixed with the water, and the resulting liquid mixture is thrown up into the air by the rain-maker.[10] The sorcerers among the Dieri in Central Australia place such trust in the efficacy of these conjurations as to believe that all rainfalls are produced thereby, generally through the intermediate action of ancestral spirits. If rain falls in a locality where no proceedings of the kind have taken place, then it is supposed that they have been initiated in some contiguous territory, a merely spontaneous and natural rainfall being out of the question. The clouds indeed generate the rain, but it will not be brought to the earth except by magic art. In the complicated magic ceremonies of these Dieri rain-makers, two large stones are employed; after a ceremonial, in the course of which the blood drawn from the two chief sorcerers is smeared over the bodies of the others, the stones are borne away by these two sorcerers for a distance of about twenty miles, and there put far up on the highest tree that can be found, the object evidently being to bring them as near to the clouds as possible.[11]

Rock-crystal as a rain-compeller finds honor among the wizards of the Ta-ta-thi tribe in New South Wales, Australia. To bring down rain from the sky one of them will break off a fragment from a crystal and cast it heavenward, enwrapping the rest of the crystal in feathers. After immersing these with their enclosure in water, and leaving them to soak for a while, the whole is removed and buried

---

[10] F. Stuhlmann, "Mit Emin Pascha im Herz von Africa," Berlin, 1894, p. 588.

[11] S. Gason, "The Dieyeric Tribe" in "Native Tribes of South Australia," pp. 276 sqq.; see also: A. W. Howitt, "The Dieri and Other Kindred Tribes of Central Australia."

in the earth, or hidden away in some safe place.[12] The widely spread fancy that rock-crystal is simply congealed water may have something to do with the choosing of this stone as a rain-maker.

Sumatrans of Kota Gadanz use a stone whose form roughly resembles that of a cat in their invocations of rain, a live black cat being supposed in some parts of this island to have certain rain-producing virtues.[13] Perhaps the electric fur of the animal may have suggested a connection with thunder-storms. Stones of this type, indeed a great many of those to which magic properties are attributed, are in many cases smeared with the blood of fowls, or have incense offered to them, this treatment of such stones being observed by the peasants in Scandinavia and other parts of Europe as well as in the Far East.

Stone crosses have sometimes been utilized as rain-bringers, as in the case of one belonging to St. Mary's Church in the Island of Uist, one of the outer Hebrides, off the Scottish coast. When drought prevailed here the peasants would set up this cross which usually lay flat on the ground, in the confident belief that rain would ensue. Of course, sooner or later, it was sure to come, and then the cross, having done its duty, was quietly replaced in its former horizontal position.[14]

A mysterious stone mentioned in Rabbinical legend is called the *shamir*. This word occurs three times in the Old Testament (Jer. xvii, 1; Ezek. iii, 9; Zech. vii, 12), and in each signifies a material noted for its hardness. In the first

---

[12] H. L. P. Cameron, "Notes on Some Tribes of New South Wales." Journ. of Anthrop. Inst., vol. xiv (1885), p. 362.

[13] J. L. van der Toorn, "Het animisme bij den Minangkabaner der Padangsche Bovenland," Bijdragen tot de Taal-Land-en Volkerkunde van Nederlandsch Indie," vol. xxxix, 1890, p. 86.

[14] Martin, "Description of the Western Islands of Scotland," in Pinkerton's "Voyages and Travels," vol. iii, p. 594.

of these passages there is express indication that the *shamir* was a pointed object used for engraving, and the word is translated "diamond" in our Bible; in the two other cases it is rendered "adamant" and "adamantine stone," respectively, thus leaving the determination of the substance an open question. However, as it is almost certain that the Hebrews were not familiar with the diamond, *shamir* most probably signifies one of the varieties of corundum, the next hardest mineral to the diamond, and extensively used in classic times for engraving on softer stones.

In the luxuriant growth of legend that sprang up in Rabbinical times, the *shamir* is not forgotten. It is said to have been the seventh of the ten marvels created at the end of the sixth day of creation. In size, it is described as being not larger than a barley-corn, but it had the power to split up the hardest substances, if brought in contact with them, or even in their neighborhood. Some of the legends ascribe to it even more wonderful magic powers, so that, like Aladdin's lamp, great buildings could be constructed by its help, Solomon having used it in the erection of the temple and other buildings. The etymology of the word indicates a pointed object, similar to our diamond-point, but in legend it is almost invariably described as a small worm, probably because of a fancied connection between this word and another designating a species of worm. Many have associated the Hebrew *shamir* with the Greek σμίρις, or emery.

The Hebrew *shamir* and the Greek ἀδάμας were both used metaphorically of hardness of heart and implacability. The Hebrew prophet Zechariah (vii, 12) says of the disobedient Jews that "they made their hearts as an adamant stone" (*shamir*), and the Greek poet Theocritus (fl. 228 B.C.) calls Pluto, the god of the infernal regions, "the *adamas* in Hades." This clearly shows that invincible hardness was the common characteristic of the material designated by these words. However, it appears probable that while *shamir* signifies a form of corundum, the word *adamas*, as used by the early Greek writers, denoted a hard, metallic substance. Possibly, when iron first became known to the Greeks, the adjective ἀδαμάντινος, "indomitable," was applied to it, and later the noun *adamas* was formed from this adjective and was used by the poets to signify an imaginary substance even harder than iron; hence, when the diamond became known in Greek lands, its extreme hardness suggested the application to it of this name.[15]

An Arab legend concerning the fabled *shamir* stone is related by Cazwini in his cosmography. When King Solomon set about building the temple in Jerusalem, he commanded Satan to dress the stones that were to be used, but the work was performed with such demoniac energy that the people round about complained bitterly of the dreadful noise. To remedy this trouble, Solomon sought the council of the leading scribes and also that of the evil spirits known as Ifrites and Jinns. None of them, however, was able to help him in this difficulty, but one of them advised him to question an apostate named Sahr, who sometimes had special knowledge of such things. When called upon for his opinion, Sahr declared that he knew of a stone that would do the work required, but did not know where it could be found; nevertheless he believed that, by a stratagem, he could secure possession of it. He thereupon ordered that an eagle's nest with its eggs should be brought to him, and also a bottle-shaped vessel made of very strong glass. Into this he slipped the eggs, put them back into the nest, and had nest and eggs replaced where they had been found. When the

---

[15] See Pinder, "De adamante," Berolini, 1829, pp. 70 sqq., where the use of the word *adamas* to designate iron is said to have been conjectured by Schneider, in his "Analecta ad hist. rei met. vet.," pp. 5, 6. Adamas as a man's name occurs in the "Iliad," xii, 140 and xiii, 560.

eagle returned to the nest it encountered this obstacle. In vain it struck at the vessel with claws and beak; after repeated efforts it flew away, but came back on the second day holding a piece of stone in its beak, which it let fall upon the vessel, breaking the latter into two halves without producing any sound. Upon this, Solomon, who knew the language of beasts and birds, asked the eagle where it had secured the stone. The bird answered: "O Prophet of God, in a mountain in the West called the Samur Mountain." This was indication enough to the wise king who, summoning the Jinns to his aid, soon had in Jerusalem a plentiful supply of these *samûr,* or *shamir* stones, with which the work of shaping and polishing the blocks for the temple was noiselessly performed.[16]

Full and precise directions are given by the old authorities as to the proper way to secure possession of the stone called *corvia.* On the Calends, or first day of April, eggs are to be taken out of a crow's nest and boiled until they are quite hard; they are then to be allowed to cool off and are replaced in the nest. The female bird notes that the eggs have been tampered with and flies away in search of the corvia-stone. When she has found it, she bears it to the nest, and as soon as it touches the eggs they become fresh and fertile again. This is the auspicious moment for securing the stone, which must be quickly taken from the nest else it would lose its virtue.[17] The lucky owner of the stone is promised increase of wealth and honors, and the power to read the future.

The fabled gem-bearing dragons of India were said to have sometimes fallen victims to the enchanter's art. Cer-

---

[16] Julius Ruska, " Das Steinbuch aus der Kosmographie des Muhammad ibn Mahmud al Kazwini," Beilage to the Jahresbericht of the Oberrealschule Heidelberg, 1895–96.

[17] Camilli Leonardi, " Speculum lapidum," Venetia, 1502, fol. xxix.

tain mystic characters were woven in thread of gold upon a scarlet cloth, and this cloth was spread by the hunters before the dragon's den. When the creature emerged, his eyes were fascinated by the strange letters in which the enchanter had infused a wonderful soporific power. Hypnotized by the sight, the dragon would fall into a deep slumber and the hunters would rush upon him and sever his head from his body. Within the head were found gems of brilliant hue, some of these possessing the power of rendering the wearer invisible.[18]

The "Gem of Sovranty," or the "Gem of the King of Kings," may have been a purely poetic Hindu fancy, or possibly may have been the diamond. Its surpassing quality is emphasized by the declaration that though the earth produced the sapphire, the cat's-eye, the topaz, the ruby, and the two mystic gems, the favorite of the sun, and the favorite of the moon, the Gem of the King of Kings was acknowledged to be the chief of all "for the sheen of that jewel spreads round about for a league on every side." To King Milinda the following question was put: "Suppose that on the disappearance of a sovran overlord, the mystic Gem of Sovranty lay concealed in a cleft on the mountain peak, and that on another sovran overlord arriving at the supreme dignity it should appear to him, would you say, O King, that the gem was produced by him?" "Certainly not, sir," replied the monarch, "the gem would be in its original condition. But it had received, as it were, a new birth through him." [19]

The Arabian author, Ibn Al-Beithar (b. ca. 1197 A.D.), describes a stone called in Arabic *hajer al-kelb,* or "dog-stone." These stones had such attraction for dogs of a

[18] Philostrati, "Vita Apollonii," Lib. iii, cap. 8.

[19] "The Questions of King Milinda," trans. by T. W. Rhys Davids; Sacred Books of the East, vol. xxxvi, Oxford, 1894, pp. 14, 303.

certain breed that when cast before them they would snap them up, bite them, and hold them in their jaws. The magicians saw in this a proof that the stones would produce enmity and ill-will among men. Having selected seven such stones they marked them with the names of any persons between whom they wished to stir up strife. The seven stones were then thrown one by one before a dog of the requisite species, and, after he had bitten them, two were chosen and were placed in water of which the persons who were to be set at variance were sure to drink. We are assured that the experiment had the desired evil result.[20]

In ancient times there was found in the river Meander a stone satirically named *sophron,* "temperate." If it were placed upon the breast of any one, he immediately became enraged and killed one of his parents; however, after having appeased the Mother of the Gods, he was cured of his temporary madness.[21]

A most singular stone is described by Thomas de Cantimpré under the name of "piropholos." This substance, according to Konrad von Megenberg's version, was taken from the heart of a man who had been poisoned, "because the heart of such a man cannot be burned in fire." If the heart were kept for nine years in fire this wonderful stone was produced. It gave protection from lightning, but its principal virtue was to guard the wearer from sudden death; indeed, we are told that a man could not die so long as he held this stone in his hand. However, it did not preserve him from disease, but only prolonged his life. The stone was said to be of a light and bright red color.[22]

---

[20] Traité des Simples of Ibn Al-Beithar, in Notices et Extraits des Manuscrits de la Bibliothèque Nationale, vol. xxiii, p. 409; Paris, 1877.

[21] De Mély, "Le traité des fleuves de Plutarche," in Revue des Études Grecques, vol. v (1892), p. 332.

[22] Konrad von Megenberg, "Buch der Natur," ed. by Dr. Franz Pfeiffer, Stuttgart, 1861, p. 456.

After enumerating all the well-known precious stones, Volmar, in his "Steinbuch," proceeds to relate that there is one which produces blindness, another that enables the wearer to understand the language of birds, still another that saves people from drowning, and, finally, one of such sovereign power that it brings back the dead to life. However, we are told that because of the miraculous virtues of these stones God hides them so well that no man can obtain them.[23] About a century earlier Saint Hildegard of Bingen wrote that "just as a poisonous herb placed on a man's skin will produce ulceration," by an analogous though contrary effect "certain precious stones will, if placed on the skin, confer health and sanity by their virtue."[24]

Persian records tell of a "royal stone" found in the head of the *ouren bad,* a kind of eagle; this preserved the wearer from the attacks of venomous reptiles. If a deadly poison had been administered to a person, he would be immediately cured by taking one drachm's weight of the stone. It thus appears that its virtues were those of the far-famed bezoar.[25] Persia evidently had good store of "wonder-workers" of this kind, for the Persian romance entitled "Hatim Tai and the Benevolent Lady," written about the beginning of the eighteenth century, recites the marvellous virtue of a stone called the *Shah-muhra.* If this were fastened on the arm the wearer became endowed with miraculous vision and all the gold and precious stones beneath the earth's surface were revealed to him.[26]

For ten centuries or more, countless thousands, although feeling assured of spiritual immortality, were none the less eager to have eternal youth and vigor and the power to peer

---

[23] Volmar, "Steinbuch," ed. by Hans Lambel, Heilbronn, 1877, p. 24.

[24] St. Hildegardæ, "Opera omnia," in Pat. Lat., ed. J. P. Migne, vol. cxcvii, col. 1260.

[25] D'Herbelot, "Bibliothèque Orientale," La Haye, 1778, p. 230.

[26] Clouston, "A Group of Eastern Romances," Glasgow, 1889.

into the future. Hence Ponce de Leon's quest for the "Fountain of Youth" in our Florida. But in addition to this, there has ever been an intense desire to find something by means of which gold could be made out of the baser metals, for youth and vigor, if coupled with poverty, are only half-blessings. The search for the "Philosopher's Stone" appears to have been a more or less aimless pursuit of this end; but there can be no doubt that this search led to the discovery of many new substances and reactions, and helped to lay the foundation of our modern chemistry. Whether the conscious aim of the alchemist was the discovery of an actual stone, or merely the discovery of some process for turning a valueless substance into one of great value, is not clearly ascertainable from the purposely vague and obscure treatises on alchemy.

The "Philosopher's Stone," the fond dream of so many who delved into nature's mysteries in the past, does not seem so improbable to-day as it did twenty years ago. The recent discovery of the element radium, which is produced from the element uranium, and the story of the strange and protean changes of radium into helium, neon and argon, according to the environment in which it is placed, have given the death-blow to the old idea of the immutability of the elements. Still, while we have been allowed this peep into the storehouse of nature's secrets, and are growing to believe that in eons of time the various different elements may have been evolved, successively, from one another, the power to provoke this change at will and in a brief space of time is as yet withheld from us, and may never be given to us, just as little as the power to send messages to the distant spheres, whose bulk, density and composition we can estimate with a considerable degree of accuracy.

Numerous specimens still exist of what is alleged to be artificial gold made by the alchemists of a past age. Of all these the most striking is a large medallion, bearing in relief the heads of Emperor Leopold and his ancestors of the House of Hapsburg. It is related that on the name day of the emperor in 1677, this medallion, originally of silver and weighing 7250 grains, was transmuted into gold by Wenzel Seiler, a noted alchemist of that time. This wonder was performed in full view of the emperor and his courtiers, by dipping the medallion in a solution. As there are four notches on the edge, it has been conjectured that these were made to secure material for testing the quality of the transformed metal. However, the simple test of specific gravity shows that the metal cannot be gold, for according to Bauer's calculation made in 1883, the medallion has a specific gravity of 12.67, between that of silver (10.5) and that of gold (19.27). This might indicate that in some unexplained way the alchemist had succeeded in precipitating a coating of gold upon the face of the object. It seems probable that the deception was soon discovered, for Seiler, who had been knighted on September 16, 1676, was exiled by order of Emperor Leopold, not long after the date on which the supposed transmutation is said to have taken place.

An exceedingly rare medal, and one of great interest to students of alchemy, was struck in 1647 by order of Emperor Ferdinand III from gold produced in his presence by Johann Peter Hofmann, a master of the alchemical art. A specimen of this medal is in the Imperial Cabinet of Coins in Vienna.[27] On the obverse, around two shields, one bearing eight fleurs-de-lis and the other the figure of a lion, are two hermetic inscriptions: LILIA CUM NIVEO COPULANTUR FULVA LEONE (yellow lilies lie down with the snow-white lion), and SIC LEO MANSUESCET SIC LILIA FULVA VIRESCENT

[27] "Nützliche Versuche und Bemerkungen aus dem Reich der Natur," Nürnberg, 1760; cited by Bolton.

(thus will the lion be tamed and thus will the yellow lilies flourish). Around a crown surmounting the two shields appear the initial letters I. P. H. V. N. F., indicating Latin words the sense of which is "Johannes Petrus Hofmann a Nurembergian subject made it," and also the letters T G V L, intended to signify *tinturæ guttæ v. libram,* or "five drops of the tincture [transmuted] a pound." The reverse has Latin words denoting that iron was the base of this tincture, the symbols used for lead, tin, copper, mercury, silver and gold being each accompanied by a cryptic declaration that Mars (iron) had controlled the respective metal.[28]

Besides the "Philosopher's Stone," the chief object of their quest, the alchemists believed that several other stones possessing magic virtues could be produced. Among these was the "angelical stone," which gave power to see the angels in dreams and visions, and also the "mineral stone," a substance by means of which common flints could be transmuted into diamonds, rubies, sapphires, emeralds, etc.[29] Possibly some alchemists were glassmakers, and fused the quartz with various mineral salts into imitations of the gems, having the colors, but not the hardness or other properties.

One of the strangest fancies as to the medicinal efficacy of stones is that held by the native Australians, who believe that "crystals" are embedded in the bodies of their medicine-men. This belief is encouraged by the medicine-men themselves; indeed, they are supposed only to retain their power so long as these *atnongara* or *ultunda* stones remain in their bodies, and a share of their might can be transmitted by transferring certain of the stones from their

---

[28] Bolton, "Contributions of Alchemy to Numismatics," New York, 1890, pp. 17, 18.

[29] Ashmole, "Theatrum chemicum Brittanicum," London, 1652, pp. 4–6.

own bodies to that of another. The ceremony proceeds as follows:[30]

> The Nung-gara [medicine-men] then withdrew from their bodies a number of small clear crystals called Ultunda which were placed one by one, as they were extracted, in the hollow of a spear-thrower. When a sufficient number had been withdrawn, the Nung-gara directed the man who had come with them to clasp the candidate from behind and to hold him tightly. Then each of them picked up some crystals, and taking hold of a leg, gripped the stones firmly and pressed them slowly and strongly along the front of the leg and then up the body as high as the breast-bone. This was repeated three times, the skin being scored at intervals with scratches, from which blood flowed. By this means the magic crystals are supposed to be forced into the body of the man. . . . After which each of them pressed a crystal on the head of the novice and struck it hard, the idea being to drive it into the skull, the scalp being made to bleed during the process. . . .
>
> One of the Nung-gara then withdrew from his skull just behind his ear (that is, he told the novice that he kept it there) a thin and sharp Ultunda, and taking up some dust from the ground, dried the man's tongue with it, and then, pulling it out as far as possible, he made with the stone an incision almost half an inch in length.

The *mesticas* of the Malays represent a class of stones differing in important respects from the various types of bezoars. A principal distinction is that the *mesticas* are not supposed to owe their origin to pathological conditions in the organism wherein they occur, but rather to a superabundance of the normal and healthy constituents of the animal or plant. It is probably due to this that the virtues of these particular concretions are rather talismanic than therapeutic, and that they are believed to endow the finder, or one who receives them by gift, with courage, immunity from injury, and also with cunning and shrewdness in the affairs of life. Especially by warriors are these stones highly valued, for they are supposed to protect the wearer from wounds; indeed, this belief sometimes went so far as

[30] Spencer and Gillen, "The Native Tribes of Central Australia," London, 1899, pp. 525–529.

to lead the Malays to think that absolute invulnerability was conferred on one who carried several of them bound so closely to the skin that in some cases they even penetrated the flesh. The typical *mestica* is described as a hard stone, brilliant but seldom transparent; it is found in the flesh or fat, in the heart or on the legs of animals, and also sometimes in plants.[31]

Rumphius declares that many extraordinary cases were related of warriors who could not be injured by any weapons until the *mestica* had been cut out of their flesh, wherein it had become embedded. Indeed, he states that Dutch officers of proved veracity had confidently asserted that they had encountered such men among their native antagonists. While Rumphius feels himself therefore forced to admit the truth of the invulnerability of these men, he hastens to add that such powers could not be inherent in any piece of stone, but must owe their origin to diabolical agencies.[32] The fact that the Mohammedans had their *mesticas* blessed by the priests of their faith, and burned incense beneath them on Fridays, the Mohammedan equivalent of the Christian Sunday, did not probably shake the belief of Rumphius that the Devil had something to do with these substances.

The medicine-men of the Kainugá Indians of Paraguay mutter incantations over the bodies of the sick, and then, after many struggles and contortions, proceed to extract stones from their mouths, claiming that they have taken the patient's disease into their own bodies, the stones being regarded as the seat of the ailment. In one case, the medicine-man produced five of these stones before the patient admitted that his pain was relieved. After the cure was

---

[31] Rumphius, "D'Ambonische Rariteitskamer," Amsterdam, 1741, p. 291.

[32] Rumphius, "D'Ambonische Rariteitskamer," Amsterdam, 1741, pp. 291, 292.

INDIAN MEDICINE-MEN

From "Histoire Générale des Céremonies Religieuses de tous les Peuples du Monde," by Abbé Banier and Abbé Mascrier, Paris, 1741.

completed the sorcerer was clever enough to feign extreme exhaustion, as though his vital forces had been subjected to a tremendous strain.[33]

In British New Guinea similar tactics are resorted to by the native doctors. A native who was suffering from lumbago fully believed the tale that his disease was caused by a stone embedded in his flesh. When the sorcerer made passes over this man's back and then exhibited a stone which he pretended to have taken thence, the sufferer was convinced that the disease had left his body, and he began to feel relief. When examined, his back showed some superficial cuts at the spot where the stone was said to have been extracted. In another case, however, when a child was to be operated upon in a like way, the child's father became suspicious and seized the operator's hands before they came into contact with the little one's body; the result being that the disease-laden stone was found concealed in the operator's hand.[34]

Pebble-mania or lithomania is an inherent trait in all mankind. From the most primitive man to the most modern, especially those of optimistic and investigating tendencies, this trait is present in a greater or lesser degree. That is, curious people would collect pebbles for their bright colors, or markings, for their transparency or translucence, and those of an investigating turn of mind, under the impression that the find was perhaps a diamond or a gem of some kind. In modern times this kind of collecting has developed into a regular industry, pebbles found on the shores of the United States and which are either pure white, transparent or translucent quartz, being cut and offered for sale. These pebbles

---

[33] Vogt, "Die Indianer des oberen Paranâ," Mitteilungen d. Anthrop. Gesellsch. in Wien, 1904, vol. xxxiv, pp. 206, 207.

[34] Hovorka and Kronfeld, "Vergleichende Volksmedizin," vol. ii, p. 900; communication from Dr. Rudolf Pöch.

are gathered, and are valuable to those who make a business of selling them, because the white opaque pebbles become translucent after cutting, or rather, during the process of cutting, and they are then passed off for moonstones, which are worth from one-third to one-half more than the cost of cutting the quartz pebbles, the purchaser being led to believe that he is getting a moonstone, although this could not be possible, since moonstones have never been found on either the eastern or the western coast of the United States. As for the cut moonstones which are brought back by the tourist, under the impression that he is getting native material and workmanship, these all come from Europe.

Pebble-mania is not confined to mankind alone. Birds and animals possess it. The magpie picks up and hides away bright objects, including odd pebbles, or carries them to its nest. The stones known as *aetites* were said to be found in eagles' nests, although they may have been swallowed by the birds for digestive purposes, just as the hen's crop is full of stones, many of them being transparent, a proof that the fowl had been attracted by them, and had swallowed these in preference to other, duller ones. Notable instances of transparent pebbles are the *alectorii,* or "cock-stones."

The great Italian goldsmith and sculptor, Benvenuto Cellini (1500–1574), relates that when a youth he often shot cranes with his arquebuse, and that in several instances he found in their entrails not only fine turquoises, but also fragments of the so-called plasma-emerald and even occasionally small pearls. This serves to indicate that the pretty exterior of such objects exerted an influence upon these birds in some degree analogous to the impressions aroused in mankind on viewing them.[35]

[35] Benvenuto Cellini, "Due trattati, uno intorno alle otto principali arti dell' oreficeria," etc., Fiorenze, Valente Panizzi & Marco Peri, 1568, fol. 10 recto.

In seventeenth century Denmark there seems to have been no lack of "magic stones," for it is related that one day as King Christian II was strolling along the beach, he picked up a shining pebble by the aid of which he could render himself invisible at will. Similar power was said to exist in stones that could be found in ant-hills if hot water were thrown onto them on St. Walpurgis Day, or St. Hans' Day. The Danes of the time also shared in the belief that the stone from the lapwing preserved from illness and sorrow as did the "swallow's-stone" as well.[36]

It has frequently been maintained that the source of pebbles could be broadly determined by their form and surface; for example, well-rounded specimens of fairly uniform size would be classed as marine pebbles, while river-pebbles would be subangular and usually flat; pebbles of glacial origin, on the other hand, would have faceted, rounded edges, their surfaces being polished and striated. However, although these rules might hold good in many cases, careful observation has demonstrated that pebbles of all these supposedly distinct types can be found among those of marine, fluviatile, or lacustrine origin. This is explicable by the fact that while the constant, unhindered action of sea or river would probably produce pebbles of distinct type, the local conditions often interfere with this. For instance, on a low sea-coast, with weak wave-action, pebbles frequently became buried in the sands, thus retaining their form practically unchanged, and even where the waves are stronger, so that the pebbles are more or less constantly exposed to their force, it must be borne in mind that some of these coast pebbles have been swept down by rivers, or have already been affected by glacial action. In these cases the force of

[36] Axel Garboe, "Kulturhistoriske Studier over Ædelstene, med særligt Henblik paa det 17. Aarhundrede," Kobenhavn og Kristiania, 1915, p, 225; citing a manuscript in the Royal Library at Copenhagen.

the waves will indeed modify the form, but along the lines of that already produced by the earlier agencies. Broadly stated, those that were round or oval would generally remain so, rectangular fragments might have their angles worn away and become elliptical, while flat fragments would not exhibit any notable change in shape.[37]

When a group of pebbles have been long exposed to attrition by the waters of a powerful stream, especially where the current is intermittent, and where a large quantity of sand has been worked or blown into the stream by freshet or wind storm, they may become rounded by the erosive action of the water or by the abrasive power of the sand, as well as by the attrition consequent upon their sharp contact with one another. This is exemplified in the case of boulders in a river bed, it having been noted in certain streams on the Navajo Reservation that while the upstream sides of the boulders were polished and rounded, and even sometimes faceted and etched, but little change was observable on the downstream sides. This has been tested experimentally, holes an inch in depth having been drilled in opposite sides of sandstone boulders, and on examination five years later in five different localities where this had been done, the deepest hole remaining on the upstream sides measured but four-tenths of an inch, while in one locality the holes had entirely disappeared, and yet so trifling was the effect of the water on the downstream side that a blue-pencil mark had not been washed away. Of course, the erosion of quartzite and limestone boulders tested in this way proved to be a much slower process, amounting to less than one-hundredth of an inch annually. Another important consideration in the shaping of pebbles by river-water is the swiftness of the current,

[37] See Herbert E. Gregory, "Note on the Shape of Pebbles," in The American Journal of Science, vol. xxxix, pp. 300–304; March, 1915; also for two succeeding paragraphs.

it having been noted, for instance, that those which have been washed down the steep slopes of the Navajo Mountain and the edge of the Black Mesa are somewhat better rounded than those that have been borne along for a much greater distance by less swift-flowing water.

That striated, faceted, or polished pebbles are always of glacial origin, or that those of glacial origin usually offer these characteristics is far from the fact; indeed, it may rather be said that they are generally missing. The fluvio-glacial drift is much more widespread than ground moraine, and the pebbles found in the former rarely present these aspects; indeed, it has been noted that in an hour's search through the glacial drift of Connecticut, only a single such specimen may be met with. On the other hand, many pebbles of this type have been found under conditions plainly showing that the striation was due to other causes, in some instances, as with those occurring in conglomerates, to pressure and differential movement.[38]

The burying of white stones or lumps of quartz with the dead was not infrequent in early times in Ireland. The peasants of the north of Ireland call these Godstones. A cist found at Barnasraghy, County Sligo, was nearly filled with quartz pebbles, and not long since a white stone was found in a primitive burial place near Larne, County Antrim. That this was a usage confined to the earlier period of Irish history is generally admitted, and the discovery of such white stones in a grave is accepted as an indication that it belongs to an early date.[39]

It has been suggested that these white stones were used for burials because of the symbolic meaning of the color,

---

[38] See Herbert E. Gregory, "Note on the Shape of Pebbles," in The American Journal of Science, vol. xxxix, pp. 303, 304; March, 1915.

[39] W. G. Wood-Martin, "Traces of the Elder Faiths of Ireland," London, 1902, vol. i, p. 329.

which to the minds of many primitive peoples was that of purity, as indeed it is still among most modern peoples, although the symbolism may not always be consciously accepted. White marble seems to most of us the most appropriate and beautiful stone for monuments, and if to a very considerable degree granite is now used as a substitute, this is principally because of its greater resistance to the deteriorating effect of atmospheric changes. Already in prehistoric times, the cave-dwellers showed a fondness for gathering quartz crystals and fragments, and specimens of those taken from the Auvergne Mountains have been found in the cave-dwellings of Les Eyzies; they may have been used as amulets or talismans.[40]

A legend of the great Irish saint, Columba, gives an instance of the curative use of white pebbles. After this saint had vainly entreated Broichan the Druid to free a Christian bond-maiden, as a last resort he menaced the druid with approaching death. The prediction or curse was speedily on the way to fulfilment, Broichan sickened unto death, and in his terror consented to free the maiden. Hereupon St. Columba went to the river Ness and picked up out of its shallows several white pebbles, announcing that they would, by the Lord's power, work the cure of heathen people. One of the stones was blessed by the saint and placed in a vessel filled with water, on the surface of which it floated, and as soon as Broichan had taken a draught of the liquid he was restored to perfect health.[41]

A famous Scotch amulet was a polished globular mass of white quartz, an inch and three-quarters in diameter, owned by the chiefs of Clan Donnachaidh and known as the

[40] Ibid., 1902, vol. i, op. cit., p. 330.

[41] Nona Lebour, "White Quartz Pebbles and their Archæological Significance"; reprint from Transactions of the Dumfriesshire and Galloway Natural History and Antiquarian Society, January 30, 1914, p. 11.

"Stone of the Banner." It had been accidentally found by a chief of this clan, who, on his way to join Robert Bruce in 1315, before the battle of Bannockburn, noted a glittering stone embedded in a clod of earth that had become attached to his flagstaff. It was looked upon as a powerful talisman in battle, and water in which it had been dipped was said to cure diseases. Tradition asserted that this white stone of Clan Donnachaidh was identical with that used long before by St. Columba.[42] As such white stones were often deposited in graves, sometimes even being placed in the mouth of a deceased person, it has been suggested that perhaps the sparks emitted by the quartz on percussion were believed to shed some faint gleams along the dark pathway of the departed in his journey to the underworld. In Christian times there can be little doubt in regard to the influence exercised by the text in Revelation: "To him that overcometh . . . I will give a white stone, and in the stone a new name written, which no man knoweth save he that receiveth it."[43]

Crystal balls are not only valued for the visions to be seen, or supposed to be seen in them, but are sometimes worn as amulets against illness. In some parts of Japan they are thought to ward off dropsy, and their wear is also recommended to guard from all wasting diseases.[44] The likeness of rock-crystal to congealed water may well be credited, in the doctrine of sympathy, with its putative power of preventing the watery infiltration from which a dropsical patient suffers. As the Japanese make many choice crystal balls, these objects are generally more or less familiar in that land

---

[42] Ibid., pp. 13 and 14, citing Proceedings of the Society of Antiquaries of Scotland, 1860–1, vol. iv, pt. i, p. 219.

[43] Ibid., p. 12, citing Proceedings of the Society of Antiquaries of Scotland, 1860–1, vol. iv, pt. i, p. 219.

[44] William Thomas and Kate Pavitt, "The Book of Talismans, Amulets and Zodiacal Gems," London, 1914, p. 52.

and have thus appealed as well to those who were superstitious as to those who appreciated things beautiful in themselves.

In Yucatan quartz crystals were not only used for divining, but also to ensure the success of the crops. The fact that such crystals have been found in the Indian mounds of Arkansas, North Carolina, and elsewhere, may warrant the supposition that they had been worn as talismans and then interred with the deceased persons as a most intimate part of their property. The writer's personal observation in Garland and Montgomery counties, Arkansas, demonstrated that quartz crystals were to be found in mounds together with chipped arrow-points of chalcedony, although the crystals did not appear to have been worked in any way. The region about Hot Springs, Arkansas, has furnished some of the finest rock-crystal found in the United States. From North Carolina also have come many remarkable specimens, the largest of which, found in 1886, was unluckily broken up by the person who discovered it. In its crystal state it must have weighed about 300 pounds, and if cut would have furnished a crystal ball 4½ or 5 inches in diameter. This splendid crystal came from Phœnix Mountain, Chestnut Hill township, in Ashe County, North Carolina, and from the largest fragment recovered, weighing 51 pounds, several slabs 8 inches square and from half inch to one inch in thickness were cut. Nearby a crystal weighing 285 pounds was found, and another weighing 188 pounds. Some of the crystals from this locality had on one side a green coating of chlorite, and when this was not removed, the effect was as though one saw a green moss growing beneath a pool of water. The rock-crystal slabs have an advantage over glass when used for mirrors, as they more truly reflect the tints of a fine complexion. Brilliant crystals from Lake George and its neighborhood have been called "Lake George

Diamonds.'' In marked contrast with the large examples we have noted, many crystals of quartz are so small that 200,000 would have an aggregate weight of but one ounce and yet many are perfect crystals and doubly terminated.

The presence of white quartz pebbles in some graves of the Indian Moundbuilders, appears to be indicated to a satisfactory extent in the case of certain specimens from the Etowah Mound in Georgia; these pebbles, which form part of the Steiner collections in the United States National Museum, were not, however, worked or polished in any way, nor are there any traces of use for ornament or decoration. On the other hand, white quartz pebbles from the Pueblo region of the Southwest offer undeniable signs of having been long used and are of frequent occurrence; some of these have been found in graves. In connection with the probable reasons determining their presence the designations ''fire stones'' or ''charms'' have been given them; some specimens of this worked quartz had evidently been worn as pendants, while others had probably been regarded as fetishes.[45]

It is most interesting to note that the superstitious use of these objects in burials was so widespread as to prove that it must have been due to some inherent property or properties in white stones, and especially in pebbles of white quartz, which appealed very strongly to the mind of primitive man. That, as has been noted above, the conception of purity should be associated with whiteness, in its contrast to any obscure color, is natural enough, and rests upon the association of spotless cleanliness with moral purity, and very probably the sparkles of light emitted by a bright piece of quartz, normally or on percussion, brought this material into some connection with the worship of fire, or of fire-gods.

[45] From letter of Mr. Neil M. Judd, Assistant in Archæology in the United States National Museum, communicated by Dr. W. H. Holmes, Head Curator of the Department of Anthropology in that institution.

To another possible conception along the same lines we have already alluded.

An instance is reported where a very curious quartz pebble, one-half white and the other black, was found within the hand bones of the skeleton of an Indian; the finder carried it about with him for many years as a "lucky stone," but it appears that his personal experience of its effects, if these can be judged from what happened to the bearer of such a talisman, has been of a kind to shatter the most robust faith in the protective power of his Indian charm. Possibly the strange relic may have symbolized night and day for the Indians, and thus have been believed to guard the wearer or the person with whom it was buried, at all times and seasons. That pebbles of this sort were sometimes buried in the ground, disposed in circles and squares, is vouched for by some who claim to have unearthed them in ploughing, but our informant was not able to confirm these statements, as the arrangements had always been effectually disturbed before he reached the spot.[46]

In many graves of the primitive Red-paint People of Maine, small pebbles have been found. As they were not large enough to have served as paint-grinders, and as but one such pebble occurs in any single grave, the presumption is quite strong that they were considered as talismans for the dead. The fact that the practical laborers of our day who dug out these graves instinctively named the pebbles "lucky stones" goes to prove that this supposition is not too far-fetched, although there is no positive evidence to support it. The pebbles were yellow, bright red, or gray in color, the graves explored being at Orland, Maine, as well as at the outlet of Lake Alamoosook, on the south side of this lake and at Passadumkeag; indeed such graves have been

[46] Communicated by Dr. Charles C. Abbott.

met with all the way from the Kennebec Valley eastward to Bar Harbor.[47]

The respective symbolic meanings of white and black are illustrated in the designations "white magic" and "black magic," the latter denoting conjurations or spells in which the aid of the powers of darkness, of the Devil and his demons, was sought by the sorcerer, while "white magic" was to be performed by harmless and innocent means, sometimes even by religious rites. In this way it sometimes so closely approached the domain of religious miracle, that it becomes difficult to distinguish between these two conceptions of supernatural action in the material world.

Quartz of a different type with needle-like inclusions is called "Thetis's hair stone." This is a transparent or translucent quartz, but so completely filled with acicular crystals of green actinolite, or occasionally altered actinolite of a yellow-brown or brown color, as to appear almost opaque; seals and charms have been made to a small extent of this variety. Of other inclusions in quartz we may note those of a very brilliant stibnite projecting in all directions, some of the intruded crystals being very curiously bent. Exceedingly beautiful gems have been cut from this material.[48] When this quartz is cut en cabochon across the ravalette inclusions, a cat's-eye effect is produced. The yellow quartz cat's-cye of Ceylon and the green of Haff, Bavaria, are of this type. So densely set were the green actinolite inclusions in the case of a specimen found at Gibsonville, North Carolina, that it was believed by the finder to be an emerald.

An extremely beautiful effect in quartz is produced by enclosed, acicular crystals, or hair-like particles of some

[47] Warren K. Moorehead, "The Red-Paint People of Maine," pp. 42, 43. Reprint from the *American Anthropologist* (N. S.), vol. xv, No. i, January-March, 1913.

[48] See the present writer's "Gems and Precious Stones of North America," New York, 1892, p. 126.

other mineral, such as rutile, for instance, and sometimes even of gold. To specimens of this latter type may be referred the Greek name "chrysothrix," used in the Orphic poem "Lithica" and signifying literally "golden hair"; of this the verses tell us there were two varieties, that which may be identified with quartz, having a resemblance to "crystal," while the other, said to have the appearance of chrysoberyl, may have been a yellower variety. To the quartz traversed by filaments of rutile, or the red oxide of titanium, has been given the taking name of "Venus's hair stone"; a pretty French name is *Flèches d'Amour* or "Cupid's Arrows."[49]

The California beaches have furnished some of the most interesting ornamental pebbles, the greater number being of chalcedony or agate weathered from an amygdaloidal rock, while a few are of jasper or fossil coral. Their variegated color-markings made them very attractive ornamental objects in themselves, and there is reason to believe that centuries ago the Indians of this region valued them as talismans or amulets. At present the finest specimens are gathered from Pescadero Beach in San Mateo County, about twenty-four miles west of San José, Redondo Beach, fifteen miles south of Los Angeles, and also from Crescent City Beach, in the northern part of California. On Moonstone Beach, Santa Catalina Island, many beautiful quartz and chalcedony nodules have been picked up, which have weathered out of ryolite rock of sanidine feldspar and quartz. It has been quite a custom for guests of the hotels to go down to Redondo Beach and gather these pebbles, and some of those collected by enterprising natives are placed in a bottle of water to bring out the beauty of their colors. Sometimes they are drilled and strung on flexible wire to form long chains or necklaces. Several pebbles presumably from

[49] See N. F. Moore, "Antient Mineralogy," 2d ed., New York, 1859, p. 190.

By courtesy of California State Mining Bureau.

1. Chalcedony and agate pebbles from Pescadero Beach, San Mateo County, California.
2. Pebble Beach, Redondo, Los Angeles County, California.

From George Frederick Kunz's "Semi-precious Stones of California," Sacramento, 1905. Bulletin No. 37 of the State Mining Bureau.

Redondo Beach were found, in 1901, in an Indian grave, where they were probably placed as amulets for the dead.[50]

The occurrence of fluid cavities in quartz, chalcedony, sapphire, and other minerals, is due at times to cavernous structures formed during the growth of these minerals, when the crystalline substances, for some reason, instead of filling these up solid, will avoid the caverns and enclose the liquid of crystallization. In agate inclusions this is found with silicious content, possibly due to the fact that it is to an extent carbonic acid gas, or water containing salt or some other foreign substance. In agate chalcedony, whether in pebbles as minute as a pinhead, or in amygdules several feet across, the liquid is enclosed because the walls of the gas-pores in the rock, which are frequently almond-shaped, are gradually becoming smaller, or rather the walls thicken by the deposition of the silica forming agate, chalcedony, or any impenetrable layers, or else an impenetrable form of quartz; then again, frequently toward the centre or when the liquid forms less rapidly, or through some change, the quartz becomes crystalline, either colorless, smoky, or amethystine, and this is due to various inclusions. This gradual thickening of the walls means that the aperture into which the liquid penetrates becomes smaller and smaller until at last it is entirely sealed, so that it becomes enclosed in a kind of nature's water-bottle, these being sometimes as large as in the chalcedony specimens from Uruguay; this is also the case with the hydrolites and the enhydros, when they can be shaken and the water rattles as in a bottle.

An occasional small Redondo Beach, California, or Medford, Oregon pebble contains a moving bubble of air in liquid.

---

[50] George Frederick Kunz, "Gems, Jewelers' Materials and Ornamental Stones of California," California State Mining Bureau, Bulletin No. 37, Sacramento, 1905, pp. 71–73.

Most wonderful specimens of rutilated quartz are the great, rich brown, possibly titanium-colored masses in the Morgan Collection at the American Museum of Natural History, that in the Vaux Collection at the Philadelphia Academy of Natural Sciences, and a smaller mass in the British Museum; these were all obtained near Middlesex, Vermont. The rutile is a rich transparent or translucent red, varying in thinness from that of an ordinary needle to that of a knitting-needle, and even to that of a thin lead-pencil. Wonderful specimens are also found in the Alps of St. Gothard, in Madagascar, and in Alexander County, North Carolina, where they are found in quantity as minute crystals of a rich red or golden yellow.

Other curious and interesting rock-crystals with inclusions are those showing enclosed drops of water, the kind termed *enhydros* by Pliny [51] and many old writers; in some of the rarer specimens the enclosed water is present in considerable quantity. Quartz with inclusions of this type was highly appreciated in the Greco-Roman world, and one of the best poets of the Decadence, Claudian (fl. about 400 A.D.), composed a series of poetic epigrams upon them, seven of these being in Latin and two in Greek. An example of the best in each tongue, the first in the former and the second in the latter, must be of interest, although the literal prose version cannot have the charm of the original verse.[52]

The Alpine ice, already precious in its frigidity, acquires an intense hardness through the action of the solar rays, but unable to transform itself entirely into a gem, it betrays its original source by the water that still remains within it. This adds at once to the beauty of this liquid stone and to its value.

In its changeful aspect, this crystal born from snow and fashioned by the hand of man is an image of the world, of the heavens enclosing cruel ocean in their wide embrace.

---

[51] Plinii, "Historia naturalis," Lib. xxxvii, cap. 73.

[52] Collection des auteurs Latin, ed. by M. Nazaire; vol. i, Lucain, Silius Italicus, Claudien, text and French trans., Paris, 1850, pp. 737, 738.

An old superstition among the Laplanders of Sweden is that in order to avert or cure disease which may be or has been caused by sleeping in the open air on the exposed moorland, three pebbles should be gathered, one from the water, one out of the earth, and the third from the surface of the ground or "from the air." These are placed on a fire until they become red-hot, and are then thrown into water; the stone which sizzles most is that belonging to the element which has caused the illness. The whole body, or sometimes only the afflicted part, is to be moistened with the water in which the pebbles have been immersed, and each separate stone is to be carefully returned to the spot whence it was taken.[53]

Near Middleville, in Herkimer County, New York, in a calciferous limestone, gray and brownish-gray in color, there are numerous cavities varying in size from that of a pinhead to that of a man's head. In these cavities are found carbonaceous substances such as asphaltum and other hard, black hydrocarbons. These cavities also frequently show mud or sand adhering to the sides, or mud and sand mixed with the petroleum, in which are often found brilliant and transparent rock-crystals, the purest of any found in the world. They are unusually perfect hexagonal prisms with both sets of six pyramid faces; that is, with same slight modification, eighteen brilliantly polished faces. These are especially sought after on account of their great purity, and because it is considered that he who wears one will have fair weather and secure the blessing of fair sailing on the sea of life. Some of these crystals are so small, though of absolute perfection, that it would require 250,000 of them to weigh an ounce; others again are sometimes as large as from one to

[53] Torsten Kolmodin, "Lapparne och deres Land; Skildringar och Studier," Pt. III, Stockholm, 1914, p. 14.

two inches in length. When not entirely transparent they frequently contain inclusions of black asphaltum or other hydrocarbons and also contain hollow cavities which are filled with fluid, sometimes salt water and sometimes liquid carbonic acid gas. In these are moving bubbles and occasionally a heavy hydrocarbon; that is, a bubble will ascend and the hydrocarbon will sink; or else the bubble will rise and take with it a small speck of hydrocarbon, and another will sink. In a wonderful specimen now at the American Museum of Natural History there is an object like a small spider of hydrocarbon which sinks while a minute water-bubble rises. They are called fair-weather stones.

Tasmanian rain-makers use white stones in their magical rites; however, the stone by itself is not considered an effective talisman, for it must be dipped in the blood of a young girl to give it added power. After a number of white pebbles have been steeped for a time in this blood, the rainmaker ties them up in strips of bark and sinks them in some deep water-hole in which a diabolical spirit is supposed to dwell. The natives confidently assert that this ceremony is soon followed by the desired rain-fall. As the belief prevails here as elsewhere, that these white stones or pebbles to retain their power must not be looked upon by a woman, it seems a little strange that the rain-bringing stone is dipped in a young girl's blood.[54]

However, white stones have not always and everywhere been regarded as lucky, for it is stated that among the fishermen of the Isle of Man the presence of a white stone in a fishing-smack is confidently believed to portend poor fishing. Indeed it has been reported by a Scotchman, who went out in a fishing boat for several consecutive days with a party of

---

[54] Nona Lebour, "White Quartz Pebbles and their Archæological Significance"; reprint from Transactions of the Dumfriesshire and Galloway Natural History and Antiquarian Society, January 30, 1914, p. 10.

Manx fishermen, that after a succession of days marked by poor fishing they began to nickname him "White Stone." [55]

An oath taken on sacred stones was regarded by the ancient Scandinavians as peculiarly binding upon him who took such an oath; in the old Norse annals it is stated that Gudrun Gjukesdatter offered King Atle that he would take an oath on the "pure white stone." The hero Duthmaruno is said to have sworn by "Loda's Stone of Power," which represented the almighty divinity of the Norsemen.[56]

A sacred well on the north side of Lough Neagh, Ireland, lends peculiar sanctity to the yellow crystals found in great quantity near by. The belief in their miraculous quality finds expression in the legend that they grow up out of the ground on Midsummer Night, and whosoever wishes to possess them as talismans must pronounce certain magic rhymes in the act of collecting them. They then become luck-bringers of potent virtue and ensure the prosperity of the household in which they are guarded.[57]

The stone, or rather rock, named catlinite, and popularly known as "pipe-stone," was regarded by certain tribes as one of their most valuable materials,[58] and was extensively used for pipe-bowls. In color it ranges from a deep red to an ashy tint; the chief quarry is situated some three hundred miles west of the Falls of St. Anthony, on the dividing ridge between the Saint Peter's and Missouri rivers. This region was visited in 1836 by George Catlin, to whom we are indebted for the preservation of so much regarding Indian folklore and customs, and after whom the substance

---

[55] W. G. Wood-Martin, "Traces of the Elder Faiths of Ireland," London, 1902, vol. i, p. 331.

[56] Finn Magnussen, "Forsog til Forklaring over nogle Steder af Osian"; Det Skandinaviske Litteraturselskabs Skrifter, 1813, Pt. II, pp. 237, 251.

[57] W. G. Wood-Martin, "Traces of the Elder Faiths of Ireland," London, 1902, vol. i, p. 330.

[58] Kunz, "Gems and Precious Stones of North America," New York, 1890, pp. 206–210.

is named. While it is impossible to determine with any degree of certainty for how long a time the Indians were familiar with this material, there are those who believe that the quarries were worked and the material used for pipe-bowls by native sculptors long before the earliest notice we have to that effect.[59] Great skill and patience were displayed by the Indians in the making of these pipe-bowls, which were sometimes carved with various symbolical figures. We have an early record of such pipes from the pen of Jacques Marquette, a Jesuit missionary to the Indians, who saw one when visiting the Illinois Indians in 1673. He reports it as being of polished red stone, like marble, so pierced that one orifice served to hold the tobacco, while the other was fastened on the stem, which was a stick two feet long, as thick as a common cane and pierced in the middle. The whole was covered with large feathers of red, green, and other colors.

Catlin states that at the time of his visit the "pipestone" quarry was guarded with a certain religious reverence from the visit of the white man, the Indians declaring that this red stone was "a part of their flesh," and that to take it from them would be to tear out their flesh and spill their blood. This highly poetic language may or may not have signified a superstitious reverence for the substance; indeed, it may simply have voiced the fear of these Indians that they might be despoiled of what for them was an especially valuable material, which they asserted had been bestowed upon them by the Great Spirit for the making of pipes exclusively. In our day an old Ojibway Indian, especially skilled in the work, has a name signifying "he who makes pipes," and carved pipe-bowls of catlinite are usually sold for from $1 to $10 apiece; as much as $20,

---

[59] Basher, "Catlinite, Its Antiquity as a Material for Tobacco Pipes," Am. Nat., vol. xvii, p. 745, July, 1883.

HINDU WEARING A COLLECTION OF ANCESTRAL PEBBLES AS AMULETS

however, is occasionally paid for a particularly large and finely carved specimen. This substance is also worked up into charms and other small ornaments which are sold to tourists, the annual sales of all descriptions amounting to some $10,000 annually. Catlinite takes a fine polish and is easily worked; a peculiarly attractive variety is red with white and gray spots.

The popular fancy for the "Fairy Stones" from a peak of the Blue Ridge Mountains, Patrick County, Virginia, is said to be directly traceable to the tale, "Trail of the Lonesome Pine," by John Fox, Jr., who makes one of these pretty staurolite crystals exercise an important influence over the destinies of his hero and heroine. This was cleverly utilized by the manager of a New York theatre, when he gave a souvenir performance of a dramatized version of the story, by presenting one of these "Fairy Stones" to each lady in the audience, a gift not only in perfect *rapport* with the play, but one highly appreciated by the recipients, few of whom were not unconsciously influenced by the symbolic half-religious, half-mythical quality ascribed to this attractive little gem.

Collections of stones and pebbles, often of little or no intrinsic value but supposed to possess occult powers, are handed down from father to son in many Hindu families of the poorer class. The accompanying illustration shows an aged Hindu, as he appeared to a recent traveller, decorated with such stones to the number of about three hundred on a ceremonial occasion. In this case they were all pierced and threaded on cords, so as to be attached to the person, and the old man proudly declared that, thousands of years ago, one of his ancestors was a playmate of the god Krishna, who had bestowed the stones upon him as a special mark of divine favor.

The presence of erratic boulders was accounted for by

popular legend in a variety of ways. Sometimes it was declared that the Virgin or a saint, while bearing an enormous stone through the air to be used in the construction of a church, had learned on the way that the church was completed and the stone no longer needed, and immediately let it drop to the earth.[60]

A stone having the rude form of a chair or seat, and known as Canna's Stone, enjoyed repute in Wales for its curative powers. It was in a field in close proximity to the church of Llangan, Carmarthenshire, which owed its foundation to St. Canna. Near this stone is a well called Flynon Canna, the waters of which were believed to be a cure for ague. To make the cure effective, however, the patient, after imbibing the sacred water, had to sit for a time in Canna's Stone, and if he dozed while sitting there this was considered to promise a speedy recovery. The combined treatment by well and stone was often repeated for several successive days and was occasionally prolonged for two or three weeks.[61]

That a child could be cured of disease by being passed through an aperture in one of the sacred stones that had formed part of a dolmen is shown in the case of a stone of this kind preserved in the church of Villers-Saint-Sépulcre, dept. Oise, France. There is another such stone in the same department, at Trie, used in a like way for the cure of feeble children or those suffering from rachitis. This reveals in a striking way the persistence of superstitious beliefs which were already condemned in 567 A.D. by the council of Tours, which prescribed that the eucharist should be refused to those who venerated these so-called sacred stones, and at a

---

[60] Renel, "Les religions de la Gaule avant le Christianisme," Paris, 1906, p. 387.

[61] Wirt Sikes, "British Goblins; Welsh Folk-Lore, Fairy Myths, Legends and Traditions," London, 1880, p. 362.

still earlier date, in 443 A.D., a council decree pronounced those bishops guilty of sacrilege who permitted the making of vows over these stones or the deposition of offerings thereon.[62]

Some of the stones of the druidic dolmens were called by the French peasants of a later age *pierres tourniresses,* or "whirling stones," for it was solemnly asseverated that at midnight on Christmas Eve these stones gyrated on their base. A still stranger fancy was that some other stones of this class became fearfully thirsty at times, once every hundred days, or perhaps only once in a century, and then rolled off to the nearest stream to slake their thirst. Under others, again, it was believed that a hidden treasure reposed, watchfully guarded by a terrible dragon. However, on one night in the year, while the clock was striking twelve, he snatched a moment's sleep, and whoever was clever enough and quick enough to make use of this chance could acquire untold riches.[63]

A strange belief prevails in and about Dourges (dept. Aube), France. On the top of a hill near this place is a chapel built in honor of St. Estapin, and in close proximity to this chapel are rocks with many irregular hollows of such varying shapes and forms that almost any part of the human body can be thrust into the openings. On the 6th of August in each year, those from the neighborhood suffering from illness or disability of any kind come hither, and, after having made their way as best they can nine times around the chapel, proceed to the platform whereon are the wonder-working stones, and introduce the afflicted part of their body into the appropriate opening in one of the rocks. The result

---

[62] Renel, "Les religions de la Gaule avant le Christianisme," Paris, 1906, p. 369.

[63] Ibid., 1906, p. 368.

is said to be an immediate cure of the trouble, however serious this may be, one experiment being sufficient.[64]

Stones of peculiar shape or marked color are those to which popular fancy has most often attributed a certain sanctity or power. Instances of this may be found in the Scottish isles. Thus, on the island of Arran in the Firth of Clyde, a green stone of approximately spherical form had acquired great repute for its healing virtue, especially for those having pains in the side. When this stone was laid upon the seat of the trouble, the pain would disappear. This, however, was not the only use to which it was put, for oaths were taken upon it, proving the presence of a certain animistic belief in the islanders' minds, as though some spirit dwelt in or animated the stone and would take vengeance on a perjuror. A still better proof of this was the idea that the green stone of Arran would bring victory to a leader if he bore it with him and cast it into the enemies' ranks at the decisive moment of a conflict, as is said to have been done by the Lord of the Isles. Alongside of this green stone may be placed a blue stone credited in the Scotch island of Fladda with the possession of like healing power, and on which also oaths were taken.[65]

A large, flat stone in St. Andrew's on the isle of Guernsey is stated to have borne a somewhat humorously misleading French inscription. This ran: "Celui qui me tournera, Son temps point ne perdra," which has been freely rendered:

To him who turns me up I say
His labor won't be thrown away.

This tempting promise, interpreted as a sign that some buried treasure was hidden in the ground beneath the stone,

[64] Paul Sebillot, "The Worship of Stones in France," trans. by Joseph D. McGuire, *American Anthropologist*, Jan.–Mar., 1902, vol. iv, No. 1, p. 98; citing Société des Antiquaires, vol. i, p. 429.

[65] Martin, "Description of the Western Isles," in Pinkerton's "Voyages and Travels," vol. iii, pp. 646. 627.

finally induced some one to devote much toil and time to the difficult task of turning the stone over. What, however, was his chagrin and disgust when the under side presented the words: "Tourner je voulais, Car lassée j'étais" (I longed to turn, because I was so tired). Whether the practical joker who originated the inscription was present to enjoy the success of his joke is not revealed.[66]

To a mass of quartz at Jerbourg, Guernsey Island, local fancy has attached a wild legend, which finds expression in the strange designation of the stone as "The Devil's Claw." The old Chronique de Normandie, which, although written much earlier, was first printed in 1576 at Rouen, recounts under date of 797 A.D. that Duke Richard, when on his way from one of his strongholds to a manor where dwelt a damsel of surpassing beauty, was assailed by the Evil One; but, like a second St. Michael, Duke Richard overcame his dangerous antagonist. Seeing that he could not prevail by force, the Devil had recourse to one of his most perilous wiles, and changed himself into a beautiful, richly-attired maiden. In this disguise he lured Duke Richard to the seashore and induced him to enter a boat and put out to sea. He thus spirited the duke away to the lonely isle of Guernsey, and at the landing spot, where the Devil finally seized his too-confiding prey, stands this mass of quartz, a deep black splash running right across, indicating in popular fancy the mark left by the devil's claws.[67]

A solitary boulder standing on a heath in North Germany is the subject of a curious legend illustrating the superstitious reverence inspired by the thunder. Once upon a time a bridal procession was traversing the heath when a violent thunder-storm broke out. Taking no heed of this, the musicians who accompanied the procession continued to

[66] Sir Edgar McCulloch, "Guernsey Folk Lore," London, 1903, p. 150.
[67] Ibid., p. 157; fig. on p. 156.

play their gay and festive music, and as a punishment for this lack of respect the God of Thunder changed the whole party into an immense rock.[68]

An erratic boulder lying in midstream in the River Ferse, in West Prussia, at a bend it makes between Peplin and Eichwald, is known in legend as the Teuffelsstein (Devil's Stone). It can only be reached by swimming to it, the part above the surface of the water measuring 26¼ feet in circumference, the height from the bed of the stream being 8¼ feet. A thick growth of alders on the banks of the Ferse at this point casts strange and sharp shadows over the gleaming surface of the block which is a biotitic gneiss. Legend tells that the Devil once tried to wreck the tower of the church at Peplin by hurling this mass of rock at it, but just as he had it poised in the air and was about to cast it forth the church bells began to ring the call for early mass, and he was forced to let the boulder drop. Another version is that he really threw it, but that it fell short of its mark.[69]

Near Hasselager in Denmark there is an immense boulder about 150 feet in circumference and 32 feet in height. Of this stone legend tells that a witch became so enraged at the fact that the steeple of the church at Svinninge was used by sailors as a landmark, that she picked up the stone and hurled it at the church, but missed her aim. As the boulder is estimated to weigh 1000 tons, this "witch" must have been regarded as a superhuman personality. The legend seems to indicate that she profited by the shipwrecks which were only too frequent on this rocky coast, and grudged the poor sailors the good service rendered them by the prominent steeple.

[68] Kuhn, "Norddeutsche Sagen," Leipzig, 1848, p. 69.

[69] Hermann, "Die erratischen Blöcke im Regierungsbezirck Danzig," Berlin, 1911, p. 41; in vol. ii, Pt. I, "Beiträge zur Naturdenkmalpflege, ed. by H. Conwentz.

A rock in Ardmore Bay, Ireland, is known as the St. Declan Stone, after the first bishop of Ardmore, who came to Ireland even before the arrival of the great St. Patrick. This rock is believed by the peasants to be endowed with great and occult powers, and the legend tells that it was carried through the air from Rome to its present resting place in the bay, at the time St. Declan was erecting his church at Ardmore. The fact that the stone rests upon a number of smaller ones renders it possible for people to squeeze their way under it at low tide, and those who pass beneath it three times are believed to have earned the special favor of St. Declan.[70]

A mass of calcareous stone in a village called Piada de Roland, situated in the commune of Toufailles (dept. Tarn-et-Garonne), France, shares with some other similar stones in this region the curious name of Roland's Foot (Piada de Roland). The one preserved in Toufailles measures 70 cm. × 47 cm. × 50 cm., and bears a natural imprint having the form of a foot. Legend accounts for this by the tale that the hero Roland once jumped from this stone to another at Sept Albres and in taking this tremendous leap thrust his foot down so strongly upon its support as to leave an imprint on the solid rock. For a time the "Piada de Roland" was kept in a cow-house—not a remarkably honorable place of deposit—but after the death of one of the cows a sorcerer advised the stone should be broken and removed, as a precautionary measure; this is said to have happened but thirty years ago, showing how deeply rooted such superstitious ideas are among the peasantry in out-of-the-way parts of France.[71]

Another rock-imprint, this time simulating that made

[70] Walsh, "Curiosities of Popular Customs," Philadelphia, 1911, p. 325.

[71] Armand Viré, "Pierres à gravures et Pierres à légendes dans le Lot et le Tarn et Garonne"; in Compte Rendu of the Ninth Session of the Congrès Préhistorique de France, Paris, 1914, p. 349.

by the hoof of a horse, is to be seen toward the edge of the abyss of Padirac (dept. Lot). Here again a local legend has been evolved to explain the imprint. We are told that the attention of both Satan and St. Martin had been powerfully attracted to the region, each strenuously seeking to gain possession of the souls of those who died, Satan of course wishing to bear them off with him to the depths of the infernal regions, while St. Martin cherished the fond hope of bringing them to Heaven. Unhappily the sins of the inhabitants of the region so much outweighed their merits that the Devil was almost invariably successful. Once upon a time, when he was riding off to his lurid realm, bearing with him a sackful of lost souls, he met St. Martin, who was full of grief at the fact that he himself had not a single soul to carry heavenward. Knowing, however, that Satan was passionately fond of gaming, he proposed that they should play a game the stake of which should be the sackful of souls. Satan consented, trusting to his powers of trickery, but all his deceptions proved vain, and the precious souls became the property of the saint. Enraged at losing the stakes, the Devil stamped on the ground, and an immense abyss opened up, threatening to engulf St. Martin; however, the latter put up a prayer to God, and spurred on his steed to a supreme and successful effort at escape, but one of the hoofs struck the rock with such force that it made an indentation therein figuring the clear outlines of a horse's hoof.[72]

The Kiowa have a sacred stone whose form suggests the head and bust of a man. This image, called *taimé,* has long been considered a kind of palladium of the tribe. It is preserved in a box made of stiff dressed rawhide (*parflèche*) and was only shown once a year, at the annual Sun Dance. As this sacred dance has not been performed since

---

[72] Ibid., p. 350.

KILLING A DRAGON TO EXTRACT ITS PRECIOUS STONE
From Johannis de Cuba's "Ortus Sanitatis," Strassburg, 1483. See page 16.

NATURALLY MARKED STONE
From Valentini, "Museum museorum," Frankfurt am Mayn, 1714. Collection of James I, of England; now in Copenhagen. See page 45.

1887, the *taimé* of the Kiowa has not been viewed by mortal eye since that time, not even the custodian of the treasure having the privilege of opening the box, except on the occasion of the ceremonial dance above mentioned.[73] Whether this stone has been rudely fashioned into its present shape, or whether its natural form suggested its use as a simulacrum of some deity, has not been determined; it is evidently not of meteoric origin as were many of the curiously shaped stones venerated as images of the gods in ancient times, in both Europe and Asia.

In the rock of St. Gowan's chapel in Wales was a natural cavity upon which the name of the Expanding Stone was bestowed by popular tradition, because the strange fancy prevailed that this stone automatically adapted itself to the size of anyone who entered the cavity. The legend ran that once, during the Pagan persecutions, when a fugitive Christian, hotly pursued, reached this rock it opened up of its own accord so that he could slip into it, and then closed about him so as to hide him effectually from his enemies. This Expanding Stone was believed to manifest its magic power by bringing to pass the wish expressed by anyone who entered it, provided he did not change his wish while he turned around within it.[74]

The natives of the French colony of New Caledonia in the southern Pacific, attach special importance to the fortuitous shape of stones in using them for talismans or amulets. According to their form such stones are considered to procure favorable effects against famine, madness, or death; to induce sunshine or rain, or else to bring good luck in fishing or in sailing, each special use being sug-

[73] Dr. Walter Hough in "Handbook of American Indians north of Mexico," ed. by Frederick Webb Hodge, Smithsonian Inst.; Bur. of Am. Ethn., Bull. 30; Washington, 1910, Pt. 2, p. 194.

[74] Wirt Sikes, "British Goblins: Welsh Folk-Lore, Fairy Myths, Legends and Traditions," London, 1880, p. 365.

gested by some different form, the color also being in some cases a determining factor. For the purpose of securing a better yield from fruit-trees a stone having the approximate shape of the fruit or with markings similar to those on fruit or tree is the one indicated by nature as the appropriate talisman, as in the case of the cocoa-nut palm, where a stone marked with black lines is the one chosen. Sometimes two different talismanic stones are used in this practice, a smaller one figuring the unripe fruit; when the tree begins to bear, the small stone is buried at its foot, and as soon as the fruit begins to mature, the small stone is removed and the larger one, representing the ripe fruit, is buried in its place.[75]

The Scotch of a century or more ago are said to have considered that an isolated stone or boulder, firmly fixed in the earth, possessed powers of a peculiar sort, and some such stones were used to cure bruises and strains and reduce swellings.[76] As it was also thought that a blow from a stone of this type was especially hurtful, this would be another case of homœopathic treatment of which so many and various examples are afforded by the superstitious use of stones and gems, as well as of other objects to which certain advantageous qualities were attributed.

Small stone boulders have been made use of by ejected peasants in Fermanagh, Ireland, in a magical incantation designed to draw down a curse upon a merciless landlord. For this purpose the peasant would collect a number of such stones, pile them up on his hearth as he would have piled turf sods, and then put up a petition that all manner of bad luck and misfortune might befall the landlord and his descendants to remote generations. Hereupon he would gather up the stones again, and, carrying them off, would

---

[75] Father Lambert, "Moeurs et Superstitions des Néo-Calédoniens," Noumea, 1900, pp. 217, 218, 222, 292–304.

[76] See Scott's "Border Minstrelsy," vol. iv, Pt. II, p. 645.

scatter them about in bog-holes, pools or streams, so that they should never be brought together again.[77] This was evidently done in the belief that the curse could only be raised if a counter-invocation were pronounced over the same collection of stones. An allusion to a custom of turning stones about while reciting a formula of malediction is contained in the following lines by Dr. Samuel Ferguson:

> They hurled their curse against the King,
> They cursed him in his flesh and bones,
> And even in the mystic ring,
> They turn'd the malediction stones.

Of all "magic stones" none seem better to deserve this designation than those mysterious and fascinating mineral specimens, veritable *lusus Naturæ,* bearing imprinted upon them by nature's hand some likeness of the human face or form. The grandeur and the overwhelming power of the material world are probably as much or even more felt in our prosaic age than they were in the earliest times, but this sentiment is sometimes coupled with a sense of distrust —happily neither general nor permanent—as to the presence in this tremendous and inspiring aggregate of forces of any distinct and definite evidence of the working of an intelligence closely similar to our own. It seems not unlikely that to this half-distrust is in great part due the fascination exercised by these naturally designed stones. We know, indeed, that when examined critically by the mineralogist, their strange markings become explicable as the results of fortuitous stratifications and juxtapositions, but to our instinctive appreciation they offer so close and startling an analogy to the artistic reproductions consciously made by the hand of man, guided by his experience

[77] Lean's Collectanea (by Vincent Stuckey Lean), vol. ii, Pt. I, Bristol, 1903, p. 476; see W. F. Wademan in Jour. Roy. Hist. and Arch. Assoc. of Ireland, July, 1875.

and intelligence, that we are almost invariably impressed with a keener sense of our kinship with nature.

Some very characteristic and interesting specimens of these natural designs were at one time in the possession of Queen Victoria, many of them having been formerly among the treasures in the valuable and extensive collection of pearls and precious stones carefully gathered together by the famous banker and connoisseur, Henry Philip Hope. Quite recently (April 20, 21, 1914) these objects, which had passed into the J. E. Hodgkin Collection, were sold at Christie's in London. Perhaps the most remarkable is thus described by B. Hertz in the Hope Catalogue:[78]

No. 62. A very beautiful lusus, in white and brown agate, representing a miniature face and neck, with light brown hair and white chaplet, surrounded by a dark brown ground colour.

So singularly natural and artistic is this strange gem, that it is difficult to banish the conviction that we are not gazing upon a fine example of a miniature done by an impressionist.[79] Another interesting, though somewhat less notable example, was a polished flint, of a brownish-gray hue, bearing a half-front miniature of an aged head and face marked in a light brownish-white;[80] still another offered the representation of a human head, the face half turned away; this was also a flint, the groundwork of a light horn-color, the design being of a still lighter shade of the same color.[81]

While nearly all these natural designs are in the flat, occasional examples of relief or intaglio are recorded. As

---

[78] Catalogue of the collection of pearls and precious stones formed by Henry Philip Hope, Esq. Systematically arranged and described by B. Hertz, London, 1839.

[79] Op. cit., p. 106.

[80] Op. cit., No. 66, p. 106.

[81] Op. cit., No. 65, p. 106.

an instance may be noted a remarkable double gem or medallion said to have been revealed on splitting open a clump of copper ore from the Bottendorf copper mines. On each of the two halves was marked the image of a male human head, dressed with a peruke, but while on one side the representation was in relief, on the opposite half it was in intaglio.[82]

A remarkable find of three of these naturally marked stones is stated to have been made in the river Theiss, near the town of Winterhut, in 1556, "on a Monday after the festival of St. Gall." On one of these flint pebbles was depicted a cross, a sword and a rod; the two others bore respectively a cross and the Burgundian arms, all being as clearly defined as though the work of the human hand.[83]

These smaller natural pictures were, however, greatly surpassed in effectiveness by some most extraordinary representations on slabs of stone, frequently on marble slabs, the strange arrangement of the veinings constituting veritable pictures of considerable extent and marvellously deceptive quality. Thus in the church of San Lorenzo in Florence was to be seen a natural marble on which were depicted two men bearing a bunch of grapes on a rod.[84] Another marble slab, preserved in the Danish Collection in Copenhagen and originally owned by James I of England, presented in most beautiful colors an image of a crucifix.[85]

To the natural image found in a specimen of copper ore may be added a much more remarkable picture discovered in a piece of iron-ore. This was found on October 8, 1669,

[82] Valentini, "Museum Museorum, oder der Vollständige Schau-Bühne," Franckfurt am Mayn, 1713, Pt. II, p. 41; figured.

[83] Ulyssis Aldrovandi, "Museum metallicum," Bononiæ, 1648, p. 527; figured on p. 528.

[84] Valentini, "Museum Museorum," p. 42; citing description by Major in his "Tractatus de cancris et lapidibus petrifactis," p. 64.

[85] Ibid., p. 42; Pl. IX, fig. 3.

by a miner of the Innesberg mines. The clump of ore weighed about two pounds and when the miner split it open with a blow of his hammer, he was startled to see on the upper half a strange and marvellous design. Calling up a companion, he exclaimed: "Look here! Here is the Blessed Virgin on this stone!" On examining the other half, the same design appeared there also. This remarkable find is said to have been recorded in the book of the mine, the stone itself having been delivered to the German imperial inspectors.[86]

It is well to bear in mind that the number of these *lusus naturæ* seemed very much larger in the eyes of writers of a few centuries ago than to us to-day, for the numerous petrifactions, showing a great variety of animal and vegetable forms, were for a long period included in the same category with the stones bearing curiously deceptive markings or veinings. Much ingenuity was expended by early observers in the attempt to explain the cause of these phenomena. The learned Jesuit, Athanasius Kircher, for example, after having proved experimentally that designs treated with certain chemical agents could be made to impress figures upon stones, took refuge in the strange hypothesis that pictures made on wood or some soft material by primitive miners had been left in the mine and with the lapse of time had slipped down into crevices in the rock, and, becoming tightly wedged in, had impressed the design on the contact-rock; or else he suggested that the original material on which the design had been made might in process of time have, by some unknown means, been converted into marble.[87] As a striking example of a picture of this class, Kircher notes and figures an image naturally designed

[86] Ibid., p. 41; figured. From report in Miscellan. Acad. Germ. Cur., Decur. I, Ann. I, Obs. CXIII, p. 232.

[87] Athanasii Kircheri, "Mundus subterraneus," Amstelodami, 1665, vol. ii, pp. 42 sqq.

on a stone slab in St. Peter's in Rome and bearing a remarkable likeness to the Blessed Virgin of Loreto.[88]

The electric or magnetic gems, tourmaline, amber, and loadstone, possess not only great scientific interest, but demonstrate the fact that a certain energy really does proceed from some of these fair, ornamental objects, an energy that produces a positive action from without upon the human body. This may well serve to make us less resolutely sceptical as to the possible presence in gem-stones of some other forms of emanation not as yet susceptible of scientific determination.

The supersensitiveness of the innocent child-soul to the most delicate impressions, and hence to the radiations or emanations from precious stones, is well brought out in the pretty tale by Saxe Holme (Helen Hunt Jackson), entitled "My Tourmaline."[88a] The particular specimen here immortalized was one of the finest from the famous Mount Mica deposits in the State of Maine. One day, while on a country ramble, the little heroine's eye is caught by the color and sparkle of a brilliant crystal lodged in the gnarled roots of an old tree. In springing forward to secure this pretty treasure the girl trips on the outstanding roots, falls, and sprains her leg very seriously, so that she is laid up for six weeks. However, the beautiful crystal is her great consolation through the long, dreary weeks, and, strange to say, she comes to feel that it has a kind of life in it. This is manifested to her and also to some others, on touching the stone, by a pricking or tingling sensation in the hand; but to the child the sensations excited by the wonderful crystal, as perfectly formed as though cut by a lapidary, red at one end, green at the other, with a separating band of white, are much more pronounced. When it is placed in the little silken bag that has been made to hold it, and

[88] Op. cit., vol. i, p. 39; Pl. IV, fig. 6.

[88a] Scribner & Co., 1886.

is laid against her cheek, her feverish restlessness gradually disappears and gives place to tranquil sleep. More than this, she is aware of a species of subconscious sympathy with the tourmaline. So intense is this sympathy that although the child consented to part with her crystal that it might be offered as a unique specimen to a foreign museum, and was heart-broken to learn that through some carelessness it had been lost while being taken thither, she recognized its presence long years after, when, travelling in Europe as a young bride, she entered the cabinet of an enthusiastic collector to view his specimens, and was in no wise surprised when she really found her "Stonie" there among his prized tourmalines.

In connection with this pretty recital it is interesting to note that the first chance observation of the attractive qualities of tourmalines is said to have been made in Amsterdam by a group of Dutch children whose attention had been attracted by a number of tourmaline crystals brought from the Orient, and who were puzzled to see bits of ash and straw attracted to the stones. This came to the knowledge of some Dutch lapidaries, who for a time called the stone Aschentrekker, or "Ash-Attractor."[89] Our name tourmaline is derived from *turmali,* the name given the stone by the natives of Ceylon.

There seems some little likelihood that certain examples of the gem called *lychnis* and noted by Pliny may have been varieties of the tourmaline. As the first tourmalines brought to modern Europe came to Holland from Ceylon, we might conjecture that those kinds of *lychnis* said by Pliny to have been brought from India had a like origin. Of these Indian specimens, the finest examples of this gem, one kind resembled the carbuncle or ruby, while another bore the designation Ionia because its color was like that of the violet

---

[89] The Germans called it Aschenzieher.

(in Greek *ion*). The most striking peculiarity of the *lychnis* was its power to attract straws or bits of paper, when it had been heated by the sun's rays or by hand-friction.[90]

Such is the confusion in the statements made by the early Greek and Latin writers as to the emerald, under which generic name they seem to have included almost all green stones of any ornamental or other value, that we cannot absolutely reject the conjecture [91] that Theophrastus (third century B.C.), the earliest of these writers on precious stones, *might* have referred to specimens of green tourmaline, when he states that the true emerald appeared to have been produced from jasper, as one of the Cyprian specimens was said to have consisted of one-half jasper and the other half emerald, the metamorphosis as yet being incomplete.[92] We admit that if Theophrastus uses the word jasper here to signify the reddish variety, we would have the combination of green and red zones in a single crystal sometimes observable in tourmaline. How this can be reconciled with the previous statement of the same author that the Cyprian "emeralds" which came from the copper mines of that island were chiefly used for soldering gold, and hence seem to have been of the class of mineral called *chrysocolla* by ancient writers, is, however, not easy to suggest.[93]

The so-called Brazilian emeralds mentioned by the Dutch mineralogist, Johann de Laet, as having been found shortly before 1647 in mines near Spiritus Sanctus, may perhaps have been green tourmalines. These crystals were described

[90] Pliny, "Naturalis historia," Lib. xxxvii, cap. 29. In his recently published "Curious Lore of Precious Stones" the present writer suggested that Pliny's *lychnis* might have been a spinel, but while some of these "ardent stones" may have been spinels, those displaying the phenomenon of attraction must have been tourmalines.

[91] A. C. Hamlin.

[92] Theophrasti, "De lapidibus, peri tôn lithôn," ed. by John Hill, London, 1746, pp. 71–73 (cap. xlvi).

[93] Idem, pp. 68–71 (cap. xlvi); see also Hill's note on p. 69.

by Gesner as of cylindrical form, striated, and of a vitreous lustre; their color was like that of the prase and they were transparent. Although De Laet adds the assertion that the Oriental emerald (green corundum) was as hard as the sapphire, the Brazilian emeralds approached more closely to the Oriental in point of hardness than did emeralds from any other source of supply;[94] and green sapphires have never been found in Brazil, while green tourmalines have been.

The earliest published work in which the electric properties of tourmaline are noted appears to be an anonymous or quasi anonymous treatise published in 1707, certain initial letters of the quaint title being italicized to indicate the initials of the author's name.[95] The first scientist to derive the action of the so-called *Aschentrekker* or "Ash-Attractor" from electric energy is said to have been the great Linnæus, who bestowed upon the tourmaline the name of the "Electrical Stone."[96]

The attractive properties of the tourmaline are said to have been first brought to scientific notice by M. Louis Lémery, in a report made during 1717 to the French Academy of Sciences; however, Lémery was inclined to attribute them to magnetic influence. That these phenomena of attraction and repulsion were really due to the electric properties of the stone was first clearly brought out by the German physicist, Franz Ulrich Theodor Aepinus, and his conclusions were communicated to the Berlin Academy of Sciences in 1756.[97] Aepinus made his experiments upon two specimens of tourmaline from Ceylon, which had been

[94] Johannis de Laet, Antwerpii, "De gemmis et lapidibus, libri duo," Lugduni Batavorum [1647], pp. 36, 40.

[95] *Curiose Speculationes* bey schlaflosen Nächten . . . von einem *L*iebhaber der *I*mmer *G*ern *S*peculirt," Chemnitz und Leipzig, bey Conr. Stossein, 1707, 857, pp. 80.

[96] Johann Gustav Donndorf, "Natur und Kunst," Leipzig, 1790, p. 516.

[97] "Histoire de l'Académie Royale des Sciences et Belles Lettres," **vol. xii**, 1756; Berlin, 1758, pp. 105–121.

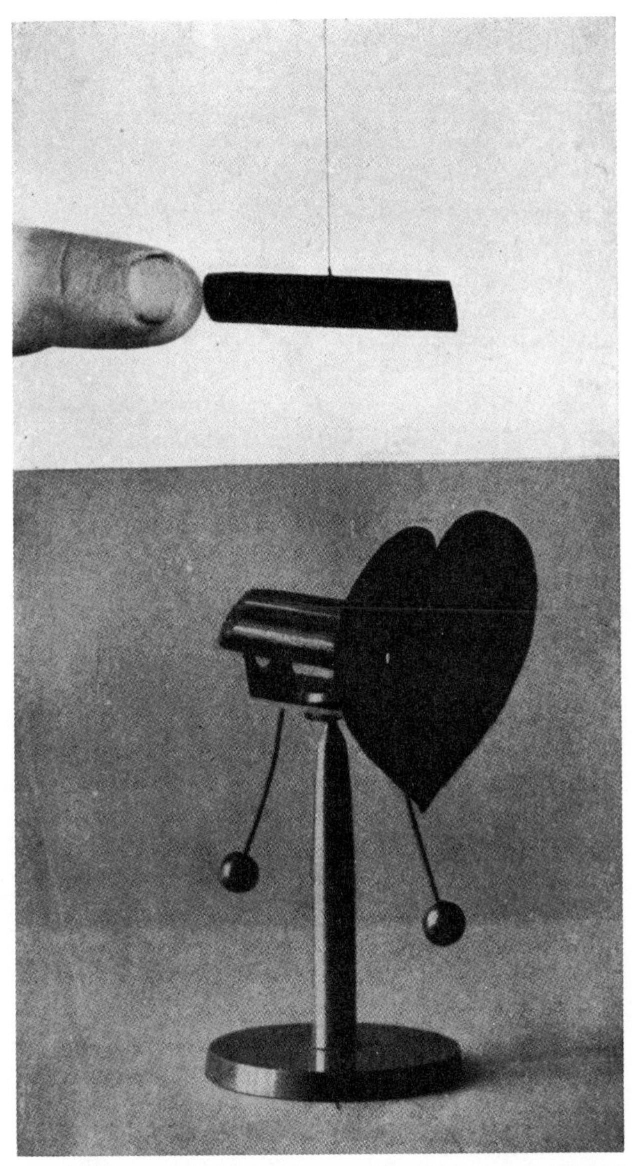

A SIMPLE APPARATUS FOR ILLUSTRATING THE ELECTRIC PROPERTIES OF THE TOURMALINE

The stone is suspended from a hollow rod and will be attracted by the finger, if the latter be brought within a short distance of the tourmaline. When the stone has been slightly heated, its positive electricity will draw toward it the heart-shaped piece of paper, just as amber attracts paper, or magnetic iron does iron filings.

furnished him by Lehmann, a fellow-member of the Berlin Academy, who, as Aepinus frankly admits, first drew his attention to the electric action of the stone. That not only friction but heat also should develop the electric energy, both positive and negative, of the tourmaline, serves to differentiate it from many other potentially electric substances, in the case of which friction alone is effective.

The specimen shown by M. Lémery to the French Academy of Sciences in 1717 is stated to have come from "a river in the Island of Ceylon," and is described as being of small size, flat, orbicular, quite thin, of a brown color, and smooth brilliant surface.[98] Its peculiar property of attracting and then repelling ashes or iron filings as well as bits of paper, was duly noted. This specimen had cost M. Lémery 15 livres. After reciting the constant repulsion and attraction exercised by a magnet upon the needle, the attraction by the opposite pole, and repulsion by the same pole, he proceeds to remark that this Cinghalese stone acted quite differently, since it first attracted and then repulsed the same object presented in the same way. This intermittent or irregular action was in his opinion to be explained by the theory that a vortex was intermittently developed in the substance. As it begins the small bodies are attracted, when it ceases they remain stationary, but when it is renewed "and there emanates from the stone a material analogous to the magnetic emanation" then the bodies are repulsed. Another peculiarity was that the body which had been repulsed could not again be attracted, whence the conclusion was arrived at that the stone's repellent force was superior to its attractive power. These necessarily somewhat inexact observations are interesting as marking one of the earliest attempts to

[98] See Historie de l'Académie Royale des Sciences Année mdccxvii Paris, 1719, pp. 7, 8.

explain these phenomena, even although the explanation is faulty.

The great French crystallographer, Abbé Haüy, relates his experiments on a tourmaline crystal.[98a] He set this crystal in steel clamps, with a long stem which was inserted in a wooden handle, and then subjected the tourmaline to the heat of a brasier. As the heat augmented and penetrated the stone, its natural electric force became decomposed, the two component fluids being forced to separate from each other. It was now necessary to cool the tourmaline off a little; when too much heated the electrical phenomena were interrupted; they were also diminished in intensity when the stone became cool again. The perfect crystal chosen for experiment clearly showed the negative and positive electrical poles; even the smallest pieces showed this, and, indeed, if a very small piece were broken off the positively electric side of a crystal, it would preserve this positive electricity and soon develop a negative electricity also.

We may be somewhat loath to doubt the tale that little Dutch children were the first to note what to them was the queer action of some bits of tourmaline, but preference should probably be given to the statement that the discovery of the electric phenomena induced by heating in these stones was due to the fact that some Dutch jewellers put specimens of tourmaline in the fire to test their hardness, and then found that the stones attracted or repelled the ashes of the fire.[99]

Toward the middle of the eighteenth century Dr. Haberden, of London, confirmed the deductions of Lémery and the somewhat later experiments of the German physicist Aepinus, and the gay world of London took up the idea,

---

[98a] Abbé Haüy, "Trattato dei caratteri fisici delle pietre preziose," Ital. trans. by Luigi Configliachi, Milano, 1819, pp. 135–138; see Plate II, fig. 49.

[99] Aepinus, l. c.

causing the new stone to become a great favorite with the fashionable. One of Hogarth's inimitable designs depicts a spendthrift fop who has just been arrested while his attention was riveted on the strange phenomena shown by the tourmaline.

In view of the important experiments made by Benjamin Franklin in the then almost unexplored field of electricity, it is easy to understand that the accounts of the newly-discovered electric properties of the tourmaline should have possessed considerable interest for him. This is testified to by a letter he addressed to Dr. William Haberden, June 7, 1759.[100] Herein he expresses his thanks for two tourmalines his correspondent had sent him, and states that he is returning the smaller one. Of the electric phenomena he writes that he had heard some "ingenious gentlemen abroad" had denied the negative electricity displayed by one side of a tourmaline, but he believes the failure to observe could be explained by defective cutting of the specimens used, the positive and negative planes having perhaps been obliquely placed; to obviate this he suggests that the positive and negative sides should be accurately determined before the operation of cutting begins. The larger of the specimens sent by Dr. Haberden was retained by Franklin, who had it mounted on a pivot in a ring, so that either side could be turned outward at will. He notes as a curious circumstance that when he wore this ring, the natural heat of the finger sufficed to charge the stone, causing it to attract light bodies. Several of his experiments were made with a cork ball suspended by a thread, and he claims that the attractive force of the positive face was increased by coating it with gold-leaf attached to the stone by white of egg. This greater effect he supposed "to be occasioned by the united force of

[100] The Complete Works of Benjamin Franklin, ed. by John Bigelow, New York and London, 1888, vol. x, pp. 282–285.

nt parts of the face collected and acting together through the metal."

While the various corundum gems, ruby, sapphire, Oriental topaz, Oriental amethyst, etc., offer a remarkable instance of the many varieties of beautiful coloration observable in a practically identical substance, no single gem-mineral can be said to equal tourmaline in this respect, more especially, however, in the combination of several colors sometimes disposed in bands, at other times in concentric circles in the same crystal. When to this we add its peculiar electric qualities, we may truly say that a fine tourmaline answers our idea of what a talismanic gem or a gem-amulet should be better than any other of the beautiful crystals with which bountiful nature has provided us. These most attractive stones are to be found in widely separated regions on the earth's surface, as fine examples have been discovered in the State of Minas Geraes, Brazil, and in our own land, in Maine and California especially. Where the color is homogeneous we may have the splendid red or rose-colored variety called rubellite, from its resemblance to the ruby, or the blue tourmaline gem named indicolite.

In times of old there was a belief that stones of various kinds would guard against the assaults of evil in the form of witchcraft, disease, and other disagreeable visitations. It was a warlike period in which peace was an unheard-of doctrine, and now that the idea of peace has become one of the ideals of present-day conditions, it is interesting to know that nature has furnished us with a stone at once beautiful, interesting, and illustrating the great fundamental principle of unity and peace.

The Peace Stone is formed by the union in one crystal of the green and the red tourmaline, with an intervening band or zone of white, the latter strikingly beautiful effect being due to the combination at this point of the red coloring matter, manganese, and the iron constituent, the source of the green hue; these two materials, by their union, neutralize each other, furnishing the transparent, colorless vein or zone. A slightly different combination of colors appears in a fine crystal, found some years ago at Mount Mica, Oxford County, Maine; this even offers a kind of "triple alliance," as it shows blue in its lower half, passing through white and pink to a grass-green at the upper end.[101]

These three hues combined in one body, in indissoluble union in spite of the differences of quality and color, yet represent one principle. This action of manganese in neutralizing the iron is well known to glass-makers; otherwise white glass could not be made. It would all be greenish in tint were it not for the use of oxide of manganese, or "glass-maker's soap," as it is termed, which neutralizes the production of a green tint by the iron and makes the white hue.

This beautifully symbolic stone is found in Paris, Maine, in San Diego County, California, and in Brazil. At times the outer edge of the stone is green, a transparent white zone surrounding the interior red zone, the whole looking for all the world like a section of watermelon, and hence it is sometimes called the "Watermelon Stone." Then again, the colors are joined in longitudinal strips, showing them side by side. This variety of tourmaline, although rare, is not especially costly, and is one more addition to the stones of sentiment, and more especially to those appropriate as symbols of our fair ideal, universal peace.

We can see symbolized in them the great and consoling fact that, however marked may be the differences between any two peoples, they need not be cause for enmity, but may instead become true and enduring sources of peace and bonds

[101] See the writer's "Gems and Precious Stones of North America," New York, 1890, Pl. 4, and also his "Precious Stones" in 20th Annual Report of the U. S. Geological Survey, Pt. VI, Washington, 1899, p. 577.

of union. The characteristic talents of each one will supplement and complete those of the other, so that working together in harmony they may accomplish far more for each other and for humanity in general than either could do singly.

At an early date amber was brought from the Baltic coast to Rome, and Tacitus states that those who collected it called it *glæsum,* a name later applied to the glass introduced into that region by Roman traders. The natives knew nothing of the nature or growth of amber, and had no use for the material, only collecting it for export to Rome, where it commanded such a high price as to excite their astonishment. Tacitus gives in the following words his theory of the origin and character of amber—his chief error being due to his belief that the substance was of very recent formation.[102]

> Now you must know that amber is a juice of trees, since various creatures, some of them winged, are often found in it. They have become entangled in the liquid and then inclosed when the matter hardened. Therefore I believe that, as incense and balsam are exuded in the remote East, so in the luxuriant groves and islands of the West are juices which are forced out by the sun close to them. These flow into the neighboring sea and are washed up by the tempestuous waves on the opposite shore. If you test the quality of amber with fire, it may be lighted like a torch and burns with a small, well-nourished flame; then it is resolved into a glutinous mass resembling pitch or resin.

Both Juvenal[103] and Martial[104] relate that effeminate Romans used to hold balls of amber in their hands to cool them during the summer heat. If any such agreeable sensation was really experienced, it must have been due to the well-known electric properties of this substance. It is stated that the Chinese often place pieces of amber on or in their

---

[102] Cornelii Taciti, "Libri qui supersunt," vol. ii, Lipsiæ, 1885, p. 243.
[103] Sat. vi, 572; ix, 50.
[104] Lib. v, 37, 9; xi, 8, 6.

pillows,[105] a use that may have been suggested by the same considerations.

As a proof of the extravagant value set upon amber by the Romans of the first century, Pliny notes that a very diminutive figure of a man, cut out of this substance, sold for a higher figure than did a healthy, vigorous slave. The popularity of this material was also attested by the fact that in the gay world of Rome the term "amber hair" was used to designate a rare and peculiar shade that became fashionable in this period.[106] It seems probable that this modish shade was somewhat lighter than the "Titian hair" once so much favored, although the difference may not have been very great.

A change of hue in amber was thought to portend a waning of love on the part of the giver, as is shown by the following not especially melodious lines from "The Fruits of Jealousy" published by Richard Tofte in 1615: [107]

> Thy tokens which to me thou sent
> In time may make thee to repent;
> Thy gifts do groan (bestow'd on me)
> For grief that they thee guilty see.
> The amber bracelet thou me gave
> (For fear thou shouldst shortly wave [108])
> From yellow turned is to pale,
> A sign thou shortly will be stale.

Not only for curative purposes and for general use as an amulet was amber prized, but an amber necklace was sometimes regarded as an especially auspicious decoration for a bride at her wedding, as is shown by an exceptionally fine necklace of facetted amber beads from Brunswick, Germany, made in the eighteenth century.

---

[105] Pfizmeier, Sitzungsbericht d. phil.-hist. Kl., Wien, 1866, vol. xliii, p. 195.
[106] Plinii, " Naturalis historia," Lib. xxxvii, cap. 12.
[107] Lean's Collectanea, vol. ii, Pt. II, Bristol, 1903, p. 640.
[108] Waver. Especially interesting as all amber changes in time.

Our earliest authority on the curative use of amber, the great encyclopædist Pliny, states that in his day the female peasants of the valley of the Po, in northern Italy, might be seen wearing amber necklaces, principally as ornaments, but also because of their remedial powers; for even at this early period it was generally believed that amber had most excellent effects in diseases of the throat and tonsils. The peasants of this region were especially subject to such disorders, and Pliny conjectures that they were caused by the different sorts of water in the neighborhood of the Alps.[109] He probably refers not only to diseases of the throat, properly so called, but also to a swelling of the glands of the neck, the *goître* with which so many of the peasants living on the slopes of the Alps, and in other mountainous regions of central Europe, are afflicted.

The golden-hued amber was called *chryselectrum* by Callistratus, as cited by Pliny. This was said to attract the flame and to ignite if it came in contact with the fire. If worn on the neck it was a cure for fevers; if powdered and mixed with honey and oil of roses it was beneficial for dimness of vision, and its powder, whether taken by itself or in water with gum mastic, remedied diseases of the stomach.[110] In ancient and medieval times the fear of poison being administered in food or drink was very great, and any substance that was credited with the power to show the presence of poison, by some change in clearness or color, was highly valued. An amber cup was said to reveal the admixture of any of the various kinds of poison with the liquid it contained.[111]

The use of amber as a preventive of erysipelas finds a defender in Rev. C. W. King, who writes as follows:

[109] Plinii, "Naturalis historia," Lib. xxxvii, cap. 11.

[110] Plinii, "Naturalis historia," Lib. xxxvii, cap. 12.

[111] Severus Sammonicus, "Preceptes médicaux," text and French trans. by L. Baudet, Paris, 1845, pp. 84, 85.

NECKLACE OF FACETED AMBER BEADS
German. Eighteenth century.

That the wearing an amber necklace will keep off the attacks of erysipelas in a person subject to them has been proved by repeated experiments beyond the possibility of doubt. Its action here cannot be explained; but its efficacy in defence of the throat against chills is evidently due to its extreme warmth when in contact with the skin and the circle of electricity so maintained.[112]

The electrical property of amber was remarked as early as 600 B.C. by the Ionic philosopher Thales, and from this observation may be dated the beginnings of the study of electric phenomena.

That faith in the magic powers of amber beads still exists is illustrated in the case of an old Russian Jewess who recently died in one of our charitable institutions. This woman is said to have reached the age of one hundred and six years, and she ascribed her extraordinary longevity to the possession of a necklace of very large amber beads, which had been given her by her mother, who also lived more than a hundred years. The daughter, a few days before her death, bestowed this treasured heirloom upon *her* daughter, for it is generally believed that the virtues of gems largely depend upon their being received as gifts.

In northern Germany, also, for more than a century a string of amber beads was looked upon as a favorite and necessary gift. The writer has seen hundreds of these strings, many of which have been worn for one, two, and sometimes more generations. The beads are round and usually facetted; however, they have been abraded against each other for so long that they are often flat disks, and a string originally fifteen or sixteen inches long will be twelve, and often only nine inches in length, so much of the original spheres having worn away.

A well-known physician of the sixteenth century, Johann Meckenbach, claimed, in 1548, to have discovered the process

[112] King, "Natural History of Precious Stones," etc., London, 1865, p. 334, note.

of producing oil of amber. Although Meckenbach was not entitled to the credit he claimed, as the experiment had already been successfully made, he gained great repute by this means, and when he communicated to Duke Albrecht of Prussia the secret of his process, the rulers of other lands overwhelmed the duke with requests for a supply of the precious remedy. Ferdinand, Archduke of Austria, sent a special messenger the long journey to Berlin, twice in a year, for a few flasks of the oil, which was regarded as a cure for many diseases.[113] The oil of amber—*oleum succini* of the Pharmacopœia—has maintained its repute as a cure for various affections up to the present day. In some forms of gout and rheumatism it relieves the inflammation and pain in the joints; and its antispasmodic action makes it a valuable remedy in cases of asthma, whooping-cough, hysteria, bronchitis, and infantile convulsions.[114]

An early version of the strange tale that ships were attracted by masses of rocks, or even mountains of loadstone, is given by Palladius (c. 367–c. 431 A.D.). He relates that the loadstone was produced on a group of islands called the Maniolæ, which were on the route to Taprobane (Ceylon), and continues, "if any ship constructed with iron nails approached these islands they were drawn by the power of the loadstone and their course was arrested. For this reason those voyaging to Taprobane use ships especially put together with wooden pegs." Probably the legend arose from the fact that wood was often used in the case of vessels trading in this region, because iron was scarce and expensive. This is the view of Procopius, who found the same story still current in the sixth century.[115]

---

[113] Raumer, "Historisches Taschenbuch," I Ser., vol. vi, Leipzig, 1835, p. 366.

[114] Pyle, "The Therapeusis of Precious Stones," in his "Medicine," Detroit, 1897, vol. iii, p. 115.

[115] Palladii, "De gentibus Indiæ," ed. Bissæus, London, 1665, p. 4.

It has been noted as a curious fact that none of the ancient writers who treat of the loadstone recognized that the attractive energy exerted by this substance on iron was also exerted by iron upon the loadstone; on the contrary, they constructed many ingenious hypotheses to explain why this was not the case.[116] The strange fancy that in the presence of a diamond a piece of loadstone was robbed of its attractive force, must have arisen from an observation of the well-known electric properties of the first-named stone, and from the idea that the much more valuable stone should have the greater power. Here, as in many other cases, we see how little interest was taken in actual experiment by ancient writers, a pre-conceived idea of the eternal fitness of things being the main criterion.

Spaniards of the thirteenth century believed that the magnetic power of the loadstone would depart from it if it were steeped in the juice of leek or onion for three days; but the virtue would return to the stone if it were bathed in goat's blood. This recalls the queer notion that the diamond could only be broken when moistened with goat's blood, both fancies having their origin in the idea that goat's, or rather ram's blood, was endowed with warmth and vitality to a higher degree than other blood.

An ingenious magnetic oracle is described by De Boot.[117] This consisted of a round board, about the edge of which were marked the letters of the alphabet, while in the centre there stood a small wooden figure, set on a pivot, and holding extended in one hand a little wand. One foot of this figure was slightly advanced and within it was concealed a small iron ball. The experimenter held in his hand a wooden sceptre, with a powerful loadstone at its top, and as he

---

[116] Martin, "Observations et théories des anciens sur les attractions et la répulsion magnétiques," in Atti dell' Accademia Pontefici dei Nuovi Lincei, vol. xviii, p. 18 (1864–65).

[117] "Gemmarum et lapidum historia," Lug. Bat., 1636, p. 466; Lib. II, cap. 204.

touched with his sceptre the lower side of the board, beneath the spot on which any one of the letters was marked, the attraction exercised by the loadstone on the iron made the figure revolve on its pivot so that the little wand pointed toward the letter indicated. In this way any word could be spelled out and appropriate answers given to any question. The device would be too obvious at present, but in De Boot's time it would have served well enough to mystify the spectators.

That the loadstone was highly esteemed in the sixteenth century was well versified by Robert Norman in "The Newe Attractive."

THE MAGNES OR LOADSTONES CHALLENGE

Give place ye glittering sparkes, ye glimmering Diamonds bright,
Ye Rubies red, and Saphires brave, wherein ye most delight.
In breefe yee stones enricht, and burnisht all with gold,
Set forth in Lapidaries shops, for Jewels to be sold.
Give place, give place I say, your beautie, gleame, and glee,
Is all the vertue for the which, accepted so you bee.
Magnes, the Loadstone I, your painted sheaths defie,
Without my helpe, in Indian Seas the best of you might lye.
I guide the Pilots course, his helping hand I am,
The Mariner delights in me, so doth the Marchant man.
My vertue lies unknowne, my secrets hidden are,
By me the Court and Common-weale, are pleasured very farre.
No ship could sayle on seas, her course to runne aright,
Nor compasse shew the ready way, were Magnes not of might.
Blush then, and blemish all, bequeathe to mee thats due,
Your seates in golde, your price in plate, which Jewellers doo rewe.
Its I, its I alone, whom you usurpe upon,
Magnes my name, the Loadstone cald, the prince of stones alone.
If this you can denie, then seeme to make reply,
And let the Painefull sea-man judge, the which of us doth lye.

THE MARINER'S JUDGMENT

The Loadstone is the stone, the only stone alone,
Deserving praise above the rest, whose vertues are unknowne.

THE MARCHANT'S VERDICT

The diamond bright, the Saphire brave, are stones that beare the name,
But flatter not, and tell the troath, Magnes deserves the same.[118]

It was reported in the seventeenth century that ruptures were cured in Belgium by the help of the loadstone. The patient was first given a dose of iron filings, reduced to a very fine powder; thereupon a plaster made of crushed loadstone was applied externally to the affected part. This was said to produce a cure in the space of eight days.[119] Probably the plaster was believed to draw the iron filings or some emanation from them through the affected parts toward the surface.

In medieval Europe this mineral was greatly valued for its therapeutic virtues. Trotula, the first of the female physicians connected with the celebrated School of Salerno, the centre of medical culture in Europe in the Middle Ages, and who wrote a treatise on female diseases, recommended the use of the loadstone in childbirth. The stone was to be held in the right hand, and the learned lady asserted that the wearing of a coral necklace would aid its beneficent effect. Both these substances are prescribed for this use by the Oxford teacher, John Gadesden (1300), in his "Rosa Anglica." Francisco Piemontese, who taught in Naples about 1340, also recommends the loadstone, but he directs that it be strewn with the ashes obtained by burning the hoof of an ass or a horse; according to this last authority, the stone should be held in the left hand.[120]

That wounds caused by burning could be healed if powdered loadstone were sprinkled over them was confidently taught even in the seventeenth century. However, some ill effects were occasionally remarked when the substance was used medicinally, for it sometimes produced melancholia.

---

[118] From Robert Norman's "The Newe Attractive," London, 1581.
[119] Aldrovandi, "Museum metallicum," Bononiæ, 1648, p. 566.
[120] Ploss, "Das Weib," Leipzig, 1895, vol. ii, p. 350.

In this case an antidote was found in the emerald, and we are assured that if a solution made from this stone were taken thrice a day for nine consecutive days, the melancholia would pass away.[121]

In the sixteenth century in India, it was believed that a small quantity of loadstone taken internally preserved the vigor of youth, and Garcias ab Orta relates that a king of Ceylon, when an old man, ordered that cooking utensils of this material should be made for him, and had all his food cooked in these. Garcias claims to have this information direct from a Jew, Isaac of Cairo, who was ordered to make the vessels.[122]

A loadstone amulet for the cure of gout is stated to have been worn by a native of the English county of Essex. The stone was sewed up in a flannel covering to which was attached a black ribbon for suspension from the neck. Of course it was worn beneath the clothing, although the encasing flannel must have prevented direct contact with the skin. This piece of magnetic iron ore measured about an inch and a half in width, and was two-tenths of an inch thick. The patient, a Mr. Pelly, was an elderly man, who had suffered for some time from annually recurring attacks of gout which prostrated him for from three to four months. Learning of the reputed virtues of loadstones, more especially of those of Golconda, he sent to India for one and he is said to have been thereby relieved of his disease.[123]

In Persia a certain stone received the name of *Shahkevheren* or "King of Jewels," for it was reputed to attract all other precious stones, as the loadstone did iron. The great-

[121] Aldrovandi, "Museum metallicum," Bononiæ, 1648, pp. 564, 566.

[122] Garcias ab Orta, "Aromatum historia" (Latin version by Clusius), Antverpiæ, 1579, p. 178. See also Valentine Ball in Proc. Roy. Ir. Soc., 3d Ser., vol. i, p. 662; Colloquy xliii, of the work of Garcias, translated from the Portuguese original.

[123] William Jones, "Credulities Past and Present," London, 1880, pp. 160, 161; citing "Panorama," vol. vii.

est of the Sassanian monarchs, Khusrau II (590–628), had occasion to test the power of this wonderful stone. He had lost a ring of great price in the river Tigris, near the spot where some time later the Mohammedans founded the city of Bagdad. Taking a *shahkevheren* the monarch attached it to a line and literally fished for his ring, using the magic stone as a bait. We are told that the ring was recovered, and this must have greatly added to the reputation of the "King of Jewels." [124]

In the ninth century Arabic treatise, translated from an earlier Syriac text and falsely attributed to Aristotle, a number of fabulous stones are noted. All of these were said to have attractive properties, and as the loadstone attracted iron, they attracted various substances, each having its special affinity. First, we are told of the stone that attracted gold, then, in turn, of stones that attracted silver, copper, and other metals.[125] Probably the legend of the finding of these stones is based upon the employment of certain mineral substances in the purifying of gold, silver, etc. Among other fabulous or almost fabulous stones was one called *askab*, which, although of mean appearance, was able to break the diamond just as the diamond broke all other stones.[126] Have we here an allusion to the polishing of the diamond by its own dust? It is not improbable that this art, in an incomplete form, was known to the Hindus long before it was practised and perfected in Europe.

The stone that attracted hair was the lightest of all stones and very fragile; a piece as large as a man's fist weighed but a drachm. It looked like a piece of fur, but when touched was found to be a stone. The strange powers of this extraordinary substance could easily be demon-

[124] D'Herbelot, "Bibliothèque Orientale," La Haye, 1778, p. 229.

[125] Rose, "Aristotle de lapidibus und Arnoldus Saxo," in Zeitsch. für D. Alt., New Series, vol. vi, 1875.

[126] Ibid., p. 358.

strated, for if placed on a hairy spot of man or beast the hair was extracted, while if it were rubbed over a bald spot the hair was made to grow.[127] Probably the appearance of certain minerals covered with fine, hair-like spines, suggested the idea that the body of the stone had attracted hair to itself, and thus gave rise to this strange belief in the depilatory power of the stone, or it may have been a form of amber that, owing to its opacity, was not recognized as being the same as the transparent variety.

The Arabic Aristotle relates many wonderful tales of stones found by Alexander the Great during his Asiatic campaigns (327–323 B.C.). While these are all apocryphal, there can be no doubt that it was subsequent to these campaigns that western Europe was first made familiar with many of the precious stones of Persia and India. One of the stones reported by "Aristotle" bore the name *el behacte* or *baddare,* rendered in a Hebrew version *dar* (pearl?). This was the stone that attracted men, as the loadstone attracted iron. A quantity of these stones were found on the seashore by the soldiers of Alexander's army, but the men were so fascinated by their aspect as to be unable to gather them up. Therefore Alexander ordered that the soldiers should veil their faces, or close their eyes, and, after covering the marvellous stones with a cloth, should take them away without once looking at them. Hereupon Alexander gave commands that a wall should be built around "a certain city." [128] Possibly we have here a distant echo of the pearl gates of the New Jerusalem.

Two other strange stones are described, one of these appearing on the surface of the water only during the night, while the other shows itself during the daytime and sinks beneath the surface as soon as the sun sets. The "day-

---

[127] Ibid., p. 370.
[128] Ibid., p. 379.

DE TAVRO

ra de plomo a q̃ dizẽ en arauigo aqob. ⁊ en latin estanno q̃ quebranta
esta manera de piedras desta guisa. q̃ si enuueluẽ el estanno en
derredor dela piedra et dan cõ el martiello: q̃ebra luego. ⁊ des q̃ la
an quebrada si fazen mortero ⁊ majadero deste plomo: pueden la
y moler ⁊ fazer della poluos. ⁊ si dellos meten cõ alguna cosa al q̃
a piedra en la uexiga: q̃branta gela luego ⁊ guaresce. ⁊ otro tal
faze si toman un pedaço pequeño della ⁊ lo ponen en somo de un
fierro delgado ⁊ lo metieren al omne q̃ a la piedra en la natura de
guisa q̃ la taga: q̃branta la luego. pero esto nõ se deue fazer: si nõ quan
do los omnes son en dubda de nõ sanar. Et los q̃ quieren foradar o entallar
las otras piedras: toman desta pedaços pequeños muy delgados ⁊
agudos ⁊ ponen los en somo de unos alfileres de plata o de cobre ⁊
foradan o entallan cõ ellos las piedras q̃ quieren entallar o fazer en
ma fecho. Pero esta piedra es assi tossigosa. por razõ daq̃llas ani
malias posonadas q̃ se crian o ella nasce. ⁊ por q̃ estas piedras
son siempre quadradas ⁊ agudas matan se aq̃llas animales a ellas
⁊ reciben dellas ponçon. assi q̃ quando los omnes las meten en las bocas

De la piedra que a nombre aguquirpaz.

El segundo grado del
signo de tauro es la
piedra a que dizen
aguquirnaz. que q̃e
re dezir tanto en cal
deo: como ueedor
de engendramiento
en este romanz. Es
ta es de natura ter
renal fria ⁊ seca. ⁊
muy fuerte en estas
dos compliziones. ⁊ su color es blanca ⁊ a en ella got
tas negras. o si es toda negra: a en ella gotas
blancas. assi que nunqua las fallan si no mezcla
das de negro ⁊ de blanco. Es fuerte ⁊ dura de q̃bran
tar. ⁊ oscura de luz que la non passa el uiso. pero q̃n

Vignette from the "Lapidario de Alfonso X, Codice Original" (fol. 12). Published in Madrid, 1881. This design shows the finding of the "Stone of Sterility." Author's library.

By courtesy Soule Photo Co.

THE "MADONNA DI FOLIGNO," BY RAPHAEL

In the Vatican Collection, Rome. The white curve in the middle of the background shows the passage of the meteor to the earth.

stones,'' according to the legend, were quite useful to Alexander in his campaigns, for if they were attached to the necks of horses or beasts of burden, the horses would not neigh, and the other animals would be equally mute as long as they bore the stones, so that the passage of the army would not be revealed to the enemy. The ''night-stones,'' on the other hand, produced an entirely opposite effect, for when wearing them the animals uttered their respective cries unceasingly. We are not told that Alexander ever used them to provide an animal symphony as martial music for his soldiers.

Referring again to the subject of amber, as the objects placed in Roman sepulchral urns were always chosen because of some supposed religious or talismanic quality, there is considerable significance in the fact that an urn of this type, preserved by Cardinal Farnese, contained a piece of amber carved into the figure of an elephant. Coming down to modern times, there is record that the Macdonalds of Glencoe handed down as heirlooms four amber beads said to cure blindness, and there seems reason to conjecture that this substance was sometimes credited with being an antidote for the poison of snake-bites, as a small perforated stone used as late as 1874 in the Island of Lewis for this purpose appears to be a semi-transparent amber.[129] Indeed, amber set as a jewel to cure rheumatism is said to be offered for sale in London to-day, and the writer has learned that the late Rev. Henry Ward Beecher long carried amber beads with him to ward off this malady.

---

[129] Nona Lebour, "Amber and Jet in Ancient Burials," reprint from Transactions of the Dumfriesshire and Galloway Natural History and Antiquarian Society, Nov. 27, 1914, pp. 4, 5.

II

On Meteorites, or Celestial Stones

IT IS somewhat difficult to obtain trustworthy accounts regarding the occurrence of meteorites in medieval and ancient times, as there was a strong tendency to confuse the real meteorites with flint arrow-heads and hatchets derived from the stone age. A number of interesting facts bearing on the history of certain real or supposed aerolites were given in a recent lecture delivered by Prof. Hubert A. Newton in New Haven, Conn.[1] Some of the more striking instances are here presented.

As an illustration of the way in which meteorites may have come to be reverenced in former times, we have the modern instance of a stone that fell in the region north of Zanzibar, on the East African coast, and was seen and picked up by some shepherd boys. At first all the efforts of the German missionaries to buy this stone were fruitless, because the neighboring Wanikas looked upon it as a god, and, after securing possession of it, proceeded to anoint it with oil, clothe it with apparel and decorate it with pearls. They also built a temple wherein the stone received divine honors. This worship endured for some time, but when, three years later, the nomad tribes of the Masai swooped down on the Wanikas and burned their villages and massacred many of the inhabitants, the Wanikas lost all respect for the stone and were glad to part with it. This conduct was, after all, not entirely unreasonable, since the fetish had failed to prove its divine power.

This occurrence in the nineteenth century may well be

[1] American Journal of Science, 4th Ser., vol. iii, pp. 1–13, New Haven, 1897.

typical of what must have happened in past times. A case from the fifteenth century, narrated by Professor Newton, is very interesting, since the treatises on precious stones of that period and somewhat later contain many notices of supposed meteorites. We are told that, on November 16, 1492, a stone weighing 300 pounds fell at Ensisheim, in Alsace. Emperor Maximilian, who was then in Basel, caused the stone to be brought to the neighboring castle and summoned a state council to determine the character of the divine message associated with its fall. The council decided that the event signified some important occurrence in the approaching conflict between the French and the Turks, and the stone, with an appropriate inscription, was suspended in the church, the strictest injunctions being given that it should not be removed. Conrad Gesner, in his treatise, "De figuris lapidum,"[2] states that a fragment of this stone was given to him by a friend and that it resembled ordinary sandstone.

We are told that nineteen years later a shower of stones fell near Crema, east of Milan; these stones fell in French territory and at that time the Pope was engaged in hostilities with the French. During the following year, the French, who had long threatened the States of the Church from their possessions in Lombardy, were forced to withdraw from Italy. In the celebrated painting by Raphael, known as the Madonna di Foligno, one of the greatest treasures of the Vatican, this Crema fire-ball is depicted.

Naturally the recitals from ancient times are not as easily controlled as the more modern accounts and it is always possible that stones other than meteorites were given a celestial origin by superstitious zeal. The black stone of the Kaabah, which is probably noted by early Greek writers and was an object of adoration for the Arabian tribes be-

[2] Tiguri, 1565, f. 66.

fore the time of Mohammed, was believed to have dropped from heaven together with Adam, and in many Greek legends images were said to have fallen from heaven. Of course in the case of real statues this is simply a vague superstition, but the stone venerated in Phrygia as an image of Cybele may possibly have been a genuine meteorite.

The following facts in relation to this stone are presented by Professor Newton:

> It was a conical mass bearing a rude resemblance to a human head, and was said to have fallen near Pessinus. It was placed in the Temple of Cybele and worshipped as her image. During the second Punic war, in 205 B.C., because of Hannibal's prolonged invasion of Italy, the downfall of the Roman state was feared, and the Romans were terrified by a shower of stones from the sky. On consulting the Sibylline books, some verses were found to the effect that a foreign enemy could be driven from Italy if the Idæan mother (Cybele) was brought from Pessinus in Phrygia to Rome. An embassy was sent to King Attalus of Pergamos to request his consent to the transfer of the stone, and although he even refused obedience to the commands of the Delphic oracle, which required him to surrender the stone as an act of hospitality, he at last yielded when a violent earthquake shook the country, and the voice of the goddess was heard, enunciating these words: "It is my will. Rome is a worthy place for any god; delay not."[3]

Herodian, who relates this story, proceeds to narrate the arrival of the stone at Rome, where Scipio Africanus was chosen to bear it to the Temple of Victory. A silver image of the goddess was made, the conical stone serving as the head. For five hundred years this image, later transferred to the Temple of the Great Mother of the Gods, was an object of Roman worship. It has been described very fully by Arnobius (fl. 300 A.D.).[4] He states that it was a small stone which could be easily and lightly carried in the hand; it was of a black hue and of rough surface, and had many irregular projecting angles. As it was naturally marked

---

[3] Titi Livi, "Ab urbe condita," lib. xxix, cap. 11.

[4] "Adversus Gentes," lib. vii.

with the form of a mouth, it was inserted in the face of an image of the goddess to figure that feature.

As the stone was valueless, modern explorers long hoped that it might not have been carried off from Rome by the spoilers, but the search for it has been in vain. In a rare volume describing excavations made in the Palatine hill in 1730, Professor Lanciani is stated to have found a stone that had been unearthed at that time in a chapel, lacking any inscription to indicate the divinity to whom it was dedicated. This stone was said to be "of a deep brown color, looking very much like a piece of lava, and ending in a sharp point." The similarity of this description to that of Arnobius indicates that the Cybele stone may really have been found in 1730, but it has since disappeared. It would have been extremely interesting for mineralogists if they could have been enabled to examine this supposed meteorite, perhaps the very earliest regarding which we have such definite information.

To throw it into greater relief it was surrounded by a silver rim. When first brought to land from the ship on which it had been transported to Rome, the sacred stone was confided to the care of a company of Roman matrons who passed it on from one to another as it was solemnly borne to the Temple of Victory.[5]

Whether this stone was really a meteorite, as tradition taught, or whether it was a fossil of the type later known as *hysteriolithus,* as was conjectured by M. Falconnet, in 1770,[6] remains doubtful. Its light weight, upon which quality Arnobius lays stress, and its peculiar form seem to favor somewhat the latter supposition. A similar stone to which divine honors were paid was in a temple on Mount Ida.

[5] Prudentius "Hymnus X," 11, 156, 157. This writer was born in 348 A.D. and died about 410.

[6] "Dissertation sur la pierre de la Mère des Dieux," in Mém. de l'Acad. des Inscrip. et Belles Lettres, vol. xxxviii, p. 370; Paris, 1770.

In prehistoric times meteorites were quite naturally supposed to possess a special sanctity, and were indeed regarded as animated by the very essence of some divinity. The name bætylus, given to these stones by Greeks and Romans, is derived from the Hebrew בֵּית-אֵל (bethel) or "house of God," a term indicating clearly enough the belief held by the ancient Hebrews in regard to meteorites, or supposed meteorites. However, long before this designation had reached the Greeks, certain meteorites had been accorded a peculiar reverence, and even worship. One of these was a black stone, called the Omphalos of Delphi. This was said to be the stone given by Rhea to Kronos when she substituted a stone for her offspring Zeus, to save him from being devoured by his father, Kronos. Zeus himself (or Kronos) threw it down to the Earth and the spot where it struck was supposed to be the centre of the Earth, hence the name Omphalos, or "navel-stone." Meteorites probably played an important part in the development of civilization, for it is believed that the earliest iron tools and weapons were made from meteoric iron, apparently the only supply available before the art of treating iron ores had been evolved.[7]

While there is admittedly but scant evidence of the existence of a Stone Age in China, and still less to indicate that Chinese civilization passed through such a period, a certain number of stone artefacts, all polished, have been found within the limits of China. However, curiously enough in view of this state of things, we find that here, as almost everywhere else, these objects were popularly regarded as "thunderbolts." Thus Chien Tsang-Ki, the author of a Materia Medica, composed in the first half of the eighth century of our era, states that objects of this

[7] Miers, "Fall of Meteorites in Ancient and Modern Times," Science Progress, vol. vii, No. 8, July, 1898, p. 351.

kind "have been found by people who explored a locality over which a thunder-storm had swept and dug three feet in the ground"; and he adds that some of these stone implements have two perforations. They were named *pi-li-chen*, "stones originating from the crash of thunder," and a still earlier writer, Chang (232–300 A.D.) applies a similar designation to stone axes and wedges "frequently seen among the people." Several centuries later Shen Kun (1030–1093 A.D.) testifies that the people of his time found many stone "thunder-wedges," in all cases after a thunder-storm; these were unperforated. It is generally believed that most of these stone implements had been made by a Tungusian tribe, akin to the Manchus.[8]

This is partly due to the fact that it was natural, after a thunder-shower, for a search to be made. Then again, as thunder-showers are usually heavy rains, they were apt to loosen the soil and leave on the surface heavy objects, more especially such materials as jade, of the density of 2.9, or jadeite, of the density of 3.3. These are much heavier than the quartz, feldspar and other ingredients of the soil, which vary from 2.6 to 2.7 and are washed away. Finally, there is the natural disinclination on the part of the Chinese to dig, from their belief that it is wrong to explore the soil, and this disinclination on their part has done much to prevent a better knowledge of the Stone Age, and our knowledge of the races which must have preceded the civilization of China; many facts of mining interest have been neglected, as well, on account of this prejudice. Perhaps within the next twenty years we may learn something about a prehistoric race in China, for as traces of the existence of such races have been found in every other country of the

[8] Laufer, "Jade: A Study in Chinese Archæology and Religion," Chicago, 1912, pp. 54, 55, 57, 63, 64; Field Museum of Natural History, Pub. 154, Archæological Series, vol. x.

world, there can be little or no doubt that such a race existed in China, although as yet we have no distinct evidences of it.

The Babylonian royal astrologers taught that the mere fact of the passage of a meteor across the heavens, whether its course were from east to west, or from north to south, was a good omen, portending victory and the successful issue of the royal projects. Especially favorable was the augury when the meteor was very brilliant and left behind it a trail that might be likened to the tail of a scorpion. This not only foretold joy for the ruler and his house, but for the entire country; evil would be overcome, righteousness would reign supreme, and prosperity would prevail. A meteor of this type is recorded as having appeared at the time Nebuchadnezzar laid waste Elam about 1150 B.C. This refers to the elder Nebuchadnezzar.[9]

A curious series of cuneiform texts treats of the prognostics to be drawn from the transformations of stars into various animals, metals, stones, etc. This is explained as referring to the apparent form or hue of the meteor itself, or of the trail it left behind. The transformations into stones concern the dushu-stone, porphyry (or some other dark red or purple stone) and lapis lazuli. This omen is invariably a favorable one.[10]

The Old Testament offers abundant testimony of the ancient belief that certain stones were animated by a divine spirit. In regard to this, Benzinger writes: [11] "It was not Yahweh who found Jacob at Bethel but rather Jacob who found Yahweh there. He anoints the stone; that is, he sacrifices to it, for the divinity residing in the stone has caused his dream." According to Benzinger's opinion the Ark of the Covenant originally served as receptacle for a

[9] Morris Jastrow, Jr., "Die Religion Babyloniens und Assyriens," vol. ii, Pt. II, Giessen, 1912, pp. 689, 690.

[10] Ibid., pp. 692–694.

[11] Benzinger, Hebräische Archäologie, Freiburg i. B., 1894, p. 370.

stone of this type, and was hence regarded as sheltering a divinity.

One of the very earliest references to meteorites appears in the Book of Joshua (chap. x, verse 11), where we read, in the account of the battle fought by the Israelites against the Amorites and their allies, that "the Lord cast down great stones from heaven" upon the Amorites, so that more of the latter were killed by these stones than by the weapons of the Israelites. Admitting the historical character of the account, this fall of meteorites probably took place in the twelfth century B.C. In an Assyrian cuneiform inscription, there is mention of the seven black stones of the city of Urka in Chaldea. These were *bætyli* and were regarded as representations of the seven planets.[12]

The fall of meteors is noted frequently in Chinese records, the first instance dating from 644 B.C. Of a meteor that fell in 213 B.C., we are told that it descended as "a star which turned to a stone as it fell."[13] A meteorite that fell in China in 211 B.C. is said to have been the indirect cause of many deaths. The event took place during the reign of the tyrannical emperor Chi Hoang-ti, who had incurred the resentment of all the Chinese litterati by his wholesale burning of books. Some believer in the power of sorcery caused an inscription to be cut on this stone predicting the death of the hated emperor within a year, and when news of the fact came to the monarch's ears he gave orders to have the stone split up, and to put to death all the inhabitants of the place where it was found, this being no doubt looked upon as a most effective conjuration of the spell.[14]

In 405 B.C., Lysander won his great victory over the

---

[12] Lenormant, "Lettres Assyriologiques," Paris, 1872, vol. ii, p. 118.

[13] Miers, "Fall of Meteorites in Ancient and Modern Times," Science Progress, vol. vii, No. 8, July, 1898, p. 349.

[14] E. F. F. Chladni, "Verzeichniss der herabgefallenen Stein- und Eisenmassen," p. 5; Gilbert's Annalen der Physik, vol. l.

Athenian fleet at Ægospotami in Thrace, and Plutarch writes, in his life of Lysander,[15] that a stone which fell from the heavens a short time before the battle was regarded by many as a portent predicting the dreadful slaughter that was to ensue. At the time Plutarch wrote (circa 150 A.D.) this stone could still be seen at Ægospotami, where it was regarded with great veneration by the Chersonites. The Greek philosopher Anaxagorus is said to have predicted the fall of this meteorite, as he had observed certain perturbations in the movements of the heavenly bodies. As Anaxagorus died in 428 B.C., his prediction must have long antedated the fall of the meteorite.

A detail given in one of the early recitals might possibly have constituted the basis of a prediction by some contemporary physicist. In the latter part of his account of the phenomenon Plutarch quotes from a Treatise on Religion, by a certain Daimachus, to the effect that, for seventy-five days before the fall of the meteorite, a vast fiery body was seen in the heavens, in appearance "like a flaming cloud." This well describes the appearance of a great comet, and might be regarded as significant when we consider the latest modern theory of the origin of meteors, according to which these bodies are detached particles of a cometary aggregation. Of this meteoric mass said to have fallen at Ægospotami, Pliny states that it was as large as a wagon and of a dusky hue, adding that a brilliant comet was visible at the time of its fall. Regarding the assertion that Anaxagorus predicted the occurrence, Pliny declares that this prediction, if true, was a greater miracle than the fall of the meteor. A portion of the stone was preserved as a venerated relic in the town of Potidæa.[16]

---

[15] Plutarchi, "Vitæ," Lipsiæ, 1879, p. 394; Lysander, 12.

[16] C. Plinii Secundi, "Historia naturalis," Venetiis, 1507, fol. 8, recto; lib. ii, cap. 60.

The site of the city of Seleucia is said to have been determined by the fall of an aerolite, and this stone is figured on some of the coins of the Seleucidæ, a thunderbolt appearing in its stead on other coins.

In the Temple of Diana, at Ephesus, there was a stone partly fashioned into the conventional form of the Ephesian Diana. This, it was asserted, had fallen down from the heavens. The stone is mentioned in the Acts of the Apostles (xix. 35), where we read that the city of the Ephesians was "a worshipper of the great goddess Diana, and of the *image* which fell down from Jupiter." In this text the word "image" has been supplied by the translators, a more literal rendering being "that which fell down from the sky." This clearly shows that the stone only faintly indicated the human form.

Tacitus says of the stone sacred to the Astarte (or Aphrodite) of Paphos, that it was a symbol of the goddess, not a human effigy, since it was an obscurely formed cone.[17] In his life of Apollonius of Tyana, Philostratus, also, mentions this stone and tells us that when Apollonius visited Paphos, he admired there "the famous symbolic figure of Aphrodite."[18] These "living stones" (λιθοι ἐμψυχοι) were often covered with ornaments and vestments, and it has been conjectured that these adornments were, in some cases, changed so as to accord with the garments appropriate to certain special festivals of the respective gods.[19]

The colossal emerald of the temple of Melkarth at Tyre is designated in the fragments of Sanchoniathon as an *ἀεροπετῆ ἀστέρα*, or star fallen from heaven. It was said to have been raised up by Astarte, and this last myth is

---

[17] Cornelii Taciti, "Opera," Lipsiæ, 1885, p. 52.

[18] Philostratus, "Apollonius of Tyana," trans. by Baltzer, Rudolstadt i. Th., 1883, p. 143 (iii, 59).

[19] Lenormant, in Daremberg and Saglio's Dict. des antiq. grecques et romaines, vol. i, Paris, 1873, p. 645.

represented on the silver coins of Marium in Cyprus. Here the radiance and splendor of the object suggested a stellar or celestial origin, and we see the same tendency at work in the application of the name *ceraunіæ* (thunder-stones) to certain brilliant gems by Pliny.[20]

Virgil[21] seems to confound with thunder the detonation of a bolide, followed by a train of light, and he seems also to confound the bolide itself with a lightning flash, for he says that its fall diffused a sulphurous vapor far and wide. Seneca was more critical, for he regarded the fact of thunder sometimes accompanying the fall of a meteorite as merely a coincidence.

Although, in the absence of exact and trustworthy contemporaneous accounts of the fall of these sacred stones, we cannot be absolutely certain that they were meteorites, the testimony in several cases is sufficient to render this almost certain, while in many other cases there is no reason to doubt the substantial accuracy of the tradition. The choice of some of the *bætyli,* however, was determined by their form alone, to which was ascribed a religious significance, not exactly compatible with our religious ideas of to-day, but quite easily understood when we remember that the divine creative energy was concretely represented in ancient times by many symbols offensive to our sense of propriety.

In the treatise "On Rivers," attributed to Plutarch, a stone is said to have been found on Mount Cronius, which bore the name of "cylinder." When Jupiter thundered, this stone, terrified by the noise, rolled down from the top of the mountain.[22] This passage is interesting as suggesting one of the reasons which caused the name "thunderbolt"

[20] F. Lenormant, in Daremberg and Saglio's Dict. des antiq. grecques et romaines, vol. i, p. 645, Paris, 1873. See Fig. 739.

[21] Aen. ii, 692–698.

[22] De Mély, "Le traité des fleuves de Plutarche"; in Revue des Etudes Grecques, vol. v (1892), p. 334.

to be given to certain stones, for stones adapted to ornamental use might easily be exposed by the weathering of the rocks, and then detached by the concussion produced by heavy thunder. Of course, the cylinder-stone here mentioned must have more especially signified one of the prehistoric celts, but it is not unlikely that the name was also given to other, unworked stones, having a similar form.

Before Galba was chosen emperor, and when he was acting as governor of the Basque provinces in Spain, a thunderbolt descended upon the shore of a lake in that region. Search was made for the stones which were supposed to have fallen, and Suetonius tells us that twelve axes were found. This was regarded as a sure augury of Galba's elevation to the imperial dignity,[23] but for the archæologist the presence of the axes merely signifies that this was the site of a lake dwellers' village.

In some cases, the stone which was held to be a dwelling-place of the divinity was also regarded as a representation, or epitome, of some sacred mountain. In the earliest stage of this belief, the god was supposed to have his abode in the mountain, and later he was thought to animate the stone which had a fancied likeness in shape to the mountain. A coin of the Roman emperor Elagabalus (204–222 A.D.)[24] bears on its reverse a representation of one of the sacred stones of Astarte, namely, that worshipped at Sidon. This is shown resting upon a car, and it seems probable that it was transported from place to place, so that large numbers

[23] Suetonii, "Opera," Lipsiæ, 1886, p. 203; Galba, 8.

[24] This name signifies "Mountain-God" and its assumption by the emperor marked his devotion to the worship of the divinity animating the stone of Emesa, El Gabal, which Elagabulus had conveyed to Rome, where it remained until 222 A.D. This stone was regarded as a miniature representation of the sacred mountain near Emesa. The stone is figured on the aureus of the emperor Uranius Antonius. See Ch. Lenormant, Rev. Numismatique, 1843, p. 273. sq., Pl. IX, No. 1.

of people could have the privilege of paying reverence to it.

There seems to be fairly strong reasons for the belief that the Black Stone of the Kaaba at Mecca is an aerolite.[25] If the conjecture be correct, this stone occupies a unique place among meteoric masses, for it was an object of worship for many centuries before the advent of Mohammed, and is to-day regarded with the highest reverence by one hundred and twenty millions of Mohammedans. One of the most solemn acts performed by the pilgrims at Mecca is the kissing of the Black Stone, and should any one doubt that true religious enthusiasm is aroused by this act, he should read the following words of Ibn Batoutah:[26]

> The eyes perceive in it a wonderful beauty, similar to that of a young bride; in kissing it one feels a pleasure that delights the mouth, and whoever kisses it wishes he might never cease to do so; for this is an inherent quality in it and a divine grace in its favor. Let us only cite the words of the Prophet in this connection: "Certainly it is the right hand of God on earth."

For centuries before Mohammed's time the Kaaba at Mecca had been a famous sanctuary and a religious centre for the nomadic Arabs. It is stated that there were 360 idols in the temple, a number which suggests a connection with the year of 360 days in use among the Arabs. The most celebrated of these idols bore the name of Hobal, and was the figure of a man cut out of red agate. There was a tradition to the effect that this idol had been brought from Belka in Syria. As one of the hands was broken off, the Koreish, the Arab tribe having charge of the Kaaba, repaired this defect by attaching a golden hand, in which were held seven arrows, plain shafts without heads or feathers, similar to the arrows used for divination by the

[25] Lenormant, "Lettres Assyriologiques," Paris, 1872, vol. ii, p. 123.

[26] "Voyages d'Ibn Batoutah." Translation by C. Defremery and B. R. Sanguinette, vol. i, 3d Ed., Paris, 1893, p. 314.

THE KAABA AT MECCA

The letter A indicates the place where the Black Stone is inserted in the wall of the building. From "Histoire générale de cérémonies religieuses de tous les peuples du monde," by Abbé Banier and Abbé Mascrier, Paris, 1741.

Arabs. For some occult reason the agate was supposed to exercise a certain control over meteorological phenomena, for in Persia it was believed to ward off tempests, while prayers for rain in time of drought were made to this agate image of the Kaaba.[27]

Much has been written regarding the Black Stone, but perhaps the most satisfactory description is that given by Burckhardt, who writes: [28]

> At the North-east corner of the Kaabah, near the door, is the famous "Black Stone"; it forms part of the sharp angle of the building at from four to five feet above the ground. It is an irregular oval, about seven inches in diameter, with an undulated surface, composed of about a dozen smaller stones of different sizes and shapes, well joined together with a small quantity of cement, and perfectly smooth; it looks as if the whole had been broken into many pieces by a violent blow, and then united again. It is very difficult to determine accurately the quality of this stone, which has been worn to its present surface by the millions of touches and kisses it has received. It appears to me like lava, containing several small extraneous particles of a whitish and of a yellowish substance. Its color is now a deep reddish-brown, approaching to black.

This description seems to support the conjecture that the stone is a meteorite. The injuries it has sustained are attributed to various accidental or intentional causes. In the early part of the Mohammedan era the Kaaba was damaged by fire, and the intense heat caused the stone to break into three pieces. This injury was repaired, but some years later (926 A.D.) the heretic sect of the Carmates captured and sacked Mecca. Hoping to divert to another place the tide of pilgrims, and the riches they brought with them, the leader of the sect caused the stone to be wrenched from its place and borne away to Hedjez. During the sack of Mecca, or possibly in its violent removal, the stone was broken into two pieces,—perhaps along the line of one of

---

[27] Sale, "The Koran" (Preliminary Discourse), Phila., 1853, p. 14.
[28] Burckhardt, "Travels in Arabia," London, 1829, p. 137.

the old fractures. At first an offer of 50,000 dinars ($125,-000) was made for the return of the stone, but before many years had passed the Carmates restored it voluntarily, having been disappointed in their hope of attracting the pilgrims. The Black Stone was destined to suffer still greater injury. In 1022 A.D., Hakem, the ruler of Egypt, who suffered from megalomania and was disposed to claim divine honors for himself, dispatched an emissary to Mecca to destroy the stone. Mixing with the crowd of pilgrims, this man approached the revered relic, and crying out "How long shall this stone be adored and kissed?" struck it a tremendous blow with a club. The story runs that only three small pieces were broken from the stone, but as it is also stated that these pieces were pulverized and the powder made into a cement to fill up the cracks, the injury was probably much greater than the pious Mohammedans were willing to admit.[29]

Mohammedan tradition teaches that the Black Stone was sent from heaven and was once pure and brilliant; it only grew black because of the sins of men. Legend relates that Abraham stood on this stone during the construction of the Kaaba. This edifice was erected in a miraculous way, for the stones came of themselves, all cut and polished, from the Mountain of Arafat. However, no place was found for the Black Stone, and it was afflicted and said to Abraham: "Why have not I also been used for the House of God?" "Be comforted," replied the Prophet; "for I will see that you are more honored than any other stone of the edifice. I will command all men, in the name of God, that they shall kiss you when they pass in the procession."[30]

A fragment of the Black Stone of Mecca was brought to Bagdad in 951 A.D. by order of the Khalif Moti Lillah, and

---

[29] Burckhardt, "Travels in Arabia," London, 1829, p. 167.

[30] Chardin, "Voyage en Perse," Amsterdam, 1735, vol. iv, p. 171.

was inserted in the threshold of the main entrance to the royal palace there. From a balcony directly above the entrance was suspended a piece of tapestry taken from that in the Kaaba, and it was so hung that its lower border was about on a level with the face of anyone entering the portal. All who passed in were strictly enjoined to touch their eyes with this tapestry and also to kiss the piece of the Black Stone, upon which no one was permitted to tread. These details are given in Khondemir's life of Abu Jafer Al Mostasem, the last of the Khalifs, who died in 1258 A.D.[31]

The Kaaba at Mecca offers to the adoration of faithful Mohammedan pilgrims to the shrine, not only the famous Black Stone, which is set in the eastern corner of the building, but also another sacred stone inserted in the southern corner at a height of five feet from the ground. This is designated as the "Southern Stone." The Kaaba itself is a small rectangular structure, built of stone from the surrounding hills, and having a length of 12 metres (39.4 feet), a width of 10 metres (32.8 feet) and a height of 15 metres (49.2 feet). One of the few Europeans who have been permitted to enter the sacred enclosure, Dr. Snouck-Hurgronje, does not believe that the Kaaba owes its origin and sanctity to the Black Stone, but that its foundation was rather due to the presence of the well Zemzem, whose waters were already reported to have a therapeutic quality in the early days of Islam, and which may have earned its repute on this account. If, however, we admit that the medical properties (of a purgative nature) are due to contamination or percolation posterior to the primitive time when the well Zemzem first attracted the reverence of the Arabs of this region, then the purity of the water may account for its

[31] Giovanni B. Rampolli, "Annali Musulmani," vol. viii, Milano, 1824, p. 589, note 104.

high place in the esteem of the Arabs. Of the Black Stone, a native of Mecca who saw the stone when it had been taken out of the wall of the building, in the course of the latest restoration of the structure, states that its inner surface is of a grayish hue.[32]

The Kaaba also contained the Maquam Ibrahim, a sacred stone preserved from pre-Islamite times, and brought into connection with the history of Abraham by the Mohammedan legends. This stone, enclosed in a receptacle of like material, was at one time buried in the ground underneath the building, but receptacle and enclosed stone are now set within the iron gratings which partition off a part of the space inside the cupola over the pulpit of the Mosque of Mecca.[33]

An Oriental poem by Assmai detailing the wonderful exploits of the hero Antar, describes the way in which he became possessed of a matchless sword. One day he came upon two knights in desperate encounter; on seeing him they paused in their strife and to his question as to its cause one of the combatants told him that they were brothers, sons of a great Arab emir, recently deceased. Their father had once found a black stone, in appearance like a common pebble, but possessed of such penetrative power that when a herdsman threw it at a camel it traversed the animal's body, inflicting a gaping wound. The emir immediately recognized that the stone must be a "thunder-stone," as meteorites were called; he therefore secured possession of it and commanded his most skilful smiths to forge a sword from it. When this task had been successfully performed the emir clothed the smith in a robe of honor, and then, drawing the new sword from its sheath, cut off his head with a single stroke. This served at once as a test of

[32] Dr. C. Snouck-Hurgronje, "Mekka," Haag, 1888, vol. i, pp. 2, 4, 5.
[33] Op. cit., p. 11.

the weapon's quality and as an assurance that it would not soon be duplicated. On his death-bed the emir called to him his youngest son and said to him: "My son, take the sword and hide it from your brother, and when you shall see that he has seized my goods and is squandering them in riotous living, and sends you away, without reverence for the Lord of Heaven and Earth, take the sword away with you. If you bring it to the court of the Persian King, Khusrau Nushirwan, he will heap gifts and honors upon you, or if you elect to go instead to the court of the Byzantine Cæsar, monarch of the Servants of the Cross, he will give you as much gold and silver as you may ask for." This was the tale told by the younger knight, who added that when, after the father's death, the brother had sought in vain for the famous sword, he had resorted to torture to extract from the favored son the secret of its hiding place, and had brought the latter to this spot commanding him to find it and give it up, and when he refused so to do, had attacked him. The hero Antar, like a veritable knight-errant, took up the quarrel of the oppressed brother and slew his opponent, securing as a free-will offering of gratitude the magic sword.[34]

The forging of swords from meteoric iron was, in the opinion of the Orientalist Hammer-Purgstall, the origin of the characteristic surface given to the famous Damascus blades. A most interesting modern example of a meteoric-iron weapon is a dagger made by Von Widmanstädt for Emperor Francis I of Austria, out of the famous Bohemian siderite long preserved in the Rathaus at Elbogen and known as the "Verwünschte Burggraf." On the surface of this blade, however, the lines were angular, while on the

[34] From Hammer-Purgstall's "Fundgrube des Orients," vol. iv, Heft 3; cited by E. F. F. Chladni, "Neues Verzeichniss der herabgefallenen Stein- und Eisenmassen," p. 55; Gilbert's Annalen der Physik, vol. l.

true Damascus blade the lines are wavy.[35] An unsuccessful attempt to forge a sword from a piece of meteoric iron is reported by Avicenna in the case of a siderite that fell at Jurgan in 1009 A.D., from which swords that were ordered to be made by the Sultan of Khorassan could not be executed.[36]

n an Arabic work bearing the name of Avicenna and entitled "The Cure," the writer mentions a meteorite which fell in the Jordan, and of which Sultan Mohammed Ghazni wished to have a sword made for him, thus proving that the Sultan believed that meteorites possessed marvellous properties.[37]

A number of Greek and Roman coins bearing representations of these sacred meteorites have come down to us, and more than two hundred specimens may be seen in the section of meteorites in the Natural History Museum (Königlich-kaiserliches naturhistoriches Hofmuseum) in Vienna. These coins are of great value in determining the history of those aerolites which were preserved in the temples of certain divinities.

The Viennese collection of meteorites is the finest in the world, and this is largely due to the zeal and intelligence of the late Dr. Aristides Brezina, while superintendent of the department of mineralogy and meteorites in the Museum. In regard to the impression made upon the mind of man in ancient times by the fall of meteorites, Dr. Brezina writes:[38]

---

[35] E. F. F. Chladni, "Neues Verzeichniss der herabgefallenen Stein- und Eisenmassen," p. 58; Gilbert's Annalen der Physik, vol. l.

[36] Ibid., p. 5.

[37] Berthelot, "Histoire des Sciences: La Chimie au Moyen-âge," Paris, 1893, vol. iii, p. 225.

[38] Brezina, "The Arrangement of Collections of Meteorites"; Proceedings of the American Philosophical Society, vol. xliii, Jan.-Dec., pp. 212, 213.

The ancients supposed the stars to be the domiciles of the gods; falling stars and falling meteorites signified the descending of a god or the sending of its image to the earth. These envoys were received with divine honor, embalmed and draped, and worshipped in temples built for them.

The coins to which we have alluded were usually struck in honor of the sanctuaries wherein the aerolites were objects of adoration, and the temple is often rudely figured with the stone set up in the centre. In many cases the meteorite was preserved in its original form, which, if conical, was regarded as a phallic symbol; in other cases, the mass was rudely shaped into the conventional form of some divinity.

It is stated in Spangenberg's Chron. Saxon. that in 998 A.D. two immense stones fell at Magdeburg during a thunderstorm. One of these is said to have fallen in the town itself and the other in the open country, near the river Elbe. The description of a meteoric fall given in an eighteenth century treatise on meteors, presents a vivid picture of the phenomena attending—or believed to have attended—such a fall. We are told that on June 16, 1794, at about seven o'clock in the evening a thunder cloud was seen in Tuscany, near the city of Siena and the town of Radacofani. This

REMARKS

CONCERNING

STONES

SAID TO HAVE FALLEN FROM THE CLOUDS, BOTH

IN THESE DAYS,

AND IN ANTIENT TIMES.

BY

EDWARD KING, ESQ. F.R.S. AND F.A.S.

Res ubi plurimum proficere, et valere possunt, collocari debent.

CICERO DE ORAT. 37.

LONDON:

PRINTED FOR G. NICOL, BOOKSELLER TO HIS MAJESTY, PALL-MALL.

1796.

Title-page of one of the earliest treatises on meteorites.

cloud came from the north, and shot forth sparks like rockets, smoke rising from it like a furnace; at the same time a series of explosions was heard, not so much resembling the sound of thunder as that produced by the firing of cannon or the discharge of many muskets. The cloud remained suspended in the air for some time, during which many stones fell to the earth, some of which were found. One of them is described as being of irregular form, with a point like a diamond; it weighed about five pounds and gave out a "vitriolic smell." Another weighed three and a half pounds, was very hard, of the color of iron, and "smelled like brimstone." [39]

The following passage written in the fourteenth, or perhaps in the thirteenth century, shows considerable accuracy of observation: [40]

> There are some who fancy that the thunder is a stone, for the reason that a stone often falls when it thunders in stormy weather. This is not true, for if the thunder were a stone, it would wound the people and animals it strikes, just as any other falling stone does. However, this is not the case, for we see that the people who have been struck by thunder (sic) show no wounds, but they are black from the stroke, and this is because the hot vapor burns the blood in their hearts. Therefore, they perish without wounds.

The fall of a siderite twenty miles east of Lahore in India, on April 17, 1621, is reported in contemporary records. From this iron, which weighed about 3¼ pounds, the Mogul Emperor Jehangir ordered two sabres to be made, as well as a knife and a dagger, and commanded that the fact should be properly registered. Here, as in other similar cases, the weapons were believed to possess a quasi-

[39] King, "Remarks Concerning Stones said to have Fallen from the Clouds," London, 1796, p. 4.

[40] Megenberg, "Buch der Natur," ed. Pfeiffer, Stuttgart, 1861, p. 92. (This is based on Thomas de Cantimpré's "Liber de natura rerum," written about 1240.)

magic power because of the celestial origin of the material employed.[41]

Michele Mercato[42] (d. 1593) gives a vivid description of the fall of a meteor which was observed near Castrovilarii, in Calabria, January 10, 1583. Some men in a meadow observed a black, whirling cloud rushing through the air, and saw it descend to the earth not far from where they were standing. The noise accompanying the descent of the meteorite was so deafening that it was heard far and wide, and the poor men fell to the ground almost unconscious from terror. People from the neighborhood hastened to the spot and, after restoring the terrified witnesses of the phenomena, discovered a mass of iron weighing thirty-three pounds at the spot where the black cloud had touched the earth.

The startling phenomenon of a rain of stones from the sky which took place under rather queer circumstances is reported by the Jesuit priest Alvarus as having occurred in China in 1622. The Taoist priests of that land enjoyed the repute of being able to bring down rain from the sky by their magic or religious rites, and when, during the year mentioned, China was visited by a drought of unexampled severity, the aid of these rain-makers was invoked. Yielding, perhaps not unwillingly, to the popular entreaty, a group of priests ascended a hill and proceeded to pronounce their invocations. To the joy of the onlookers the sky became darkened and a rushing sound was heard, at first mistaken for an oncoming rain-storm, but to the dismay of all an immense shower of stones of all sizes fell upon the earth, destroying what remained of the parched fruits and

[41] E. F. F. Chladni, "Neues Verzeichniss der herabgefallenen Stein- und Eisenmassen," p. 17; Gilbert's Annalen der Physik, vol. 1. (From copy having MS. notes and emendations by the author.)

[42] Metallotheca Vaticana, Romæ, 1719, p. 248.

grain crops, and killing or maiming many persons. So terrifying was the sight that the Jesuits who were watching the result of the affair half-believed that the Last Day had come. When the panic had finally subsided, the people fell upon the unlucky Taoist priests and beat them soundly.[43]

In the "Annals of the Ottoman Empire," by Subhi Mohammed Effendi, there is an account of the fall of a meteor at Hasergrad, on the banks of the Danube, on the fourth of Saban, A. H. 1153 (October 25, 1740). The weather was fine, not a cloud was to be seen in the sky, and not a breath of air was stirring. Suddenly there arose a whirlwind, the air became obscured with clouds of dust, rain fell in torrents, and it became dark as night. While all who were out of doors were hastening to seek shelter from the storm, three terrific peals of thunder were heard, as loud as the sound of many cannon. After the storm had passed several strange masses partly of stone and partly of iron were discovered in a nearby field. The Vizier bore two of these as great rarities to the Sultan in Constantinople.[44]

The influence exerted by popular beliefs, even upon the learned, is well illustrated by the opinion given by some of the leading French physicists of the eighteenth century as to the character of meteorites. When a meteoric stone fell at Luce, Dept. Marne, France, September 13, 1768, three French scientists, among them the celebrated Lavoisier, were sent to investigate the matter. In their report to the Academy of Sciences, they state that there must have been some error in the accounts given of the event, for it was an assured fact that no such things as *pierres de foudre*, or thunder-stones, existed. This was, of course, perfectly true, but Lavoisier and his companions did not stop to think

[43] Ulyssis Aldrovandi, "Museum Metallicum," pp. 528, 529.
[44] Fundgruben des Orients, vol. iv, p. 282; Wien, 1814.

that stones might fall to the earth in some other way. The result of the investigation was summed up as follows:

> If the existence of thunder-stones was regarded as doubtful at a time when physicists had scarcely any idea of the nature of thunder, it is even less admissible to-day, when modern physicists have discovered the effects of this natural phenomenon are the same as those of electricity. There is no record that the fulgarite, the fused sand or rock struck by the lightning, has ever been used.
>
> The opinion which seems the most probable to us, and that which is most in accord with the accepted principles of physics as well as with the facts reported by Abbe Bacheley, and our own investigation, is that the stone was originally covered with a slight crust of earth and turf, and was struck by lightning and so made visible.

Chladni reports in a pamphlet published in 1794 that the mass of meteoric iron discovered by Dr. Pallas in Siberia, and known as the Pallas or Krasnojarsk iron meteorite, was regarded by the Tartars as a sacred object which had fallen from heaven.[45] As it is somewhat unlikely that this belief could be accounted for by an ancient tradition, we must seek an explanation in the conviction among primitive peoples that any mass of rock or metal of unusual appearance and differing notably from the surrounding formations must have come from the sky. In this way primitive instinct often anticipates the results of modern scientific investigation. This siderite, of irregular form and weighing some 1500 pounds, was seen by Dr. Pallas in 1772, and deposited by him in 1776; he learned that it had been found in 1749 at the summit of a mountain situated between Krasnojarsk and Abakansk, by a Cossack. Most of this famous siderite is preserved in the St. Petersburg Museum.

A singular circumstance in regard to the fall of a meteor, and one that in ancient times would have been explained in

[45] King, "Remarks Concerning Stones said to have Fallen from the Clouds," London, 1796, p. 26.

a miraculous way, is that during the desperate and bloody battle of Borodino, won by Napoleon over the Russians, September 6, 1812, a meteorite is said to have fallen near the headquarters of the Russian general. This would certainly have been regarded—after the event—as a manifestation of divine wrath, and hence a prognostic of the Russian defeat. However, had the French been defeated, the meteorite would have been looked upon as a sign of divine favor, and it would have been honored and reverenced. In modern times the natural phenomenon is taken for what it is worth, and the only interest excited is a purely scientific one.

Of all the meteorites that have been discovered, the most remarkable are undoubtedly those found at Melville Bay, about 35 miles east of Cape York, West Greenland, in 1894, by Admiral, then Lieutenant, Robert E. Peary, and brought by him to the United States in 1895 and 1897.[46] They are now to be seen in the American Museum of Natural History, New York. The first report of the existence of meteoric iron in the vicinity came from Captain Ross, who in 1818 was given two iron knives, or lance-heads, by some Eskimo of Regent's Bay. An analysis of the metal revealed the presence of nickel and immediately suggested a meteoric origin of the material; nothing more definite could be learned at the time from the Eskimo than that the metal had been taken from an "iron mountain" not far away. In 1840, the King of Denmark, whose interest had been aroused in the matter, authorized the sending out of an expedition to seek for the suspected siderites, but the search proved unsuccessful; a later attempt made by the officers of the *North Star*, a Franklin relief ship, in 1849–50, also failed. For a time the determination of the telluric origin of the supposed siderites discovered at Ovifak, Disko Island, West Greenland,

[46] Lieut. Robert E. Peary, "Northward over the 'Great Ice,'" New York, 1897, vol. ii, pp. 553 sqq.

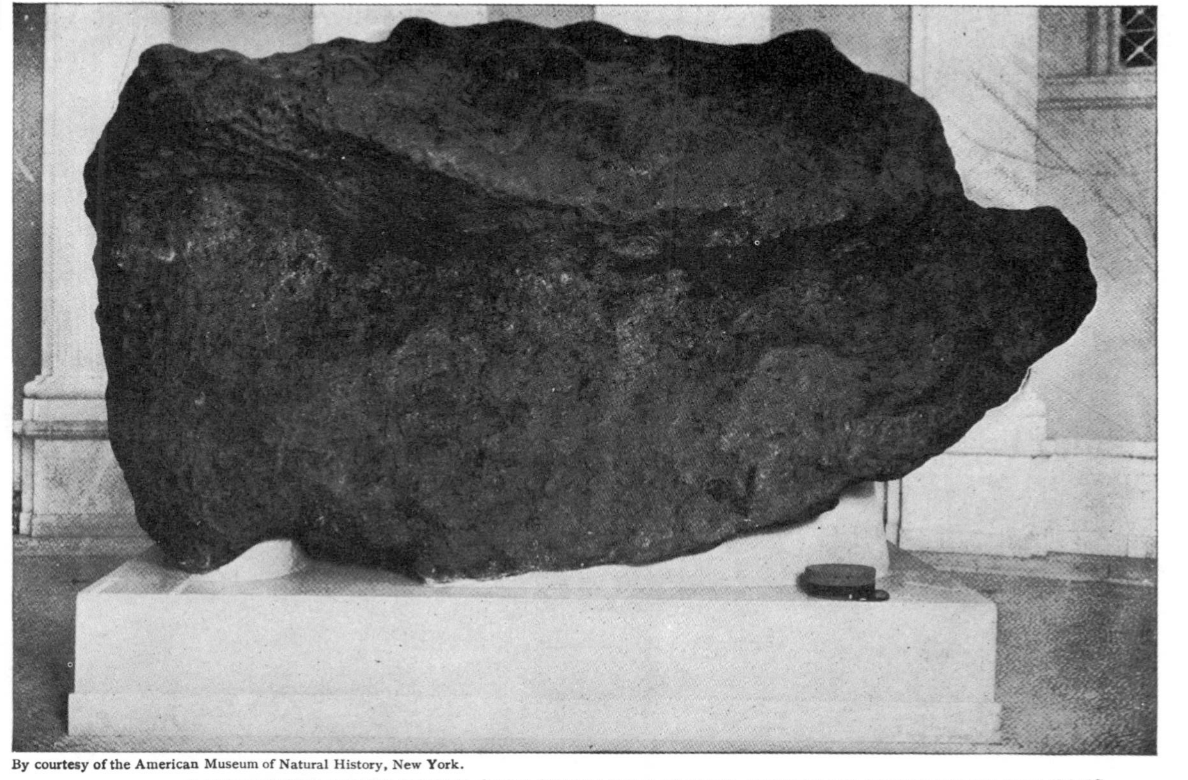

By courtesy of the American Museum of Natural History, New York.

"AHNIGHITO," THE GREAT CAPE YORK METEORITE, WEIGHING MORE THAN 36½ TONS

In the American Museum of Natural History, New York City. Obtained by Admiral Peary.

By courtesy of the American Museum of Natural History, New York.

"THE WOMAN," CAPE YORK METEORITE

In the American Museum of Natural History, New York City. Weight 3 tons. Obtained by Admiral Peary

by Baron N. A. E. Nordenskiold in 1870, cast some doubt upon the true meteoric character of the iron of which the Cape York knives had been made, and rather discouraged further searches. It was not until 1894 that these extraordinary masses of meteoric iron were at last seen and located by a European, one of the hunters of the Tellikontinah tribe of Smith Sound Eskimos serving as Lieutenant Peary's guide. The siderites were three in number, the two smaller having been named by the Eskimo "The Dog" and "The Woman," respectively, while the largest was known as "The Tent." It now bears the name of Ahnighito, that of the daughter of the explorer.

The two smaller ones reposed loosely upon gneissic rocks, but Ahnighito, found on a small island some six miles away, on a terrace 80 feet above tide-water and about 100 feet from the shore, lay almost buried in rocks and sand.

Eskimo legend had woven its web about these enigmatic meteorites and the natives saw in them an Innuit woman, who with her dog and tent had been hurled from the sky in a bygone age by Tornarsuk, the Evil One. Originally the mass called "The Woman" was said to have closely resembled the figure of a woman, seated and engaged in sewing, but by the gradual chipping away of fragments of the iron this form had almost disappeared. Peary was told that not long before, the "head" had fallen off and that a party of Eskimo had tried to carry it away, lashed to a sledge; however, as they were passing over the ice, it suddenly broke up, so that sledge, iron and dogs sank in the water and the Eskimo themselves barely escaped with their lives.

The dimensions of Ahnighito, the largest siderite ever discovered, are given as follows: length, 10 feet 11 inches; height 6 feet 9 inches; thickness, 5 feet 2 inches. It weighs something over 36½ tons. The weight of "The Woman" is 3 tons, and that of "The Dog" 1100 pounds. The chemical compositions of these three siderites, which are regarded as having originally constituted a single mass, have been determined by J. E. Whitfield. In addition to small quantities of copper, sulphur, phosphorus and carbon, the following proportions of the main constituents were ascertained:[47]

	The Dog	The Woman	Ahnighito
Iron	90.99	91.47	91.48
Nickel	8.27	7.78	7.79
Cobalt	.53	.53	.53

Though smaller and less imposing by its mass than the greatest of the Cape York meteorites, that called "Willamette" from having been found two miles northwest of the town of that name in Clackamas County, Oregon, ranks as the fourth, or possibly the third largest iron meteorite in the world, and is the largest discovered within the territory of the United States; remarkable peculiarities of form make it an especially interesting object.[48] It was a chance find, made in 1902 by two prospectors in their search for gold or silver. Noting what appeared to be a very slight rock projection they tapped this with their hammers and the sound of the blow revealed the presence of metal; digging down here and there, they ascertained the existence of a considerable mass of iron. Although at first no one supposed that it was a meteorite, before long this fact became known, and the finder, by very primitive methods and by dint of tireless efforts, succeeded in transporting the iron to his own land. His courageous attempt to acquire possession of it was not, however, crowned with success, as the courts decided that the company owning the land whereon it had

[47] Edmund Otis Hovey, "The Foyer Collection of Meteorites," American Museum of Natural History, Guide Leaflet No. 26, December, 1907, pp. 23–27.

[48] Henry A. Ward, "Willamette Meteorite"; Proc. Rochester Acad. of Sc., vol. iv, pp. 137–148, plates 13–18.

By courtesy of the American Museum of Natural History, New York.

"THE DOG," CAPE YORK METEORITE

In the Americam Museum of Natural History, New York City. Weight 1100 pounds. Obtained by Admiral Peary.

By courtesy of Rochester (N. Y.) Academy of Sciences.

TWO VIEWS OF THE WILLAMETTE METEORITE NOW IN THE AMERICAN MUSEUM OF NATURAL HISTORY, NEW YORK CITY

Found in Clackamas County, Oregon, near the town of Willamette. Weight 31,107 pounds.

been found possessed the right to reclaim it from the finder.

When weighed on the railroad scales in Portland, Oregon, the net weight of this siderite was shown to be 31,107 pounds. The most striking peculiarity is the abundance of pittings and hollows and their unusual size. That these resulted in part from the effects of the enormous heat generated by the swift flight of this weighty mass through the earth's atmosphere, is generally admitted; but some of the deepest pits are believed to owe their origin to the decomposition of spheroidal nodules of troilite, and the cylindrical holes to the decomposition of rod-like masses of the same substance. Willamette, which was donated to the American Museum of Natural History, by Mrs. William E. Dodge, is 10 feet long, 6 feet 6 inches high, and has a thickness of 4 feet 3 inches.[49] Chemical analyses have been made by Mr. J. M. Davison of the University of Rochester and by J. E. Whitfield of Philadelphia. Their respective determinations are here given:

	Davison	Whitfield
Iron	91.65	91.46
Nickel	7.88	8.30
Cobalt	.21	?
Phosphorus	.09	?
	99.83	99.76

The famous Cañon Diablo meteorite possesses a surpassing mineralogical interest.[50] In 1891, at the Tenth International Geologic Congress, Washington, D. C., the mineralogist Koenig announced that he had discovered some

[49] Edmund Otis Hovey, "The Foyer Collection of Meteorites," American Museum of Natural History, Guide Leaflet No. 26, December, 1907, pp. 27, 28.

[50] See the present writer's "Diamond and Moissanite; Natural, Artificial and Meteoric," a lecture delivered at the Twelfth General Meeting of the American Electro-chemical Society in New York City, October 18, 1907; here the literature on this important meteor is fully given. Two other interesting meteorites are described by George F. Kunz and Ernest Weinschenk in the American Journal of Science, vol. xliii, May 1892, pp. 424–426, figures.

microscopic diamonds in this meteorite, and later investigations by Prof. Henri Moissan confirmed this discovery and enlarged its scope. A mass of the iron weighing about 400 pounds was used by Professor Moissan; this was cut by means of a steel ribbon saw. As had been the case in Koenig's investigations, the saw soon encountered excessively hard portions that obstructed its operation, so that twenty days' labor was requisite to separate the iron into two parts, each with a section area of nearly 100 square inches. On close examination it became evident that the obstacles to the cutting consisted of round or elliptical nodules, of a dark gray to black hue, and enclosed in the bright iron. These nodules were mainly composed of troilite (iron protosulphide). After chemical treatment an insoluble residue remained, consisting of silica, amorphous carbon, graphite and diamond. Many of these very minute diamonds were black, but a few were transparent crystals, octahedrons with rounded edges.[51] The presence of this diamond material in the interior of the iron mass of the meteorite indicates their formation from carbon by the combined agencies of high temperature and great pressure, as in the case of the artificial diamonds experimentally produced by Moissan in an iron mass first subjected to intense heat in tho electric furnace and then rapidly contracted in volume by sudden chilling. The fervid imagination of early writers would certainly have attributed wonderful talismanic powers to stones like these, probably generated in some lost planet and reaching our earth through the wastes of celestial space, could they have been able to observe and distinguish them with the incomplete optical resources of their time.

The first announcement of the discovery of these dia-

[51] See Henri Moissan, "Étude de la météorite de Cañon Diablo," Comptes Rendus de l'Academie des Sciences, vol. cxvi (1893), pp. 288 sqq.; see also his paper on the Ovifak meteorite, Comptes Rendus, vol. cxxi (1895), pp. 483 sqq.

monds from the Cañon Diablo meteorite was made by Dr. A. E. Foote, and not long after Professor Koenig's determination of their character, the present writer suggested an experiment that would afford absolute proof that the material was really diamond. This was to charge a new skaif, or diamond-polishing wheel, with the supposed diamond dust obtained from the meteorite; should the material polish a diamond there could be no doubt as to its character. On September 11, 1893, this experiment was tried at the Mining Building of the World's Columbian Exposition. After the skaif had been charged with the residuum separated from the meteorite by Dr. O. W. Huntington, it was given a speed of 2500 revolutions to the minute, and in less than fifteen minutes a small flat surface had been ground down and polished on a cleavage-piece of rough diamond held against the wheel. The experiment was then repeated several times on other diamonds and always successfully. This showed conclusively that the residuum of the meteorite contained many minute diamond fragments.[52]

A most important group of meteorites were found in 1886 in Brenham township, Kiowa County, Kansas, by some of the farmers of this district in the course of their farming operations.[53] Entirely unaware of their scientific value, the finders used these objects to weight down haystacks, or for similar uses to which they would put small boulders. In all some twenty of these specimens have been recovered, varying in weight all the way from 466 pounds down to a single ounce. Most of them were taken from an area of about sixty acres, although some were scattered over a wider tract. The largest piece of the group, that on which the

[52] G. F. Kunz and O. W. Huntington, "On the Diamond in the Cañon Diablo Meteoric Iron and on the Hardness of Carborundum," American Journal of Science, vol. xlvi, December, 1893.

[53] George F. Kunz, "On Five American Meteorites," American Journal of Science, vol. xl, Oct., 1890, pp. 312–323.

farmers had bestowed the fanciful name of the "moon meteorite," had lain only three inches beneath the surface of the ground and broke a ploughshare when it was first struck; none of the masses appear to have been buried deeper down than from five to six inches. The largest mass measures twenty-four inches across the widest part and fourteen and a half at the thickest part. These Kiowa meteorites are in a sense gem-meteorites, for a number of beautiful and brilliant olivine crystals occur in them; many are in two distinct zones, the inner one being a bright transparent yellow, while the outer one is of a dark-brown iron olivine, in reality a mixture of troilite and olivine. The character and composition of the worked iron of meteoric origin found in some of the Turner group of Indian mounds, in the Little Miami Valley, Ohio, indicate that the latter may perhaps be brought into connection with this group of meteorites. For here, as in the Frozen North among the Esquimo, and in a number of other cases, the iron available for primitive man was mainly that of meteorite origin.

In view of the relatively small number of meteorites that have fallen in historical times, and of the small part of the earth's surface actually occupied by human settlements, we need scarcely be surprised at the statement that there is but one credibly recorded instance of the killing of a human being by a meteorite. This unique disaster is said to have happened at Mhow in India, and fragments of the meteorite which fell then are to be seen in museum collections. The great weight of some meteorites would have rendered them very destructive had they not fallen in the open country; the heaviest single mass actually *known* to have fallen, came to the ground at Knyahinya, Hungary, in 1866, and weighed 547 pounds; it buried itself 11 feet in the ground. Of course much heavier aerolites and siderites, satisfactorily recognizable as such, have been found, the heaviest being perhaps that at Bacubrit, Mexico, 13 feet in length with a width of 6 feet and a thickness of 5 feet; the weight of this mass is estimated to be some 50 tons. Of meteorites which have fallen in more or less close proximity to human beings, may be noted one at Tourinnes-la-Grosse, which broke the street pavement; another at Angers, which fell into a garden, near to where a lady was standing; and still another at Brunau, which passed through a cottage roof.[54]

Many other accidents caused by meteorites or what were believed to be meteorites are recorded, the credibility of some of the statements not being very convincing; others, however, appear to be quite worthy of credence. Thus the Chronicle of Ibn Alathir relates that several persons were killed by a rain of stones that fell to the earth in Africa in August, 1020 A.D.[55] In the middle of the seventeenth century the tower of a prison building in Warsaw is said to have been destroyed by a meteorite.[56] A hundred years or so before, on May 19, 1552, there was a great fall of stones, not far from Eisleben, one of which killed the favorite steed of Count Schwarzenburg, while another wounded the count's body-physician, Dr. Mitthobius, in the foot. This was witnessed by Spangenberg, who reports it in his Saxon Chronicle; he carried off some of the stones with him to Eisleben.[57] An eight-pound stone (probably a siderite) is stated by a certain Olaf Erikson to have fallen on shipboard and killed two persons, at some time about the middle of the seventeenth century; this is rather indefinite information.[58] The most remarkable happening, however, is reported from

[54] Lazarus Fletcher, in Encyclopædia Britannica, 11th ed., vol. xviii, p. 263; article Meteorites.

[55] Chladni, op. cit., p. 8.

[56] Petri Borelli, "Hist. et observ. phys.-med.," 1676; cited by Chladni, op. cit., p. 20.

[57] Chladni, op. cit., p. 14; see also Gilbert's Annalen, vol. xxix, p. 376.

[58] Chladni, op. cit., p. 19.

Milan from the end of the seventeenth or the beginning of the eighteenth century, when a very small meteorite, weighing not quite an ounce, fell into the cloister of Santa Maria della Pace (now a cotton factory) and killed a Franciscan monk. Such was the velocity of this little stone that it penetrated deep into the monk's body, whence it was extracted and preserved for a long time in the Collection of Count Settála. The greater part of this collection went later to the Ambrosian Library at Milan, but Chladni sought in vain there for any trace of the death-dealing meteorite.[59]

Among the Welsh peasants there is a belief that when a meteor falls to the earth it becomes reduced to a mass of jelly. This they name *pwdre ser*. The most plausible explanation offered for this fancy is that the autumn, the season when the largest number of meteors may be observed, is also the time of the year when the jelly-like masses of the plasmodium of Myxomycetes most frequently appear in the fields. A peasant who, after noting the apparent fall of a meteor, should go in search of it, might easily come across one of these lumps of plasma, and might well be induced to think that he had found all that was left of the meteor after its violent fall to the earth. Of course we have here to do with the apparent, not with the real, fall of a meteorite. In this connection it is interesting to note that the *medusa*, or jelly-fish, has been called a "fallen star" by sailors.[60]

This Welsh fancy that meteors or "falling-stars" turned to a jelly when they struck the earth appears to have been quite general in Great Britain, and the jelly-like substance was variously named "star-slough," "star-shoot," "star-gelly" or "jelly," "star-fall'n." The Welsh *pwdre ser* literally means "star-rot." As early as 1641 Sir John Suckling (1609–1642) wrote the following lines which well de-

[59] Chladni, op. cit., p. 22.

[60] See "Nature" for June 23 and July 21, 1910.

scribe the way in which these gelatinous substances came to be regarded as the remains of a "fallen star":

> As he whose quicker eye doth trace
> A false star shot to a mark'd place
> Do's run apace,
> And, thinking it to catch,
> A jelly up do snatch.

Sir Walter Scott also, whose familiarity with superstitions was very great, has not failed to note this one in his "Talisman," where the hermit says: "Seek a fallen star and thou shalt only light on some foul jelly, which in shooting through the horizon has assumed an appearance of splendour." Here the star itself is supposed to have had this gelatinous form.

An early writer,[61] noting this curious belief that "a white and gelatinous substance" was all that remained of a fallen star, declares that he had clearly demonstrated to the Royal Society that the mass was composed of the intestines of frogs, and had been vomited by crows, adding that his opinion had been confirmed by the testimony of other scientific men. Huxley, from a description, conjectured that the substance was nostoc, a gelatinous vegetable mass, but this seems to be somewhat doubtful. In 1744 Robert Boyle states that some of this "star-shoot" was given to a physician of his acquaintance, who "digested it in a well-stopt glass for a long time," and then sold the liquor for a specific in the removal of wens.[62]

A jelly-like mass believed by him to be the remains of a "fallen star" was found by Mr. Rufus Graves at Amherst, Mass., on August 14, 1819, and duly reported in the American Journal of Science.[63] As this gentleman was at one

[61] Merrett, "Pinax rerum naturalium Britannicarum," London, 1667, p. 219.

[62] "The Works of the Hon. Robert Boyle," vol. i, p. 244.

[63] Vol. ii, pp. 335–7, 1820.

time lecturer on chemistry at Dartmouth College, his testimony is worth heeding, but there can be no doubt that while he accurately describes what he found, he was altogether mistaken in supposing that the meteor fell precisely on the spot where he discovered the gelatinous substance. As we have noted, it has recently been suggested that these "jellies" are plasmodia of forms of Myxomycetes which do not appear to have any connection with the spot whereon they rest, but seem to have fallen from the air.[64]

Falling stars are explained by the natives of Labrador and of Baffin's Bay as being souls of the departed bound on an excursion to Hades in order to see what is going on there, while the phenomena of thunder and lightning are caused by a party of old women, who quarrel so violently over the possession of a seal that they bring the house down over their heads and shatter the lamps. These " old women " must, of course, be spirits of the upper air, not human beings.[65]

In some Australian tribes the sorcerers, or "medicine-men," taking advantage of the superstitious dread of falling stars common among the aborigines, pretend to have marked the spot where such a star has fallen and to have dug it up and preserved it in their medicine-bag. These suppositititious "fallen stars" are sometimes quartz pebbles, and in one instance the curiosity of a European investigator was satisfied by the display of a piece of thick glass, which the sorcerer strictly maintained he had dug out of the ground wherein the star had fallen.[66]

Arrow-heads encased in silver were looked upon as the solid contents of the lightning flash, and were not only thought to protect the house in which they were kept from

---

[64] Edward E. Free in Nature, Nov. 3, 1910, No. 2140, vol. lxxxv.

[65] Arnaldo Faustini, " Gli Eschimesi," Torino, 1912, p. 41.

[66] Edward M. Curr, " The Australian Races," Melbourne and London, vol. iii, p. 29.

being struck by lightning, but their protective power was believed to extend to seven houses in the immediate neighborhood. An interesting example is a neolithic silex arrowhead figured by Bellucci. This has been elegantly set in silver in modern times, and comes from Pesca Costanzo, in the province of Aquila, Italy.

The Italians are convinced that if the arrow-head, or similar object, come in contact with a piece of iron, the "essence of the lightning" departs from it, revealing itself in a spark; hence they wrap it up, carefully, in skin, cloth, or paper so as to guard it from harm. Sometimes these objects are anointed with oil, a survival of the custom of making propitiatory offerings of oil. This usage in the case of sacred stones is very general, and is met with in places as remote from each other as Sweden, India and the Society Islands.[67]

In an Iroquois myth and legend, He-no, the god of thunder, is an object of great veneration because of the powerful aid he renders to those whom he favors. He is believed to direct the rain which shall fertilize the seed in the earth, and also to give aid to the harvesters when the fruits of the earth have ripened. While traversing the celestial vault, in his journeyings hither and thither above the surface of the globe, he bears with him an enormous basket filled with huge boulders of chert rock. These he casts at any evil spirit he may encounter, and when on occasion a spirit succeeds in avoiding such a boulder, it will fall down to the earth surrounded by fire. We have here another version of the almost universal myth of thunderstones.[68]

In treating of the flint arrow-heads of the American Indians, Adair notes that in form and material they closely

[67] Bellucci, "Il feticismo in Italia," Perugia, 1907, pp. 17 sqq.

[68] Harriet Maxwell Converse, "Myths and Legends of the N. Y. State Iroquois," edited and annotated by Arthur Caswell Parker (Ga-wa-so-wa-neh), New York State Museum Bulletin, No. 125, Albany, 1908, p. 40.

resembled the "elf-stones" with which European peasants were wont to rub any of their cattle believed to have been "shot" by fairies or elves. A village in which one of these magic objects existed was considered to be particularly favored by fortune, as they not only served to protect the cattle from bewitchment but were equally efficacious in preserving human beings from the spells of witches.[69]

In East Prussia, when cows are believed to have been bewitched so that their milk is under a spell, resort is had to the powers of a perforated "thunder-stone." Such stones were ancient stone hammers with a central perforation for a handle. The stone is held beneath the cow at milking-time, and the milk is allowed to pass through the perforation.[70] By this means the spell is broken and the milk becomes harmless.

Such perforated stones are also used to protect a house from being struck by lightning. When a storm approaches nearer and nearer, the owner of one of these magic stones will thrust his finger through the hole, twirl the stone around three times, and then hurl it against the door of the room. When this has been done, the house is believed to be proof against lightning.[71]

In Westphalia the stone is laid upon a table alongside of a consecrated candle, the shrewd peasants thus assuring for their houses the protection of the church as well as that of the ancient God of Thunder.[72]

Another phase of the superstition in regard to the stone axes known in many different parts of the world as thunder-stones, because they are believed to have fallen during a thunder-storm, is given by Dr. Lund in a letter written from Logoa Santa in Brazil. He states that the inhabitants

[69] Adair, "History of the American Indians," London, 1775, p. 425.
[70] Frischbier, "Hexenspruch und Zauberbann," Berlin, 1870, p. 19.
[71] Ibid., p. 107.
[72] Hartmann, "Bilder aus Westfalen," Osnabrück, 1871, p. 144.

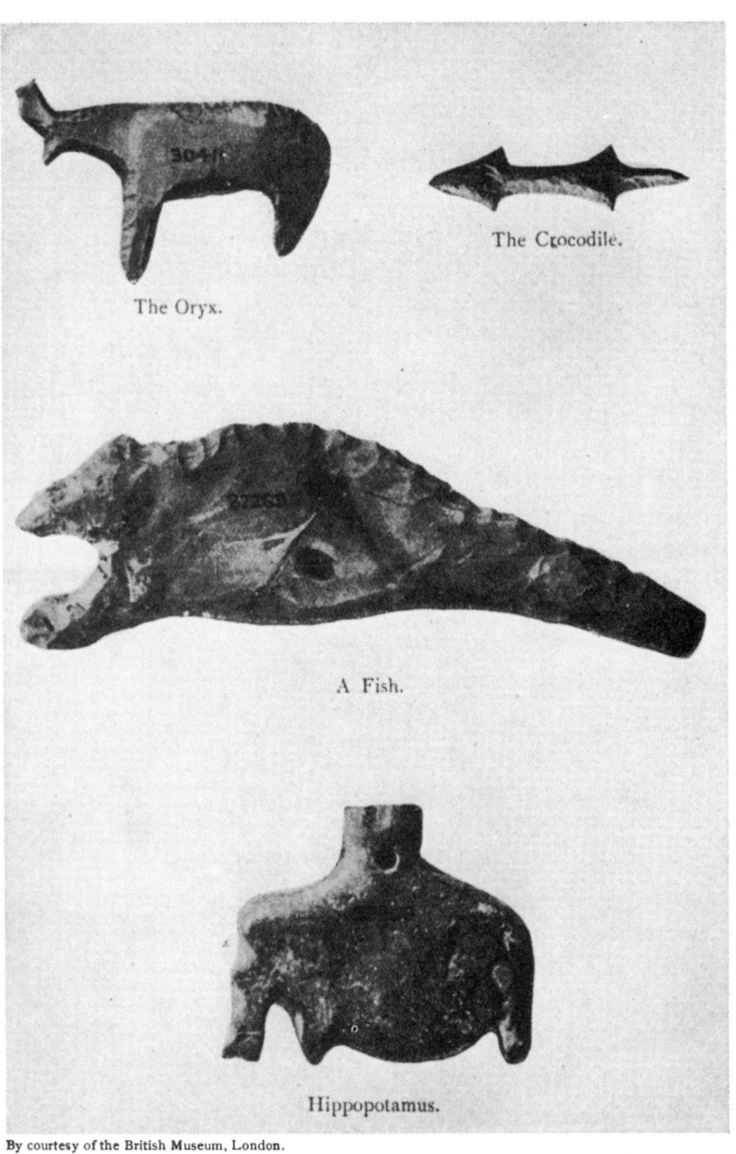

By courtesy of the British Museum, London.

FLINT AMULETS OF THE PREDYNASTIC PERIOD, EGYPT

rather look askance at these stones, believing that wherever they are found the lightning is apt to strike, "in order to seek its brother!"[73]

The stone implements of various forms found in the shell-heaps of Brazil are called by the natives *Curiscos* or "lightning-stones." The Guaranis name them "stars fallen from heaven"; the Cajuas, "stones hurled by the thunder"; and the Coarados, "axe-stones." A high price is paid for these by the gold-seekers in Brazil, who believe that, by attraction, they show the presence of gold beneath the surface, just as the divining-rod is supposed to be affected by the presence of water or by hidden treasures.[74]

The peasants of Slavonic descent in Moravia have great faith in the virtues of the "thunder-stone." During Passion Week the stone has the power to reveal the location of hidden treasures, and it is also believed that warts on man and horse will disappear if they be rubbed with such a stone before sunset. However, not only healing virtues are attributed, for if the stone be hurled at anyone and strikes him, it inflicts a mortal wound.[75]

A poetic and appropriate name has been applied to the earliest of the chipped stone artefacts of primitive man by archæologists. They are called "Dawn Stones" (eoliths), and the name characterizes these interesting relics, the first steps in the development of sculptural art, as products of the dawn of human civilization.

A curious survival of the adoration of stones is reported by the Earl of Roden in his "Progress of the Reformation in Ireland."[76] A correspondent informed Lord Roden that

---

[73] Lund, "Om de Sydamericanske Vildes Steenöxer," Annaler for Nordisk Oldkyndighed, Copenhagen, 1838–1839, p. 159.

[74] Rath, in Globus, vol. xxvi, p. 215 (Braunschweig, 1874).

[75] Koudela and Jetteles in Anthrop. Gesellsch. Wien, vol. xii, p. 159 (1882).

[76] Quoted by Sir J. E. Tennant in Notes and Queries, vol. v, 1852, p. 121 (No. 119, Feb. 7, 1852).

in Inniskea, an island off the coast of Mayo, there was, in 1851, a stone idol called in the Irish tongue Neevougi. This was said to have been preserved and worshipped from time immemorial. The stone is described as having been wrapped in so many folds of homespun flannel that it looked like a mass of that material. This is explained by the custom of dedicating a dress of this flannel to the stone whenever its aid was sought, the garment being sewed on by an old woman who officiated as the priestess of the stone. Prayers were offered to this strange idol for the cure of diseases, as it was supposed to be endowed with extraordinary powers. A stranger petition sometimes made was that a storm might arise and wreck a ship upon the coast so that the thrifty islanders might profit by its misfortune; on the other hand, with charming inconsistency, when they wished to go a-fishing or pay a visit to the mainland, the trusty stone was expected to assure them fair weather and a calm sea.

In Tavernier's time (about 1650) many poor families living in the woods and on the hillsides in India, far from any village where there was a temple, would take a stone, probably one of a peculiar shape, and would roughly paint on it a nose and eyes in red or green color. This being done, the whole family would gather about this stone and reverently adore it as their idol.[77]

In certain districts in Norway, up to the end of the eighteenth century, superstitious peasants used to preserve round stones, and set them up in a conspicuous place in their houses. At Yule-tide these stones were sprinkled with fresh ale. Some of them were worshipped as divinities, and every Thursday, or oftener, they were smeared with butter, or some similar substance, before the fire. This ointment was allowed to dry on the stone, which was then returned to its

---

[77] "Les Six Voyages de Jean Baptiste Tavernier," La Haye, 1718, vol. ii, p. 439; liv. iii, chap. xi.

place of honor. These ceremonies were supposed to insure the health and happiness of the household.[78]

The fact that special ceremonies were performed in connection with these stones on Thursday, as well as the name "Thor-stones" applied to many of them, indicates that in early times they were associated with the worship of the god Thor. The so-called thunderbolts—usually flint axe-heads—are believed to have been hurled at the trolls or elves by the thunder, so that these evil-disposed spirits might be subdued and prevented from fulfilling an old saying, according to which they would desolate the earth. Originally it was Thor himself who was believed to hurl the thunderbolt.

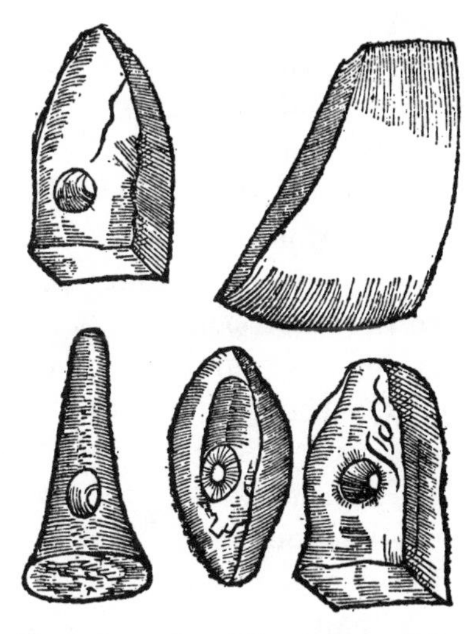

Types of ceraunia or "Thunder-stones." From "Museum Wormianum." Lugduni Batavorum, 1655.

These stones were supposed to be endowed with wonder-working powers. When a woman was in labor, ale was allowed to drip over a stone of this kind, and was then given to the woman to drink. All through the Scandinavian countries the peasants believed that if such a stone were hung up in a house or on cattle, the trolls and other malevolent spirits would be driven away, and all spells and witchcraft would be rendered harmless.[79]

In Sir William Brereton's account of his travels (1634–

[78] Magnusen, "Om en Steenring med Runeindskrift," Annaler for Nordisk Oldkyndighed, Copenhagen, 1838–1839, p. 133.

[79] Magnusen, "Om en Steenring med Runeindskrift," Annaler for Nordisk Oldkyndighed, Copenhagen, 1838–1839, pp. 132–134.

1635)[80] we read that he saw in the School of Anatomy at Leyden a stone called "*Fulminis Sagitta*, or the dart of the thunderbolt, about the size of your little finger." This was either a belemnite[81] or a stone arrow-head of somewhat similar form. It bore a Latin inscription to the following effect: "Many believe that nursing children can be cured of rupture if this stone be attached to their thighs, or if they do not suffer from this complaint, they will be preserved from it."

On the ridge-beam of an Irish cottage at Portrush was found a neolithic celt of the kind believed by the peasantry to be "thunderbolts." This celt had been placed on the roof of the cottage to protect it from being struck by lightning, a notion thoroughly in accord with the theory of sympathetic magic. In Surrey, England, a like belief is held as to the fossil belemnites, and nodules of iron pyrites such as have been found in Cretaceous formations near Cragdon are also thought to have fallen from the sky during a thunder-storm, and to possess peculiar powers in reference to the lightning.[82]

In Ireland the prehistoric stone arrow-head is believed to have been shot at man or beast by the fairies. Should an old woman be so lucky as to find one she will become highly honored in her village, and it is used as a cure for diseases produced by the wiles of evil spirits. To effect a cure, the *saigead* ("arrow") must be placed in water, which is then given to the sick person to drink.[83] Cows which have been wounded by the "fairy-darts" are also made to drink of this

[80] Brereton, "Travels in Holland, the United Provinces, England, Scotland and Ireland, 1634–1635," Chetham Soc., London, 1844, p. 41.

[81] The fossilized horny process of an extinct cuttlefish.

[82] A. E. Wright and E. Lovett, "Specimens of Modern Mascots and Ancient Amulets of the British Isles," Folk Lore, vol. xix, 1908, p. 298; Pl. VI, fig. 2.

[83] Mooney, "The Medical Mythology of Ireland," Am. Phil. Soc., vol. xxxiv, p. 143, 1887.

water. The Irish peasants wore the stone arrow-heads, set in silver, as amulets for protection against injury from like weapons at the hands of the fairies. Similar superstitions exist in the North of England.[84] Nilsson believes that the "elf-shots" (the arrow-points or axe-points) of the Irish peasantry are identical with the "Lap-shots" of the Swedish peasantry. These stones were thought to have belonged to the Laplanders, the "black elves" of the Edda, and were therefore used as a protection against the witcheries of these elves. The idea that the substance or thing that has caused an injury can effect a cure of this injury, appears in the Edda.[85]

The shepherds in the French Alps value the "thunderstones" (*peyros de tron*) very highly. They are handed down from father to son as precious heirlooms, and when the flocks are driven to the pasturage, one of these wonder-working stones is embedded in a tuft of wool on the back of the bell-wether; this is supposed to serve as a protection for the whole flock.[86] In Spain the peasants call these stones *piedros del rayo,* or "lightning-stones."[87]

The names bestowed on such prehistoric stone implements by the inhabitants of the Malay Archipelago, of Java and Sumatra, all indicate that they are believed to have fallen from the sky. In Malacca they are called *batu gontur,* "lightning-stones," and in Sumatra we have the name *anak-pitas,* "child of the lightning." In the island of Nias, near Sumatra, they are worn as amulets on the head or attached to the sword. The Watubela islanders denominate them "teeth of the thunder," a name which suggests the appellation glossopetra ("stone-tongue"), and like this is evidently

---

[84] Henderson, "Folk-lore of Northern England," pp. 185, 186.

[85] Nilsson, "The Primitive Inhabitants of Scandinavia," trans. by the author and ed. by Sir John Lubbock, 3d ed., London, 1868, pp. 200, 201.

[86] Tournier, Bull. de la Soc. d'Anthrop., 1874, p. 386.

[87] Bull. de la Soc. d'Anthrop., 1860, p. 96.

derived from the form of certain of these prehistoric celts.[88]

The Burmans have given the highly poetic name of "rainbow-disease" to the disorder known to us as appendicitis, and they use the axe-heads and other pointed or sharpened arrow-heads of the Stone Age for the cure of this malady, stroking the region affected with one of these implements. The natives share in the delusion almost universal among primitive peoples, that these stone implements have fallen from the sky during thunder-storms, and that they partake of the nature of thunderbolts; hence they are supposed to destroy the rainbow-disease, as the approach of heavy storm clouds, charged with lightning, darken the sun and put an end to the beautiful natural phenomenon.

In the island of Mindanao, one of the Philippine group, the heathen Manobos called the thunder the "speech of the lightning," and regarded the latter as a kind of wild animal, so that whenever the lightning struck the earth or a tree they believed that the animal had buried its teeth in the spot. They therefore looked upon any stone implement found there as one of these teeth.[89]

The ancient stone hammers found in Japan are called *rai fu seki,* "thunderbolts," or *tengu no masakari,* "battle-axes of Tengu," the warder of the heavens. Other stone implements bear the name "fox-axes," or "fox-planes." These peculiar designations are employed because the fox is a symbol of the devil, and the stone axes are regarded as weapons of the devil. Of course this in no wise prevents their use as amulets or medicinally; indeed, their powder is thought to be an especially effective remedy for boils and ulcers. Many such stones may be seen in the temples, where

---

[88] Morgan, "Matériaux pour l'hist. primitive," Paris, 1885, p. 484; Verhandl. Berl. Anthrop. Ges., 1879, p. 300; Von Rosenberg, "Der Malayische Archipel," Leipzig, 1878, p. 175.

[89] Semper, "Die Philippinen," Würzburg, 1869, p. 61.

they are carefully preserved and shown to the pilgrims who visit the different shrines.[90]

Even at the present day, the superstitious belief in the magic properties of the prehistoric stone implements still survives among some of the Scandinavian peasants. They believe that these offer protection against lightning, and they are very unwilling to part with them. In some regions the stone axes or arrow-heads are supposed to afford protection against lightning, and they are occasionally used to relieve the pangs of childbirth. In the latter case they are placed in the bed of the suffering woman. Another curious use to which they are put is as a cure for an eruptive disease of children. Here the flint is struck sharply with a piece of steel, so that the sparks fall upon the child's head.[91] This gives us an added proof of the association of these stone axes, etc., with fire and with the lightning flash.

The Burmese celts or stone hatchets are frequently of jade and differ from those usually met with in Europe and India, in that they are provided with a chisel-edge instead of a double-sloped cutting edge. An interesting account of the superstitions connected with these implements is given by Mr. Theobald,[92] from whom we quote the following passage. It will be noted that the Burmese ideas are in almost exact accord with those current in Europe.

> The Burmese call these implements *mo-jio,* thunder-chain or thunderbolt, and believe that they descend with the lightning flash, and, after penetrating the earth, work their way back by degrees to the surface, where they are found scattered about the fields among the lower hills, usually after rain, or on removing the crops. The true *mo-jio* is supposed to possess many occult virtues, and it is not common to find one which does not show signs of having been chipped or scraped for medicinal purposes.

---

[90] Von Siebold, Jr., Verhandl. Berl. Anthrop. Ges., 1878, p. 431.

[91] Sven Nilsson, "The Primitive Inhabitants of Scandinavia," trans. by the author and ed. by Sir John Lubbock, 3d ed., London, 1868, p. 199.

[92] Memoirs of the Geological Survey of India, vol. x, pp. 255–259.

One of the chief virtues of the *mo-jio* is to render the person of the wearer invulnerable; and many an unlucky *mo-jio* has succumbed to the popular test, which is to wrap it in a cloth and fire a bullet at it at short range. If the man misses the cloth, the authenticity and power of the charm is at once established; if the stone is fractured it is held not to be a real *mo-jio*.

Fire will not consume a house which contains one, though I never heard of this ordeal being attempted. Last but not least is the known fact that the owner of a real *mo-jio* can cut a rainbow in half with it.

Certain recent happenings have suggested that the name "aviator-stone" would be a peculiarly appropriate designation for meteorites, and indeed this new name would only serve to emphasize the legendary belief, that he who bore with him a meteorite when he was in deadly peril would escape all injury. By a strange coincidence those who are willing to take great risks and chances are generally more or less superstitious regarding small things, and a daring aviator recently remarked that on one occasion, when his machine had suddenly fallen fifty feet, he felt for his tie and said to himself: "This accident has happened because I forgot to put on my opal pin, but I have been saved from injury because I carried a meteorite." This aviator, having mentioned the incident to Harmon, a few minutes before the latter made his successful attempt to win the Doubleday-Page aviation prize, Harmon immediately took the meteorite which had been shown to him, saying: "Let me have it." He accomplished his task, and although both the competing machines were injured, the aviators themselves were saved.

A meteorite, of course, cannot be claimed to be a preventive of danger on all occasions, but several who have always carried them have seemed to escape all sorts of harm. Some years ago a meteorite was given to Edward Heron Allen, the famous writer on palmistry and the violin, and this gifted man always wore it about him. One morning he awakened to find that the entire roof above him had fallen in, except just that portion over his bed. He told the story to one of the best known ladies in Boston; one who is known for her public spirit, her love of art and her faultless manner of entertaining. This lady successfully urged Allen to give her the meteorite. A few days later, while out driving, a great truck with two runaway horses attached to it struck her carriage. Instinctively she raised her muff to protect her face; the muff was almost cut in two, but the lady was not hurt. A few days later, while she was walking under some scaffolding, it fell, and the open part where the hoists went up proved to be just where she stood. Although surrounded by ruin, she remained unharmed.

III

Stones of Healing

IN his commentary on Theophrastus, Sir John Hill touches upon the question of the medicinal virtues of precious stones. His researches regarding the causes and conditions determining color in stones, led him to the conjecture that the active principle, if it really existed, was to be sought in the coloring matter. As the opinion of a very clever student in his day, his words will bear quotation:[1]

> The greatest part of these [medicinal virtues] cannot but be seen at first view to be altogether imaginary; and as to the virtues of the Gems in general, it is now the reigning Opinion, that they are nearly all so, their greatest Friends allowing them no other than those of the common alkaline Absorbents. However, whether the metalline Particles, to which they owe their Colours, are, in either Quantity or Quality, in Condition to have any effect in the Body, is a Matter worthy of a strict and regular Tryal; and that would at once decide the Question between us and the Antients, and shew whether we have been too rash, or they too superstitious.

The so-called "doctrine of signatures" treated of the marks set by nature upon certain objects to denote their usefulness in the cure of diseases affecting different parts of the body, or their power to neutralize the effects of the bites of certain animals or reptiles. Of this theory Martius says that the "signatures" are not to be sought in a fanciful resemblance to the form of the objects with the diseased parts of the human body, but rather in the color, odor, taste, composition, etc., of the objects.[2]

---

[1] Theophrastus's "History of Stones," with an English version by John Hill, London, 1746, p. 73.

[2] Martius, "Unterricht von der Magiæ Naturali, Leipzig, 1717, p. 290.

Medieval medical literature has no more interesting example than the treatise entitled "Thesaurus Pauperum," or the "Poor-man's Treasury," written by Petrus Hispanus, who later reigned for a brief period as pope under the name of John XXI (1276–1277). The birthplace of the author was Lisbon in Portugal, and he studied for some time at the University of Paris, where his learning earned him high praise. Prior to his election as pope, he served for a time as first physician to Pope Gregory X (1271–1276). Most of the remedies prescribed in this little treatise are naturally such as had long been popular among the peasantry, and the ingredients of which could easily be secured; vegetable growths, plants, herbs and flowers, and certain parts of the more common animals, served here, as in Pliny's day and earlier still, as those most highly favored. Of the comparatively few mineral substances whose use is recommended may be noted the red variety of *chelidonius* or "swallow stone," for the cure of epilepsy; the powder of the "iris" (probably an iridescent variety of quartz) was also a cure for epileptics. Then we find, strange to say, a recommendation of such costly remedial agencies as emerald and sapphire, either of which if touched on the eye would heal diseases of that organ. Cold stones placed on the temples and tightly bound on were said to arrest bleeding from the nose, and coral was a great help in syncope. For stone in the bladder two mineral substances, "humus" and "songie," are warmly recommended (the former can scarcely be held to signify mere "soil"), as are also "stones found in the gizzards of cocks" (the *alectorius*) and those from the bladders of hogs. All these were to be reduced to powder, dissolved in liquid, and taken in the form of potions. The use of stones and coral rather as amulets or talismans than as remedies is occasionally mentioned. Thus the loadstone, if worn, is said to remove discord between man and woman;

coral, if kept in the house, destroyed all evil influences, and if a woman wore touching her skin a concretion taken from the stomach of a she-goat that had not had young, this woman would never bear a child.[3]

The curious old medical treatise in verse called the "Schola Salernitana," was translated into English by Sir James Harington in 1607. The following lines give advice that is as appropriate to the conditions of our own age as to those of any other:[4]

> Use three physitians still, first doctor Quiet,
> Next doctor Merry-man and doctor Dyet.

Whether with or without intention, the translator has omitted to render the qualification given in the original: "Si tibi deficiant medici" (if other doctors are lacking).

The terrible plague known as the Black Death is said to have claimed 13,000,000 victims in Europe in the years 1347 and 1348. A contemporary, Olivier de la Haye, in a poem describing this fearful visitation, gives a number of recipes used, or to be used as remedies. In one of these there appear as ingredients pearls, jargoons, emeralds and coral, one-sixth of a drachm of each of these materials entering into the composition of the prescription.[5] The symptoms of this form of the plague, as described by the old writers, are said to resemble closely those of the disease that was prevalent not long ago in some parts of Asia, especially in northern China and Manchuria.

A famous class of medical remedies used in medieval

---

[3] From a fourteenth century Italian MS. translation of the treatise in the author's library; see fol. 8, recto, col. 2; fol. 9, recto, col. 1; fol. 10, recto, col. 2; fol. 14, verso, col. 1; fol. 17, verso, col. 1; fol. 25, verso, col. 1; fol. 26, verso, col. 1; fol. 26, verso, col. 2; fol. 29, verso, col. 2.

[4] Regimen sanitatis Salernitanum, ed. Sir Alexander Cooke, Oxford, 1830, p. 125. This edition contains reproductions of many curious woodcuts from the old German editions of Curio, published in 1559, 1568 and 1573.

[5] Havard, "Histoire de l'orfévrerie," Paris, 1896, p. 359; Olivier de la Haye, "Poème sur la grande peste de 1348," verses 3162 sqq.

times bore the generic name *theriaca,* or theriac, this designation being derived from the Greek *therion,* signifying a beast, more specifically a poisonous animal and hence also a serpent. These preparations were primarily antidotes for poison, but were also freely administered for any form of "blood-poisoning," for malarial infection, malignant fevers and the like. Principal ingredients were the "Armenian stone" (a friable, blue carbonate of copper), pearls, charred stag's-horn, and coral. The Veronese physician, Francesco India, confidently affirms that this remedy not only cured the plague, but also protected those who had partaken of it from contracting the disease; this was said to be more especially true of the *theriaca Andromachi,* or Venice treacle as it was popularly called, which purported to be the invention of a Roman or Greek physician, Andromachus, who composed some medical poems dedicated to Cæsar.[6]

In medieval Bohemia the knowledge of precious stones and their employment for curative purposes is well attested. There exists a Bohemian manuscript list of precious stones dated in 1391, in which no less than 55 different gems are noted. Their medicinal use in Bohemia at this time is vouched for by the Synonima Apothecariorum where precious stones are listed among the materials of the apothecaries' art.[7]

In the testaments of royal and princely personages, medical stones are often bestowed as precious legacies. Thus in the will of the Hessian prince, Henry VIII of Fürstenberg, the following stones are mentioned as especially costly objects: a "crabstone" (Krebstein), a bloodstone, and a gravel-stone, the latter being a piece of jade or nephrite.[8] The crabstone, sometimes called crab's-eye, is a chalky concretion which forms on either side of the stomach

[6] Francisci Indiæ, "Hygiphylus sive de febre maligna dialogus," Veronæ, 1593, pp. 125, 126.

[7] Dr. B. Jézak, "Aus dem Reiche der Edlesteine," Prag, 1914, p. 65.

[8] Kobert, "Ein Edlestein der Vorzeit," Stuttgart, 1910, p. 36.

of a crab or other crustacean during the moulting period, and this was and is still used as an eye-stone for the removing of foreign bodies that have entered the eye, the eye-stone

Interior of fifteenth century pharmacy. From Johannis de Cuba's "Ortus Sanitatis", Strassburg, 1483.

being introduced under the eyelid. This results in a rapid flow from the tear-ducts which often washes away the foreign bodies, the passage of the stone across the eyeball occasionally aiding in the work by rubbing off the body.

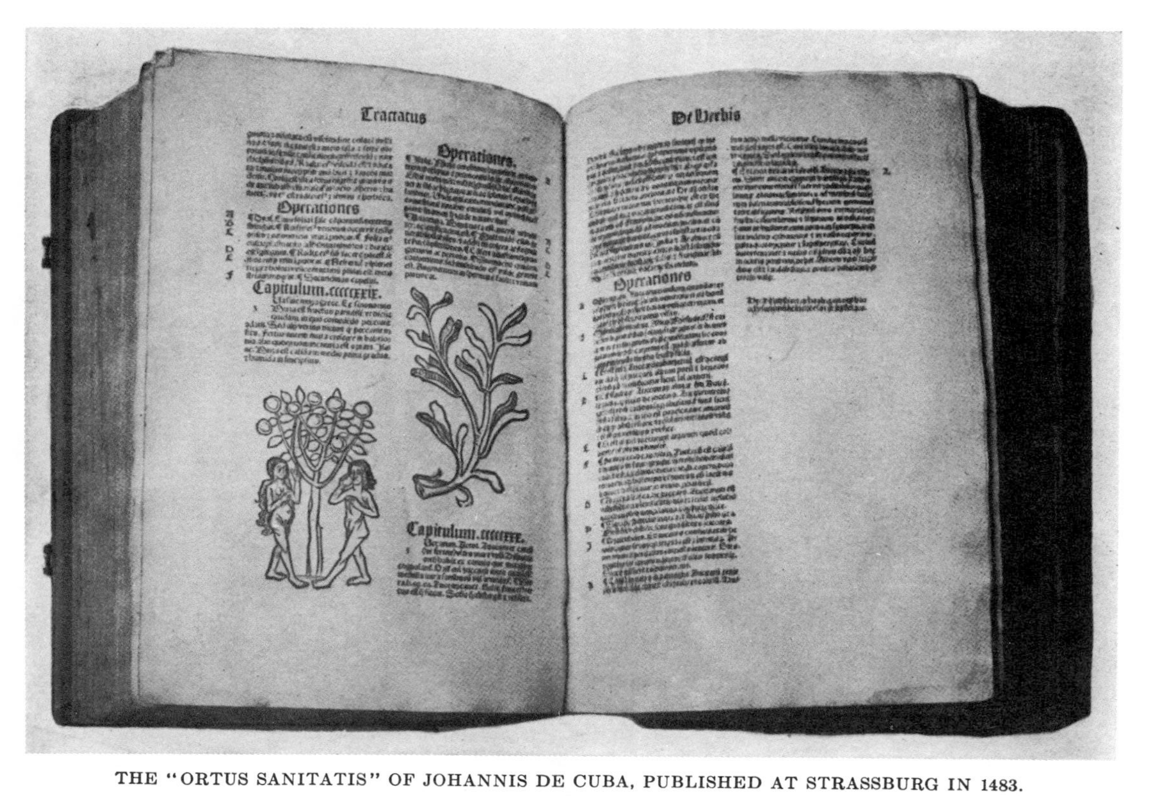

THE "ORTUS SANITATIS" OF JOHANNIS DE CUBA, PUBLISHED AT STRASSBURG IN 1483.

The woodcut depicts Adam and Eve beneath the "Tree of Knowledge."

In the sixteenth century sapphires, emeralds, rubies, garnets, jacinths, coral and sardonyxes were used in all tonics prescribed to protect the heart against the effects of poison and of the plague. As it was noted that these remedies were frequently ineffectual, an explanation was sought in the fact that spurious stones were often used, the apothecaries either not having the knowledge to recognize the genuine stones, or being moved by a desire to profit by the substitution of some inferior substance. Hence physicians were warned to be on their guard against such deceptions, and only to employ thoroughly trustworthy apothecaries for the compounding of their prescriptions. A substitution frequently made was that of the so-called yellow chrysoprase (cerogate), a stained chalcedony, for the jacinth, although the true jacinth of the ancients was of the color of the amethyst. The grinding of coral in a brass mortar, instead of in one of marble, was also regarded as a very dangerous proceeding, which would have the worst possible results for the unlucky patient who took the powder, for some particles of the brass might be rubbed away and mix with the coral. This was said to have often produced very serious illness.[9]

In a price-list of a firm of German druggists, printed in 1757, all the precious stones still appear. Here the cost of a pound of rock-crystal is six groschen ($.18); the same quantity of emerald was priced at eight groschen ($.25), while the pound of sapphire was quoted at sixteen groschen ($.50), of ruby at one thaler ($.75), and of lapis-lazuli at five thalers ($3.75). This indicates quite clearly the quality of the emerald, sapphire and ruby offered for sale. A pound of Oriental bezoar commanded the highest price, sixteen thalers ($12).[10]

[9] Andrea Matthiolus, "Commentaries sur Discoride," Lyon, 1642 (written in 1565), p. 538.

[10] Fühner, "Lithotherapie," Berlin, 1902, p. 44.

Regarding the length of time during which various preparations retained their strength, Braunfels [11] states that, according to the opinion of the Arabian physicians, the solution of lapis Armenus lasted for ten years, while that of lapis lazuli could be preserved only about three years. A list of the indispensable materials which should be in every good pharmacy included the following precious stones:

Jacinth	Magnes
Sapphire	Coral
Emerald	Hematite
Topaz	Aetites
Margaritha (pearl)	Jasper

The supposed medicinal properties of precious stones are subjected to a searching criticism by the Veronese physician, Francesco India, writing in 1593.[12] After establishing the distinction between alimentary and medicinal substances, he proceeds to exclude from the latter category the jacinth, emerald, sapphire, etc., because although they could be reduced to a powder, they could not be dissolved, so that when taken in a potion they could be absorbed in the human system.[13] Hence no such effects could properly be ascribed to them as were to be expected from the regular and normal medicinal agencies. This writer ascribes the original use of such stones as remedies for malignant fevers and other dangerous diseases to the Arabs, adding that "had they not made this mistake and thus led many physicians into error, they would have been better worthy of praise."[11] In fact he does not hesitate to pronounce the emphatic opinion that these stones are not remedial agents fit to be

[11] Braunfels, "Reformation der Apptecken," Strassburg, 1536, fol. XIV b, XX b.

[12] Francisci Indiæ, "Hygiphylus, sive de febre maligna dialogus," Veronæ, 1593.

[13] Op. cit. pp. 115 sqq.

administered or used by any rational physician.[14] That powdered hematite (red oxide of iron) possesses an astringent quality and may really be looked upon as a medicine, he fully recognizes, more particularly its efficacy for the cure of diseases of the eye, but neither these nor similar qualities can be credited to sapphires, emeralds, or jacinths. At the same time he is not disposed to deny that these stones may have some subtle effect upon the body when worn, or when held in the mouth for a time. Thus he agrees with Avicenna (Ben Sina) that a jacinth worn over the heart may strengthen that organ, for he knows of the power inherent in jasper to check a hemorrhage. In a word his argument is principally directed against the internal use of powders made from these hard and unassimilable stones.[15]

Robert Boyle, writing in 1663, attempts to show that the theory of the therapeutic action of precious stones is not incompatible with observed facts. In this connection he says:[16]

> I am not altogether of their mind, that absolutely reject the internal use of Leaf-Gold, Rubies, Saphyrs, Emeralds, and other Gems, as things that are unconquerable by the heat of the stomach. For as there are rich Patients that may, without much inconvenience, goe to the price of the dearest Medicines; so I think the Stomach acts not on Medicines barely upon the account of its heat, but is endowed with a subtle dissolvent (whence never it hath it) by which it may perform divers things not to be done by so languid a heat. And I have, with Liquors of differing sorts, easily drawn from Vegetable Substances, and perhaps unrectified, sometimes dissolved, and sometimes drawn Tinctures from Gems, and that in the cold . . . But that which I chiefly consider on this occasion is, that 'tis one thing to make it *probable,* that is, *possible,* Gold, Rubies, Saphyrs, etc., may be wrought upon by humane Stomach; and another thing to shew both that they *are wont* to be so, and that they *are* actually endowed with those particular

[14] Op. cit., p. 116.

[15] Op. cit., pp. 118–122.

[16] Boyle, "On the Usefulness of Experimental Philosophy," Oxford, 1664, p. 108.

and specifick Virtues that are ascribed to them; nay and (over and above) that these Virtues are such and so eminent, that they considerably surpass those of cheaper Simples. And I think, that in Prescriptions made for the poorer sort of Patients, a Physician may well substitute cheaper Ingredients in the place of these precious ones, whose Virtues are no half so unquestionable as their Dearnesse.

Whether the somewhat mysterious illness and death of the popes Leo IV and Paul II could have been caused by the great quantity of pearls and precious stones they were in the habit of wearing was a question seriously discussed by Johann Wolff, the supposed lethal effect being attributed to the coldness of such objects.[17] Indeed, the frigidity of precious stones was adduced by certain writers as one of the chief reasons for their remedial use in fevers.[18]

Not only to King Frederick III of Denmark himself, to whom on his death-bed in 1670, a dose of pulverized bezoar was administered, but to his queen and their children such remedies were given, there being record that on September 19, 1663, a prescription containing red coral and pearl powder was compounded by the Court Pharmacy for the queen, while a few years earlier the inevitable bezoar and also a tonic pearl-milk were administered to some of the royal offspring.[19]

Some interesting details as to the use of precious stone remedies for the cure of illness appear in the manuscript notes of lectures given at the Leyden Hospital by the seventeenth century physician, Lucas Schacht, in 1674 and 1675.[20] This shows that these remedial agents were there and at that time only used as a last resort, when the patient's con-

[17] Johannis Wolffii, "Curiosus amuletorum scrutator," Francofurti et Lipsiæ, 1692, p. 564.

[18] J. B. Silvatici, "Controversiæ medicæ," Francofurti, 1601, p. 223.

[19] Axel Garboe, "Kunsthistoriske Studier over Ædelstene," Kjbenhavn og Kristiania, 1915, p. 254.

[20] See Axel Garboe, "Kulturhistoriske Studier over Ædelstene, med særligt Henbilk paa det 17. Aarhundrede," Kjbenhavn og Kristiania, 1915, pp. 141 sqq.

FAMOUS PEARL NECKLACE OF THE UNFORTUNATE EMPRESS CARLOTTA, WIDOW OF EMPEROR MAXIMILIAN OF MEXICO.

dition had become desperate, and the physician is usually obliged to record the fact that death ensued shortly afterwards. Thus we are told of the case of a certain Ludovicus Carels who was suffering from difficulty of breathing and purulent expectoration; his body was so distended that he could scarcely move his limbs, and he also had a severe diarrhœa. This was his condition on November 12, 1674, and the symptoms steadily grew worse under a treatment of herb decoctions, until a few days later, on November 21, it is noted that "he only thinks of death." Still the doctors waited until November 24 before they decided to administer a compound remedy consisting in part of the elixirs of jacinth and pearl; three days later the patient died. In general the chief symptoms which justified the use of such remedies were those of high fever or great weakness.

Although by the middle of the eighteenth century the belief in the special curative powers of precious-stone material had almost entirely disappeared, giving place to a more scientific conception of the chemical composition of these bodies, still, we find, even in so capable a writer as the German mineralogist, U. F. B. Brückmann, a lingering trace of the old idea, for while he declares that all intelligent physicians have abandoned their use, he adds, "if, however, any stone of this kind has more effect than an ordinary earthy substance, it is the lapis lazuli, but we have a hundred other remedies equally efficacious and much cheaper." He also testifies to the fact that very little genuine material was to be had from the apothecaries, he himself having often seen a yellow feldspar offered instead of a jacinth, and poor garnets as substitutes for rubies.[21]

Toward the end of the eighteenth century, a famous cordial medicine, called "Gascoign's Powder," after the

---

[21] U. F. B. Brückmann, "Abhandlung von Edelsteinen," Braunschweig, 1757, pp. 4, 5 of preface.

physician who compounded it, had an immense vogue in England. This man is said to have got more than £50,000 ($250,000) from the sale of this single remedy. It is stated to have contained Oriental bezoar (the most important ingredient), white amber, red coral, crab's eyes, powdered hartshorn, pearl and black crab's claws; certainly a most incongruous mixture and one well calculated to test the resisting powers of the person to whom it was administered.[22]

A modern writer finds in the homeopathic theory of medicine an explanation of the apparent therapeutic effects of precious stones.[23] For if the smaller the dose the greater the effect, then such super-subtle emanations as are thought to proceed from precious stones must have effects still more powerful than those of the most highly diluted tinctures administered by homeopathists of the old school. Christian Science, however, with its bold denial of the existence of disease, and with its purely spiritual treatment of the "mental error" that is supposed to be at the root of all morbid symptoms, could even more easily account for the apparent cures wrought by merely wearing precious stones. The belief in their remedial virtue would serve to remove the morbid impression, and would restore the mind to its normal and healthy state.

An instance from our own day of the application of a mineral substance externally for the cure of disease, appears in the use of the uranium pitchblende occurring in Joachimsthal, Bohemia. This is enclosed in leather bags and applied to the head for the cure of headache. The most violent pains are said to be relieved in a short time by this treatment,

[22] John and Andrew Van Rymsdyk, "Museum Brittanicum," 2 ed. revised and corrected by P. Boyle, London, 1791, p. 51.

[23] Fernie, "Precious Stones for Curative Wear," Bristol, 1907, p. 256.

the effect being produced by the radium contained in the pitchblende.[24]

Agate

Treating of the medicinal virtues of agates, Pliny distinguishes between the Indian agates, which were a remedy for diseases of the eyes, and those from Egypt and Crete, which were especially adapted for curing the bites of spiders or scorpions.[25] This latter quality was probably attributed to the agate because it was believed to have a cooling influence upon the body. Damigeron directs that when used to cure the bites of venomous creatures the stone should be reduced to a powder, which was to be strewn over the wound; sometimes, however, this powder was dissolved in wine and administered internally.[26] As an agate, if held in the mouth, was supposed to quench thirst, it was recommended at an early period for the cure of fevers and inflammatory diseases.[27]

In Byzantine times the use of agate for inflamed eyes and for headaches is still advised by Psellus (eleventh century), who adds that it checks menstruation and prevents the accumulation of water in cases of dropsy. This he attributes to the wonderful absorbent power of the stone.[28] It seems most probable that here some kind of hydrophane has been confounded with the agate. The other use, that of checking hemorrhages, presupposes the use of a red variety of agate.

---

[24] Von Hovorka and Kronfeld, "Vergleichende Volksmedizin," Stuttgart, 1908, vol. i, p. 355. Communication of Dr. Christof Hartungen, Jr.

[25] Damigeron, "De lapidibus," ed. Abel, Berol., 1881, p. 177.

[26] Plinii, "Naturalis historia," lib. xxxvi, cap. 54.

[27] Orphei, "Lithica," ed. Abel, Berol., 1881, vs. 610 sqq.

[28] Pselli, "De lapidum virtutibus," ed. Bemond, Lug. Bat., 1745, p. 10.

Beryl

Thomas de Cantimpré[29] tells us that the beryl cures quinsy and swollen glands in the neck if the affected part be rubbed with the stone. It is also useful as a remedy for diseases of the eye, and if water in which it has been steeped be given to anyone suffering from an attack of hiccoughs, relief will be afforded.

The beryl was warmly recommended as a cure for injuries to the eyeball, even of the most serious kind. For use in such cases the stone was to be pulverized in a mortar, and this powder then passed through a fine sieve. Of the minute particles thus secured, a small quantity was to be introduced each morning into the injured eye, the patient being in a recumbent posture. He was then to keep properly quiet with his eyes shut for a considerable length of time after this operation. Although it was not indeed claimed that where the power of sight had been destroyed it could thus be restored, still even in case of such severe injury the eyeball was healed sooner and assumed a better appearance. In less serious cases a cure was considered to be assured.[30]

Carbuncle

Many virtues are attributed to carbuncles. It is related that those who wear them can resist poisons and are preserved from the pest. They dissipate sadness, control incontinence, avert evil thoughts and dreams, exhilarate the soul and foretell misfortunes to man by losing their native splendor.[31]

---

[29] Konrad von Megenberg's fourteenth century version, "Buch der Natur," ed. by Dr. Franz Pfeiffer, Stuttgart, 1861, p. 436.

[30] Andreæ Baccii, "De Gemmis et Lapidibus Pretiosis" (Latin version by Wolfgang Gabelchover of the Italian original), Francofurti, 1603, pp. 100, 101, Note of Gabelchover.

[31] Johannis Braunii, "De Vestitu Sacerdotum Hebræorum," Amstelodami, 1680, pp. 672–3.

Chalcedony

Perforated, spherical beads of milky-white chalcedony are worn at the present day by Italian peasant-women to increase the supply of milk. Hence the Italian name for such a bead, *pietra lattea.* Perforated beads of white steatite, belonging to the early Iron Age, have been found near Perugia, where the chalcedony beads are worn, and it is believed that these steatite beads were borne for the same purpose.[32]

Coral

Coral and safran, if wrapped in the skin of a cat, were believed to have marvellous powers; and when emeralds were added to the coral the talisman would drive off a mortal fever. To have the proper effect, however, it must be attached to the neck of the patient.[33] As a cure for hydrophobia, dog-collars set with flint and Maltese coral were recommended in Roman times; "sacred shells" and herbs over which magic incantations had been pronounced were also attached to, or enclosed in these collars. The use of coral in this case appears to have been due to the belief in its power to dissolve the spell cast by the Evil Eye, for Gratius, who flourished in the first century A.D. and was a contemporary of the poet Ovid, asserts that if such collars were put on dogs suffering from hydrophobia, the gods were appeased, and the charm cast by "an envious eye" was broken.[34]

The Hindu physicians found that coral tasted both sweet and sour, and they asserted that its principal action was

[32] Belucci, "Catalogue de l'Exposition de la Société d'Anthropologie" (Ex. de 1900), pp. 278–279.

[33] Severus Sammonicus, "Preceptes médicaux," text and trans. by L. Baudet, Paris, 1845, pp. 76, 77.

[34] Gratii Falisci, "Cynegeticon"; collection des auteurs Latin, ed. Nizard, vol. xvi, Paris, 1851, p. 786, lines 401–405.

on the secretions of the mucous membrane, on the bile and on certain morbid secretions.[35] Although the chemical constituents of coral have but slight medicinal value, it is quite possible that some effects upon the secretions may have been observed experimentally after the administration of a dose of powdered coral.

An old pharmacopœia gives elaborate directions for the preparation of the "Tincture of Coral." A branch of very red coral was to be buried in melted wax, and allowed to remain over a fire for the space of two days, "after which time you will see that the coral has become white, while the wax has assumed a red hue." A fresh branch of coral is then to be put into the partially colored wax, and the above operation repeated; the wax will then be "redder than before." It is now to be broken into crusts, which are to be steeped in alcohol until the liquid has extracted the coloring matter from the wax and has become reddish. In this way, after the removal of the wax by filtration, etc., a tincture was obtained which is represented to have been an excellent tonic, and to have had the power to expel "bad humors," by inducing perspiration, or by its diuretic action.[36] We strongly suspect that in this, as in many modern "tonics," the contents of spirit was the active principle.

An apparent confirmation of the widespread belief of former centuries that red coral changed its hue in sympathy with the state of the wearer's health, caused perhaps by the exudations or sweats arising from fevers or other ailments, is given from personal experience by the German physician, Johann Wittich. Writing toward the end of the sixteenth century, this author relates that he was called in to attend a youth named Bernard Erasmus, son of the burgomaster of

[35] Garbe, "Die indische Mineralien"; Naharari's "Rajanighaṇṭu," Varga XIII, Leipzig, 1882, p. 76.

[36] Lémery, "Cursus Chymicus," Latin version by De Rebecque, Geneva, 1681, p. 338.

Arnstadt. As the youth sickened unto death a red coral which he was wearing turned first whitish, then of a dirty yellow, and finally became covered with black spots. To the anxious questions of the youth's sister, Wittich could only give a mournful answer, telling her to take away the coral, for death was surely approaching, and this prognostication proved to be only too true, as in a few hours young Erasmus was dead.[37]

A rosary of coral beads was sometimes called in France a *pater de sang*, or "blood-rosary," since it was believed to check hemorrhages. An anonymous author of an eighteenth century treatise on superstitions, assuming that this effect could be produced only by thickening the blood, asserts that such a rosary might do more harm than good, for if it possessed this power at one time, it must possess it constantly, and its action would be very injurious.[38] Pearls and corals were still freely used as therapeutic agents in the last half of the seventeenth century, for we are told that Louis XIV (1638–1715), in 1655, took tablets containing gold and pearls, which had been prescribed for him by his physician Vallot, and, in 1664, a remedy composed of pearls and corals was recommended by the same authority.[39]

Corundum

A stone, which from the description seems to have been an almost colorless variety of corundum with a faint reddish tint, is recommended in the Syrian Aristotle for the alleviation of diseases of the breast. To have the proper effect

---

[37] Johannes Wittichius, "Bericht von den wunderbaren Bezoardischen Steinen," Leipzig, 1589, p. 56, cited in Axel Garboe's "Kunsthistoriske Studier over Ædelstene," Kobenhavn og Kristiania, 1915, p. 98.

[38] "Histoire critique des practiques superstitieuses; par un prêtre de l'Oratoire," Paris, 1702, p. 326.

[39] Hovarka and Kronfeld, "Vergleichende Volksmedizin," Stuttgart, 1908, vol. i, p. 107.

this stone was to be worn on the region affected by the malady.[40]

Diamond

The Hindu physicians claimed that they had found that the diamond had six flavors; it was sweet, sour, salty, pungent, bitter, and acrid. Since the stone united all these apparently contradictory qualities, we have no reason to be surprised that it should be supposed to cure all diseases and lessen all ills. An elixir of great potency, stimulating and strengthening all the bodily functions, was made from the diamond.[41]

The author of the Jawâhir-nâmeh (Book of Jewels), written about a century ago, gives some of the prevalent Hindu ideas regarding the diamond. He asserts that the similarity of this stone and rock-crystal led to the belief that the latter was only an incomplete or "unripe" form of the diamond. For this reason rock crystal was called *kacha*, "unripe," and the diamond, *pakka*, "ripe." The same writer, after noting the general belief that if a diamond were put in the mouth it caused the teeth to fall out, states that some were not disposed to admit this, as diamond-dust had been used as a tooth-powder without any bad effects.[42] It might certainly serve to whiten the teeth, but any one who trusted to this very drastic dentifrice would soon be sadly in need of the dentist's help.

As a proof that the diamond was not much prized as an ornamental stone in the Middle Ages, although some of

---

[40] Rose, "Aristoteles De lapidibus und Arnoldus Saxo," in Zeitsch. für D. Alt., New Series, vol. vi, pp. 378, 379.

[41] Garbe, "Die indische Mineralien"; Naharari's "Rajanighaṇṭu," Varga XIII, Leipzig, 1882, p. 80.

[42] "Oriental Accounts of the Precious Minerals," trans. by Raja Kalikishan, with remarks by James Prinsep; Journ. Asiat. Soc. of Bengal, vol. i, Calcutta, p. 354.

the praise bestowed upon it by Pliny and other classical writers was copied and recopied in a more or less perfunctory way, we may cite the few lines devoted to the stone by Psellus, who lived in Constantinople in the eleventh century A.D. This writer simply remarks of the diamond that it is hard and difficult to pierce, adding, as its chief virtue, that it would quench the heat of the "semi-tertian" fever.[43] The belief in this cooling quality of the diamond was suggested by its lack of color coupled with its extreme hardness, the latter quality being thought to augment the refrigerant power supposed to be inherent in colorless crystals which resembled ice.

Emerald

The emerald is especially commended for amulets to be suspended from the necks of children; it is believed to preserve them from epileptic convulsions and to prevent the falling sickness; but if the violence of the disease is such that it cannot be overcome by the stone, the latter breaks up. Bound to a woman's thigh it is said to hasten parturition; hanging from the neck it drives off vain fears and evil spirits. It strengthens the memory, restores the sight, reveals adultery and gives a knowledge of the future, produces eloquence and increases wealth.[44]

Besides the usual designation *marakata* which Garbe believes to be derived from the Greek σμάραγδος, the Sanskrit has several distinguishing names for the emerald. One of these, *açmagarbhaja,* signifies "sprung from the rock," and well describes the emerald in its matrix. Another name is *garalari,* "enemy of poison," indicating the great repute enjoyed by this stone in India as an antidote for all animal,

---

[43] See Pinder, "De adamante," Berolini, 1829, p. 66.

[44] Johannis Braunii, "De Vestitu Sacerdotum Hebraeorum," Amstelodami, 1680, p. 659.

mineral and vegetable poisons.[45] In Mexico the emerald[46] bore the name Quetzalitzli, "stone of the quetzal," because its color resembled the brilliant green of the plumes of the bird called in the Mexican tongue *quetzal*. These plumes were worn as insignia of royalty by the sovereigns of Mexico and Central America, and hence the emerald was regarded as an essentially regal gem, although its use was not confined to royalty.

The tincture of emerald is recommended by the Arab physician Abenzoar as an internal remedy for the cure of dysentery, the dose prescribed being six grains. He also claims to have cured one of his patients suffering from this disease by making him wear an emerald.[47] This illustrates the use of the stone in Moorish Spain in the early part of the eleventh century, the period of the highest development of Moorish civilization, for Abenzoar, or Abû Meruân, as he is sometimes called, was born in Seville about 1091 A.D. and died in 1161 or 1162.

Hematite

The curative properties of the hematite were generally recognized by the early writers, and in this case they were not so much at fault, as this substance possesses considerable astringent properties. Galen recommends its use for inflamed eyelids, following in this the teachings of the Egyptian schools of medicine. If there were tumors on the eyelids, the hematite was to be dissolved in white of egg, and if the tumors were very large it was to be boiled with fenugreek (fœnum græcum); if, however, there were no tumors, but simply a general inflammation of the eyelids, a

[45] Garbe, "Die indische Mineralien"; Naharari's "Rajanighaṇṭu," Varga XIII, Leipzig, 1882, p. 76.

[46] The emerald of Mexico was evidently the jade or the *piedra del hijada.*

[47] Gabriel Colin, "Avenzoar, sa vie et ses œuvres," dissertation for doctorate in Univ. of Paris, 1911, pp. 164, 165.

solution in water sufficed. At the outset a few drops of a weak solution were to be poured into the eye through a glass tube; should this treatment not prove effective, the solution was to be made thicker and thicker, until at last it had to be dipped out on the point of the tube. If ground to a fine powder in a mortar, hematite cured spitting of blood and all ulcers. Galen advises great care in judging of the quality and strength of the powder, which was to be poured on or spread over the sore, but in his own case he admits that he trusted to his sense of taste to determine its quality.[48]

Sotacus as quoted by Pliny distinguishes five kinds of hematite, each one of which possessed special medicinal virtues. The best was the Ethiopic, which was a valuable ingredient in lotions for the eyes, and for burns. The second kind was called androdamus and came from Africa; this was very black, and was exceedingly hard and heavy, whence its name "conqueror of man"; it was reputed to attract silver, brass and iron. If rubbed with a moistened whetstone it gave forth a red juice, and was considered to be a specific for bilious disorders. The third kind was brought by the Arabs; this gave scarcely any juice when rubbed with the whetstone, but occasionally a little of a yellowish hue, and was useful for burns and for all bilious disorders. The fourth kind was called elatite in its natural state and melitite when burned; and the fifth appears to have contained an admixture of schist. These shared in the general virtues of the hematite, three grains of whose powder, when taken in oil, would cure all blood diseases.[49]

That the cause of the friendship between Hector and Dolon was the latter's ownership of a hematite is asserted in the Greek Orphic poem "Lithica." This statement must

---

[48] Claudii Galeni, "Opera omnia," ed. Kühn, Lipsiæ, 1826, vol. xii, pp. 195, 196; De simplic. med., lib. vii, cap. 2.

[49] Plinii, "Historia Naturalis," lib. xxxvi, cap. 38.

be derived from some annotation to the Iliad made in the Alexandrine schools, for Homer himself knows nothing of it. In the fateful encounter of Hector with Achilles, the form and aspect of Dolon are assumed by Athena to deceive Hector into the belief that his friend was at his side to aid him in the unequal struggle. The blood of Uranus when wounded by Kronos is stated in "Lithica" as the generating cause of hematite, and the stone is recommended as a cure for eye-diseases.[50]

Jacinth

A peculiarly stimulant and tonic effect exercised by the jacinth was noted by Ben Sina (Avicenna), and to this is attributed its value as an antidote for poisons. Not, however, to the material composition of the stone was this effect to be attributed, for it proceeded from the mass in the same way as did the virtue of the magnet. Hence Ben Sina is opposed to the theory that the natural warmth of the body acted upon the jacinth, when taken internally, producing a transmutation, dissolution and mingling of its substance with the volatile spiritual essence.[51]

In Constantinople, at a time when the plague was exceptionally prevalent, the citizens used to wear jacinths, because of the special virtues these stones were supposed to possess as guardians against the plague. That jacinth amulets intended for therapeutic use were occasionally to be found in pharmacies, is attested by Ambrosianus, who states that a jacinth the size of a human nail, and set in silver, was kept in a "pharmacy in Poland." This stone, if held to a wound, was said to prevent mortification.[52]

---

[50] "Lithica," lines 636 sqq.

[51] Avicennæ, "Liber canonis," Basileæ, 1556.

[52] Aldrovandi, "Museum metallicum," Bononiæ, 1648, p. 965.

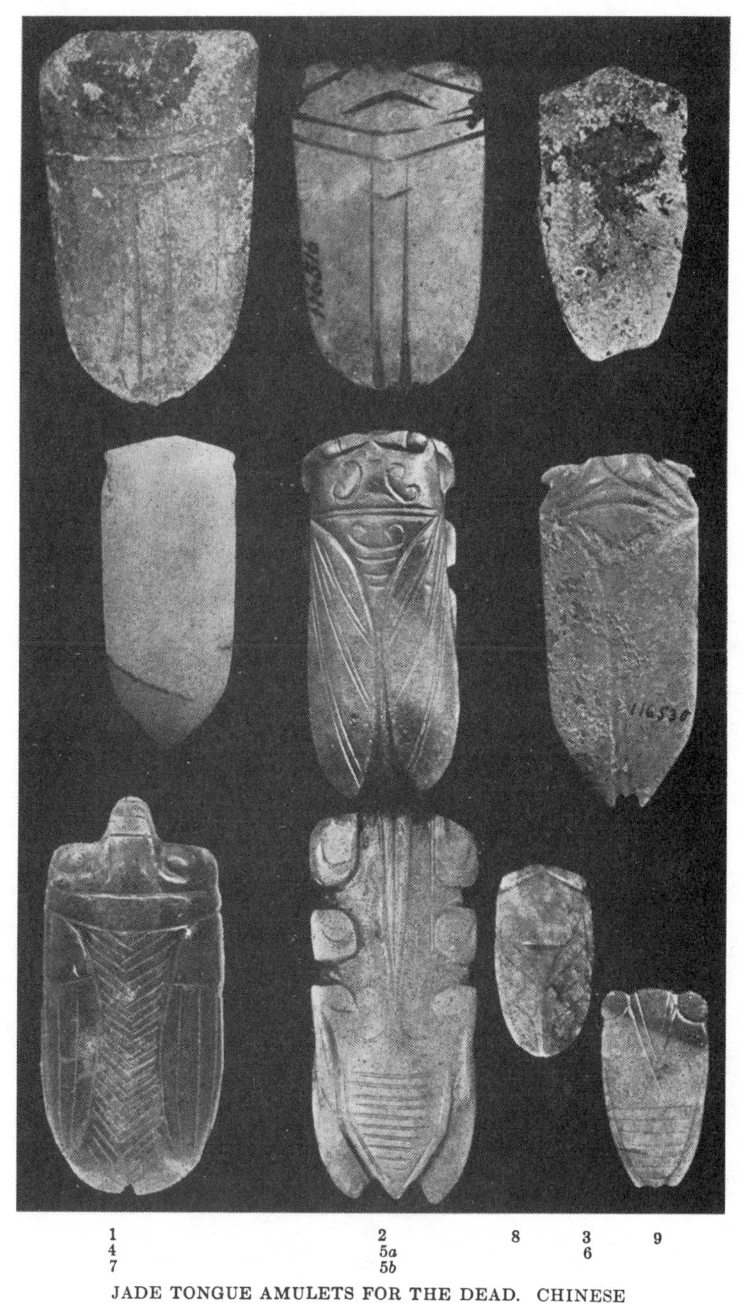

1	2	8	3	9
4	5a		6	
7	5b			

JADE TONGUE AMULETS FOR THE DEAD. CHINESE

Figs. 1-4, plain types; Fig. 5, carved in shape of realistic cicada (*a*, upper, *b*, lower face); Figs. 6-9, conventionalized forms of cicada. From "Jade," by Berthold Laufer.

By courtesy of the author and Field Museum of National History, Chicago.

FRONTISPIECE OF MUSEUM WORMIANUM

Printed in Leyden in 1655, showing a part of the remarkable collection of specimens illustrating natural history owned by Olaus Wormius of Copenhagen.

Jade

The first mention of this material is made by Monardes, who says:[53]

> The so-called nephritic stone is a species of stone, the finest of which resemble the emerald crystal, and are green with a milky hue. It is worn in various forms, made in ancient times, such as the Indians had; some like fish, some like the heads of birds, others like the beaks of parrots and others again round as balls; all, however, are perforated, since the Indians used to wear them attached for nephritic or gastric pains, for they had marvellous efficacy in both these infirmities. Their principal virtue regards the nephritic pain, and the passing of gravel and stone, in such sort that a gentleman who owns one, the best I have ever seen, wearing it bound on his arm, passed so much gravel that he often takes it off, thinking that it may be injurious for him to pass such a quantity; and, indeed, when he removes the stone he passes much less. . . . This stone has an occult property, by means of which it exercises a wonderful prophylactic effect, preventing the occurrence of nephritic pain, and should it nevertheless ensue, removing or alleviating it. The duchess my lady, having suffered three attacks of this malady during a short period, had one of these stones set in a bracelet and wore it on her arm, and from the time she put it on, she has never felt any pain, although ten years have past. In the same way it has served many, who have realized the same benefit. Therefore, it is highly prized and it cannot now be worn so easily as in former times, as only caciques and noblemen own it, and rightly, since it has such wonderful effects.

The Chinese Taoist adept T'ao Hung Ching, who flourished A.D. 500, directs that when powdered jade is prescribed by a physician, carved jade must not be used, nor unwrought jade that has been buried in tombs. While sometimes a very fine powder was recommended, the usual plan was to reduce the jade by pounding it into pieces the size of small pulse. When administered in this form the Chinese physicians asserted that the powder passed unchanged through the system, but that the essential principle, the innate virtue, was absorbed by the patient. It relieved heart-burn and

[53] Monardes, "Delle cose che vengono portate dall'Indie Occidentali," Venetia, 1575, Bk. II, chap. XIV, p. 46.

asthma and stilled thirst. Taken regularly for a long period it acted as a powerful general tonic, and had the special effects of strengthening the voice and rendering the hair glossy; but all these good effects could only be secured by the use of unwrought jade.[54]

The *lapis nephriticus* (jade) was held to be a remedy for œdematous affections of the feet. As this stone was so highly in favor in Europe for a century or two after it had first been brought from America by the Spaniards, many were of the opinion that it should be constantly worn to exert its full curative power. There were some, however, who argued that with this as with other remedies, constant and unremitting use weakened the effect, so that when the wearer was suddenly attacked by some disorder for which jade was a cure, his system would have become so habituated to its action that it would no longer work as a remedy.[55]

Of the *lapis nephriticus* the old Danish writer, Caspar Bertholin, relates in 1628 that four prominent citizens of Copenhagen, whom he had recommended to wear it to break up the calculi with which they were afflicted, could testify to its worth, adding, somewhat naïvely, "at least two of them can, for the two others are dead—but not of the stone." He himself, however, although he had sent for specimens at great expense, to Venice, Nuremberg and Batavia, could not gain any relief from his trouble, but nevertheless, firm in his conviction of the special curative power of jade, he asserts that the calculi which tormented him must have been exceptionally hard and flint-like, so that they could not be broken up. The vogue enjoyed by this supposed remedy in the Denmark of the time is illustrated in the case of the reign-

[54] T'ang Jung-tso, "Yü-shuo" (a discourse on jade), trans. by Stephen W. Bushell; Investigations and Studies in Jade, The Bishop Collection, New York, 1900, pp. 329, 330.

[55] Jacobi Wolff, "Curiosus amuletorum scrutator," Francofurti et Lipsiæ, 1692, pp. 218, 219; citing principally, Bartholini, "De lapide nephritico."

ing sovereign, Christian IV, who wore on his person a green nephrite until the day of his death. This stone is still preserved in the Rosenborg Museum collection among the relics of this king.[56]

Johannes de Laet was much impressed with the virtues of the *lapis nephriticus* as were most of his learned contemporaries, since he assures his readers that an oblong, smooth, moderately thick stone in his possession, having the color of honey and a very oily surface, had given his wife great relief from the severe pains caused by renal calculus, when the stone was bound upon her wrist. This particular specimen he sent a few years later to his Danish friend, Ole Worms, for the latter's cabinet of natural history. De Laet writes that all the virtues claimed for nephrite by Monardes in 1574, were observable in his specimen.[57]

As late as 1726, there were some who retained faith in the curative power of jade, for a record of that date informs us that the traveller Paul Lucas had just come back to Paris from the Orient, and had brought with him a specimen of the lapis nephriticus which he intended to have cut up into thin slabs to bestow upon such of his friends as were suffering from gravel or calculus, or similar troubles.[58]

After relating that a specimen of American jadeite had been sent to him prior to 1602, Cleandro Arnobio states that when he showed it to a Signor Michele Mercato, "a man well versed in medicine and in the knowledge of minerals and herbs," the latter immediately recognized it and called it "nephite," from its virtues, saying also that he had found it useful in aiding parturition. A pharmacist, to whom it

[56] Axel Garboe, "Kulturhistoriske Studier over Ædelstene, med særligt Henblik paa det 17. Aarhundrede," Kobenhavn og Kristiania, 1915, pp. 204, 205; citing Caspari Bertholini, "De lapide nephritico opusculum," 1628.

[57] Johannes de Laet, "De gemmis et lapidibus libri duo," Lugduni Batavorum [1647], p. 84.

[58] "Sammlung von Natur und Medicin-wie auch hierzu gehörigen Kunst- und Literatur-Geschichten," Breslau, 1726, p. 262.

was shown in turn, declared that he had used the stone in this way but did not know its name. This is perhaps the earliest use of the name nephrite, the form occurring in the Italian text being either due to a typographical error, or to Arnobio's ignorance of the correct spelling.

Proceeding to dilate upon the many virtues of this stone, Cleandro quotes Aldobrando, "a physician, physicist and philosopher of Bologna," who described it as having usually a purple shade, almost like porphyry, with various figures of herbs, flowers, knots and Arabic characters in a yellow color. There were, however, according to the same authority, some of a darker hue, with protuberances and bands of yellow and also black spots, as though the stone were a section of the spleen. This kind was recommended and used in diseases of the spleen. In another variety, in the midst of the purple color might be seen a yellow stain with pittings and hollows; this was thought to figure a section of the liver, spattered with bile, and such stones were employed with good effect to cure those suffering from bilious disorders. To discharge the bile a dose of four grains was administered, the powdered stone being thoroughly dissolved in wine. Still another kind, of a reddish hue, "like coagulated blood," full of pittings and veinings, was thought to be more especially valuable as a remedy for disorders of the blood and for checking hemorrhages.[59]

The learned Ko Kei asserts that the body of a man who had taken nearly five pounds of jade did not change color after his death and states that the body having been exhumed several years later did not show the slightest alteration. Besides this, it was observed that there were gold and jade around the tomb. Since then (in China), in the Kan period, the custom was followed of embalming the dead bodies of the emperors, and of preserving them in a gar-

[59] Cleandro Arnobio, "Tesoro delle Gioie," Venetia, 1602, pp. 139–141.

ment ornamented with pearls and enclosed in a case of jade.[60]

The Indians of Brazil prize the so-called Amazon-stones (jade) more highly than any other of the ornaments they wear. This is not chiefly because of their ornamental quality, but rather because these *ita ybymbae* (green stones) have in many cases been handed down from generation to generation for many centuries. They are of cylindrical, tabular or other regular form and polished, and are believed to be amulets affording protection against many diseases as well as against snake bites. They are worn suspended from the neck and are regarded as valuable aids in difficult parturition. Because of their remedial virtues they are sometimes called *ita poçanga,* or "medicine stones." They are also found with the natives of the Caribbean islands and are there called "the smooth stones from the far-off continent." [61]

As in all superstitions, so in those concerning jade in China, the fact that ill luck instead of good luck fortuitously resulted from the use of the material was explained in a way that did not do violence to the fundamental idea. We are told that on the road near Kneha, in Turkestan, there lies a block of jade from the quarries of Raskam-Darya, in Eastern Turkestan. This block was on its way to Pekin, when orders came from the imperial court not to forward any more jade from this quarry. The reason was that the heir apparent had been taken ill after having slept on a couch made of Raskam jade.[62]

---

[60] "Les Lapidaires," etc., F. de Mély, vol. i, Les lapidaires chinois, Paris, 1896, p. 178.

[61] Martius, "Beiträge zur Ethnographie und Sprachkunde Amerika's zumal Braziliens," Leipzig, 1867, vol. i, p. 729.

[62] Grombtchewski, Berichte der Geog. Gesellschaft zu St. Petersburg, vol. xv, p. 454 (1889).

Jasper

In the collection of the Biblioteca di Ravenna there is a red jasper amulet engraved with a device representing Hercules strangling the Nemæan Lion. Amulets of this type are recommended for the cure of the colic by the Greek physician Alexander Trallianus, who flourished in the first half of the sixth century A.D. He directs that this design be engraved on a "Median stone," which is then to be set in a gold ring and worn by the patient.[63] The fact that the constellation Leo was believed to rule over the stomach, and possibly over the liver also, probably determined the selection of the design. On the reverse of the Ravenna amulet are inscribed the letters K K K, which are believed to stand for Κωλική, "colic."[64]

After noting the power of the jasper (probably the red variety) to check hemorrhages from any part, and its general effect upon the circulation of the blood in reducing the pulse, thus calming desire and quieting the restless mind, Cardano turns to another of the reputed virtues of this stone, that of rendering the wearer victorious in battle. The true reason for this he finds in the stone's tendency to diminish passion, and hence to render the wearer timid and cautious, for "the timid usually conquer, since they avoid a doubtful contest if possible." Gesner states that he saw "in the possession of a writer of Lausanne," a green jasper, bearing the image of a dragon with rays, similar to the gem described by Galen.[65]

Of the jasper, De Boot relates,[66] from his own experience, that for checking hemorrhages the red variety is the most effective, and, in this connection, he describes the case of a young woman in Prague, who had suffered for six

[63] Alexandri Tralliani, "De medicamentis," Basileæ, 1556, p. 593.
[64] Revue Archêologique, 3rd ser., vol. i, pp. 299 sqq.
[65] Gesneri, "De figuris lapidum," Tiguri, 1565, fol. 113, verso.
[66] "Gemmarum et lapidum historia," Lugd. Bat., 1636, pp. 251–3.

years from hemorrhages. Many different remedies had been tried without avail, and when De Boot was called in to attend the case, he advised the woman to wear a red jasper. As soon as this stone was attached to her person the hemorrhage ceased. After wearing the jasper for some time, the woman thought she could safely lay it aside, but whenever she did so the hemorrhage returned after a longer or shorter interval, while it always ceased immediately she resumed wearing the stone. This seemed to prove conclusively that it checked the flow of blood. Eventually the woman was so effectively cured that she was able to give up wearing the stone. Green jasper, if worn attached to the neck so as to touch the gastric region, was, according to De Boot, a cure for all diseases of the stomach. The same writer alludes to the belief that the virtue of this stone was enhanced if it were engraved with the image of a scorpion while the sun was entering the constellation Scorpio, but he rejects this belief as entirely superstitious and futile, while admitting that, to obtain the best results, the jasper should always be set in silver.

Pear-shaped pieces of red jasper seem to have been more especially favored for use as amulets. Italian amulets of to-day show this, and Bellucci finds that the form is chosen as representing a drop of blood, and thus aiding, by sympathetic magic, in the cure of hemorrhages or wounds, and preventing the infliction of the latter. Sometimes such amulets of red jasper are attached to the bed-post by a red ribbon. In the case of a particularly valued amulet of this type, Bellucci was informed by the peasant owner that it owed its great virtue to having been blessed by the parish priest. Thus the traditional power of a pagan amulet received the sanction of the church and the object was associated with purely Christian amulets.[67]

[67] Bellucci, "Il feticismo primitivo in Italia," Perugia, 1907, pp. 87–90.

Jet

Jet, the *gagates* of the ancients, was said to have been first found in the river Gagates in Lycia, whence its name was derived. Galen, the greatest physician of ancient times, reports, however, that he searched in vain for this river, although he sailed in a small vessel along the whole coast of Lycia, so that he might closely observe it. Still, he did not give up his search for the material, even when he failed to find its reputed source, and in Cælo-Syria, on a hill on the eastern shore of the Dead Sea, he came across certain black, crustaceous stones, which emitted a slender flame when placed in the fire. These must have been small masses of bitumen, and, according to Galen, they were used for chronic swellings of the knee-joint "which are difficult to cure."[68]

The fumes of jet are mentioned as a remedy for the pest in one of the earliest Greek medical treatises, written by Nicander, who flourished in the second century B.C. He declares that the most virulent pestilence could be driven away if the bedrooms were fumigated with the smoke of the slow-burning jet.[69] The plague was called the black plague and naturally the aid of a black substance was sought to cure it.

For Pliny, jet was endowed with many medicinal virtues. Its fumes were a cure for hysteria and were said to reveal the presence of a latent tendency to epilepsy; connected with this in some way was the curious belief, repeated by later authors with certain variations, that these fumes could also be used as a test of virginity. When powdered and mixed with wine, jet relieved the pains of those suffering from toothache, and if the powder were combined with wax,

[68] Claudii Galeni, "Opera omnia," ed. Kühn, Lipsiæ, 1826, vol. xii, p. 207; De simplic. med., lib. vii, cap. 2.

[69] Nicandri, "Theriaka," Parisiis, 1557, p. 2.

a salve was produced that gave very beneficial results in cases of scrofula.[70] Even as a toilet preparation jet was recommended for use, and a most excellent dentifrice is said to have been made from it. In this connection jet was credited with tonic as well as cleansing properties, as is shown by the words of Bartholomæus Anglicus, who declares that this material was especially beneficial for "feeble teeth and waggyng," since it strengthened them and made them firm.[71]

The delusions and hallucinations of melancholic subjects were believed to be put to flight by the power of jet, either in its solid form or when reduced to a solution. The fact that this material was often used for the beads of rosaries was thought to have some connection with its supposed virtues, since the bad dreams or dreadful hallucinations sometimes accompanying melancholia were designated as "demons," and thus the prayers counted off on jet beads might be supposed to have the greater power to banish the devil and his black angels. The old writer who cites these particulars about jet, adds that there was to be found in the river Nile a black stone the size of a bean, at sight of which dogs would stop barking, and which also drove away evil spirits. Here we have another among many instances of the curious blending of the doctrines of sympathy and antipathy, the black stone repelling the imps of darkness and nullifying the spells of the Black Art.[72]

Lapis Armenus

The *lapis Armenus* was well known to the Arabs under the name *hajer Armeny,* and their medical writers describe it quite accurately and distinguish it from the somewhat

[70] Plinii, "Naturalis historia," lib. xxxvi, cap. 34.

[71] Bartholomæi Anglici, "De proprietatibus rerum," London, Wynkyn de Worde, 1495, lib. xvi, cap. 48; De gagate.

[72] Johannis Baptistæ Portæ "Phytognomica," Francofurti, 1591, pp. 170, 171.

similar lapis lazuli, with which it was often confused in ancient times. Ibn Beithar states that if properly prepared it would not provoke nausea, as was otherwise the case. It was said to cause a very abundant evacuation of bile and must have been regarded as an efficient remedy for the bilious disorders so general in warm climates.[73]

A "blue amulet" against vertigo, melancholia and epilepsy could be made up of the following ingredients: shavings from an elk's horn and from a human skull, to be reduced to a fine powder, the excrement of a peacock, white agate, lapis lazuli or *lapis Armenus,* of which enough was to be used to give the required sky-blue tint. The whole mass was then to be softened by the addition of gum tragacanth, and formed into heart-shaped tablets, which were to be dried out in the air, and then smoothed on a turning-lathe. These amulets were to be worn attached to the neck or the arm, sometimes they were enclosed in a little receptacle of silver or of red sandal-wood and suspended from the neck.[74]

Lapis Lazuli

In Papyrus 3027 of the Berlin Museum, a record that dates from about the fifteenth century B.C., and appears to be contemporaneous with the celebrated Papyrus Ebers, we have directions for the curative use of three stones as amulets; namely, lapis lazuli, malachite (Amazon stone?) and, probably, red jasper. The interpretation of the text offers considerable difficulty, but it seems that the stones were worked into the form of beads and then strung on a cord and suspended from a sick child's neck. Thereupon a formula was recited, calling upon the disease to pass

[73] Ibn el Beithar, "Traité des simples;" French trans. of L. Leclerc in "Notices et Extraits de MSS. de la Bib. Nat.," etc., vol. xxiii, Pt. 5, Paris, 1877, pp. 418, 419.

[74] "Der Römisch Kaiserlichen Akademie der Naturforscher . . . Abhandlung, Siebenter Theil," Nürnberg, 1759, p. 90.

through the beads and disperse itself through water and air, or, more literally, to attach itself to the denizens of water and air. The translation of Dr. Adolph Erman is as follows:[75]

> [A red bead? of lapis-lazuli thereon.]
> . . . a green bead? of malachite is thereon.
> a red bead of jasper? is thereon
> O, ye beads! fall upon the haunches [of the . . .] in the flood; on the scales? of the fish in the stream; on the feathers of the birds in the heavens. Hasten forth! *nšw*, fall upon the earth
> Let this text be recited over the beads?, one of lapis-lazuli, the other of jasper?, the other malachite, which are drawn on a string of . . . and hung upon the neck of a child.

Erman does not venture to translate the name of the disease (nšw), but says that another word derived from the same root signifies a discharge from the nose. Possibly we have to do with croup or some similar disease of the respiratory organs.

A curious prescription for the cure of cataract is given in the Ebers Papyrus,[76] dating from about 1600 B.C. The six ingredients are as follows: genuine lapis lazuli, verdigris salve, a resinous substance perhaps similar to what is to-day called tabasheer, milk, stibium, and "crocodile-earth," the slime of the Nile. It is possible that the word *chesbet*, which usually signifies lapis lazuli, was understood in this case as indicating some other stone, such as that known by the name of *lapis Armenus*—this latter is a carbonate of copper and really possesses astringent properties.

For remedial use a lapis lazuli (*cyanus*) of deep hue is

[75] Erman, "Zaubersprüche für Mutter und Kind," Philosophische und Historische Abhandlungen der König. Pr. Akad. d. Wissenschaften, 1901, Berlin, p. 9.

[76] "Papyrus Ebers, Die Maase und das Kapitel über die Augenkrankheiten," by Georg Ebers. In the Abhandl. d. phil. hist. Klasse der Königl. sächs. Gesell. d. Wissenschaften, vol. xi, Leip., 1890, p. 318.

recommended by Dioscorides. This stone was to be burned thoroughly and the resultant powder moistened so that a kind of paste was obtained. This was claimed to have an astringent and caustic effect, and was freely used as a counter-irritant.[77] Probably here as in other cases a sulphate of copper has been confused with the lapis lazuli. The ancients did not favor the administration of lapis lazuli internally, and Braunfels [78] therefore regarded the free use of pills of lapis lazuli which was common in his time as a source of grave danger. The *lapis Armenus,* however, if well prepared and properly washed, was less to be feared; but, unfortunately, the genuine stone was rarely to be found in the apothecaries' shops.

Malachite

Many medicinal virtues were ascribed to malachite. Worn as an amulet, it averted attacks of faintness, prevented hernia, and saved the wearer from danger in falling. In this latter respect similar powers seem to have been admitted in the case of the green malachite as were attributed to the light blue or greenish-blue turquoise. If malachite were reduced to a powder, dissolved in milk and taken as a potion, it cured cardiac pains and colic; mixed with honey, and applied with a linen cloth to a wound, it stanched the flow of blood, and cramps were relieved if this solution were applied to the affected part; lastly, if mixed with wine, it was a cure for virulent ulcers.[79]

Powdered malachite was sometimes administered medicinally, with what results we have little definite information; certainly, if not very carefully used, the effect would

---

[77] Dioscoridis, "De materia medica," lib. v, cap. 106.

[78] Braunfels, "Von Edelsteinen," Strassburg, 1536, fol. xlviii, a.

[79] De Boot, "Gemmarum et lapidum historia," Lug. Bat., 1636, p. 264, lib. ii, cap. 113.

have been anything but favorable. A friend of De Boot once told the latter that a dose of six grains of powdered malachite acted as a purgative, but the wary doctor confesses that he never ventured to test the efficacy of this prescription.[80] In Bavaria, at the present time, mothers and midwives are fond of wearing pieces of malachite set in rings or strung for use as necklaces. These are believed to help the dentition of children and are also thought to bring more clients to the midwives. Amulets of this and other kinds were sold in Bavaria, in the seventeenth century, by wandering students and by gypsies.[81]

Median Stone

Of the so-called Median stone we read, in Konrad von Megenberg's "Buch der Natur,"[82] that it had powers of good and evil; "for when dissolved in the milk of a woman who has borne a son, it restores sight to the blind." It also cured gout and insanity. If, however, anyone were so ill-advised as to dissolve the stone in water and partake of the solution, he would die of hasty consumption; or if he simply bathed his forehead with the liquid, he would be robbed of his sight.

Onyx

A famous medicinal stone was at one time in the Abbey of St. Alban, founded in 793 A.D. by Offa, King of Mercia, in honor of the British protomartyr. In 1010, under Abbot Geoffrey de Gorham, a sumptuous shrine was erected to receive St. Alban's body; this shrine was principally of silver, and was richly adorned with precious stones, chosen

[80] Ibid., loc. cit.

[81] Höfler, " Volksmedizin und Aberglaube," München, 1893, pp. 38, 39.

[82] Konrad von Megenberg " Das Buch der Natur," ed. by Dr. Franz Pfeiffer, Stuttgart, 1861, p. 452.

from among those in the treasury of the monastery. The records state that one of these stones "was so large that a man could not grasp it in his hand." It was believed to give great help to women in childbirth. Hence, it was not set in the shrine, but was left free, so that it might be taken from house to house as required. The size of this stone and the fact that it was not used for ornamentation might have induced the belief that it was one of the singular "eagle-stones," so celebrated in ancient and medieval times, but it is expressly described as an onyx-gem, the gift of King Ethelred II (968–1016) to the monastery. From the description we learn that on one side of this onyx was cut an image of Esculapius, the god of healing, and on the other that of "a boy bearing a buckler." As the art of gem-cutting was practically unknown in Europe in the tenth century, this must have been an antique gem, and may have served as a pagan amulet many centuries before it was placed upon the shrine of a Christian saint and used as a Christian amulet.[83]

An old manuscript of Matthew Paris [84] gives a sketch of the gem from this author's own hand. As the special power exerted by this talisman was to aid women in their confinements, it was loaned out from time to time to such as were considered worthy of the honor. In one case, however, it came into untrustworthy hands, for the favored lady failed to return the gem when her immediate need of its help had passed, retaining it in her possession until her death, when she bequeathed it to her daughter. During her lifetime the latter appears to have had no prickings of conscience, but on her death-bed, possibly through the exhortations of her confessor, she made provision that the long-lost sardonyx

[83] Dugdale, "Monasticon Anglicanum," London, 1819, vol. ii, pp. 184, 185; also extract from Cotton MS., Nero D vii, on p. 217.

[84] De vit. abbot.

should be returned to the Abbey. It is said to have borne the name Kaadman, which Mr. Thomas Wright regarded as a corruption of *cadmeus* or *cameus,* early forms of our "cameo." [85]

Pyrite

In Geneva and in the neighboring regions great virtues are ascribed to a cut and facetted iron (pyrite), very hard, susceptible of a high polish and of resplendent lustre. This is cut to resemble the rose or brilliant form of diamond, and is set in rings, buckles, and other ornaments. In appearance it resembles polished steel and is called *pierre de santé,* or "health-stone," for it is believed to grow pale when the health of the wearer is about to fail.[86] This substance is known as marcasite and is a bisulphide of iron. In the time of Louis XVI it was largely used for ornamental purposes; at present steel has almost entirely taken its place, although it is still utilized to a limited extent. Many believe that this is the material to which Victor Hugo alludes in his great romance, "Les Miserables," as having been manufactured by Jean Valjean.

Rock-crystal

Medical men in Rome, in the first century, attested that no better cautery for the human body could be used than a crystal ball acted upon by the sun's rays,[87] and this use of the material seems to have been very general at that time.

In his commentary on Andrea Bacci's gem-treatise, Wolfgang Gabelchover, the German translator, says that a German name of rock-crystal in his time, the early sixteenth century, was *Schwindelstein* ("vertigo-stone"), be-

[85] Thomas Wright, "On Antiquarian Researches in the Middle Ages," in Archæologia, vol. xxx, London, 1844, pp. 444–446; cut on page 444.

[86] Collin de Plancy, "Dictionnaire Infernal," Bruxelles, 1845, p. 415.

[87] Plinii, "Naturalis historia," lib. xxxvii, cap. 10.

cause it was believed to preserve the wearer from attacks of dizziness. Other remedial or physical effects of rock-crystal are also noted. Taken as a powder in dry wine, it was a cure for dysentery, and the physician, Christopher Barzizius, taught that if its powder were mixed with honey and administered to mothers, they would be the better able to nurse their offspring.[88]

The following lines by Robert Wilson (d. 1600), a popular sixteenth-century comedy writer, credit amber and rock-crystal with qualities not commonly ascribed to them, although the fancied growth of rock-crystal from a piece of ice probably explains its supposed styptic virtue:[89]

> LUCRE: And if they demand wherefore your
> wares and merchandise agree,
> You must say, jet will take up a straw;
> amber will make one fat;
> Coral will look pale when you be sick,
> and crystal stanch blood.

That a remedial tincture of rock-crystal could be made was firmly believed by the Danish chemist, Ole Borch (Olaus Borrichius, 1626–1690), and in his chemical lectures he gives the following directions as to the processes to be employed. A rock-crystal was to be heated to a high temperature and then cast, while still warm, into cold water; it would thereupon break up into small fragments. By heating these particles together with tartaric salts, the whole mass would be reduced to a liquid solution. Half of the quantity, after cooling off, was to be put into a distilling glass with the best "spirit of wine" and was to be digested in a bath of luke-warm water. It would then be seen that the solution became

[88] Andreæ Bacii, "De gemmis et lapidibus pretiosis" (Latin translation by Wolfgang Gabelchover of Italian original), Francofurti, 1603, p. 103.

[89] Wilson, "The Three Ladies of London," 1584. The three female characters are symbolical or allegorical and are named respectively, Lucre, Love, and Conscience.

red. This process is repeated several times, and finally the tincture is concentrated by distilling off the spirit of wine, leaving the pure rock-crystal tincture. Its remedial quality is stated to have been applicable to dropsy, scrofula, or hypochondriac melancholia, if it were taken in doses up to forty drops in a proper medium.[90]

To make the *magisterium* of rock-crystal, a pound of the substance was to be heated to a high temperature and then dipped into spirits of vitriol. After this operation had been repeated ten times, the rock-crystal was to be ground, on a marble slab, to a very fine powder, which was a sure remedy for gout and for calculi formed in any of the bodily organs. The spirits of vitriol in which the rock-crystal had been dipped was sometimes filtered through blotting-paper and sold as crystal spirits of vitriol; this was asserted to be a powerful diuretic, from seven to ten drops being given at a dose in a cup of meat broth.[91]

As late as the last half of the eighteenth century a Dr. Bourgeois recommended the use of rock-crystal, calcined and ground, as a very excellent astringent in the most obstinate cases of diarrhœa. In reporting this, Valmont de Bomare (1731–1807) adds that it would be desirable to know the nature of the acid in rock-crystal and its state of combination.[92] Here, as in all cases where some of the constituents of precious stones may really possess certain curative powers, a better result can be attained by using these constituents in other forms or combinations.

The wonderful therapeutic virtues of a Scotch lake named Loch-mo-naire are explained by a local legend as

[90] From MS. of Borch's lectures of 1685, in the Royal Library at Copenhagen, Thottske Collection, 744; cited in Axel Garboe's "Kulturhistorisk Studier over Ædelstene," København og Kristiania, 1915, p. 215.

[91] "Der Römisch Kaiserlichen Akademie der Naturforscher . . . Abhandlungen, Siebenter Theil," Nürnberg, 1759, pp. 162, 163.

[92] Valmont de Bomare, "Dictionnaire raisonné universel," Paris, 1775, vol. iii, p. 118.

having arisen from certain magic crystals which had been cast into its waters. These crystals, if placed in water, rendered the liquid a potion of great curative power. They were the property of a woman who had gained by their possession a great reputation as a healer, but her success attracted the envy of a neighbor who determined to secure for himself the woman's wonder-working stones. In pursuance of this design he came to her, feigning illness. She saw through his deception and sought safety in flight, but he pursued her and was gaining rapidly on her, when she threw the stones into the waters of the lake, crying out the Gaelic word *noire*, "shame," and uttering the wish that its waters should be rendered powerful to cure the sick, all except those of the clan Gordon to which the would-be thief belonged. As the correct translation of the name of the lake is said to be not "Lake of Shame" but "Serpent Lake," the legend appears to have no good foundation, but is perhaps as true as any of the popular tales purporting to explain the origin of the virtues of healing springs or waters.[93]

To many stones was attributed the power of transmitting a certain remedial virtue to water or other liquid in which they were immersed. This, as we have related, was the case with the white stone that St. Columba sent to King Brude at Inverness when the king's druid priest Broichan was suffering from disease. A peculiarity of this stone was that if it were required in the case of a person about to die, it would disappear from view. Thus its remedial powers could never be put to test unless success were assured.[94]

There can be no reasonable doubt that some remarkable cures have been effected by means of relics, or by drinking the waters of a spring believed to have been pointed out by some divine vision. From a purely scientific standpoint

---

[93] Walsh "Curiosities of Popular Customs," Philadelphia, 1911, p. 624.
[94] MacCulloch, "Religion of the Ancient Celts," Edinburgh, 1911, p. 332.

this can be explained as the result of an extraordinary stimulation of the nerve-centres, caused by the rapt enthusiasm of religious faith. The relics, or the pure water, simply serve as an object about which this faith crystallizes, so to speak, and gains a concrete and external form, which in turn reacts upon the mind of the believer. It is a well-known fact that a great shock, or imminent peril, has sometimes suddenly restored the power of motion to those who have long been paralyzed. This view does not, however, necessarily exclude a religious interpretation of these phenomena when they are produced by religious impressions, for the divine will manifests itself by natural means, and a true understanding of the regular and normal working of these means should give us a deeper, truer, and purer faith.

Sapphire

As a substance for medicinal use, the Hindus declared the sapphire to be bitter to the taste and lukewarm. It had a remedial action against phlegm, bile and flatulence.[95] A similar action is ascribed to several other precious stones, the medicinal qualities attributed to them being less differentiated among the Hindus than they were with the Greeks and Romans, or in medieval times.

To drink of a potion made from the sapphire was said to be helpful for those who had been bitten by a scorpion, and for those suffering from intestinal ulcerations, or from growths in the eye; it also prevented boils and pustules, and healed ruptured membranes.[96] Here we see that the sapphire shared with the emerald the power of strengthening the sight, and one authority asserts that if anyone looked long and intently at a sapphire, his eyes would be protected

[95] Garbe, "Die indische Mineralien"; Naharari's "Rajanighaṇṭu," Varga XIII, Leipzig, 1882, p. 83.

[96] Johannis Braunii, "De vestitu sacerdotum Hebræorum," Amstelodami, 1680, p. 659; citing pseudo-Dioscorides.

from all injury, and nothing harmful could befall them.[97]

A medieval test of the antitoxin quality of the sapphire was to place a spider in a vessel to whose mouth a sapphire was so suspended that it would swing backwards and forwards just above the spider. The supposedly venomous insect was not long able to resist the power of the stone and fell a victim to its virtues. Wolfgang Gabelchover gravely asserts that this experiment had often been successful.[98]

The removal of particles of sand or dust from the eye was said to be successfully accomplished by "warming" a sapphire over the eye, the virtue of the stone thus passing into the eye and giving the organ the strength necessary for the ejection of the troublesome foreign body.[99] This attribution of a chemical action to the sapphire in eye-trouble may be added to the many statements of its general curative powers in eye-diseases.

Topaz

The thirteenth century Hindu physician Naharari states that the topaz tastes sour and is cold. It is a remedy for flatulence and is a most excellent appetizer. Any man who wears this stone will be assured of long life, beauty and intelligence.[100] Many a curious legend has been woven about the old belief that the topaz quenched thirst. However, popular fancy does not endow any and every topaz with this power. One of these thirst-removing topazes is said to have been in the possession of a celebrated Hindu necromancer, whose services had been sought by one of the petty rajahs of India on the day of a decisive battle. Either this necromancer's art must have failed him at the critical

---

[97] Aldrovandi, "Museum metallicum," Bononiæ, 1648, p. 972.

[98] Andræ Baccii, "De gemmis et lapidibus pretiosis," Francofurti, 1603, p. 68. Note of Gabelchover to his Latin version of the original Italian.

[99] Frederici Jacobi Schallingi, "*ΟΦΘΑΛΜΙΑ* sive disquisitio hermetico-galenica de natura oculorum," Erffurdt, 1615, p. 125.

[100] Garbe, "Die indische Mineralien"; Naharari's "Rajanighaṇṭu," Varga XIII, Leipzig, 1882, p. 79.

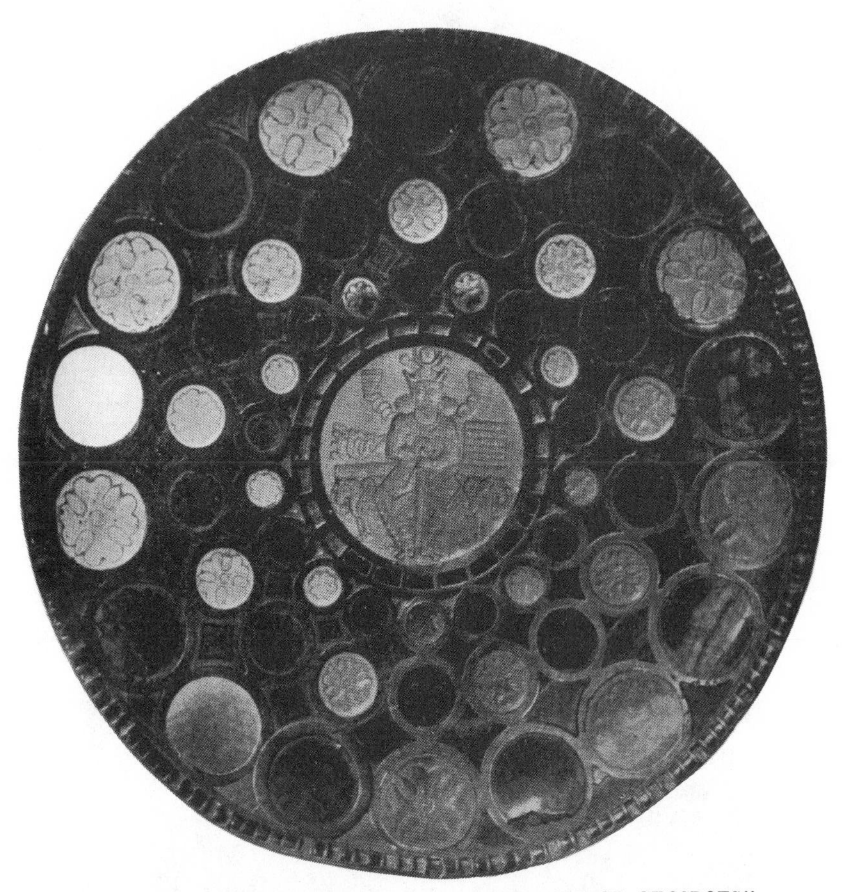

ANCIENT PERSIAN RELIC KNOWN AS THE "CUP OF CHOSROES"

The engraved rock-crystal medallion in the centre depicts Khusrau II, Parwiz (A. D. 591-628), in the peculiar nd characteristic garb of the Sassanian monarchs. The strange wing-like adornments rising from each shoulder, nd the moon crescent and sun-disk above the head, are especially noteworthy. In the Royal Museum, ucharest, Roumania.

1. Emerald that belonged to the deposed Sultan of Turkey, Abdul Hamid; weight 45.33 carats. Auctioned December 11, 1911, Paris.
1½. Side view of the emerald.
2. Almandite garnet (transparent) fashioned into a knuckle bone; on the upper surface is engraved an eagle with outspread wings, above which are the Greek characters *κακγ*. Charm seal of some early knuckle-bone player.
3. Sardonyx idol-eye of a Babylonian bull, pierced for suspension. Engraved at a later period with the head of a Parthian king.
4. Aquamarine seal (transparent). Sassanian Pahlavi. Found in ruins of Babylonia.

moment, or else a more powerful enchanter guided the fortunes of the enemy, for the latter prevailed and the owner of the potent topaz was left dying upon the field of battle. Alongside him was a poor wounded soldier who was clamoring for a drop of water to quench his burning thirst. Hearkening to this prayer, the dying necromancer threw his topaz to the soldier, telling him to place it upon his heart. No sooner did he do so than his thirst passed away, and we must suppose that his wounds were also healed, for we are told that on the morrow he sought everywhere on the battle-field for the corpse of his benefactor but could find no trace of it.

Tavernier, the great French Seventeenth Century jeweler-traveler, the first European to visit the ruby mines, took with him a number of emeralds, generally large. These were often cut from the top of the crystal, usually darker in color, and simply domed off, preserving the original hexagonal shape. Remarkable specimens are in the Indian Museum and the South Kensington Museum, part of the jewels of Thebaud, King of Burma. The finest emeralds of this type belonged to the late Sultan of Turkey; one of the finest, a remarkable gem, cut rounded en cabochon, was with the Bijoux du Sultan, S. M. Abd-Ul-Hamid II, sold at the Galerie Georges Petit, November 28, 1914. It weighed 44 $^3/_{16}$ carats (old system) or 45.29 carats (metric system). (See color plate.)

A remarkable charm is a hemispherical, transparent aquamarine, with figure of hump bull, found in ancient Babylonia. (See color plate.)

A quaint, ancient amulet is carved out of fine knuckle bone, an eagle with spread wings engraved on one side; portrait of a Parthian King. (See color plate.)

A Babylonian idol's eye, of sardonyx, was pierced and worn as charm against the Evil Eye; later engraved with portrait of a Parthian King. (See color plate.)

IV

On the Virtues of Fabulous Stones, Concretions and Fossils

NOT only precious or semi-precious stones were used as charms or talismans and for curative purposes; a large number of animal concretions also were and are still somewhat in favor. These concretions, variously composed but usually containing a quantity of carbonate of lime, are found in different parts of animals' bodies, and they were believed to contain a sort of quintessence of the nature of the animal in which they occurred. For this reason the *alectorius,* from the body of the cock, one of the most widely-known of the animal stones in ancient times, was thought to confer valor upon the wearer, and is said to have been worn by athletes in their contests.

In the case of venomous, or supposedly venomous, creatures, such as the toad and certain snakes, the stone was used as an antidote for poisons. This virtue was thought to be notably present in the so-called bezoar stone, taken from the stomach of a species of goat, as well as from some other animals. As we shall see, legend sought to account for the peculiar qualities of the bezoar by the tale that the animals in whose bodies the stones were formed had been bitten by serpents. Indeed, it seems not unlikely that the belief in the curative properties of the bezoar stone originally owed its existence to the finding of some such concretion in the body of an animal that had died from the effects of snake-bite.

As is well known, certain pathological conditions induce the formation of stones of various kinds and shapes in the human body also. Here the tendency has been to use these stones to counteract the disease which produced them. Renal or vesical calculi, for instance, were recommended for diseases of the kidneys and bladder, a treatment quite in accord with the popular idea of the homeopathic theory.

Another class of animal substances, namely, the fossil teeth of the shark, enjoyed a tremendous vogue at one time, and were known by the name of *glossopetræ*. These were usually regarded as stones, and because of their peculiar form were frequently assimilated to the belemnites and even to the flint arrow-heads and other prehistoric flint instruments, which were dug up in many places. All these flint artefacts were believed to have been precipitated to the earth by the discharge of electricity during a thunder-storm; in other words, they were "thunder-bolts."[1] The same idea was frequently held as to the origin of the *glossopetræ*, and those found on the island of Malta were brought into connection with an incident of St. Paul's visit to that island.

In many different countries, especially in the north of Europe, these flint arrow-heads and the fossil remains of similar form, were called fairy-darts or elf-shots, and were believed to be the enchanted weapons of the elves and fairies, who, in the old folklore, are represented as beings of a very different quality from the fairies and elves of the tales of our childhood. In some parts of Europe at the present day, for example in Ireland, the peasantry talk with bated breath of the doings of the "good people," for they shrink from using the word "fairy" lest it might offend these mysterious and generally malevolent beings. The designation "good people" is therefore used to placate and flatter them.

Various shell fossils were also used as talismans. Here the form generally determined the virtues they were supposed to possess. Some of these strange forms lent them-

[1] See Chapter II, pp. 106–116.

selves to an interpretation in line with the primitive adoration of the life-giving forces of nature, and suggested the use of such fossils to cure certain special diseases. Other of these petrifactions retaining the form of the enclosing shell, especially those of circular shape, and with concentric rings, were believed to be of meteoric origin and to have fallen during thunder or rain; hence the names of *brontia* and *ombria*. A certain class of these fossils, with convolutions on the surface resembling the form of a snake, were called snake-eggs (*ova anguina*), and, very naturally, enjoyed the repute of preserving the wearer from poisons. All these varieties will be described in this and the following chapters.

Extracting toad-stone. From Johannis de Cuba's "Ortus Sanitatis," Strassburg, 1483.

While some believed that the toad-stone was vomited by the animal, others held that it constituted a part of the toad's head. That this was the popular belief in Shakespeare's time is shown by the well-known lines in his "As You Like It" (Act II, sc. 1):

> Which like the toad, ugly and venomous,
> Wears yet a precious jewel in his head.

De Boot, whose treatise was published about the time that Shakespeare wrote these lines, gives the following account of the result of his efforts to obtain a toad-stone according to the prescribed method: [2]

I remember that, when a boy, I took an old toad and set it upon a red cloth that I might secure a toadstone; for they say that it will not give up its stone unless it sits upon a red cloth. However, although I watched the

[2] Anselmi Bœtii de Boodt, "Gemmarum historia," Hanoviæ, 1609, p. 52.

toad for a whole night, it did not eject anything, and from this time I became convinced all the tales concerning this stone were merely fond imaginings.

A stone called simply the "Indian Stone," and said to be light and porous, is noted by pseudo-Aristotle, and to it is attributed the power to relieve those suffering from dropsy, by drawing the water to itself. If weighed after having been applied to the patient, the stone was found to have increased in weight in proportion to the amount of water absorbed, and when it was placed in the sun, water of a yellowish hue exuded, until, finally, the stone resumed

BVFONITES

Toad-stones. Natural concretions of claystone and limonite. From Mercati's "Metallotheca Vaticana," Romæ, 1719.

its original appearance and weight.[3] Another and perhaps earlier authority gives the name "toad-stone" to this material.[4]

The toad-stone was not only an antidote for poisons, but was also thought to give warning of their presence by becoming very hot. To fully profit by this strange quality, the wearer of such a stone was advised to have it so set in a ring that it would touch the skin; in this way he would be

[3] Rose, "Aristoteles de lapidibus und Arnoldus Saxo," Zeitschr. für d. Alt., New Series, vol. vi, 1875, pp. 373, 374.

[4] Petra, "Specilegium Solesmense," Parisiis, 1855, p. 370.

sure to have timely notice, if any poisoned food or drink were offered to him.[5] The writer who mentions this adds the following tale of the discovery of a toad-stone:

> A clerk once found a toad which had a round knob on its head, wherefore he thought that there must be a toad-stone. So he took up the toad and tied it firmly in the sleeve of his coat. When he returned from the fields and searched for the toad he found it not, although the sleeve of his coat was tightly bound below and he could not discover any opening through which the creature could have passed. This shows us that it is a great help to prisoners in jail.

Another early authority, Thomas de Cantimpré, says of the toad-stone:

> If one take the stone from a living and still quivering toad a little eye can be seen in the substance; but if it be taken from a toad that has been some time dead, the poison of the creature will have already destroyed this little eye and spoiled the stone.

If the toad-stone be swallowed at meal-time it passes through the system and carries off all impurities.[6] Here the substance may have been one of many concretionary materials,—bauxite, impure pearls, concretionary limestone, stalagmite, or even the eye-stones from the crawfish; indeed, any material, white or gray, that had a semblance to a toad color, and was then sold by the vendor of charm stones as coming from a toad's head.

The great Erasmus (1465–1536) made a pilgrimage to the famous shrine of the Virgin in the church at Walsingham, in Kent. In his description of what he saw there he expressly notes a wonderful toad-stone:

> At the feet of the Virgin is a gem for which there is as yet no Latin or Greek name. The French have named it after the toad [crapaudine], because it represents so perfectly the figure of a toad that no art could do this

[5] "Le Grand Lapidaire de Jean de Mandeville." From the edition of 1561, ed. by J. S. del Sotto, Vienne, 1862, p. 90.

[6] In Konrad von Megenberg's "Buch der Natur," ed. by Dr. Franz Pfeiffer, Stuttgart, 1861, p. 437.

so well. The miracle is all the greater that the stone is so small, and that the exterior surface has not the form of a toad, the image showing through it as though inclosed within.[7]

As we see, the stone of Erasmus contained the form or image of a toad. This was not usually the case with the concretions that bore this name, and it appears probable that the "crapaudine" of the shrine at Walsingham owed its peculiarity rather to art than to nature. A rather far-fetched explanation of the origin of these substances is given by Ambrosianus, who relates that, in order to investigate the quality and character of toad-stones, he killed a number of toads and took out their brains. Although these were not hard when extracted, they became, in time, as hard as stones.[8]

A toad-stone which appeared to represent the form of this animal was preserved as an heirloom in the Lemnian family. It exceeded the size of a walnut and was often seen to dissipate the swelling caused by the bite of a venomous creature in any part of the body, if it were rubbed quickly over the swelling. It, therefore, seemed to possess the same quality as was attributed to the animal from which it was taken, namely, to draw out and annul all poisons. If any neighbor of the Lemnian family were bitten by a mouse, a spider, a dormouse, a wasp, a beetle, or any such creature, he soon sought the aid of this stone.[9]

We have noted De Boot's unsuccessful attempt to secure a toad-stone, but he does not seem to have used the orthodox method for obtaining it. According to one authority,[10] the creature should be placed in a cage covered with a red cloth

---

[7] Erasmi, "Colloquia," Lipsiæ, 1713, p. 596.
[8] Aldrovandi, "Museum metallicum," Bononiæ, 1648, p. 814.
[9] Lemnii, "De miraculis occultis naturæ," Francofurti, 1611, pp. 212, 213.
[10] Mizauld, "Hundert curieuse Kunst-stücke," in Martius' "Unterricht von der Magiæ Naturali," Leipzig, 1717, p. 290.

and then set in the hot sunshine for several days, until thirst forced the poor toad to eject his precious stone, which was to be removed as soon as possible lest it should be swallowed again. Another method proposed is so cruel that it is a comfort to know that the whole matter is little more than a fanciful conceit. In this case, the toad was to be enclosed in a pot with many perforations, and the vessel with its unlucky inmate was then to be placed in an ant-hill and left there until nothing remained of the toad except his bones and the coveted stone. It is quite probable that any stone found in an ant-hill after this procedure would be termed a "toad-stone," since the toad was put away in order to find one. In some instances they may have been bony concretions from the head of the toad, or even pebbles that the toad had swallowed.

While it is quite possible that some of the so-called toad-stones may really have been concretions found in the head of the toad, by far the greater part were probably small pebbles sold as "toad-stones" to those who believed in the magic virtues of such a stone and were ready to pay a good price for one. Where there is a demand there will always be a supply, and the rarer the genuine article is, the greater is the incentive to imitation or substitution. In the case of some of these "toad-stones" set in rings to serve as amulets, the material has been found to be the fossil palatal tooth of the ray, a species of fish.[11]

The small share of material prosperity that fell to the lot of wits and literary men in the England of the sixteenth century, even in the age of Elizabeth, induced Thomas Nash (1567–1601) to liken the fate of the wit to that of the toad-stone, or, as he writes, of "the pearl," which was said to be in the head of the toad, this "being of exceeding virtue, is enclosed with poison; the other, of no less value, compassed

[11] Smith, "Jewellery," London, 1908, p. 151.

about with poverty."[12] A writer of the same period affirms that if the toad-stone were touched to any part, "envenomed, hurt, or stung with rat, spider, wasp, or any other venomous beast," the swelling and pain were diminished.[13]

The bones of the lizard were supposed to have medicinal virtues similar to those attributed to various "stones" found in animals. The following directions are given by Encelius for securing these bones: "Put a green lizard, while still alive, in a closed vessel filled with the best quality of salt. In a few days the salt will have consumed the flesh and the intestines, and you can easily gather up the bones."[14] These were used as remedies for epilepsy and were considered to be as efficacious as the hoofs of the elk, a recommendation which seems to have been regarded as sufficient to convince the most sceptical of the remedial virtues of the lizard's bones.

The crab furnished the stone called the crab's-eye, because in form it resembled an eye. Like almost all the animal concretions, it was principally used as a remedy for those suffering from vesical calculi, and no other concretion was believed to be so efficacious in breaking up or dissolving the calculi in the case of those who had long been afflicted with them. Those referred to by Encelius were from the crawfish and are often used as eye-stones.[15]

In the last joint of a crab's claw was sometimes found a small concretion closely resembling in size and appearance a grain of millet-seed; it was in no wise like the "lapillus" found in crab's eyes. We have the testimony of Cardanus that he had preserved two such concretions, one of which he had himself come across, while the other had been found

[12] "Anatomy of absurditie," 1589; p. 40 of Collier's reprint. Lean's Collectanea, vol. ii, Pt. II, Bristol, 1903, p. 643.

[13] Lupton, "One Thousand Notable Things."

[14] Encelii, "De re metallica," Francofurti, 1557, pp. 219, 220.

[15] Idem, pp. 218, 219. See also p. 121 of the present book.

by a colleague. They were smooth and light, and of a reddish-white color. Because they were very rarely met with, the circumstance was regarded as of good augury for the finder.[16]

A round concretion (a calculus) from the liver of the ox is described by Ibn Al-Beithar as being of a yellowish color and composed of successive superimposed layers. If secured at the time of the full moon it was believed to promote *embonpoint,* and was much prized by the Egyptian women for this virtue. The effect was to be attained by taking two grains of the pulverized concretion, either with the bath or directly after bathing, and thereupon a "fat hen" was to be eaten.[17] The latter prescription, if regularly and frequently administered, might be thought to suffice without the powdered calculus.

From the second stomach of heifers was sometimes obtained a dark brown or blackish concretion of very light weight and as round as a ball. This was credited with great remedial virtues provided it had not fallen to the ground.[18] There seems to have been a belief that the curative or talismanic properties of animal concretions, or of the teeth of animals, were weakened, or destroyed, if these objects came in contact with the earth. This belief was perhaps due to the idea that the mysterious power of the substance was originally derived from earth currents, or emanations, and that the active principle would return to the earth if the object came in contact with it.

The *lapis carpionis* or carp-stone, a triangular mass, was taken from the jaws of the carp. It was smaller or larger according to the size of the fish. The principal remedial use was against calculi, or for the cure of bilious dis-

[16] Cardani, "De subtilitate," Basilæ, 1554; lib. vii, p. 211.

[17] Traité des Simples of Ibn Al-Beithar in "Notices et Extraits des Manuscrits de la Bibliothèque Nationale," vol. xxiii, pp. 416–417; Paris, 1877.

[18] Plinii, "Naturalis historia," lib. xi, cap. 79.

eases and colic.[19] These are bony plates from the upper part of the mouth of the carp. Such so-called "stones" were also said to check bleeding of the nose, a quality they owed to their astringent properties, quite noticeable if anyone tasted the powder made from them.[20]

The *cinædias,* a white and oblong concretion, had in Pliny's time the reputation of possessing extraordinary powers, announcing beforehand whether the sea would be clear or stormy.[21] In what way this weather prediction was manifested we are not told; perhaps the surface of the concretion may have become dull or grayish when there was much humidity in the air. The cinædia were said to be found in pairs in the fish of that name; one pair being taken from the head of the fish and another pair from the two dorsal fins. Power to cure diseases of the eye was conferred upon these concretions by putting nine of them, duly numbered, in an earthen jar together with a green lizard. Each day one of the "stones" was taken from the vessel in the numerical order, and on the ninth day the lizard was liberated. Evidently it was thought that to kill the animal would interfere with the transmission of its virtue to the concretions.[22]

The eye of the hyena was supposed to furnish a stone called *hyænia* and Pliny writes that these animals were hunted to secure possession of it. Like rock-crystal and many other decorative stones, this *hyænia* was thought to give the power to foretell the future, if it were placed beneath the tongue.[23] Because of the hyena's uncanny habit of feeding on carrion, and unearthing dead bodies from

---

[19] Encelii, "De re metallica," Francofurti, 1557, p. 218.

[20] Lemnii, "De miraculis naturæ," Francofurti, 1611, p. 213.

[21] Ibid., lib. xxxvii, cap. 56.

[22] Ibid., lib. xxix, cap. 38.

[22] Ibid., lib. xxxvii, cap. 60.

graves, it has often been associated with necromancy and with evil spirits.

The *lacrima cervi,* or "stag's tear," is not to be confounded with the bezoar stone according to Scaliger, who maintains that it was a bony concretion that formed in the corner of a stag's eye only after the animal had passed its hundredth year; as the stag never attains this age he might as well have said that the existence of this "tear" was a fable. However, he describes it as though he had carefully inspected a specimen, saying that it was so smooth and light that it would almost slip through the fingers of anyone who held it in his hand. It had similar powers to those of the bezoar, being a powerful antidote to poisons and a cure for the plague if powdered and given with wine; these good effects resulting from the excessively profuse perspiration that followed the administration of the dose.[24]

These fabled stag's tears, though often praised as substitutes for the bezoar, were not believed in by all the early writers, one of them, Rollenhagen, giving expression to a caustic opinion that might do credit to a writer of our own day. Alluding to the many reports of the existence of such "tears," shed by the animals because of the pains they suffered after indulging in a diet of serpents, he notes that all those who make these statements are careful to place the habitat of these eccentric stags as far away from their own land as possible, always "somewhere in the Orient," probably at "Nowheretown," as he adds.[25]

The *chelonia* is said by Pliny to have been the eye of the Indian tortoise. The magicians asserted that this was the most marvellous of all "stones"; for if bathed in honey and then placed in the mouth, when the moon was either full

[24] Danielis Sennarti, "Epitome naturalis scientiæ," Francofurti, 1650, lib. v, cap. 4, pp. 438, 439; citing Scaliger, Exercit. 112.

[25] G. Rollenhagen, "Wahrhaffte Lügen von Geistlichen und Naturalichen Dingen," Wahrenberg, 1680, p. 93.

or new, it conferred the power of divination, and this power lasted for one entire day.[26] This virtue was not, however, altogether peculiar to the *chelonia,* for it was shared by several other substances; in each case the stone was to be placed in the mouth, thus coming into more immediate contact with the organs of speech, and stimulating to prophetic utterance. A later writer states that it was the uterine stone from the tortoise that gave the gift of prophecy. That from the head cured headaches and averted lightning, while the stone taken from the liver, if administered in solution, was a remedy for ague.[27]

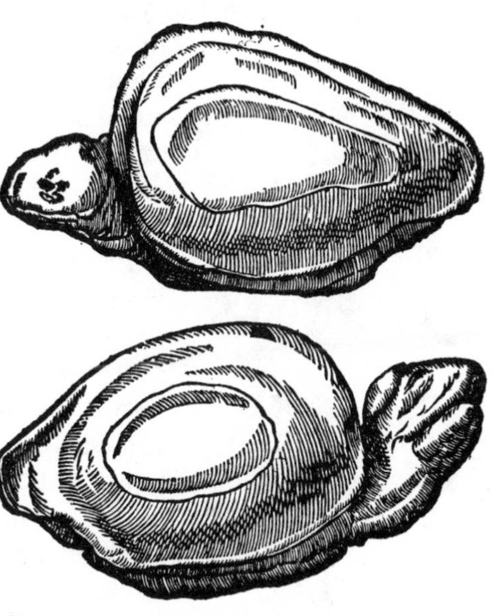

Types of *cheloniæ* (tortoise-stones). Natural concretions. From Aldrovandi's "Museum metallicum," Bononiæ, 1648.

The wild ass was another of the animals that furnished concretions prized for their talismanic and medicinal powers. That taken from the animal's head cured headache and epilepsy; that from the jaw made the owner indefatigable, so that he yielded to none in battle. It was also a remedy for ague and for the bites of venomous creatures, as well as a marvellously efficacious vermifuge for children.[28] Very likely the story of Samson, who wrought such slaughter

---

[26] Plinii, "Naturalis historia," lib. xxxvii, cap. 56.
[27] Leonardi, "Speculum lapidum," Venetia, 1502, fol. xxviii.
[28] Ibid., fol. xxiv.

among the Philistines when armed with the jawbone of an ass, may have suggested the fancy that the concretion from the ass's jaw would give victory to the wearer.

Pliny notes the opinion that a stone taken from the body of a young swallow, if worn attached to the human body, helps to strengthen the brain, and he adds that the stone is said to be found in the young bird even when it has just broken the shell.[29] According to Thomas de Cantimpré the swallow-stone is a talisman for merchants and tradesmen.[30] The merits of the *chelidonius,* as this stone was called, were fully recognized in Saxon England and are given due prominence in an Anglo-Saxon medical treatise, dating from the first half of the tenth century. When these "swallow-stones" had been obtained they were to be carefully protected from contact with water, earth, or other stones. To secure the best results *three* of them were to be applied to the person who stood in need of their remedial effects. Not only did they cure headache and eye-smart, but they banished the dreaded nightmare, rendered futile the wiles of goblin visitors, and dissolved all fascinations and enchantments. The seekers after these wonderful stones are stoutly assured that they can only be found in "big nestlings."[31]

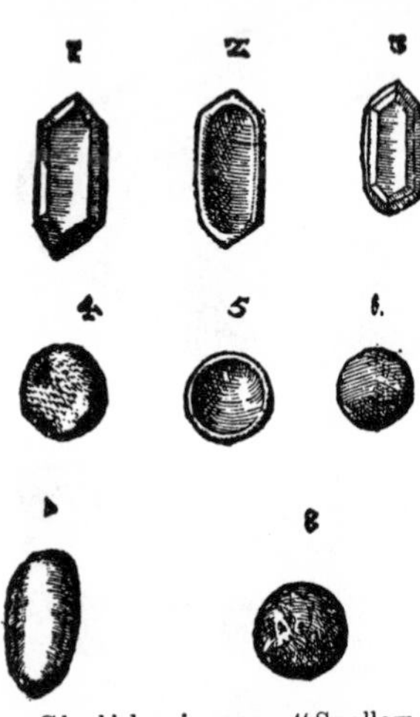

Chelidonius, or "Swallow-stones." From "Museum Wormianum," Lugduni Batavorum, 1655.

[29] C. Plinii Secundi, "Naturalis historia," ed. Janus, Lipsiæ, 1880, p. 249, lib. xxx, cap. 11.

[30] In Konrad von Megenberg's version "Buch der Natur," ed. Pfeiffer, Stuttgart, 1861, p. 440.

[31] Rev. Oswald Cockayne, "Leechdoms, Wortcunning and Starcraft of Early England," London, 1865, vol. ii, p. 307 (Bk. iii, cap. i, of "Laece Boc").

The *ætites* (eagle-stone) is first mentioned by Pliny who states that it was found in the nests of eagles of a certain species, and adds that some called this stone *gangites*. Fire had no power over it and it was a useful remedy for many diseases. Its special virtue, however, was to prevent abortion, this use being suggested by the character of the stone itself, which "was as though pregnant, for when it was shaken another stone rattled within it, as though in a womb." The curative virtues of the *ætites,* like that of the swallow-stone, only existed when the stone was taken from the bird's nest. This was probably a story told by the vendors of such geodes to enhance the value of their wares, although there may have been some foundation for it in folklore.

They are really hollow concretions of an iron stone, containing a piece of loose iron or hardened sand, or a concretion of some kind that rattles, and is called by the Italians *bambino* or "babe." Such concretions are found at many places on every continent, many fine ones having been found in Delaware. They vary in size from one to six inches across. The small ones of a hard, smooth exterior that have become polished from wear, are especially valued as charms.[32]

A passage in the treatise on stones by Theophrastus, pupil of Aristotle, might seem to indicate that the *ætites* was already known in the third century B.C. The words he employs are as follows: "The most astounding and greatest power of stones (if indeed this be true) is that of bearing progeny." As both Pliny and Dioscorides name this stone or geode and fully describe its character, laying especial stress upon the loose, rattling material enclosed in its hollow interior, this fact giving rise in later time to the half-poetic

[32] "Naturalis historia," lib. x, cap. 4, and lib. xxx, cap. 44.

name of "the pregnant stone," there is every reason to believe that it was already known of three or four, or even more centuries before their time.[33]

Marbodus of Rennes calls this stone "the guardian and defender of nests."[34] Enclosing as it did one or more smaller stones, it was thought to be symbolically designated as an aid to parturition. According as it was attached to the left arm or to the left thigh, it either retarded or accelerated the natural processes. This, however, by no means exhausted the virtues of the stone, for when worn on the left arm of man or woman, it conferred sobriety, increased riches, and moved the wearer to love; it also brought victory and popularity, and preserved children from harm. In addition to all its other powers this stone seems to have possessed a certain detective quality, to judge from the following words of Aetius, who wrote in the sixth century A.D.:[35]

> The ætites serves to discover thieves, if anyone places it in the bread which they eat; for whoever has committed a theft is unable to consume the bread. It has also been stated that, if cooked with any kind of food, the ætites unmasks thieves, since they cannot eat such food. If taken with wax from Cyprus, with fresh olive oil, or with any other calefacient, this stone greatly helps those suffering from rheumatism and paralysis.

The loose, enclosed concretion was named in Latin *callimus,* and we have a detailed description from the sixteenth century of one of these, which belonged to Georgius Fabricius. Because of its curious markings he had it set on a pivot in a ring, so that both sides of the stone could be easily seen. The material was in part as clear as a rock-crystal, evidently a very translucent chalcedony, but the

---

[33] Theophrasti, "De lapidibus" (Peri lithôn), ed. by John Hill, London, 1746, p. 16; cap. 10; see Hill's note, pp. 16–19.

[34] Marbodei, loc. cit.

[35] Aëtii, Tetrabiblos, Basileæ, 1542, p. 77.

chief interest centred in the images or figures traced by nature upon the stone. These showed what seemed to be two forms, one of a cowled monk, and the other that of a tall, beardless man; there was also a third, showing an undefined form. On the under side of this *callimus* was marked the outline of a crescent moon.[36]

Ætites. From Johannis de Cuba's "Ortus Sanitatis," Strassburg, 1483.

A seventeenth-century writer, not otherwise uncritical, does not hesitate to declare that he had himself witnessed, in the case of a fig-tree, an instance of the special power exercised by the *ætites*. One of these stones having been attached to this tree, all the fruit dropped off in the space of ten hours, although the tree had apparently lost nothing of its vigor, its foliage remaining as luxuriant as before.[37]

An old treatise on the *ætites* gives the following names as applied to it in various languages:[38]

Italian: Aquilina, pietra d'aquila, pietra aquilina, ethite.
French: Pierre de l'aigle.
Spanish: Piedra de l'aguila.
Polish: Orlovi Kamyen.
Swedish: Oernarsteen.
English: Eagle-stone.
German: Adlerstein.
Flemish: Adelersteen, arensteen.
Arabic: Hager achtamach.

---

[36] Conradi Gesneri, "De figuris lapidum," Tiguri, 1565, pp. 142, 143; with figures of ring. Pliny already mentions the *callimus*, "Naturalis historia," lib. xxxvi, cap. 39.

[37] Bauschii, "De lapide ætite," Lipsiæ, 1665, p. 64.

[38] Ibid., p. 9.

Syriac: Abno dneshre.
Chaldaic: Abno dineshar, or abno denishra.
Hebrew: 'Eben ha-nosher.

Some said that this stone might be found not only in the eagle's nest, but also in that of the stork. This idea was, however, entirely erroneous in Bausch's opinion, for though he had caused diligent search to be made by all those who encountered such nests, no "eagle-stone" could ever be found. To the supposed "stork-stones" had been given the name *lychnites,* as they were believed to be luminous, their light serving to frighten off any snakes which might be seeking the new-laid eggs.[39]

Bausch enumerates and rejects a number of explanations to account for the supposed presence of the *ætites* in the nests of eagles. One theory was that these stones served to give stability to the nest, and enabled it better to resist the assaults of the wind; others asserted that the coolness of the stones lowered the unduly high temperature of the eggs and of the parent bird's body; others again were inclined to attribute to them a mysterious formative and vivifying power exerted on the eggs, or else a talismanic power protecting these from injury. While rejecting all these notions, as we have stated, and indeed denying the truth of the assertion that such stones were ever found in eagles' nests, Bausch cites the authority of St. Jerome, in his commentary on Isaiah, chap. lxvi, that the amethyst had been found with the young of the eagle, being placed with them in the nest to protect them from venomous creatures.[40]

That the "eagle-stones" were not always hollow is shown by a specimen owned in the eighteenth century by the English family Postlethwayte. This was solid, and had been cut into the shape of a heart, a hole being pierced at the

---

[39] Ibid., pp. 9, 10.
[40] Ibid., pp. 11, 12.

upper end so that the stone could be worn suspended. In a curious letter written April 25, 1742, by Martha Postlethwayte, sister of Sir Thomas Gooch, who successively presided over the episcopal sees of Bristol, Norwich and Ely, to her daughter Barbara Kerrick, the writer advises her correspondent, in order to avoid a repetition of former misadventures, to "wear the eagle-stone and take Mrs. Stone's receit," and adds: "I hope it may have good effect and make me a good grandmother." The result was favorable, and must naturally have affirmed the faith in the powers of the stone.[41]

An inventory of the furniture, plate, jewels, etc., of Charles V of France, made in 1379,[42] describes two stones preserved in a case of cypress-wood which the king always carried about with him. One of these was called the "holy stone" and aided women in childbirth. This was probably an "eagle-stone." It was set in gold and the setting was adorned with four pearls, six emeralds and two balas-rubies. The other stone, which cured the gout, was an engraved gem bearing the figure of a king and an inscription in Hebrew characters. This description suggests one of the Gnostic gems so common in the early Christian centuries. The gem was suspended from a silver cord, so that it could be worn on the neck, or perhaps attached to some other part of the body. We find in the *comptes royaux* of 1420 an electuary composed of powdered precious stones, for the cure of the infirmities of Isabel of Bavaria, who was fifty years old and had been for several years obese and a valetudinarian.[43]

In some parts of the Orient the superstitious notion exists that the *ætites* occasionally emits a wailing sound during the night, and this is said to be either an expression of the

[41] Albert Hartshorne, F.S.A., in Proceedings of Society of Antiquaries of London, Sec. Series, vol. xxii, p. 517, May 27, 1909.

[42] MS. 8356 of the Bibliothèque Nationale, f. LXXII, verso.

[43] F. de Mély La Grande Encyclopédie, vol. xxvi, p. 884.

birth-pangs of the mother stone, or else the cry of its new-born offspring, the small stones enclosed within the geode, for the story goes that each night some of these are generated.[44]

These "eagle-stones" still retain their repute in Italy, where they are called *pietre gravide,* or "pregnant stones," and are considered by many of the peasants as almost indispensable aids to parturition. They are in such demand that the lucky owners rent them for the nine months during which they are worn. As soon as one case has been happily concluded, the amulet is passed on to some other woman who is in need of it. A fee of five lire, or one dollar, is paid in each case, and a pledge worth a hundred lire ($20) is required before the stone is handed over. Some amulets of this class bear Christian symbols.[45]

Geodes of this description consisting of limonite are to be found in many places. Some of them are of relatively recent formation, and one of these shows curiously enough that in addition to its other virtues the *ætites* can on occasion perform the functions of a savings-bank. This strange specimen was found in 1846, at Périgueux, department Dordogne, France. On opening the geode there appeared within some 200 silver coins dated in the fifteenth and sixteenth centuries; all of these were encrusted with the material forming the enclosing mass.[46]

Long, white, rough stones, calcareous shell growths, were sometimes taken from snails and cockles. These were believed to have a marked diuretic action, and were therefore strongly recommended for certain diseases of the kidneys and the bladder. They were also believed to be helpful in

---

[44] Julius Ruska, "Das Steinbuch des Aristoteles," Heidelberg, 1912, p. 4, citing Petermann, "Reisen im Orient," vol. ii, p. 132.

[45] Bellucci, "Il feticismo in Italia," Perugia, 1907, p. 94, note. (Figures on pp. 94 and 95.)

[46] Lacroix, "Minéralogie de la France," Paris, 1893–1910, vol. iii, p. 399.

cases of difficult parturition. Although no details are given, it seems most probable that the stones were reduced to a powder from which some sort of potion was concocted,[47] this having no more action than so much ground shell or marble dust.

The *alectorius* or "cock-stone" is one of the most famous of those real or supposed animal concretions that were known in ancient times. From the age of Pliny—and unquestionably long before his time—there was a popular belief that this stone was only to be found in the gizzard of a cock which had been caponed when three years old, and had lived seven years longer. This was believed to allow the substance to acquire its boasted virtue, for the longer it remained in the body of the capon, the greater its power. Such a "cock-stone" never exceeded the size of a bean. From its association with the pugnacious fowl, the *alectorius* became a favorite stone with wrestlers, and the great and invincible Milo of Croton is said to have owed many of his victories to the possession of one, for if held in the mouth, it quenched the thirst and thus refreshed the combatant.

Extracting an alectorius. From Johannis de Cuba's "Ortus Sanitatis," Strassburg, 1483.

Many other virtues of this stone are recorded; it rendered wives agreeable to their husbands, dissolved enchantments, brought new honors and powers in addition to those already enjoyed, and helped kings to acquire new dominions. How persistent was the faith in the virtue of the *alectorius* is shown by the fact that the great astronomer Tycho Brahe

[47] Lemnii, "De miraculis naturæ," Francofurti, 1611, p. 213.

greatly valued a stone of this kind, not larger than a bean, and believed that it brought him luck in gambling and in love. Thomas de Cantimpré[48] says that the name signifies an allurer or enticer, because the stone excites the love of husbands for their wives.[49] In order to secure the due effect it should be held in the mouth, possibly because this would render the wife less eloquent.

A specimen of the *alectorius* is listed in the inventories of Jean Duc de Berry (1401–1416). It is called there a "capon-stone" and is described as having red and white spots. Several other objects to which talismanic virtues were ascribed are also noted, such, for instance, as the

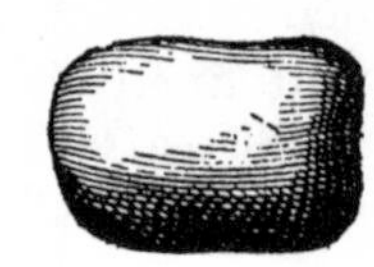

ALECTORIVS

Alectorius. From Mercati's "Metallotheca Vaticana," Romæ, 1719.

"molar of a giant," set in leather; probably the tooth of a hippopotamus, or the fossil tooth of some antediluvian creature. There is also what is termed a "tester," composed of several "serpent's teeth" (*glossopetræ?*), horns of the "unicorn" (narwhal's teeth) and stones regarded as antidotes to poison. These were all suspended by golden chains, and were valued at seventy-five livres tournois.[50]

As a companion piece to the "cock-stone," the hen furnished a concretion possessing special virtues. This came from the fowl's gizzard and was of a sky-blue color; its

[48] In Konrad Von Megenberg's version, "Buch der Natur," ed. by Dr. Franz Pfeiffer, Stuttgart, 1861, p. 435.

[49] The writer erroneously derives the name from the Latin verb *allectare*, the true derivation being from the Greek ἀλέκτωρ, a cock.

[50] Guiffrey, "Inventaires du Duc de Berry," vol. i, p. 166.

Arabic name was *hajar al-ḥattaf.* If it were worn by an epileptic, the attacks of his malady would cease; it favored procreation and also nullified the effects of the Evil Eye, and it kept children from having bad dreams if placed beneath their heads when they were sleeping. Thus the effects it was fancied to produce differed from those ascribed to the *alectorius.*[51]

In medieval times bunches of dried "serpent's tongues" were sometimes hung around salt-cellars or attached to spits; but frequently, for royal or princely use, such tongues, or the jawbones of snakes, were set with valuable precious stones and constituted a peculiar jewel termed in old French a *languier,* or *épreuve* (tester); for these utensils, often very rich and tasteful specimens of the goldsmith's art, were believed to show in some way the presence of the much-dreaded poison in any viands with which they were brought in contact.[52]

The Indians and Spaniards in South America made remedial use of a stone said to be obtained from the cayman or alligator, at Nombre de Dios, Cartagena, etc. This was employed as a cure for various intermittent fevers. Monardes writes that he applied two of these *lapides caymanum* to the temples of a young girl suffering from an attack of fever, and found that the fever was alleviated thereby; but he doubts that fevers could be entirely cured by this treatment.[53]

From New Spain was also brought the *lapis manati,* taken from the manatee, or sea-cow. This does not appear

---

[51] Julius Ruska, "Das steinbuch aus der Kosmographie des Muhammad ibn Maḥmud al-Kazwînî," Beilage to the Jahresbericht of the Oberrealschule, Heidelberg, 1895–96, p. 15.

[52] Chabœuf "Charles le Téméraire à Dijon," 1474; in Mém. de la Soc. burg. géog. et hist., vol. xviii, p. 137.

[53] Monardes, "Semplicium medicamentorum ex novo orbe delatorum historia" (Latin version by Clusius), Antverpiæ, 1579, p. 51.

to have been a stone, but rather the cochleæ of the animal, the small bones in the head which transmit the auditory vibrations to the sensorium. They were highly valued by the Indians for their remedial action in cramps and colic, and the Spaniards collected them and brought them to Spain to enrich their very miscellaneous pharmacopœia. Sometimes they were taken internally, but often they were set in rings or worn suspended from the neck as amulets. This stone, or bone, is described as oval in shape and of a hue

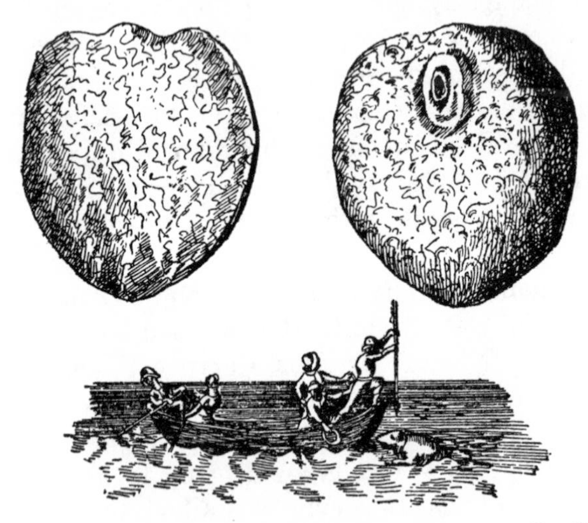

Lapis manati. From Valentini's "Museum Museorum, oder Vollständige Schau-Bühne," Frankfurt am Main, 1714.

resembling that of ivory. When pulverized and dissolved, the solution was odorless and tasteless. They are in size often as large as a woman's clinched fist.[54]

The ear-bones of fish, almost invariably in pairs, are still used as amulets in Spain and Italy. One of their chief virtues is to protect children from the Evil Eye, as well as

---

[54] Valentini, "Museum museorum, oder Vollständige Schau-Bühne," Frankfurt am Main, 1714, Bk. III, cap. 27, §§ 1, 4.

from accidents of any kind. They are also believed to preserve the wearer from deafness or diseases of the ear.[55] This is quite in accord with the primitive fancy that the different parts of the animal body had prophylactic or curative powers in relation to any disease of that portion of the human body.

Even the spider was supposed to produce a stone having remedial power, especially that variety called by the Germans Kreuzspinne ("cross-spider"). The belief was general in Germany, in the sixteenth century, that it was very unlucky to injure one of these spiders; indeed, Encelius writes that although he had never seen a "spider-stone," he had never dared to dissect one of the spiders to seek for the stone. He also remarks that it was in no wise strange this should have such power, since spider-webs were used as remedies for many diseases. Naturally enough the "spider-stone" was an antidote against poisons, and a belief was current that in a year when the plague was raging no Kreuzspinne was to be seen.[56]

Lapis malacensis, stone of the hedgehog or porcupine. From Mercati's "Metallotheca Vaticana," Romæ, 1719.

An attempt to induce one of these spiders to secrete or produce its stone or calculus is told by Simon Paulli. On his return from France in 1630, he stopped for the summer with his revered master, Sennart, at Wittenberg, in order to pursue his studies. One day they found by chance that an enormous spider had wandered into the rain-water holder, and the extraordinary size of the creature—it was as big as a muscat nut—suggested the idea of making it the subject of experiment. It was therefore put into a glass jar

[55] W. L. Hildburgh, "Further Notes on Spanish Amulets," in Folk Lore, vol. xxiv, No. 1, p. 70, March 31, 1913. Sec. Plate I, Fig. 27.

[56] Encelii, "De re metallica," Francofurti, 1557, p. 219.

with a quantity of powdered valerian root, this material (or salt) being reputed to have a favorable influence in the production of the stone. However, the experimenters were doomed to disappointment, for the poor spider was unable to live up to its reputation. Tired of waiting for nothing, recourse was finally had to the drastic measure of dissection, but no stone of any kind could be found. This convinced the observers that all the talk about spiders' stones was mere foolishness or deception. In a note in the Miscellanea Curiosa, under date of 1686, the statement is made that such stones could indeed be found, but only in the autumn season and in no other part of the year.[57]

A small golden amulet, having the form of a heart and set with various stones, was strongly recommended to ward off the plague by Oswald Croll, a writer of the early part of the seventeenth century. On the upper side of the heart-amulet should be set a fair blue sapphire; above, beneath, and at either side of this should be put a toad-stone, or a "spider-stone," so as to give a cross effect. The "spider-stones" were asserted to be powerful enemies of the plague. On the under side of the heart a good-sized jacinth was to be set, the jacinth also being credited with great virtue against plague or pestilence. The gold heart was to be hollow within. To give a finishing touch to the efficacy of the amulet it was necessary to take a living toad and keep the creature suspended by its hind-legs until it died and dried up so that the body could be reduced to a powder. This powder was then to be kneaded into a sort of paste with a little very sharp vinegar and introduced into the hollow interior of the gold heart.[58]

The "fretful porcupine" also contributed its stone to the

---

[57] See text in Axel Garboe's "Kulturhistoriske Studier over Ædelstene," Kjbenhavn og Kristiana, 1915, p. 56, note from Simon Paulli, "Quadripartitum botanicum," Argentorati, 1667, p. 163.

[58] Oswaldus Crollius, "Basilica chymica," Frankfurt, 1623, p. 213.

series of concretions; this was usually found in the animal's head, and was considered to be even superior to the bezoar as an antidote against poison. If steeped in water for a quarter of an hour, the water became so bitter that "there was nothing in the world more bitter." Another stone supposed to be found in the animal's entrails possessed like properties, but was said to lose none of its weight when placed in water, while the first-mentioned stone became lighter. Tavernier bought three of these stones, paying as much as five hundred crowns for one of them.[59]

A jewel made of ambergris, in the J. Pierpont Morgan collection, is said to be the only specimen of its kind that has been preserved for us from medieval times. The perfumed material has been skilfully carved into the symbolic figures of a woman and three children. At one time believed to symbolize Charity, the later theory is that these figures have a less pure significance and rather denote the reproductive energies, for ornaments of this material were credited with aphrodisiac powers; however, they were also believed to cure stomachic disorders. The delicate perfume they exhaled was one of their chief titles to admiration, and after the lapse of more than three centuries, this particular jewel still emits a fragrant aromatic odor when it has been held for some time in a warm hand. The style of the workmanship indicates that this is a piece of cinquecento Italian work. It was at one time in the Wencke Collection, in Hamburg, and later formed part of the Spitzer Collection, until the sale of the latter in 1893.[60]

While many of the reports of the finding of immense masses of ambergris (in one the weight of the mass is given as three thousand pounds) may be classed as at least highly

[59] "Les six voyages de Jean Baptiste Tavernier," Pt. II, Paris, 1678, p. 470; liv. ii, chap. 24.

[60] Williamson, "Catalogue of the Collection of Jewels and Precious Works of Art, the Property of J. Pierpont Morgan," London, 1910, pp. 12–14.

improbable, still there is abundant unmistakable evidence that very large pieces have really occasionally been found. In Rome and in the Santa Casa of Loreto costly and artistically shaped pieces of ambergris were to be seen, which clearly indicated that the weight of the original unworked mass must have greatly exceeded that of the ornamental object. There can be no doubt of the authenticity of the details regarding a great piece of ambergris weighing 182 pounds bought in the year 1693 from King Fidori by the Dutch East India Company for 11,000 rigsdalers or nearly $12,000 at the current valuation of the coin of that time. In form it resembled a tortoise-shell, was 5 feet 8 inches thick, and 2 feet 2 inches long. After being long kept in Amsterdam as a curiosity, and having been viewed there by thousands of persons, it was finally broken up and sold at auction.[61] A lump extracted from a whale in the Windward Islands weighed 130 pounds and was sold for $3500, or nearly $27 a pound.

The livers of certain animals provided concretions called haraczi by the Arabs; these were much used as remedies for epilepsy. The Turkish butchers, when slaughtering animals, always examined the livers carefully so as to secure these stones. As the Jews were said to suffer much from melancholia and epileptic disorders they valued the liver-stones very highly.[62]

The use of fossils as talismans and for the cure of diseases was mainly due to their strange and various forms. As color played the most important part in the case of precious stones, each color being looked upon as possessing a certain symbolic significance fitting the stone for some special use or uses, so in the case of fossils the form was

---

[61] Caspar Neumann, "Disquisitio de ambra grysea," Dresden, 1736, pp. 80, 81.

[62] Gimma, "Della storia naturale delle gemme," Napoli, 1730, vol. i, p. 479.

the determining factor. Sometimes it was as the form of some creature held by the superstitious to be particularly endowed with mysterious qualities beneficial to mankind, at other times the fossil form suggested some part of the human body, and was therefore believed to afford protection to this part, or to cure any disease affecting it. This will be made clearer by a brief notice of some of the principal fossils which were favored in ancient and medieval times, either by popular superstition or by those who from interested motives made use of these superstitions for the purpose of gain, although they may have only half believed in the real virtue of the objects they sold.

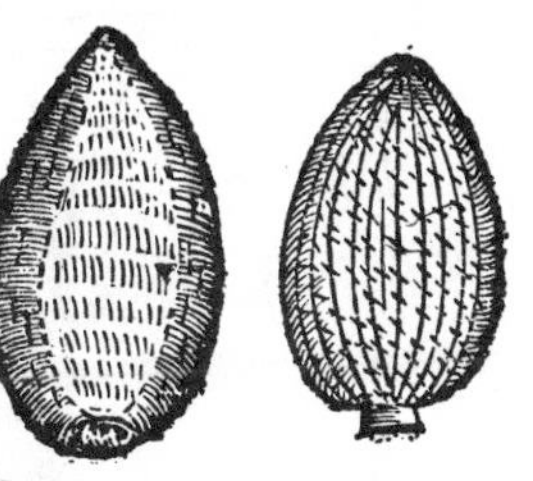

Lapis Judaicus. Pentremite heads. From "Museum Wormianum," Lugduni Batavorum, 1655.

The remedial quality of fossils, which were believed to have been formed from shells and marine animals deposited during the deluge, is ascribed by Mentzel to the fact that they had been produced by the action of fire, and hence had the same quality as though prepared and calcined by the chemist's art. They were therefore believed to have great medicinal virtues in the cure of diseases.[63]

The lapis Judaicus [64] is described as of oval form, in shape like an olive, and sometimes provided with a stem at the upper part as though it had grown on a tree. The stone was soft and friable and in color either white or grayish. The "male" variety had several rows of equidistant spines, while the "female" was quite smooth. The description and the figured representations of the lapis Judaicus show that it was a form of pentremite—that is, a form of crinoid. This fossil, which was said to come from Syria and Palestine, was taken in solution as a remedy for calculus. The larger, male

[63] Christiani Mentzelii, "Lapis Bononensis," Bilefeldiæ, 1675, p. 47.
[64] Mercati, "Metallotheca Vaticana," Romæ, 1719, p. 227.

stones, were regarded as the better for renal calculus and the smaller, female stones, for vesical calculus. Hence this fossil was sometimes called tecolithos, from τήκειν, to dissolve, and λίθος, stone.[65] Pliny also states that this name was applied to certain concretions found in sponges and supposed to possess similar virtues.[66] Of the remedial use of this stone, or fossil, Galen states that when prescribed for vesical calculi, it was pulverized in a mortar, and the

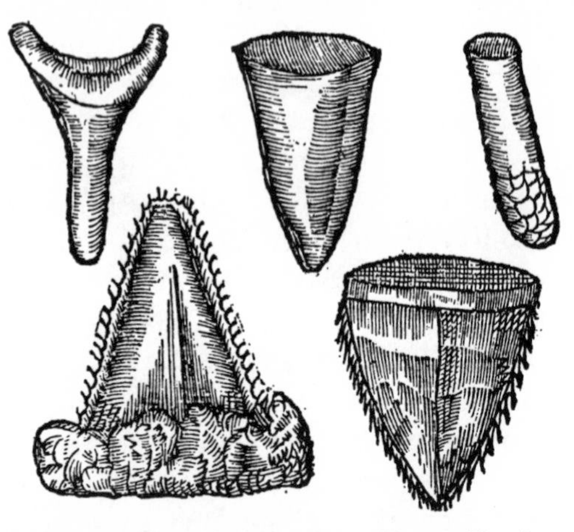

Glossopetræ. Fossil shark's teeth. From "Museum Wormianum," Lugduni Batavorum, 1655.

powder being mixed with water, three glasses of the solution were given. He adds, however: "I must say that as far as I have seen they have no effect, but they are efficient in the case of renal calculi."[67]

No fossils were more prized than the so-called *glossopetræ* or "tongue-stones." Although these were really the fossilized or petrified teeth of a species of shark, Pliny and

[65] Plinii, "Historia Naturalis," lib. xxxvii, cap. 68.

[66] Ibid., lib. xxxvi, cap. 35. See also Dioscorides V, 155; Ætius II, 19.

[67] Claudii Galeni, "Opera Omnia," ed. Kuhn, Lipsiæ, 1826, vol. xii, p. 199. De simplic. med., lib. vii, cap. 2.

his sources believed them to be meteorites, which "fell from the sky when the moon was waning." This was, indeed, a prevalent fancy regarding all dart-shaped, pointed or sharpened fossils, or flints. Because of this celestial origin, the *glossopetræ* were said to control the winds and even to affect the motions of the moon. At a later time the chief source of supply for these petrified teeth was the island of Malta, and they were therefore sometimes called *lingues Melitenses,* or Maltese tongues; the Germans named them *Steinzungen,* or "stone-tongues." According to popular belief these so-called Maltese tongues were petrified snakes' tongues and they were brought into connection with the miraculous adventure of St. Paul on the island of Malta, when he shook off a viper that had fastened on his hand, and sustained no injury from the bite (Acts, xxviii, 3–5). This was taken to signify that the poison had been taken from all the snakes on the island.[68]

The material called "St. Paul's Earth," said to be derived from "St. Paul's Cave," in the island of Malta, was reduced to a fine powder and made into tablets. These were stamped with the Maltese cross; sometimes on the opposite side some other figure was impressed. As there was temptation to sell other material for the genuine, the purchaser was warned to be on his guard. The virtues of this powder—which was dissolved in wine or water—were numerous, and were the same as those ascribed to the "tongues" (*glossopetræ*) and to the "eyes"; for it was believed to be an antidote for poisons, cured the bites of venomous creatures, and remedied many other ills. The "eyes" were set in rings so that the material touched the wearer's skin; the "tongues" were worn attached to the arm or suspended from the neck. Sometimes vessels were made from the earth. These were

[68] Valentini, "Museum museorum, oder Vollständige Schau-Bühne," Frankfurt am Main, 1714, lib, i, cap. 24, § 2.

filled with wine or water, the liquid being allowed to stand until it had absorbed the virtues of the earth; it was then taken as a potion with good effects. The "tongues" and "eyes" were often dipped in wine or water and were supposed to transmit their curative powers to the liquid.[69]

In the fifteenth and sixteenth centuries a strange belief was prevalent among the ignorant to the effect that the fossil sharks'-teeth, the "tongue-stones," were the teeth of witches who sucked the blood of infants; these "vampires" were called *lamiæ* in ancient times.[70] Probably the fact that a certain species of shark bore the name *lamia* gave rise to this idea, which was therefore merely due to a confusion of names. Nevertheless we can easily understand that this popular belief added to the repute of the *glossopetræ,* for the more dreaded the object the greater the power it was credited with possessing. In the seventeenth century De Laet (d. 1649), the Dutch naturalist and geographer, received in Leyden certain *glossopetræ* sent him by a friend in Bordeaux, who wrote that they would cure any one suffering from soreness of the mouth, whether this were the result of having eaten impure food, or were produced by some derangement of the secretions. The "tongues" were to be dipped in spring water and would cause bubbles to form therein; as soon as these disappeared, the water was to be used as a gargle, and the mouth was to be washed with it two or three times. De Laet's friend assured him that this treatment would cure the disorder in twenty-four hours.[71]

A seventeenth-century amulet of a fossil shark's tooth, mounted in silver and found in an excavation at Salzburg, Austria, was among the objects exhibited by the writer for the New York branch of the American Folk-Lore Society, in

---

[69] "Museum Wormianum," Lug. Bat., 1655, pp. 7–9.
[70] Aldrovandi, "Museum metallicum," Bononiæ, 1648, lib. iv, cap. 10, p. 600.
[71] "Museum Wormianum," Lug. Bat., 1655, p. 65.

the Department of Ethnology of the Columbian Exposition held in Chicago, in 1893. They are frequently found at Lake Constance but are from the ancient fossiliferous formations and not from the lake. They are often sold as amulets.

Fossils whose form suggested that of a more or less acutely pointed shaft, were thought to possess special powers, sometimes offensive as against enemies, and again defensive for the protection of the wearer. Thus the belemnites,[72] considered to represent the form of a dart, when dissolved and taken as a potion, were said to prevent nightmare and to guard against enchantments. They are often either ash-colored or whitish, and sometimes reddish-black. All these varieties were frequently found during the sixteenth century in Hildesheim, and in the marble grotto near the castle of Marienburg, called the "Dwarf's Grotto."[73]

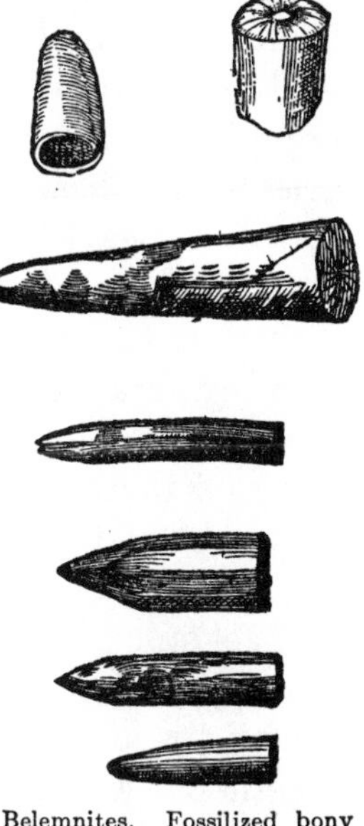

Belemnites. Fossilized bony end of extinct cuttle-fish. From Aldrovandi's "Museum metallicum," Bononiæ, 1648.

The umbilicus marinus, a fossil shell, which in form bore a great likeness to the human navel, was called "sea-bean" by sailors. Usually of a pale saffron hue, some specimens have a reddish or blackish tinge. In the sixteenth century it was believed to have astringent properties. We are also told that women used it as one of the ingredients of a cosmetic for whitening the complexion.[74]

---

[72] This is the fossilized horny part of the tail of an extinct cuttlefish, and numerous specimens have been found in the marl of New Jersey as well as in many other places.

[73] Gesneri, "De figuris lapidum," Tiguri, 1565, fol. 89, verso, 90, recto.

[74] Mercati, "Metallotheca Vaticana," Romæ, 1719, pp. 138–139. Figure on p. 138.

Certain echinites (fossil sea-urchins) found on the Baltic coast are called by the peasants *Adlersteine* and *Krallensteine* ("eagle-stones" and "claw-stones"), since they believe that while the substance was soft eagles had seized them with their talons, thus producing the peculiar forms and markings. Whoever had a fossil of this description on his table while a thunder-storm was raging ran no risk of being struck by lightning.[75]

Reich describes another variety of echinite, which was popularly known as a "toad-stone," the specimen he figures having been given him by a certain Johannis Krauss. In this appeared some large cavities, whose presence Reich found it very difficult to explain, until Krauss informed him that they had been made by a former owner of the fossil who had scraped out a few grains of the substance each year for medicinal use. He was persuaded that his long life—he attained the age of eighty—was entirely owing to his employment of this remedy.[76]

The *trochites* and *entrochus,* named Räderstein, or "wheel-stone," by the Germans, are other fossils to which remedial or talismanic virtue was accorded in popular fancy. These "wheel-stones," while detachable, fitted as closely together in the original formation as though they had been skilfully adjusted by a clever artisan.[77] De Laet states that when immersed in oil they gave forth bubbles and moved about spontaneously. Still another of these fossils believed to be amulets was the *enastros,* which De Boot terms the *asteria vera,* or genuine asteria, since it not merely showed a star-shaped marking as did the fossil coral bearing the name

[75] Andree, "Ethnographische Parallelen und Vergleiche," New Ser., Leipzig, 1889, p. 33.

[76] Reichii, "Medicina Universalis" [Vratislaviæ, 1691], p. 76. See Fig. 4, opp. p. 72.

[77] De Boot, "Gemmarum et lapidum historia." ed. Toll, Lug. Bat., 1647, p. 410; lib. ii, cap. ccxxvii, and also De Laet, "De gemmis et lapidibus," Lug. Bat., 1647, p. 138.

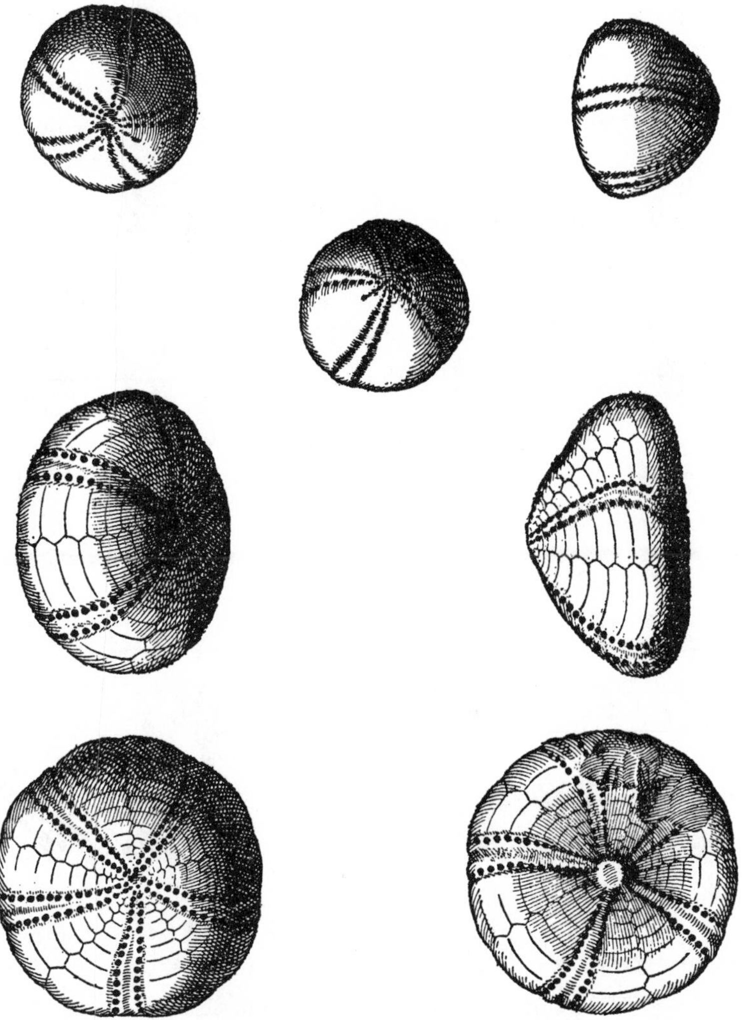

Brontia. Fossil sea urchins. From Mercati's "Metallotheca Vaticana," Romæ, 1719.

astroites, but was shaped like a five-pointed star. As with the *trochites,* chains of these little stars were found, closely joined together but separable from one another. Some called them "star-seals," because the stellar imprint was sharp and clearly defined as though the work of an engraver or gem-cutter.[78] These fossils are types of encrinites.

The sections of the stem-like fossils called *entrochus* by the older writers have been named St. Cuthbert's beads in

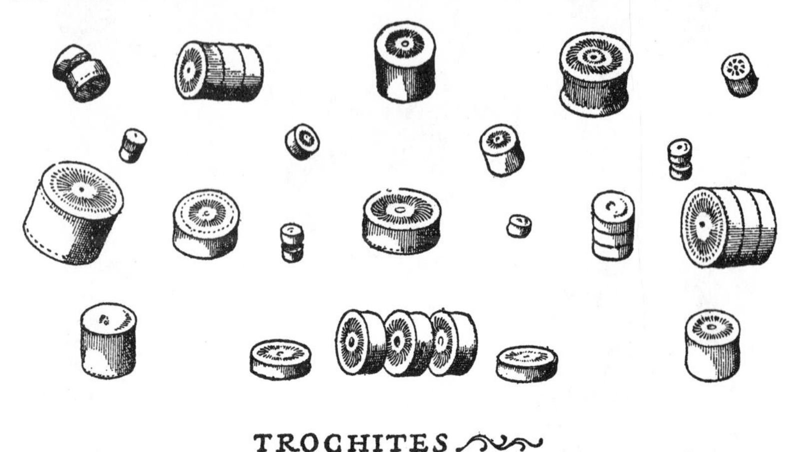

Aloysius Gomier. sculp.

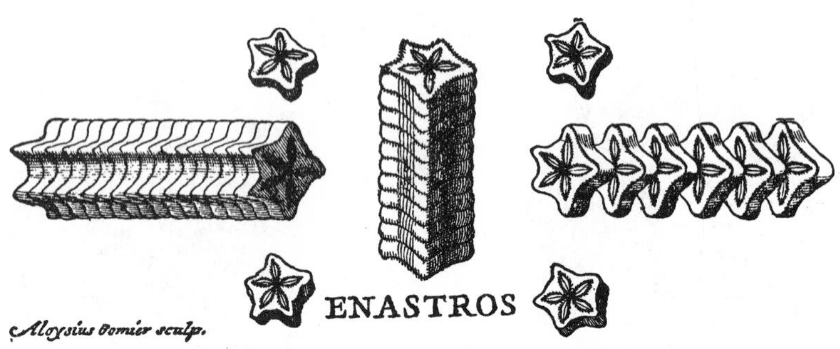

Trochites } Fossil Crinoid Stems. Enastros } From Mercati, "Metallotheca Vaticana," Romæ, 1719.

later times, while the fossil called *lapis Judaicus* has borne the name of "stone-lily," because in form it resembles the lily. Ages ago the stem and flower-like head united consti-

[78] Ibid., p. 300; lib. ii, cap. cxlviii.

tuted a crinoid (a marine zoophyte). These aquatic creatures—half-plant and half-animal—usually twine their roots about some shell in the depths of the waters, but sometimes they become detached and then, moving their delicate tentacles, they creep along the bottom of the sea.

In olden times parts, or segments, of an animal were worn as a protection against harm from that particular creature, or else to endow the wearer with some of its real or fancied qualities. In modern times this tendency finds expression in the wearing of jewels of animal form, wherein precious stones are grouped and arranged so as to constitute different parts of the creature's body. Such jewels are often looked upon as "mascots."

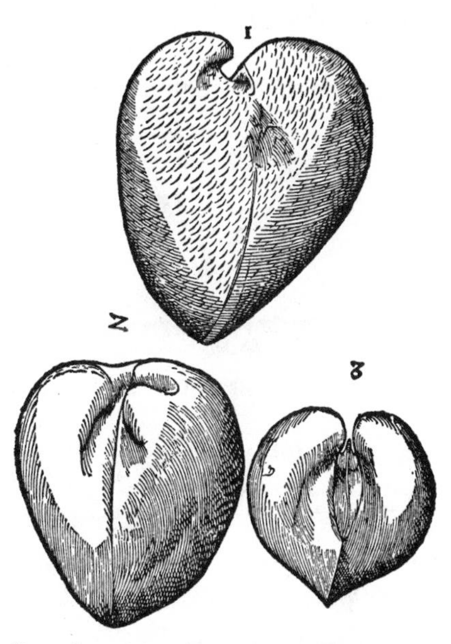

Bucardites triplex. From Aldrovandi's "Museum metallicum," Bononiæ, 1648.

A peculiar fossil was known to the Germans by the name of Mutterstein, and is called *hysterolithus* in the Latin treatises of Agricola, De Boot, etc., a word of Greek derivation signifying the resemblance of the object to an organ of the body. These fossils are formed from the contents of certain shells, and retain the shape of the enclosing shell, which has broken away. Some of these formations were called *enorchi* from a fancied resemblance to another organ and were regarded as phallic emblems, while others were thought to figure the heart, especially large specimens being named *bucar-*

dites, or "ox-hearts." This name is already employed by Pliny. The *hysterolithus* was used to cure various female diseases, and to the *bucardites* was accorded among other virtues that of increasing the wearer's courage.[79] The *hysterolithus* is believed to be the same as the *autoglyphus* mentioned by pseudo-Plutarch as having been found in the river Sagaris, in Asia Minor. Its peculiar shape was regarded as symbolizing Cybele, the mother of the gods, and the story ran that if one of the unfortunate male victims of Eastern jealousy should obtain a stone of this kind he

Types of Ombria (Fossil Sea Urchins). From Mercati's "Metallotheca Vaticana," Romæ, 1719.

would become reconciled to his sad lot and would cease to regret his lost manhood.

If we were inclined to accord the title of precious stones to stones greatly esteemed for their talismanic virtues, a high place in this category would be assigned to the sâlagrâma-stone of the Hindus.[80] Among the aboriginal inhabitants of India this was regarded as a symbol of the female principle in nature, and of its representative the goddess Prakrti, and in the later Hindu belief the stone was looked upon as the special emblem of the god Vishnu, the "Preserver," the second personage of the Hindu Trimurti. It is therefore ardently revered by those who are more espe-

---

[79] Valentini, "Museum museorum, oder Vollständige Schau-Bühne," Frankfurt am Main, 1714, vol. ii, p. 11.

[80] See, in regard to this stone, Oppert, "Der Salâgrâma-Stein," Zeitschrift für Ethnologie, XXXIV Jahrgang, Berlin, 1902, pp. 131–137.

cially devoted to the worship of Vishnu. These stones are fossil formations, either of ammonites or univalve mollusks of a spiral order, and consist of a number of spirals surrounding a circular, central perforation. They are generally the hardened filling of the shell itself, which has entirely weathered away. For the stone to be an effectual talisman, the diameter of the perforation should not exceed one-eighth of the total diameter of the sâlagrâma. The best specimens are said to be found in Nepal, on the upper course of the Gandakî, which flows into the Ganges from the north, and is called the Salagrama River, because the sacred stone is found in it.

There can be little doubt that we have here a substance similar to the fossils described by Pliny and his successors under the names *brontia, ombria, ovum anguinum,* and *cornu ammonis,* and it is most probable that in India, as in Europe, these fossils were believed to have fallen from heaven, and were associated with the thunder-bolt. Hence they would be regarded by the Hindus as more especially sacred to Vishnu, who was originally a divinity representing the various forms of light, one of his manifestations being the lightning.

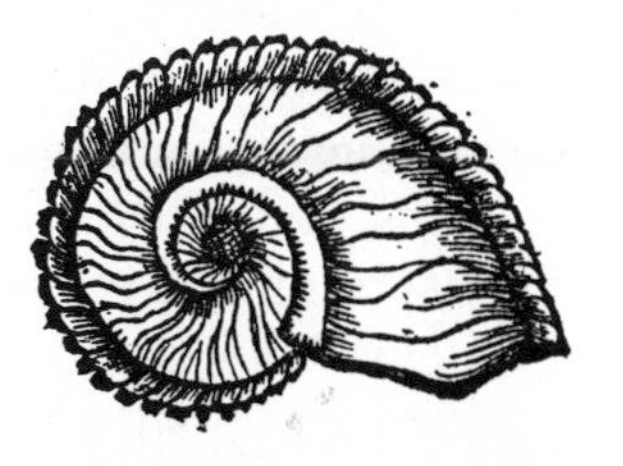

Cornu ammonis (Fossil Nautilus.) From "Museum Wormianum," Lugduni Batavorum, 1655.

The sâlagrâmas must be carefully chosen, for not all of them are luck-bringing, some being bearers of ill-fortune. A black sâlagrâma brings fame to the owner, and a red one, a crown; but one with an unduly large perforation would cause dissension and strife in a family, one with irregularly formed spirals portends misfortune, and a brown one would bring to pass the death of its owner's wife. Each faithful worshipper of Vishnu has one of these stones, but two may not be in the same house. To give away a sâlagrâma would be equivalent to casting away every prospect of good-fortune. However, only one who belongs to the three highest castes is entitled to become an owner of the sacred stone, in which the very spirit of Vishnu is supposed to dwell; neither a Sudra nor a Pariah enjoys this privilege, which is also denied to women.

The sâlagrâma is carefully wrapped in linen cloths, and must be often washed and perfumed. The water with which it has been washed becomes a consecrated drink. The master of the house must adore the stone once each day, either in the morning or in the evening. As the sâlagrâma not only brings happiness in this world but also insures felicity in the future world, it is held over the dying Hindu while water is allowed to trickle through the orifice. This ceremony appears to have a certain analogy to the rite of extreme unction administered in the Catholic Church.

It is stated by Finn Magnusen that in Iceland, toward the beginning of the last century, he saw superstitious peasants carefully guard small stones of peculiar appearance in pretty bags filled with fine flour. They treated these stones with great reverence and either wore them on their persons or placed them in their beds or other furniture.[81]

The fossils known as *brontiæ*, *ombriæ* and *chelonites* were all believed to be antidotes for poison and also to make the wearer victorious over his enemies. Hence they were sometimes set in the pommels of swords. That these objects were equally potent in peace, is shown by the fact that Danish peasant women placed them in their milk pails to ward off the effects of any spell that might have been cast over the cow's milk by a malevolent witch.[82]

---

[81] Magnusen, "Om en Steenring med Runenindskrift," Annaler for Nordisk Oldkyndighed, Copenhagen, 1838–1839, p. 133.

[82] Valentini, "Museum museorum, oder die vollständige Schau-Bühne," Frankfurt am Main, 1714, vol. ii, p. 12.

David Reich notes the four kinds of astroites, or "victory stones," given by De Boot; the first, marked with small stars; the second, with rose-like figures; the third, with wavy lines, like the convolutions of a worm; the fourth, with obscure and indefinite markings. To these varieties Reich adds a fifth, the convex side of which was marked with black crosses, while the other, flat side, showed larger crosses surrounded by circles; all these markings were so perfect that an artist could scarcely imitate them; this specimen he

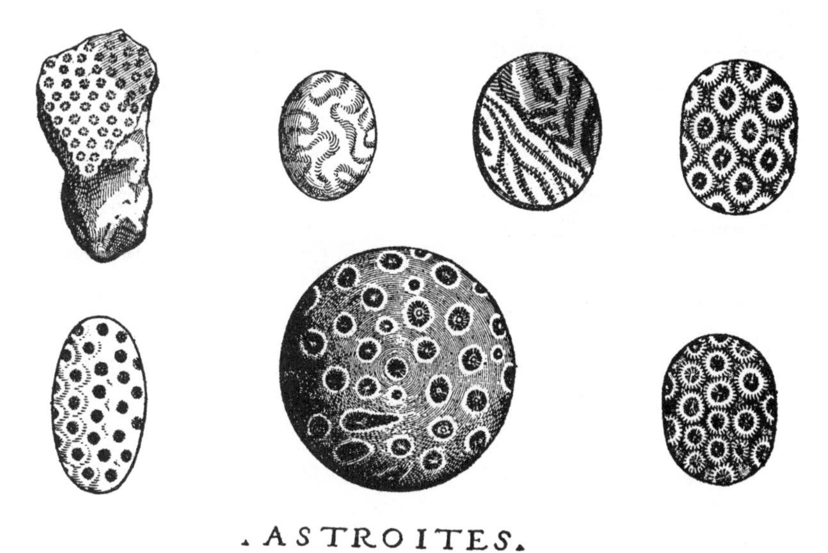

Specimens of Astroites (asteria), or fossil coral. From Mercati's "Metallotheca Vaticana," Romæ, 1719.

had set, with other precious gems, in a silver cross, the flat side of the fossil, at the back of the cross, being covered by a heart-shaped topaz.[83] These were all specimens of fossil coral.

The saga of Dietrich of Bern relates of King Nidung that

---

[83] Reichii, "Medicina universalis" [Vratislaviæ, 1691], p. 75. See Fig. 3, opp. p. 72.

on the eve of a battle in which his forces were much inferior to those of the enemy, he was filled with despair to find that he had left his "victory stone" in his castle, miles away from where he had pitched his tent. Overmastered by his desire to regain possession of his stone at this critical time, Nidung offered a large sum of money and his daughter's hand to anyone who would bring it to him before the battle began. The distance was so great and the time so short that the task seemed utterly impossible, and a young esquire, Velint by name, was the only one willing to risk the enterprise. He was favored in his quest by having a horse of wonderful strength and endurance, by whose help he barely succeeded in making the long journey to the castle and returning in time. King Nidung, wearing his invincible stone, was the victor in the battle, and he did not fail to carry out his rather rash promise.[84]

Amulets of fossil coral are freely used in Italy, especially in the province of Aquila, and are called "witch-stones" (*pietre stregonie*). These are similar to one type of the "asterias" worn as amulets in ancient and medieval times. Many of the Italian amulets are incised or engraved with Christian subjects, one figured by Bellucci bearing the head of Christ on the obverse, and Christ on the cross on the reverse side; on others appears the image of the Virgin Mary.[85]

Crystalline quartz will sometimes show a star either at base or apex, if cut *en cabochon*. This is due to the presence of acicular crystals of rutile or to air spaces. Those specimens from Albany, Maine and other places present this phenomenon, and Starolite and Astrolite or "star stone" has been suggested as an appropriate name for this variety.

---

[84] Peringskiold, "Wilkina Saga eller historia om Konung Diedrich of Bern," Stockholmis, 1715, pp. 57, 58.

[85] Bellucci, "Il feticismo in Italia," Perugia, 1907, pp. 100–104.

V

Snake Stones and Bezoars

THE bezoar stone, according to the usual belief, was taken from the intestines or the liver either of the goat or of the deer. The Arabs told a strange tale as to the generation of this stone.[1] They said that at certain seasons the deer were wont to devour snakes and other venomous creatures, whereupon they would straightway hasten to the nearest pool and plunge into it until only their nostrils were above the water. Here they remained until the feverish heat caused by the poison they had swallowed was alleviated. During this time stones were formed in the corners of their eyes; these dropped as the deer left the pool, and were found on its banks. The stones were a sovereign antidote for poisons of all kinds. When reduced to a powder and taken internally, or when simply bound to the injured part, they effected a cure by inducing a profuse perspiration. It is curious to note that this tale foreshadows, in a fanciful way, the latest progress of medical science; namely, the use of a substance generated in the body of a diseased animal as an antidote for the disease from which the animal suffered.

We are also told that Abdallah Narach narrates the case of the Moorish king of Cordoba, Miramamolin, as Monardes gives the name, to whom a violent poison had been administered and who was cured by means of a bezoar stone. The king, overcome with gratitude for the preservation of his life, gave his royal palace to the man who had brought him the stone. Monardes remarks: "This certainly was a royal gift, since we see that at this day the castle of Cordova is

[1] Nicolo Monardes, "Delle cose que vengono portate dall'Indie occidentali," Venetia, 1575, pp. 95–6.

something rare and of great value and the stone must have been highly prized when such a price was paid for it."[2]

The first mention of the bezoar stone is by the Arabic and Persian writers. In the Arabic work attributed to Aristotle, and which was certainly written as early as the ninth and possibly in the seventh century, it is even described among the precious stones. The same is true of the oldest Persian work on medicine, namely, that of Abu Mansur Muwaffak, composed about the middle of the tenth century. A valuable monograph on the bezoar was written in 1625 by Caspar Bauhin, a learned professor and physician of Basel; this work contains all that was then known of the various qualities ascribed to this substance by the older authors.

Application of a bezoar to cure a victim of poisoning. From Johannis de Cuba's "Ortus Sanitatis," Strassburg, 1483.

The bezoar does not appear to have been used medicinally in Europe before the twelfth century, when the so-called pestilential fevers became very prevalent. In their distress people turned to the lapis bezoar, which was so highly recommended by the Arabic physicians whose works were, at that time, becoming more widely known through the intercourse between the Spaniards and the Moors. Caspar Bauhin writes:[3] "Even to-day princes and nobles prize it very highly and guard it in their treasures among their most precious gems; so that the physicians are forced, sometimes

[2] Ibid., pp. 104–5.

[3] Caspari Bauhini, "De lapidis bezaaris ortu natura," etc., Basileæ, 1625, p. 3.

against their better judgment, to employ it as a remedy. So great are its virtues that many imitations are made."

The name bezoar, derived from the Persian *padzahr* (*pad*, expelling; *zahr*, poison), or some of its many variants, was often used to designate any antidote for poison, so that the Arabs would say that such or such a substance was the bezoar for a particular poison. This should be understood to signify that the stone received its name because it was regarded as a specially powerful antidote.

The various authors give many different sources for the bezoar. We have already cited Monardes and repeated his account; other writers asserted that this concretion came from the heads of certain animals, others again said that it was taken from their livers, and still others stated that it was formed in the eye of the stag. Naturally, concretions of a similar form and quality may well have been obtained from any of these sources. Indeed, one of the most potent bezoars was that taken from the monkey. A specimen of this kind is described and figured in the Museum Brittanicum [4] with the following description:

> A Monkey's Bezoar, very much resembling one from the goat, of an oblong shape broke in two, with a long straw, or some such like substance in its centre; its colour brown, pink, or deep yellow. I found it set as generally they are for preservation in a little chest, or case, of what is called *Lignum Lævisiunum;* the pith or medula of which appears to resemble the common elder, and may, for what I know, be as curious as the stone itself.

Toll quotes [5] Jacob Bontius to the effect that these monkey bezoars, which were rounded and a little longer than the finger, were considered the best of all.

As the chief quality claimed for the bezoar was that it induced a profuse perspiration, we might understand that it could have a beneficial effect in some cases. It was

---

[4] Museum Brittanicum, John and Andrew van Rymsdyk, London, pp. 50–51.
[5] De Boot, "De lapidibus," ed. Toll, Lug. Bat., 1636, p. 367.

also remarked that the solution of the stone blackened the teeth and those who used it were therefore obliged to take great care that the medicine should not touch their teeth.

We learn that a genuine stone was valued at 50 gold crowns (about $125) in Calcutta; another is said to have brought 130 crowns ($325). De Boot states that a drachm of the powdered stone was worth two ducats ($5) in Lower Germany and four ($10) in Upper Germany; why, he does not say.

Monkey bezoar. From Valentini's "Museum Museorum oder Vollständige Schau-Buhne," Frankfurt am Main, 1714.

Garcias ab Horto, a Portuguese physician of Goa, in India, describes a variety of the bezoar called the Lapis Malacensis, used as an antidote for poisons in Malacca. This was found in the liver of the hedgehog, and the substance was held in such esteem that of two found in the fifteenth century, one was sent as a very valuable gift to the Portuguese Viceroy at Goa. Garcias describes this as being of a light purple hue, bitter to the taste and smooth as the skin of a toad. The custom was to steep the stone in water for some time and then to give this water to the patient as a medicinal draught. A specimen was brought to Rome from Portugal by Cardinal Alexandrinus, and Mercato states that he had seen a test of its virtues as an antidote for poisons. In the opinion of De Boot: "As an antidote for any poison which may have been administered, nothing more excellent than the bezoar stone can be had."[6] It

[6] "De lapidibus," Lug. Bat., 1636, p. 370. See also Mercati, "Metallotheca Vaticana," Romæ, 1719, p. 179, with figure of stone from hedgehog.

was even asserted that if a bezoar set in a ring were frequently placed in the mouth and sucked, this would afford a cure for poison by inducing a profuse perspiration.[7] Besides its exceptional quality as an antidote for poisons, this stone was regarded as a panacea for all chronic and painful diseases, especially if taken each morning for several days, after the use of a cathartic.

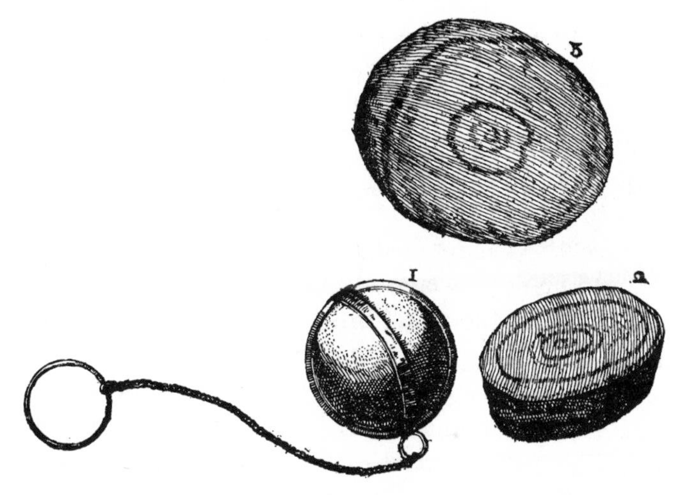

1. Hedge-hogstone from Malacca. 2, 3. Spurious stones of this type manufactured in Ceylon. From Kaempfer's "Amoenitatum exoticarum fasciculi V," Lemgoviæ, 1712.

Besides this use as a remedy or antidote, the bezoar was credited with the powers of an elixir of life, for some of the Hindus employed it as a preservative of youth and vigor. Twice a year, after dosing themselves with a strong cathartic medicine, they would take ten grains of powdered bezoar daily for fifteen days, and they are said to have derived great benefit from this treatment.[8]

The celebrated practical test of the bezoar's power as

[7] Aldrovandi, "Museum metallicum," Bononiæ, 1648, p. 809.
[8] Ibid., p. 809.

an antidote to poison, recorded by the famous French surgeon, Ambroise Paré (1510–1590), was performed in Paris with one which had been brought from Spain to Charles IX of France. Clearly the only perfectly satisfactory means of ascertaining whether the reputed virtues of this curious concretion were really present was to make an experiment therewith upon a living human being. Now it chanced that just at this time there was in the royal prison a cook who had stolen two silver dishes from his master, and who, in accord with the pitiless laws of that period, had been condemned to death for this offence. Here was an excellent opportunity, therefore, to make a trial of the bezoar, but as the adjudged legal penalty could not well be arbitrarily changed to some other form of death, the matter was first laid before the condemned man himself, with the promise that should he not succumb to the poison he would be given his liberty. As at the worst this was taking a chance of life in exchange for certain death, the cook readily consented. The necessary preparations having been made, the poison was administered and immediately thereafter the man was given a dose composed of a part of the bezoar reduced to powder and dissolved in liquid. The effects of the poison were soon manifested by violent retching and purging, and when Paré was called in an hour later, he found the man in great agony, with blood issuing from his nose, ears and mouth, and from the other bodily apertures. He piteously complained that he felt as though consumed by an inward flame, and before another hour had passed he expired, crying out that it would have been much better to have died by hanging. From his report, Paré seems not to have been present when the poison was given and not to have been informed of its character, as he merely states that from the results of his autopsy and from the symptoms he had observed, he concluded that it was corrosive sublimate. Probably, conscientious and truly religious as he was, he was unwilling to take an active part in such an affair. The king ordered that his discredited bezoar should be cast into the fire and destroyed. As an illustration of Ambroise Paré's humility and piety we may cite his remark on the recovery of one of his patients: "I treated him and God cured him."[9] It was Paré who operated upon Admiral Coligny after the unsuccessful attempt on the latter's life made a few days before his assassination on St. Bartholomew's Day, August 24, 1572, at the outset of the dreadful massacre.

Alluding to the ill-success attending the experiment performed by Ambroise Paré, in order to test effectively the supposed virtues of the substance as an antidote for poisons, Engelbert Kaempfer remarks that Paré's bezoar may have been of inferior quality, and, moreover, bezoars could not be successfully used to counteract mineral poisons, but were only useful when vegetable poisons had been taken. This opinion was probably due to the fact that the bezoar itself is largely or in the main a vegetable substance. That the interior layers of a specimen should be inferior in quality to the external layers was not for Kaempfer a proof of its spurious character, but might easily be accounted for by a change of pasturage in the case of the creature in whose body the concretion had formed.

This writer asserts that he considered those bezoars to be genuine which were of a partly resinous and partly mineral composition, so that when pulverized they could be dissolved in nitric acid, the solution having a reddish hue. The Persians not only attributed to bezoars the same virtues as did the Europeans, but also recommended the administration of the bezoar elixir to persons in health, that they might avoid contracting disease and prolong their lives,

[9] Ambroise Paré, "Œuvres Complètes," Paris, 1841, vol. iii, pp. 341, 342.

more especially if the dose were taken at the beginning of the year. In general, however, he found that where Europeans used the bezoar as a remedy, the Persians gave a dose of pearl tincture instead; but as rarities, or perhaps as talismans, bezoars were even more highly prized in Persia than in Europe, for there was hardly a Persian of note who did not preserve one of these concretions among his treasures. The price depended upon perfection of form and color, as well as upon size, one weighing a mishkel (about 75 grains Troy) was commonly valued at one toman, the equivalent of 15 ounces of silver (about $20), according to Kaempfer's computation, but the price rose rapidly with the size of the bezoar in a proportion similar to that observable in the case of pearls. As Persian bezoars were so costly in Persia, and the home demand for them so great, those sold by this name in Europe must have had another origin.[10]

Of several experiments made with criminals to whom poison was administered and then a dose of bezoar to test its virtues as an antidote, one of the most interesting has to do with a criminal incarcerated in the prison at Prague, in the reign of Emperor Rudolph II. To this man a drachm of the deadly poison *aconitum napellus* was administered. Five hours were allowed to elapse before the bezoar was given, so that the poison should have full time to be absorbed by the system. During this time the effects were fully manifested, oppression at the chest, pain in the gastric region, dimness of vision and dizziness. When the five hours had expired five grains of bezoar were given to the man in a little wine. After taking the dose he felt some relief and vomited, but the bad symptoms soon returned and even became aggravated, as though a supreme conflict for the mastery between poison and antidote were in progress. There

[10] Engelberti Kaempferi, "Amœnitatum exoticarum fasc. V," Lemgoviæ, 1712, pp. 402, 403.

was delirium, extreme tension of the abdomen, repeated vomiting, and an irregular, feverish pulse; finally an acute inflammation of the eyes supervened, causing such intense pain that the man declared he would rather die than endure it longer. However, at the end of eight hours' time from the administration of the poison—three hours after the dose of bezoar had been given—all the morbid conditions passed off, the patient was able to eat food with relish and he slept quietly. In the morning he was perfectly well, and never realized any subsequent bad effects. The emperor released him from prison and even bestowed a handsome reward upon him.[11]

A strange experiment to determine the character and quality of bezoars is related by Kaempfer on the authority of Jager. The latter asserted that while in Golconda he had the opportunity of examining recently captured gazelles for the presence of bezoars, and that by compressing their abdomens he could distinctly feel two such concretions in the case of one of the animals and five or six in the case of the other. They were kept some days for further observation, but as they absolutely refused all food, it was decided to kill them rather than have them starve to death. This was done, but when the bodies were opened no trace of any bezoar could be found, and Jager conjectures that the substance of these concretions had been absorbed into the system of the animal for lack of any other nourishment.[12]

In his memoirs, Jehangir Shah relates that an Afghan once brought from the Carnetic two goats said to have bezoar stones [pâzahar] in their bodies. Jehangir was much surprised to note that these animals were fat and healthy

[11] Andreæ Baccii, "De gemmis et lapidibus pretiosis," Francofurti, 1603, p. 193; Latin version by Wolfgang Gabelchover of the original Italian.

[12] Kaempferi, "Amœnitatum exoticarum fasciculi V," Lemgoviæ, 1712, pp. 400, 401.

looking, as he had always been told that those having bezoars were invariably thin and wretched in appearance. However, the Afghan was shown to be correct in his conjecture, for when one of the goats was killed and the body opened four fine bezoars were brought to light.[13]

About the beginning of the eighteenth century, Charles Jacques Poncet, a French physician, was called to the court of the Abyssinian monarch of that time. One of the favorite remedies of this Frenchman was a kind of artificial bezoar, which he claims to have used with great success in cases of intermittent fever. This so-called bezoar he administered to the sovereign and to two of his children, and he also revealed to the Abyssinian king the secret of its composition. He tells us that this "Emperor of Ethiopia," as he terms him, showed great interest in medical science, and listened eagerly to explanations of the character and operation of the various remedies.[14]

The Indians of Peru had their own theory as to the genesis of the bezoar-stone. In relation to this Joseph de Acosta writes:[15]

> The Indians relate from the traditions and teachings of their ancestors, that in the province of Xaura, and in other provinces of Peru there are various poisonous herbs and animals which empoison the waters and pastures where they [the vicuñas, etc.] drink and eat. Of these poisonous herbs, one is right well known by a natural instinct to the vicuña and to the other animals which engender the bezoar, and they eat of this herb and thus preserve themselves from the poison of the waters and pastures. The Indians also say that the stone is formed in the stomachs of these animals from this herb, whence comes the virtue it possesses as an antidote for poisons, as well as its other marvellous properties.

---

[13] The Tûzuk-i-Jahangîrî or memoirs of Jehangir trans. by Alexander Rogers, London, 1909, p. 240; Orient. Trans. Fund, N. S., vol. xix.

[14] "Voyage d'Ethiopie"; in Lettres édifiantes et curieuses, IV Recueil, Paris, 1713, p. 103.

[15] De Acosta, "Histoire Naturelle et Morale des Indes," tr. by Cauxois, Paris, 1600, f. 206 r. and v.

Of the mineral bezoar, which was also regarded as an antidote against poisons, Mohammed ben Mançur relates that various ornamental figures were formed from it, such as small images of the Shah or little female figures; these were perhaps regarded as talismans. Knife-handles were also made of this material,[16] and here the use may have been connected with the belief in the curative power of the bezoar, if brought into direct contact with the skin, as would be the case when the knife-handle was grasped in the hand.

A mineral bezoar bearing a close likeness to the animal concretion was found in Sicily. This stone was usually round, sometimes oblong like an egg, and sometimes compressed; its usual size was about that of a pigeon's egg, the largest stone not surpassing the size of a hen's egg. It was commonly white, occasionally of a somewhat ashy hue, and the surface was generally smooth, though now and then it was rough with small protuberances. Its taste resembled that of the white *bolus armenus*. The composition of this stone was similar to that of the Oriental bezoar of animal origin, having the same layers, and in the centre a small mass of sand over which nature had imposed from eight to ten layers, just as in the animal bezoar.[17]

A peculiar bezoar is reported from Indrapura, India. This was said to have been found in the skull of a rhinoceros, and was of light weight and of a black hue, varying to pale red when held against the light; it was hard enough to cut glass. The owner believed it to be a panacea for all ills. For blood-spitting it was held in the mouth; for rheumatism, bruises, or burns, it was rubbed over the affected part; and for the bites of venomous creatures it was simply laid

[16] Von Hammer, "Auszüge aus dem persischen Werke, Buch der Edelsteine, von Mohammed ben Manssur," in Fundgruben des Orients, vol. vi, p. 134; Wien, 1818.

[17] Boccone, "Recherches et observations naturelles," Amsterdam, 1674, pp. 238, 239.

upon the wound; even those at the point of death were revived by it.[18]

An amulet set with a bezoar stone is said to have possessed such a power to prevent bleeding that when a Malacca prince was killed in a battle with his rebellious subjects, no blood was flowing from any of his numerous wounds. On stripping the body a golden armlet set with a bezoar came to view, and the moment this was removed blood began to flow freely from the wounds.[18a]

Mercato writes of a marvellous Occidental bezoar, sent from Peru to Rome in 1534, as a gift to Pope Gregory XIII. It weighed no less than fifty-six ounces, although it was defective, since a large portion of the exterior crust was missing, the second layer was partly broken away, and even the third layer was damaged in some places. This wonderful concretion had been dedicated to one of the Peruvian gods, as a rare and precious object, and it was taken away by the Spaniards when they spoiled the temple. Mercato says that this bezoar was "of a truly monstrous size, unheard of in all previous centuries, and it is still the largest in the whole realm of nature."[19]

The bezoars of the New World seem to have differed considerably from those of India. They had a rough surface, were usually of a gray color, of various sizes and forms, and composed of a number of superimposed, coalescing layers, much thicker than those of the Oriental, or Indian, bezoar. They were usually of considerable size, either hollow within or containing seeds, needles and similar substances. They came from the West Indies, especially from Peru, and were brought thence by the Spaniards and Portu-

---

[18] F. Nix, in Tijdschrift voor Ind. Taal, Land en Volk, vol. v, p. 151.
[18a] Julii Reichelti, "De Amuletis," Argentorati, 1676, p. 75.
[19] Mercati, "Metallotheca Vaticana," Romæ, 1719, p. 175.

guese. The greater number were found in a kind of chamois; however, we are told that the bezoar was not found in all these animals, "but only in the old ones."[20]

A letter written in the sixteenth century by one who had travelled extensively in India and in Peru, illustrates the ideas of that time regarding both Oriental and Occidental bezoars:

> A gentleman living about twenty-eight years in these Countries, writes to his Friend, that he saw those Animals out of which comes the Bezoar, and saith, they are very like *Goats,* only they have no Horns; and are so swift, that they are forc'd to shoot them with guns. He tells us, that he and some Friends, on the 10th of *June* 1568, hunted some of these Creatures, and in five Days kill'd many of them; and that in one of the oldest of them, they made diligent Search for the stone, but found it not, neither in the Ventricle, nor in any other Part of the Animal. They ask'd the Indians that attended upon them, where the Stones lay; they denied they knew anything of them, being very envious and unwilling to disclose such a Secret. At length (he saith) a Boy about twelve years old perceiving us to be very inquisitive, and to be very desirous of Satisfaction in that Particular, shew'd us a certain Receptacle and (as it were) a *Purse,* into which they receive their eaten herbs, which afterwards when churned, they convey into the Ventricle.[21]

The same circumstances were observed by this informant in regard to the Peruvian bezoars, and from the "pouch" of one of these animals were taken no less than nine stones, "which, by the help of nature, seemed to be made of the Juice of those salutiferous Herbs, which were crammed up into this little Pouch."[22]

While the Occidental bezoar from South America enjoyed a special repute in Europe in the sixteenth and seventeenth centuries, when bezoars were so freely used as poison-

[20] Valentini, "Museum museorum, oder Vollständige Schau-Bühne," Frankfurt am Main, 1714, bk. iii, cap. 13, §§ 1, 2, p. 446.

[21] Pancirollus, "The History of Many Memorable Things," London, 1715, p. 288.

[22] Ibid., loc. cit.

antidotes, and for the cure of fevers and other diseases, it has been doubted whether the aborigines of South America ever valued them in any way before the time of the Spanish Conquest. What seems, however, to be a proof that they sometimes did so, is afforded by the discovery of a bezoar, probably taken from the body of a llama, in a tomb at Cojitambo, in the Cañari region of Ecuador. In spite of the contrary opinion expressed by Garcilasso de la Vega, there is reason to believe that such animal concretions were used by these Indians in magic practices. The Quichua name is *illa,* and Holquin in his Quichua dictionary says that the natives believed that bezoars were luck-bringing stones. Another name, *quicu,* is vouched for by Arriaga, who states that the Spaniards found some bezoars stained with the blood of sacrificial victims, thus showing that they were thought to possess a certain religious or mystic significance. Another author, Don Vasco de Contreros y Vievedo, writing in 1650, states that the most highly valued of these concretions among the natives of South America were those taken from the American tapir, which they called *danta.*[23]

The comparative value of Oriental and Occidental bezoars was still an open question toward the end of the sixteenth century. In a letter written by Sir George Carew to Sir Robert Cecil, on October 10, 1594, the former states that he had submitted a bezoar from the West Indies to a London jeweler named Josepho, who had told him that had the substance come from the East Indies he would value it as high as £100, but that never having made trial of West Indian bezoars, he would not venture on an estimate, although he did not doubt but that they were quite as good.

[23] R. Verneau and P. Rivet, "Ethnologie ancienne de l'Equateur," Paris, 1912; vol. vi of Mission du service géologique de l'armée pour la mesure d'un arc de méridien équatorial en Amérique du Sud, 1899–1906, pp. 235, 236; figure (nat. size) on p. 235.

Nevertheless he would not care to buy this one before having tested its virtues experimentally.[24]

That good Queen Bess shared the beliefs of her age as to the virtues of stones is well known, and she appears to have regarded her bezoars as worthy of a place among the treasures of the Crown, for in the inventory of the jewels made at the accession of James I we read:

> Also one greate Bezar stone, sett in goulde that was Queene Elizabeth's, with some Unicorne's Horne, in a paper; and one other large Bezar stone, broken in peeces, delivered to our owne handes, by the Lord Brooke, the two and twentith day of Januarie, one thousand sixe hundred and twenty and two.[25]

After the death of Rudolph II, in 1612, the Venetian envoy, Girolamo Soranzo, wrote to the Doge, "No other monarch has ever accumulated so many jewels." He also communicates the fact that some at least of these gems were to follow him to the grave, for when interred, his head was covered with a cap adorned with many valuable precious stones. However, Rudolph's fondness for the more splendid gems and jewels was accompanied by a very particular taste for the collection of Oriental bezoars, of which a large number are noted as in his possession at the time of his death. These ranged in weight from 1 loth (½ oz. Troy) to 25½ loth (a little more than one pound Troy); most of them were provided with a rich gold setting, and one especially prized bezoar, weighing about 8 ounces, reposed in a silver box decorated with 32 diamonds and 26 rubies. Another of very singular shape, resembling "four toes," is also entered on the list. Besides these the imperial collection included several other curious animal concretions, probably

---

[24] Historical Manuscripts Commission, MSS. of the Marquis of Salisbury, Pt. V, London, 1894, p. 3.

[25] Archæologia, vol. xxi, p. 153, London, 1837. From Warrant of Indemnity given by King James I to the guardians of the crown jewels.

regarded as having therapeutic virtues, such, for instance, as a "stone" from the body of a doe; this had been found by a certain Helmhardt Jörger and by him presented to the emperor; another of these treasured concretions came from the stomach of a stag. A specimen of the famed "eagle-stone" is also listed; this had a double gold setting, and on it were inscribed the words "Piedra Geodas," showing that the real character of this stone as a geode was then well understood.[26]

Some of the gold-mounted bezoars of Rudolph II are still to be seen in the Hofmuseum, at Vienna. One is surrounded by a gold band with a scroll pattern; another has a capping of gold and stands upon a golden base, and still another, capped and belted with gold, is attached by a chain to a golden bowl. This was probably to be used as a test of the freedom from poison of any beverage in the vessel. A bezoar of the eighteenth century is mounted upon a tree of gold, against the trunk of which a wild boar is leaning. This may be only a decorative adjunct, or it might be an indication of the particular animal source of this special bezoar.[27]

The bezoars of Borneo are taken either from monkeys or porcupines. For medicinal use, the gratings are dissolved in water and the solution is administered as required. Skeats relates that he was once asked $200 by a native for a small stone, erroneously asserted to be a bezoar. This stone was carefully wrapped up in cotton and preserved in a tin box with some grains of rice, the owner firmly believing that the stone fed on the rice. A red monkey (semnopithecus) furnishes many of these bezoars, but those from the porcupine are supposed to be so much the more efficacious that the Sultan of Saik claims all bezoars of this kind found in

[26] Jahrbuch der kunsthistorischen Sammlungen des allerhöchsten Kaiserhauses, vol. xx, Pt. II, pp. lxv, xcvii, Wien, 1899.

[27] Figured in Jeweler's Circular Weekly, Dec. 17, 1913, p. 53; Charles A. Brassler, "Gold Mounted Specimens of Bezoar."

BEZOARS OF EMPEROR RUDOLPH II, NOW IN THE HOFMUSEUM, VIENNA

his dominions as his personal property; nevertheless, many are said to be surreptitiously taken out of the country by Malayan or Chinese traders. A remarkably fine specimen in the possession of the Sultan is valued at $900; small ones may be worth no more than $40, but the value increases very rapidly with the size of the concretion. Though it is confidently believed that the bezoars work wonderful cures in diseases of the bowels and of the respiratory organs, the natives value them chiefly as aphrodisiacs, this action being secured either by wearing them or by taking them in solution.[28]

The Chinese work entitled P'ing-chou-k'o-t'an, by Chu Yü, written in the first quarter of the twelfth century, mentions the *mo-so* stone (the bezoar) and states that it was worn in finger rings. Should anyone have reason to suppose that he had taken poison, all he had to do in order to escape any bad effects was to lick the bezoar-stone set in his ring. The Chinese writer adds that it might thus be justly called "a life preserver."[29]

The Dayaks of Borneo have a method for producing bezoars which they call *guligas*. This is to shoot an animal with an unpoisoned arrow. When the wound heals, there is often a hardening of the skin, which finally results in the formation of a *guliga*. In some of these concretions the point of the arrow still remains. The *guligas* of natural formation are frequently found between the flesh and the skin of apes and porcupines.[30]

In the eighteenth century Valmont de Bomare reports that the bezoars of the hedgehog commanded the highest

---

[28] Skeat, "Malay Magic," London, 1900, pp. 274 sqq.

[29] Chau Ju-Kua, "Chu-fan-chi" ("A Description of Barbarous Peoples"), trans. by Friedrich Hirth and W. W. Rockhill, St. Petersburg, 1911, p. 16, and p. 90, note 7.

[30] Von Dewall, "Aanteekeningen omtrent de Noordoostkust van Borneo;" Tijdschrift voor Ind. Taal. Land en Volk, vol. iv, p. 436.

price. These were greasy and soapy, both to the eye and to the touch, and of a greenish or yellowish color; a few were reddish or blackish. They were so highly valued in Holland that a Jew in Amsterdam asked 6000 livres ($1200) for a specimen in his possession as large as a pigeon's egg; and such bezoars were even rented in Holland and Portugal, at the rate of one ducat ($2.50) a day, to those who were exposed to contagion, and believed that the bezoars, if worn as amulets, would protect them from the danger.[31]

In a letter to the Macon, Georgia, *Journal and Messenger* of August, 1854, Major J. D. Wilkes, of Dooley County, relates that while hunting he shot down a fine buck. He states that on cutting up the animal he found a stone of a dark greenish color, about where the windpipe joins the lights. It was from an inch and a half to two inches long, and quite heavy for its size, although it appeared to be porous. Major Wilkes says that he had heard of similar stones from old hunters, and had been told that they possessed the power of extracting poison, but that they were rarely found. The communication proceeds to relate a case where this stone was successfully applied to a dog which had been bitten by a rattlesnake. · We have here one of the few notices extant regarding an American bezoar stone.[32]

An American bezoar taken from the stomach of a deer killed in the Chilhowee Mountains, in Tennessee, was reported in 1866 by Prof. David Christy. In extracting this concretion the hunter had damaged the outer layer, but when this was removed there remained a perfectly smooth, round body, about the size and shape of a hen's egg, and of a light brown color. When Professor Christy obtained it,

[31] Valmont de Bomare, "Dictionnaire raisonné universel," Paris, 1775, p. 556.

[32] Edwards, "History and Poetry of Finger Rings," New York, 1855, pp. 110, 111.

this bezoar had already acquired the reputation of possessing great though somewhat undefined virtues; he presented it to Professor Wood of the Ohio Medical College in Cincinnati.[33]

Writing of bezoars in the year 1876, Dr. Learned states that Signor Korkos, of Morocco, showed him one for which he had paid twelve dollars. It was as large as a small walnut, the surface being smooth and cream-colored; a section revealed the presence of the concentric circular layers characterizing the formation of this concretion. For remedial use it was rubbed on a stone until a sufficient quantity of its powder was obtained, which was then diluted in liquid and administered as a potion. Strict dieting and absolute rest in the house for seven days were an essential part of the treatment, the bezoar powder being more especially recommended in diseases of the heart, liver or other internal organs, but for sore eyes and for rheumatism its virtues were praised. This illustrates a modern employment of the concretion in Mohammedan Morocco.[34]

Some medical authorities of the sixteenth century were disposed to regard the calculus produced by the human subject as superior in medicinal efficacy to the far-famed bezoar. One of their arguments was that as man was the highest type of organized being a human product must exceed in value one from an animal source; then again, his food was of the best, superior in quality to that taken by the animals furnishing the bezoars. For every theory a proof can be found if one is on the lookout for it, and therefore we need not be surprised if the virtues of calculi or gravel were also supported by evidence. In 1624 or 1625 the Dutch city of Leyden was visited by the plague, and to the great regret of the physicians there was no supply of bezoars on hand. Here-

[33] "Scientific American," vol. xv, No. 19, p. 299; November 3, 1866.
[34] Dr. Learned, "Morocco and the Moors," 1876, p. 281.

upon they were driven to make use of human gravel, and found to their astonishment that this was an even more excellent sudorific than the bezoar itself.[35]

Although there is no direct relation between bezoars and the hair-balls sometimes found in the stomach or intestines

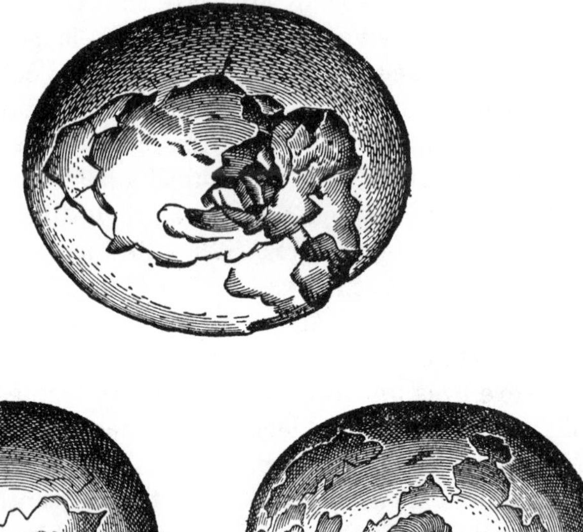

Calculi taken from the bladder of Pope Pius V. From Mercati's "Metallotheca Vaticana," Romæ, 1719.

of human beings, there is some slight analogy, as the animal bezoar concretions seem to have been formed about a nucleus consisting of some indigestible material that has been swallowed by an animal. From the report of hospital surgeons, it appears that these hair-balls, which result from a long-

[35] S. de Vries, "Curieuse Aenmerkingen der byzonderste Oost en West-Indische Verwonderens-waerdige Dingen," Utrecht, 1682, Pt. II, pp. 912, 913.

continued habit of swallowing hair, are almost exclusively found in the bodies of women, generally of very young girls. The large size which they sometimes attain is very surprising; in several instances they have so filled up the stomach that they are moulded by it into its exact shape. Although when a hair-ball has reached this size, and indeed long before, the most alarming symptoms set in, frequently recurrent vomiting being the most characteristic, we cannot but wonder how it is possible for *any* food to enter and pass through the stomach under such conditions, the only explanation being the great power of dilation this organ possesses. Its disposition to patiently tolerate foreign bodies where it cannot expel them, renders it often a poor guide in a diagnosis based upon the patient's personal experience. These hair-balls accumulate and lodge not only in the stomach but also in the intestines, and in either case the eventual result is almost certain to be fatal unless the obstacle is removed by operation. Very occasionally only does nature react sufficiently to expel the impediment without surgical aid. Of course all treatment is vain unless the morbid habit of hair-swallowing can be overcome. This does not seem to be an accompaniment of a distinctly diseased mental condition, although that is sometimes coincident, but must assuredly result from some derangement or abnormality of the nervous centres, inducing a morbid and unnatural craving.[36]

The serpent-stone, called by Pliny *ovum anguinum,* or "serpent's egg," is said to have been worn by the Druid priests as a badge of distinction. Pliny relates that he had seen one of them which was as large as a moderate-sized apple, its shell being a cartilaginous substance. It was sup-

[36] See Ledra Hazlit, M.D., "Hair-balls of the Stomach and Intestines," Jour. A. M. A., vol. lxii, No. 2, pp. 107–110, with illustration; and G. A. Moore, "Hair Cast of the Stomach with Respect of a Case," Boston Medical and Surgical Journal, Jan. 1, 1914.

posed to be generated in midsummer out of the saliva and slime exuding from a knot of interwined serpents. When

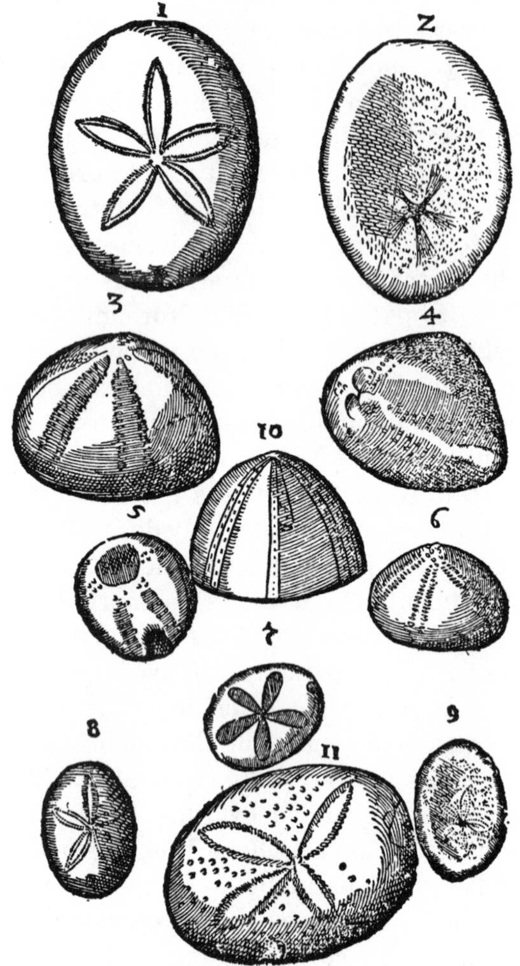

Types of the Ovum Anguinum. Echinites (sea-urchins). From Aldrovandi's "Museum metallicum," Bononiæ, 1648.

the moisture had coagulated and formed into a sphere, this was tossed in the air by the hissing snakes, and, in order to preserve its efficacy as a talisman, the finder had to catch it in a linen cloth before it fell to the ground. Such "serpent's eggs" were in high favor with the Romans, who believed they procured for the wearers success in all disputes and the protection of kings. So great was the faith reposed in their magical virtues that Claudius is said to have condemned to death a Roman knight, one of the Vecontii, simply because he had an *ovum anguinum* concealed in his bosom when he appeared in court during the trial of a lawsuit in which he was involved. In order to enhance the value of this amulet, the story was circulated that great dangers were incurred in securing it; for the snakes pursued any one who seized the egg and he could only escape by fording a river, across which they could not swim.[37] In later accounts of this amulet it is described as a ring, sometimes composed of a blue stone with an undulating streak or stripe of yellow, thought to represent a snake.

Certain so-called floating-stones have been found in a branch of Mann Creek, a tributary of the Weiser River, which flows into the latter near its confluence with the Snake River in Idaho.[38] These are hollow quartz globes, with a shell so thin that the air in the cavity more than makes up for the specific gravity of the quartz. Some formation similar to this may possibly have been intended by Pliny in his description of the *ovum anguinum* or serpent's egg of the Druids, which floated if thrown into a stream, although it is perhaps more probable that these "serpent's eggs" were shells of the sea-urchin, as they are figured by De Boot and other writers.

The snake-stone, legends regarding which are met with in so many different parts of the world, is known to the Lapps of northern Europe, and strange to say, some of the

---

[37] Plinii, "Naturalis Historia," lib. xxix, cap. 12.
[38] Kunz, Dept. of Mining Statistics.

elements of Pliny's old recital touching the "serpent's egg" come out in the account given of it by this primitive race, in general so far removed from any notion of classical tradition. Anyone in search of this stone must resort, according to the Lapps, to the pairing place of snakes, for here they throw the stone, which is small and white, back and forth to one another; he must steal along quietly until he is quite near to the snakes and then snatch the stone as it flies through the air, and run away with it as fast as he can to the nearest piece of water. Should he reach the water before the snake does—for the reptile pursues him—he gains the ownership of the stone; if, however, the snake first reaches the water, this is very dangerous for the man. Hence he should carefully search out the nearest water before snatching the stone, and as the snake will not immediately know what has become of it, and will hunt for it awhile before starting in pursuit of the thief, the latter will have time to come first to the water.[39]

Tertullian writes that the wearing of stones taken from the head of a dragon or of a serpent was especially reprehensible in the case of a Christian; for how could a Christian be said to "bruise the head" of the Old Serpent (Gen. iii, 15) while wearing such a stone about his neck or on his head, and thus testifying to a kind of serpent worship?[40]

The Greek poem "Lithica," belonging to the fourth century B.C., also celebrates the virtues of a "snake-stone," which is to be pressed closely on the bitten spot; but besides this application, the drinking of undiluted wine in which the stone *ostrites* had been pulverized, is recommended. This shows that the therapeutic value of alcohol as a stimulant to

---

[39] Johann Turi, "Muittalus samid birra; en bog om Lappernas liv."; text, and Danish trans. by Emilie Demnant, Kjøbenhavn, 1911, p. 184 (p. 62 of text).

[40] Tertulliani, "Opera Omnia," Parisiis, 1879, vol. i, col. 1425, De cultu feminarum.

revive the nerve-centres, paralyzed by the animal poison, was recognized at this time. An unusually precise description is given of the *ostrites;* it was round, hard, black and rough, and was marked by many wavy lines or veins. Some one of the many varieties of banded agate seems to answer best to this description.[41]

The legend that St. Patrick drove out all snakes from Ireland sometimes took the form that the saint had transformed them into stones. This belief is noted by Andrew Borde, physician and ecclesiastic, who, writing in 1542, mentions some strange stones he had been shown on that island:

> I have sene stones the whiche have had the forme and shape of a snake and other venimous wormes. And the people of the countrie sayth that such stones were wormes, and they were turned into stones by the power of God and the prayers of saynt Patrick. And English merchauntes of England do fetch of the erth of Irlonde to caste in their garden's, to keepe out and to kyll venimous wormes.[42]

The legendary serpent-stone is usually one taken from the reptile's head, but Welsh tradition tells of one extracted from the tail of a serpent by the hero Peredur, and having the magic property that anyone holding it in one hand would grasp a handful of gold in the other. This stone was generously bestowed upon Etlym by the finder, who only secured it after vanquishing the serpent in a dangerous conflict.[43]

The snake-stone (or "mad-stone"), in Arabic *ḥajar al-ḥayyat,* is described by the Arab writer Kazwini, as being of the size of a small nut. It was found in the heads of certain snakes. To cure the bite of a venomous creature the

---

[41] "Lithica," lines 336 sqq.

[42] The fyrste boke of the introduction of Knowledge made by Andrew Borde of Psysycke Doctore. Ed. by Furnival, London, 1870, p. 121. Early English Text Soc., Extra Series No. X.

[43] Wirt Sikes, "British Goblins: Welsh Folk-lore, Fairy Myths, Legends and Traditions," London, 1880, p. 366.

injured part was to be immersed in sour milk, or in hot water, and when the stone was thrown into the liquid it would immediately attract itself to the bitten part and draw out the poison.[44] The homeopathic idea plays a considerable rôle in the superstitions of the Arabs of northern Africa. To cure the bite or sting of the scorpion, the creature is to be crushed over the wound it has inflicted. If anyone is bitten by a dog, he should cut off some of the animal's hair and lay this on the bitten part; if, however, the dog was mad, it must be killed, its body opened and the heart removed. This is then to be broiled and eaten by the person who has been bitten.[45]

Many beautiful glass beads of Roman, or perhaps of British fabrication, have been found in Great Britain and Ireland. Upon some of these are bosses composed of white spirals, the body of the bead being blue, red, yellow, or some other brilliant color. These have been called "holy snake beads." Probably most of them are merely ornamental productions and were not intended to represent serpent-stones. The curious test of the genuineness of an *ovum anguinum* mentioned by Pliny, namely, that even if set in gold, it would float up a stream against the current, indicates a very porous structure; perhaps some of these serpent's eggs were hollow, vitrified clay balls with wavy lines on the surface.

De Boot, in his treatise on stones and gems,[46] figures the *ovum anguinum*, and says that its form was either hemispherical or lenticular. In his opinion the name "serpent's egg" was given to the stone because on its surface

---

[44] Julius Ruska, "Das Steinbuch aus der Kosmographie des Muḥammad ibn Mahmud al-Kazwînî," Beilage to the Jahresberichte of the Oberrealschule, Heidelberg, 1895–96, p. 15.

[45] Edmond Doutté, "Magie et Religion," Alger, 1909, p. 145; quoting Largeau, "La Sahara algérienne," p. 80.

[46] Gemmarum et lapidum historia," Lug. Bat., 1636, pp. 347–349.

there appeared five ridges, starting from the base and tapering off toward the top. These bore a certain resemblance to a serpent's or adder's tail. The stone was believed to protect the wearer from pestilential vapors and from poisons.

The so-called "snake-stones," many specimens of which have been found in British barrows, bear in the Scottish Lowlands the designation "Adder Stanes." They are also sometimes called adder-beads or serpent-stones. For the Welsh they were *gleini na droedh* and for the Irish *glaine nan druidhe,* the meaning being the same, "Druid's glass." Many interesting examples were added to the collection of the Museum of Scotch Antiquaries, one of these being of red glass, spotted with white; another of blue glass, streaked with yellow; other types were of pale green and blue glass, some of these being ribbed while others again were of smooth and plain surface. That the glass "snake-stones" were objects of considerable care and attention is indicated by the mending of a broken specimen shown by Lord Landesborough at a meeting of the Society of Antiquaries in 1850. This broken bead had been repaired and strengthened by the application of a bronze hoop.[47]

The supposed snake-stones are also to be found among the Cornishmen, who sometimes call these objects *milprey* or "thousand worms," and they even lay claim to the power of forcing a snake to fabricate the "stone" by thrusting a hazel-wand into the spirals of a sleeping reptile. In another version it is not a bead that is formed but a ring which grows around a hazel-wand when a snake breathes on it. If water in which this ring has been dipped be given to a human being or an animal that nas been bitten by a venomous creature,

[47] Daniel Wilson, "The Archæology and Prehistoric Annals of Scotland," Edinburgh, 1851, pp. 303, 304. Two specimens figured on p. 304.

all ill-effects of the bite will be warded off, the water acting as a powerful antidote to the poison.[48]

The belief that the snake-stone of Welsh legend—in reality either a fossil or a bead—was evolved from the venom or saliva ejected by a concourse of hissing snakes, gave rise to a peculiar popular saying among the Welsh to the effect that people who are whispering together mysteriously, and apparently gossiping, or perhaps hatching some mischief, are "blowing the gem."[49]

Many of the glass beads known as "snake-stones" or "Druid's glass" are perforated, and this is fancifully explained as being the work of one of the group of snakes which forms the bead. This particular snake thrusts its tail through the viscous mass before it has become hardened into a glass sphere. In various parts of Scotland such beads are treasured up by the peasants; according to the testimony of an English visitor of 1699, who reports that they were hung on children's necks as protection from whooping-cough and other children's diseases, and were also valued as talismans productive of good fortune and protective against the onslaught of malevolent spirits. To guard one of these precious beads from the depredations of the dreaded fairies the peasant would keep it enclosed in an iron box, this metal being much feared by the fairies.[50]

A type of snake-stone used in Asia Minor is described as being of a pearly white hue, rounded on one side and flat on the other. Toward the edge of the flat side runs a fine, wavy, bluish line, the undulations of which are fancied to figure a serpent. The victim of a snake-bite first had the spot rubbed with some kind of sirup; then the stone was

---

[48] John Brand, "Observations on the Popular Antiquities of Great Britain," London, 1849, vol. iii, p. 371.

[49] Wirt Sikes, "British Goblins: Welsh Folk-Lore, Fairy Myths, Legends and Traditions," London, 1880, p. 360.

[50] J. G. Frazer, "Balder the Beautiful," London, 1913, vol. i, p. 16.

applied to the bitten spot, and it would adhere to the inflamed surface for eight days; at the expiration of this time it would fall off. The bite would be entirely healed and would not be followed by ill effects of any kind.[51]

A novel theory in regard to the formation of a type of snake-stones is given by an old Chinese writer. This is that snakes, before they begin to hibernate, swallow some yellow earth and retain this in the gullet until they come forth again in the springtime, when they cast it forth. By this time the earth has acquired the consistency of a stone, the surface remaining yellow, while the interior is black. If picked up during the second phase of the moon this concretion was thought to be a cure for children's convulsions, and for gravel, and was powdered and given in infusion. The infusion could also be applied with advantage externally to envenomed swellings.[52]

An old manuscript found in a manor house in Essex, England, contains a translation, made in 1732 by an Oxford student, E. Swinton, of some details on the snake-stone, taken from a work published in the same year at Bologna by Nicolo Campitelli. After noting that these stones came from the province of Kwang-shi in China and from different places in India, their appearance and qualities are described. In color they were almost black, some having pale gray or ash-color spots. The test of the genuineness of such a stone was to apply it to the lips; if not a spurious one, it would cling so closely to the membrane that considerable force must be exerted to separate it therefrom. The usual directions are given for its employment in the cure of snake bites, but its usefulness by no means ended here; its curative power was also exhibited in the case of "Scrophulous Erup-

[51] Arakel, "Livre d'histoire," chap. liii; in Collection d'historiens armeniens, French transl. by M. Brosset, St. Petersburg, 1874, vol. i, p. 545.

[52] F. de Mély, "Les lapidaires de l'antiquité et du moyen âge," vol. i, "Les lapidaires chinois," Paris, 1896, pp. 237–238.

tions and Pestilential Bubos,'' and it could be used in the treatment of malignant tremors, venereal disorders, etc. With the manuscript was found a specimen snake-stone. This was described as being a thin oval body, about an inch in length and three-quarters of an inch broad; the color was gray with light streaks, and the surface was bright and polished. It was of the consistency of horn, and the writer of the note in the ''Lancet'' believes that it was part of a stag's antler or some similar substance, from which the animal matter had been removed by the action of heat; many of the Oriental snake-stones are of this type, but, as we have already seen, a great variety of more or less porous materials have been and are still used in this way in different parts of the world. A practical experiment was made in 1867 by Dr. John Schrott, who excited six cobras to bite a number of pariah dogs. Without delay the snake-stones were applied to the wounds, but they proved absolute failures, death resulting as speedily as though nothing had been done.[53]

Jean Baptiste Tavernier, the great Oriental traveller of the seventeenth century, gives the following description of the ''snake-stones'' found in India:[54]

Finally, I will mention the snake-stone, which is about the size of a doubloon, some approximating to an oval form, being thicker in the middle and tapering toward the edges. The Indians say that it forms on the head of certain snakes, but I rather believe that the priests of these idolators make them think this, and that this stone is a composition of certain drugs. However this may be, it has great virtue to draw out all the poison, when anyone has been bitten by a venomous creature. If the part that has been bitten has not been punctured, an incision must be made, so that the blood can flow out, and when the stone has been applied, it does not fall off until it has absorbed all the poison which gathers about it. To clean it, woman's milk is used, or should this be lacking, cow's milk, and after ten or twelve

[53] "Account of the Snake Stone," in Lancet, vol. 177, London, July–Dec. 1909, p. 1478.

[54] "Les six voyages de Jean Baptiste Tavernier," Pt. II, Paris, 1678, pp. 410, 411; Bk. II, ch. xxiv.

hours steeping, the milk which has drawn out all the poison takes on the color of pus. Having dined one day with the Archbishop of Goa, he took me into his museum, where he had several curious objects. Among other things he showed me one of these stones, and having told me of its properties, he assured me that but three days before he had seen them tested, and presented the stone to me. As he was traversing a marsh on the Island of Salsate, whereon Goa is situated, to go to a country house, one of those who bore his palanquin, and who was almost entirely naked, was bitten by a snake and was immediately cured by this stone. I have bought several of them, and they are sold only by the brahmins, which makes me think the brahmins themselves make the stones. There are two methods of testing whether the stone is good or the product of some deception. The first of these tests is to place it in one's mouth, for then, if it be good, it springs up and cleaves to the palate; the second test is to place it in a glass full of water; if it is not sophisticated, the water begins to seethe, small bubbles rising from the stone at the bottom to the surface of the water.

Thevenot, a French traveller who visited India in 1666, about the time Tavernier was there, asserts that the famous "Stones of the Cobra" were manufactured in the town of Diu, in Guzerat, and that they were made "of the ashes of burnt roots, mingled with a kind of Earth they have, and were again burnt with that Earth, which afterwards is made up into a Paste, of which these Stones are formed." After describing the process employed for cleaning the stones after they had been used, Thevenot adds that if not freed from the absorbed venom the stones would burst.[55]

Dr. J. Davy examined and analyzed some of these "stones," and found one of them to be a piece of bone partially calcined. When applied to the tongue or to any other moist surface it adhered firmly. Another, which lacked all absorbent or adhesive power, was said to have saved the life of four men. It therefore appears that while some of the "snake-stones" really possessed some possible curative virtues, others were esteemed only because of a superstitious

[55] "The Travels of M. de Thevenot into the Levant," London, 1686, Pt. III, p. 32; Bk. I, chap. 18.

belief in their magical properties. Kaempfer, writing in 1712, informs us that these stones should always be used in pairs, and applied successively to the wound.[56] The belief in the efficacy of such stones is still general in India, and one of the varieties is supposed to be found in the head of the adjutant bird.[57]

Francisco Redi[58] describes the extraordinary healing power attributed to stones obtained from the heads of certain serpents, called by the Portuguese "*cobras de capello,*" found throughout Hindostan and Farther India. These stones are claimed to be an infallible remedy for the bites and stings of all kinds of venomous reptiles or animals, and likewise for wounds made by poisoned arrows, etc. He repeats the usual tales of their adhering powerfully when applied to the bite or wound, and clinging to it like a cupping-glass until they had absorbed all the poison, when they would fall off spontaneously, leaving the man or animal sound and free. Then follows the account of steeping the stones in milk to remove the poison, the milk assuming a color between yellow and green. These wonderful stones and the narrations concerning them had been brought to Italy by Catholic missionaries, who seemed to have entire faith in their powers; so that Redi says they offered to prove the accounts by any number of experiments, such as would satisfy the most incredulous, and prove to medical men that Galen was correct when he wrote (Chapter XIV, Book I) that certain medicines attract poison as the magnet does iron. For this purpose a search for vipers, etc., was recommended; but, owing to the season being later and colder than usual, none could at that time be obtained, as they had

[56] Davy, "An Analysis of the Snake-stone," Asiatic Researches, vol. xiii, p. 318; Kaempfer, "Amoen. Exit.," pp. 395–397; cited in Yule-Burnell, "A Glossary of Anglo-Indian Colloquial Words and Other Phrases," London, 1886, pp. 643, 644.

[57] "Jungle Life in India," p. 83.

[58] Redi, "Experimenta," Amstelodami, 1675, pp. 4–8.

FRANCISCI REDI,

Nobilis Aretini,

EXPERIMENTA

circa res diverſas naturales,
ſpeciatim illas,

Quæ ex Indiis adferuntur.

Ex Italico Latinitate donata.

AMSTELODAMI,
Sumptibus ANDREÆ FRISII.
M DC LXXV.

4 FRANCISCI REDI

qui peregrinationibus ſuis mercedem virtutis quærunt & aſportant, & ubi huc pervenerunt, usque adeo benigne excipiuntur, ut fateantur, Florentiæ renatos eſſe antiquos & delicioſiſſimos hortos Phæacios, & in Sereniſſimo Magno Duce Coſmo tertio, aliisque Sereniſſimis Principibus regiam & humaniſſimam affabilitatem Alcinoi.

Ergò tibi dico, quod annò cIɔ Iɔc LXII. ſub finem veris, reduces ex India orientali, in aulam Hetruriæ, tunc Piſis venationibus occupatam, pervenerint tres Patres, venerabilis ordinis S. Franciſci, vulgo *Zoccolanti* dicti, qui ex illis regionibus multas res curioſas adferentes, id honoris obtinuerunt, ut inſpiciendi copiam darent Sereniſſimo Magno Duci Ferdinando II. æternæ & glorioſæ memoriæ, inter alia non ſine pompa oſtentantes nonnullos lapides, quos, perinde ut tu mihi ſcribis, affirmabant reperiri in capite

Experimenta naturalia. 5

pite certorum ſerpentum, à Garzia ab Horto deſcriptorum, & à Luſitanis *Cobras de Cabelo* dictorum, eosque per omnem regionem *Indoſtan*, & vaſtiſſimas duas peninſulas intra & extra Gangem, ſed ſpecialiter in regno *Quamſy*, ceu probatæ fidei experimentum, ſecuriſſimi antidoti loco inſervire, ſi imponantur morſui viperarum, aſpidum, ceraſtum, & quorumcunque aliorum animalium, qui morſu vel pungendo inficiunt: nec non ſi imponantur quibuscunque vulneribus, à ſagittis, vel alio aliquo armorum veneno infectorum genere recens inflictis. Præterea dicebant, talem & tantam, & usque adeo miraculoſam eſſe ſympathiam horum lapidum cum veneno, ut ſtatim vulneri appropinquantes, parvarum ventoſarum inſtar ſe eidem tenaciſſime applicarent, nec ante loco moverentur, quam omne venenum ſugendo imbibiſſent, quo facto ſua ſponte ſoluti in terram caderent,

A 3 re-

Frontispiece and title-page of Francesco Redi's "Experimenta naturalia," Amsterdam, 1675, and two specimen pages of this treatise, referring to the snake stones believed to be taken from the Indian *Cobras de Capello*, or hooded snakes.

FORMS OF TABASHEER
Bought at Fair at Calcutta, 1888, by Dr. Valentine Ball.

not emerged from their winter quarters. An experiment was therefore substituted, after much consultation among the learned men of the Academy of Pisa, whereby oil of tobacco was introduced into the leg of a rooster. This was regarded as one of the most fatal of such substances, and was administered by impregnating a thread with it to the width of four fingers and drawing it through the punctured wound. One of the monks forthwith applied the stone, which behaved in the regular manner described. The bird did not recover, but it survived eight hours, to the admiration of the monks and other spectators of the experiment.

Redi states that he himself possessed some of these stones, as did also Vincent Sandrinus, one of the most learned herbalists of Pisa. Redi describes them as "always lenticular in form, varying somewhat in size, but in general about as large as a farthing, more or less. In color some are black, others white, others black, with an ashy hue on one side or both," etc.

Up to the present time no one has apparently identified what Tavernier referred to in speaking of snake-stones. It, however, occurred to the writer, after receiving a quantity of tabasheer from Dr. F. H. Mallet of the Geological Survey of India, who obtained it at the bazaar of the Calcutta Fair in November of 1888, that many, if not most of the Hindu snake-stones must have been tabasheer. Tabasheer is a variety of opal that is found in the joints of certain species of bamboo in Hindostan, Burmah, and South America; it is originally a juice, which by evaporation changes into a mucilaginous state, then becomes a solid substance. It ranges from translucent to opaque in color, and is either white or bluish-white by reflected light, and pale yellow or slight sherry red by transmitted light. Upon fracture it breaks into irregular pieces like starch. As in Tavernier's account of its clinging to the palate and causing water to boil when immersed, it actually has the property of strongly adhering to the tongue, and when put into water emits rapid streams of minute bubbles of air. It has a strong siliceous odor, but after absorbing an equal bulk of water becomes transparent like a Colorado hydrophane described by the writer several years ago before the New York Academy of Sciences.

Although tabasheer is mentioned in nearly all the text-books, very little of it has reached the United States. It is highly interesting, since we have here an organic product scarcely to be distinguished from a similar opal-like body found by Mr. Arnold Hague in the geysers of the Yellowstone Park. Both tabasheer and the hydrophane were probably what was called "Oculus Beli," "Oculus Mundi," and "Lapis mutabilis" by Thomas Nicol, Robert Boyle, and other writers of the seventeenth century, and "Weltauge" by the Germans.

The great capacity of this substance for absorbing a fluid would undoubtedly render it as efficacious for the purpose of absorbing poison as any other known stone, providing the wound were open enough; and its internal use to-day as a medicine is possibly also due to this property.

Tabasheer, as known among mineralogists, is a corruption of the word tabixir, a name which was used even in the time of Avicenna, the Grand Vizier and body surgeon of the Sultan of Persia in the tenth century. It played a very important part in medicine during the Middle Ages. As to its origin, Sir David Brewster [59] says that tabasheer is only formed in diseased or injured bamboo joints or stalks.

Guibourt [60] differs from Brewster, inasmuch as he attributes the different rates of growth to the fact that when

---

[59] Edinburgh Philos. Journal, No. 1, p. 147; Philos. Trans., cix, p. 283; and "The Natural History and Properties of Tabersheer," 1828; Edinburgh Journal, viii, p. 288.

[60] Jour. de Pharmacies, xxvii, pp. 81, 161, 252; and Phil. Mag., x, p. 229.

SPECIMENS OF TABASHEER

At the upper right-hand corner is figured a hydrophane, or "Magic Stone," at the upper left-hand corner is a floating stone from Oregon. The tabasheer was bought at the Fair held in Calcutta in 1888.

there is a superabundance of sap the tabasheer is formed from the residuum. More recently, Henry Cecil[61] says, "In the onrush of tropical growth in the young shoot, nature, after flooring the knot, has poured in, as it were, sap and silica sufficient for a normal length and width of stem to the knot next above it. But by some check to the impulse, or by irregularity of conditions, the portion of stem thus provided for is shorter or narrower than intended, and the unused silica is left behind as a sediment, compacted by the drying residuum sap."

This latter view is sustained by Dr. Ernst Huth, who discusses the name, history, origin, and reputed virtues of this substance with much fulness.[62] In regard to its use in medicine during the Middle Ages, he quotes a remarkable list of applications to the ills that flesh is heir to.

Here it is cited as a remedy for affections of the eyes, the chest, and of the stomach, for coughs, fevers, and biliary complaints, and especially for melancholia arising from solitude, dread of the past, and fears for the future. Other writers speak of its use in bilious fevers and dysentery, internal and external heat, and injuries and maladies.

The writer has examined a large number of so-called madstones, and they have all proved to be an aluminous shale or other absorptive substance. But tabasheer possesses absorptive properties to a greater degree than any other of the mineral substances examined, and it is strange that it has never been mentioned as being used as an antidote. It may be confidently recommended to the credence of any person who may desire to believe in a madstone.

The writer believes that Tavernier's snake-stones may all have been tabasheer, or again, while some of them were of this substance, others may have been artificially compounded

[61] Nature, xxxv, p. 437.

[62] "Der Tabixir in seiner Bedeutung für die Botanik, Mineralogie, und Physik"; X. Sammlung. Naturwissenschaftlicher Vorträge, Berlin, 1887.

by the authorized dealers of the Brahmin caste. The instance he gives of the successful use of such a stone is not altogether incredible, as, should one of the less active poisons be sucked out of a wound shortly after this were inflicted, a cure might well be effected. In view of the great difference

> There is another Stone, which is call'd the Serpent's-Stone with the hood. This is a kind of Serpent that has a kind of a hood hanging down behind the head, as it is repreſented in the Figure. And it is behind this hood that the Stone is found, many times as big as a Pullet's-egg. There are ſome Serpents both in *Aſia* and *America* of a monſtrous bigneſs, 25 foot long; as was that, the skin whereof is kept in *Batavla*, which had ſwallow'd a Maid of 18 years of age. Theſe Stones are not found in any of thoſe Serpents that are not at leaſt two foot long. This Stone being rubb'd againſt another Stone, yields a certain ſlime, which being drank in water by the perſon that has the poiſon in his body, powerfully drives it out. Theſe Serpents are no-where to be found but upon the Coaſts of *Melinde*; but for the Stones you may buy them of the *Portugueze* Mariners and Souldiers that come from *Mozambique*.

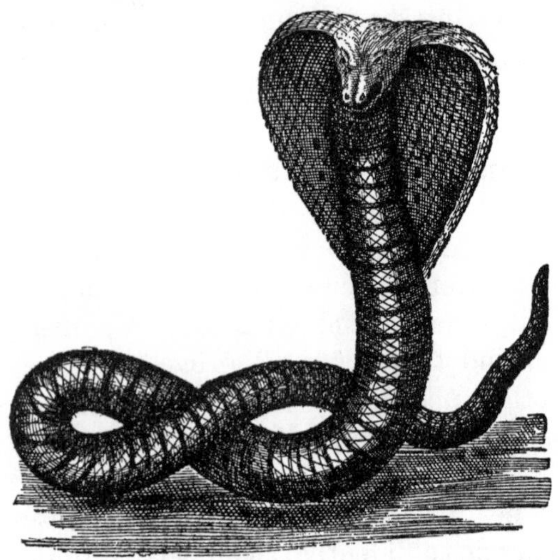

Cobra de Capello. From Tavernier's Travels, English translation by John Philips, London, 1684.

in the virulence of poisons and the varying degrees of the sensibility to toxic effects, it is not strange that the snake-stones should sometimes seem to give good results. Tavernier states that these stones were brought to India by Portuguese sol-

[63] Tavernier, "Voyages en Turquie, en Perse, et aux Indes," Paris, 1718, vol. ii, p. 392; liv. ii, chap. 24.

diers returning from service in Mozambique.[63] For successful use a pair of them were needed, so that, when applied to a snake-bite, as soon as one became saturated with the venom the other could be immediately substituted. To have them always at hand, those natives fortunate enough to own a pair of *pedras de cobra* carried them about in a little bag.[64]

A curious traditional belief is current in some parts of India, notably in Ceylon, to the effect that the male cobra, during the night, uses a certain luminous stone to lure its prey and to attract the female. This is probably the chlorophane, a variety of fluorite, a substance which shines with a phosphorescent light in the darkness, and this quality, quite mysterious in the eyes of the natives, may have induced them to associate the stone with the snake, the epitome of all subtlety and cunning. Serpent-stones were supposed to exist in both ancient and medieval times, and the belief in their existence is widespread among many races of mankind.

A chlorophane is also found in the microlite localities of Amelia Court House, Virginia. The writer made a series of experiments and noted that some of these specimens emit a phosphorescent light at a low temperature. The material occurs in Siberia, and Pallas describes a specimen from this locality. When subjected to the heat of the hand, it gave out a white light, in boiling water a green light, and when placed on a burning coal a brilliant emerald-green light, visible at a considerable distance. Similar phenomena have been observed by the writer, who has found that very slight attrition, even the rubbing of one specimen against another in the dark, will produce phosphorescence.[65]

The real or supposed virtues of the "snake-stones" of Ceylon are detailed at considerable length by the great

---

[64] Engelberti Kaempferi, "Amœnitatum exoticarum fasciculi V," Lemgoviæ, 1712, pp. 395, 396.

[65] Kunz, "Gems and Precious Stones of North America," 2d ed., New York, 1892, p. 183.

Dutch naturalist, Rumphius. After noting the old tale that the "natural" snake-stones came from the *cobra de capello* (*Serpens pilosus*), he proceeds to relate the information he had been able to gather regarding the "spurious" stones of this type. These were fabricated by the Brahmins, the process being kept a profound secret; indeed, there were those who asserted that the Brahmins themselves had lost the art, as this had been possessed by but a single family which had died out, leaving the secret unrevealed. Rumphius describes these artificial stones as usually round and flat, the size varying from that of a half-shilling piece to that of a two-shilling piece. Some were of lenticular form and a few were oblong; all had a white spot in the middle. In making the application, the bitten spot was first pricked until it bled, whereupon the stone was immediately laid on and allowed to remain until it dropped off of itself "just as a leech would do." So intense was its absorbent activity that it would sometimes break, in which case a substitute had to be quickly applied. The saturated stone was placed in milk and the absorbed venom was thus drawn out, turning the milk blue.[66]

One of the tales of the Gesta Romanorum treats of a serpent-stone of singular medicinal virtue. According to the story—which is, of course, a mere legend—a certain Theodosius, who "reigned in a Roman city," was a most prudent ruler, but was afflicted with blindness. In his care for the welfare of his subjects he had decreed that when anyone who desired justice rang the bell at the palace gate, a judge must forthwith appear and try his case. Now it happened that a serpent had its nest near the bell-rope, and one day, while the reptile was absent, a toad took possession of the nest. Returning and finding the nest occupied,

[66] Rumphius, "D'Amboinsche Rariteitkamer," Amsterdam, 1741, pp. 303–305.

the serpent,—evidently a worthy descendant of the original serpent of Paradise, "more subtle than any beast of the field,"—wound its tail about the bell-rope and pulled the bell. When the judge appeared, as in duty bound, he was struck by this strange spectacle, and reported it to the emperor, who told him to right the wrong which had been done, directing him to expel and kill the toad. Not long after, the serpent made its way into the palace and entered the emperor's room, bearing in its mouth a small stone. Proceeding to the emperor's couch, it crawled up, raised its head above the emperor's face and dropped the stone upon his eyes. As soon as the stone touched the eyes, the emperor's sight was restored. The serpent disappeared and was never seen again.[67]

A representative type of "madstone" is a concretionary calculus occasionally, but very rarely, found in the gullet of male deer. In form it bears a resemblance to a water-worn pebble and is usually of oblong shape, the largest specimens being 3 inches in length and 1½ inches in width. The chemical analysis of Dr. H. C. White showed that the chief component was tricalcic phosphate. His experiments demonstrated that while such a concretion would absorb water to the amount of 5 per cent. of its own weight, the quantity of blood or other fluid it was able to absorb only amounted to 2.3 per cent. of its weight. When immersed in water, after having been placed on a wound caused by the bite of a venomous creature, the liquid absorbed was given out so as to discolor the water, and the material exuded was found to be of toxic quality. However, experiments with animals that had been bitten by snakes or other reptiles, failed to show that the stone exercised any curative effect. Dr. White states that he has in his possession a "mad-

[67] "Die Gesta Romanorum," ed. Wilhelm Dick, Erlangen, 1890, p. 127.

stone'' dating from 1654, but this is of a different type, being a porous sandstone.[68]

Even in South Africa snake-stones are known, but it appears that the few specimens reported had been brought thither from the Dutch East Indies; one such stone had been handed down for generations in a Dutch settler's family. From their appearance some of these snake-stones were judged to be pieces of burnt hartshorn. A Boer farmer owned an amulet of this kind that he would loan from time to time to neighbors who might have need of it. On one occasion, when the daughter of an English hunter had been bitten by a snake, the father sent off a man on horseback to borrow this snake-stone. Owing to the unavoidable delay, some hours elapsed before it could be applied to the wound. The girl recovered after its use but the wound did not heal satisfactorily, and this was attributed to the length of time that had intervened between the attack of the snake and the use of the remedial stone.[69]

In December, 1887,[70] the writer described a white opaque variety of hydrophane with a white, chalky or glazed coating, which had recently been brought from a Colorado locality. The absorbent quality of this stone is quite remarkable, and when water is allowed to drop on it, it first becomes very white and chalky, and then gradually perfectly transparent. This property is developed so strikingly that the finder proposed the name "Magic Stone" for the mineral and suggested its use in rings, lockets, charms, etc., to conceal photographs, hair, and other objects, which the wearer wishes to reveal only as caprice dictates.

---

[68] Dr. H. C. White, "The Chemical and Physical Characters of the So-called 'Mad-Stones,'" British Association for the Advancement of Science, 73d Report, Meeting of 1903 at Smithfield, London, 1904, p. 605.

[69] "Lancet," vol. 164, Jan.–June, 1903, p. 343.

[70] American Journal of Science, vol. xxxiv, Dec., 1887. See also Kunz, "Gems and Precious Stones of North America," New York, 1892, p. 144.

VI

Angels and Ministers of Grace

THE veneration of angels and the attribution to them of especial days or months, as well as the idea that they were guardians of those born on those days or during those months, was the result of many factors. The belief in the existence of angels is present in all parts of the Bible, but in the earlier portions they are not individualized in any way. The angel of God, or of the Lord (*malach Elohim* or *malach Yahveh*) was simply a messenger of God, employed to communicate his will or else to accomplish some act of divine justice.

It is quite possible that the greater prominence given to angels among the Jews after the Babylonian Captivity was not solely dependent upon Babylonian or Persian influence. We learn from the historical and prophetical books of the Old Testament that the Jews had, from the earliest times, worshipped other gods besides the God of Israel, and were ever ready to assimilate the religious superstitions of the heathen world. Several of the divinities that were worshipped in Babylonia and Assyria were also objects of adoration in Israel, not indeed by the chosen spirits of the nation from whom we receive our records, but by the masses of the people. This very fact, however, served in a certain sense to maintain the purity of the national religion. As the superstitious inclinations of the populace were so fully satisfied from without, there was no necessity to develop or distort the national religion in this direction. The Babylonian Captivity changed all this. It was the élite of the

Jewish nation that was deported, and the sufferings and humiliations to which they were subjected in a foreign land only served to strengthen their faith in Yahveh and in his Law. Hence it is, that when this tried and purified remnant returned to Judæa, rebuilt the fallen temple and reorganized the state, the latter became a theocracy in a much stricter sense than ever before, and from this time we can really speak of Judaism as the religion of the whole people.

But the inevitable tendency to split up the unity of the divine force, a tendency that makes itself felt in all religions and among all peoples, soon asserted itself anew and in a different direction. As the people were no longer allowed, we may even say were no longer inclined, to go after foreign gods, they proceeded to develop the idea of divine messengers or intermediaries which had always formed part of the national faith, but had never been fully evolved. While Isaiah and Ezekiel both knew of a division of the angels into certain categories as, for example, cherubim, seraphim, hayyot (living creatures), ofanim (wheels) and arelim, there is no attempt at individualization, and the first mention of an angel's name occurs in the Book of Daniel, which later critics are disposed to assign to the second century B.C. It is most natural to suppose that such names were known and were familiar to the people long before that time. When we read in the Book of Daniel, xii, 1: "And at that time shall Michael stand up, the great prince which standeth for the children of Israel," it is easy to see that the idea that certain special qualities were attributed to this angel was deeply rooted in the popular mind. In a previous verse, x, 13, we read: "Michael, one of the chief princes, came to help me,"—a conclusive proof that a hierarchy of angels had already been thought out.

The great source of information in regard to angelology is the Rabbinical literature which had its rise about the first century B.C. and culminated in the Talmuds of Babylon and Jerusalem in the fifth century A.D. As these compilations, although nominally commentaries on the books of the Old Testament, are almost encyclopedic in their character, they throw much light on this subject. In a monograph of Kohut, entitled "Jüdische Angelologie,"[1] many extracts, belonging to an early period, are given. Seven princes of heaven were recognized and among these four were especially favored. They occupied a place near to the Throne of Light and were bathed in its radiance. We are told that "God surrounded his Throne of Light with four angels: Michael, 'Who is like God?' at the right; Gabriel, 'Might of God,' at the left; Uriel, 'Splendor of God,' before it; and Raphael, 'Salvation of God,' at the west" (Numeri Rabba, c. 2).[2] They represented various attributes of the divine: Michael, goodness and mercy; Gabriel, punitive justice; Uriel, the majesty of God, and Raphael, his providence. Michael and Gabriel are particularly prominent and are called Royal Angels (מבביהון דמלאכיא); they have especial care of Israel. As we have seen, Michael was singled out by Daniel and he was commonly regarded as chief prince. Gabriel was looked upon as the avenger and the executor of divine judgments and occupied the next place, while Uriel and Raphael are less frequently alluded to, although the latter appears prominently in the Book of Tobit.

In the New Testament, also, Michael and Gabriel are evidently regarded as the chief angels, and Revelation places Michael at the head of the hosts of the good angels in their conflict with Satan and his followers. We can see in the Gospels how widespread was the belief in demoniacal possession, and in the existence of evil spirits; it was almost inevitable that the aid of good spirits should be invoked to

[1] Leipsic, 1866.
[2] Kohut, loc. cit., p. 25.

:t them, and although both Christianity and Judaism sternly rebuked any direct worship of angels, they were regarded as ministering spirits, and it was only natural that the masses should be led to use their names on amulets and talismans, and little by little to arrive at the belief that a particular angel was entrusted with the welfare of each individual. The same tendencies were at work in both religions, but a new development was initiated for the Christian church by the growing veneration of the early martyrs and of their relics. When this became more pronounced, the saints to a great extent took the place of the angels; a passage from the writings of St. Ambrose composed in 377 A.D. shows us that this transformation of belief had already begun to make itself felt at that time. St. Ambrose writes: "We should address our supplications to the angels who are appointed to guard us; we should also address them to the martyrs, whose patronage seems assured to us by a physical pledge" (their relics).

The danger that the worshipping of angels might lead Christians away from the Church into magic practices and beliefs was clearly recognized in the early centuries, and at the Council of Laodicea, in 363 A.D., it was proclaimed that Christians should not render worship to angels outside the church, or in private assemblies or associations. Whoever was found guilty of such practices (of such idolatry, as it was called) was pronounced anathema, as he was considered to have turned away from the Lord Jesus Christ and worshipped idols. The first Council of Rome, held in 492 A.D., expressly forbids the wearing of talismans inscribed with the names "not of angels as they pretend, but rather with those of demons." Indeed, there is abundant evidence that in this age, and even earlier, those addicted to angelolatry were not satisfied with the few angels named in the Holy Scriptures, but addressed their petitions to a multitude of angels evolved from the fervid imagination of the superstitious among the Jews. Of these angels not recognized by the Church, the following prayer of a certain Aldebert, condemned by the second Council of Rome, 745 A.D., gives us a few names: "I pray and supplicate the angel Uriel, angel Raguel, angel Michael, angel Adimis, angel Tubuas, angel Sabaoth and angel Simihel." In the judgment of the Church fathers, all these names, with the exception of Michael, designated demons.[3]

A manuscript of the ninth or tenth century in the Library of Cologne gives the following "nomina angelorum," and instructs the reader as to their special virtues:

> If when it thunders you think of the Archangel Gabriel, no harm will befall you. If on awakening you think of Michael you will have a happy day. Have Orihel (Uriel) in mind against your adversary and you will prevail. When eating and drinking think of Raphael and abundance will be yours. On a journey think of Raguhel and everything will prosper. Should you have to lay your case before a judge, think of Barachahel and all will be explained. When you take part in a banquet, think of Pantasaron and all the guests will delight in you.[4]

On some medieval gems appear angel figures, one very curious specimen of this class being an onyx, engraved in intaglio. On this gem, which is in the British Museum, the engraver depicts the Annunciation, but the figure of the Angel Gabriel is precisely that of a nude Cupid; hand and foot are raised as though the little god (or angel) were dancing. It has been conjectured that this strange attempt at adapting a classic form is due to the fact that the gem was cut in Constantinople during one of the violent iconoclastic persecutions, and that the engraver thus sought to veil the true significance of his work. In this case, however,

---

[3] Dictionnaire d'Archéologie Chrétienne, ed. by Dom Fernand Cabrol and Dom H. Leclercq, vol. i, Pt. II, Paris, 1907, col. 2088.

[4] Ibid., col. 2089.

we must believe that the accompanying inscription was added at a later date, for it expressly names the Annunciation, the Angel Gabriel, and the Virgin ("Mother of God").[5]

Another interesting gem, from about the same period, is a square amethyst, measuring about 3 cm. in each direction. This bears, engraved in intaglio, a standing figure of Christ, without a halo; behind his head is the monogram ☧, and in his left hand he holds a scroll with the words (in Greek): "In the beginning was the Word"; his right hand is stretched forth in benediction, and alongside the figure are the following angels' names in Greek characters: Raphaêl, Penel, Ouriêl, Ichthys, Michaêl, Gabriêl, Azaêl, The fourth and middle name, Ichthys (fish) is the well-known anagram of the Greek words signifying "Jesus Christ, the Son of God, the Saviour," and the use of this as the name of an angel is thought to have been suggested by a passage in Isaiah (ix, 6).[6]

A "prime émeraude" among the Gorlæus gems is engraved with a design showing two souls brought before God by the two guardian angels.[7] Somewhat the same belief in the guiding or conducting of souls after death is found in Plato's "Phædon," where it is said that the *daimon* which had guided a person during life led his spirit to the place in Hades where judgment was to be rendered.

The following list from Lodge's "Wit's Miserie," printed in 1596, gives the seven good angels and sets over against them the seven bad angels, each of whom represents one of the seven deadly sins:

---

[5] Dictionnaire d'Archéologie Chrétienne, ed. by Dom Fernand Cabrol and Dom H. Leclercq, vol. i, Pt. II, Paris, 1907, cols. 2089, 2090.

[6] Dictionnaire d'Archéologie Chrétienne, ed. by Dom Fernand Cabrol and Dom H. Leclercq, vol. i, Pt. II, Paris, 1907, cols. 2088, 2089.

[7] Macarius (L'Heureux), "Abraxus seu Apistopistus," Antwerp, 1657, Plate XIX, No. 78 (Gorlæus, 1695, Pl. CCXVIII, No. 430).

Good Angels	Bad Angels
Michael	Leviathan, pride
Gabriel	Mammon, avarice
Raphael	Asmodeus, lechery
Uriel	Beelzebub, envy
Euchudiel	Baalberith, ire
Barchiel	Belphagor, gluttony
Salathiel	Ashtaroth, sloth

The curious book called in Hebrew "Sepher de-Adam Ḳadmah" and attributed to the angel Raziel, is supposed to belong to the twelfth or the thirteenth century, or at the earliest to the eleventh century,[8] although the redactor may have used some earlier materials. Legend states that it was engraved upon a sapphire and was given by the angel Raziel to Adam when the latter was driven from Paradise. Handed down from generation to generation, it finally came into the possession of Solomon. The name Raziel signifies "secret of God," in allusion to the revelations contained in the book, which was supposed to protect the house wherein it was from all danger of fire.

In this book there is an interesting list of angels, denominated the twelve princes, set over the twelve months of the year. The text of the first printed edition appears to be corrupt in some places, but the names may be transliterated as follows:[9]

Sh'efiel, "Balm of God".......Presiding over Nisan (April)
Ragael, "Balance of God"......Presiding over Ayyar (May)
Didanor, "Our Light".........Presiding over Sivan (June)
Ta'anbanu, "Answer for us"...Presiding over Tammuz (July)
Tohargar, "Whirlwind"........Presiding over Ab (August)

[8] Zunz, "Die gottesdienstliche Vorträge der Juden," Berlin, 1832, p. 167. Zunz conjectures that Eleazar of Worms (1176–1238) may have written a portion of this work.

[9] "Sepher de-Adam Kadmah," Amsterdam, 1701, fol. 34 verso. The interpretations of the several names are from Schwab's "Vocabulaire de l'angélologie," Paris, 1897, except in the case of Ragael, where Schwab gives "angel of the moment."

Morael, "Fear of God"........Presiding over Elul (September)
Hahedan, "The Brilliant"......Presiding over Tishri (October)
Uleranen, "To chant, celebrate".Presiding over Marchesvan (November)
Anatganor, "Thou art the Guardian" ....Presiding over Kislev (December)
Mephniel, "Before God".......Presiding over Tebah (January)
Tashnadernis, "Saturnus" .....Presiding over Shebat (February)
Abarchiel, "Fire of God"......Presiding over Adar (March)

The following list, while probably of later date than the one we have just given, is more frequently cited as authoritative: [10]

Orders	Angels	Tribes	Signs
Seraphim	Malchidiel	Dan	Aries
Cherubim	Asmodel	Reuben	Taurus
Thrones	Ambriel	Judah	Gemini
Dominations	Muriel	Manasseh	Cancer
Powers	Verchiel	Asher	Leo
Virtues	Hamaliel	Simeon	Virgo
Principalities	Zuriel	Issachar	Libra
Archangels	Barbiel	Benjamin	Scorpio
Angels	Adnachiel	Naphtali	Sagittarius
Innocents	Hanael	Gad	Capricornus
Martyrs	Gabriel	Zabulun	Aquarius
Confessors	Borichiel	Ephraim	Pisces

In Rabbinical writings we are told that if a man fulfilled one of the commandments, one angel was bestowed upon him; if he fulfilled two commandments, he received two angels; if, however, he fulfilled all the commandments, many angels were given him. This was a literal construction of the text Ps. xci, 11: "For he shall give his *angels* charge over thee." These angels were believed to shield the believer from the attacks of evil spirits.[11]

The Mohammedan Atlas, the angel appointed by God to bear the earth on his shoulders, was given a rock of ruby to

[10] Barrett, "The Magus," London, 1801, p. 138.
[11] Weber, "Jüdische Theologie," 2d ed., Leipzig, 1897.

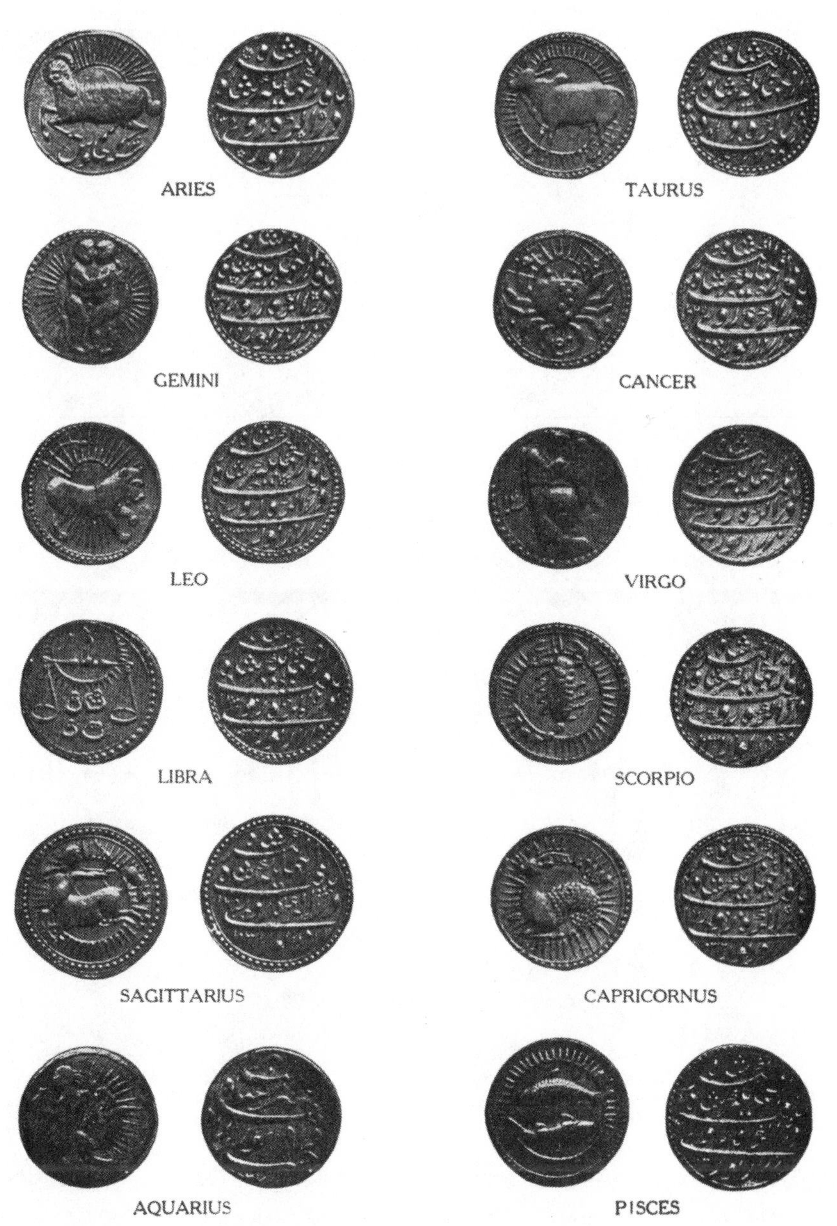

By courtesy of the American Numismatic Society, New York.

ZODIAC MOHURS, COINED BY THE MOGUL SOVEREIGN SHAH JEHAN, ABOUT 1628.

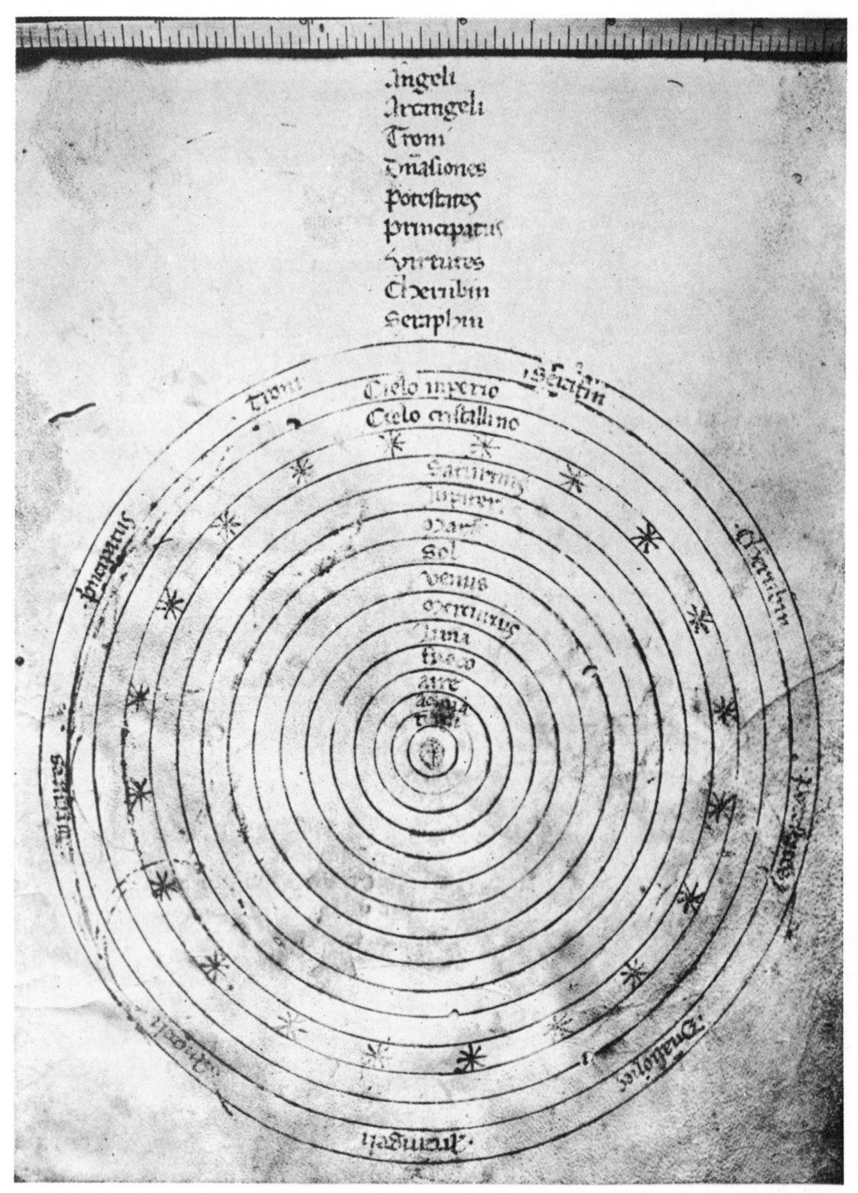

The medieval conception of the cosmos, the successive spheres of the planets, including the sun, and beyond these the crystalline heaven and the empyrean. In an outermost circle are named the great celestial powers, as recapitulated above the spheres. From a XIV century Italian MS. in the author's library.

stand upon. Beneath this ruby-rock, were, successively a huge bull, an immense fish, a mass of water, and lastly darkness.[12] Thus the grand vision of "the face of the deep" over which hovered the Spirit of God, before the creative words were spoken, giving form to the earth, is not altogether lost sight of in this Mohammedan fancy.

Luther was a firm believer in the existence of guardian angels, and he even goes so far as to assert that the angels assigned to men differed in rank and ability as did the men themselves. Of this he says:

> Just as among men, one is large and another small, and one is strong and another weak, so one angel is larger, stronger, and wiser than another. Therefore, a prince has a much larger and stronger angel, one who is also shrewder and wiser, than that of a count, and the angel of a count is larger and stronger than that of a common man. The higher the rank and the more important the vocation of a man, the larger and stronger is the angel who guards him and holds the Devil aloof.[13]

Our idea of a guardian angel is so spiritual and so pure that it is difficult for us to understand the curious results this belief has occasionally produced among the primitive peoples. A weird tale is told of a Congo negro who killed his mother so as to gain an especially powerful guardian spirit.[14] The dreadful deed was perpetrated in the full conviction that the mother's love would remain unshaken, while her power for good would be increased. Such ferocious egoism does not find an exact parallel among civilized peoples, but the underlying principle is unfortunately too often illustrated in our midst at the present day.

The belief in guardian angels has the best of Scripture warrant as offered by the text Matthew, chapter xviii, v. 10,

---

[12] Lane, Arabian Society in the Middle Ages," ed. by Stanley Lane-Poole, London, 1883, p. 106.

[13] Schindler, " Der Aberglaube des Mittelalters," Breslau, 1858, p. 4.

[14] Peschel, " Völkerkunde," Leipzig, 1885, p. 272. Quoted from Winwood Reade's " Savage Africa."

where Christ speaking of little children says: "Their angels do always behold the face of my Father who is in Heaven." Another New Testament passage testifying distinctly to the existence of this belief in the Apostolic Age, is in the Acts of the Apostles (xii, 15), where we read that after the miraculous rescue of Peter from his imprisonment, his friends could not believe the report that he had been seen standing at the door of their dwelling, and exclaimed: "It is his angel."

That not only individuals but nations also had special guardian angels was, as we have already noted, a belief held to a certain extent among the Jews after the Babylonian Captivity. To the trace of this in the tenth chapter of Daniel (vs. 13, 21), where Michael stands for Israel, may be added the evidence afforded by the Greek Septuagint version of Deuteronomy xxxii, 8, part of the "Song of Moses." Here the Revised version based on our Hebrew text reads:

> He set the bounds of the peoples,
> According to the number of the children of Israel.

The Septuagint translators, however, must have had a slightly different text before them for they render the last words: "According to the number of God's angels." It therefore seems probable that they read in Hebrew *benê Elohim* instead of *benê Yisrael.* Of the *benê Elohim* or "Sons of God" we read in Genesis, chapter vi, verse 2, that they wedded with the "Daughters of Men." This has been given a poetic form by Thomas Moore in his "Loves of the Angels." The Book of Job also, in its Prologue in Heaven (i, 6–12), introduces the "Sons of God" among whom appeared Satan, the "Adversary." Of angel names, as has been noted, there is Biblical warrant only for Gabriel, Michael, and Raphael, the last-mentioned, in the Apocryphal Book of

Tobit; to these IV Esdras (not a canonical book) adds Jeremiel and Uriel, names not admitted by the Church.

There has been preserved for us a most interesting calendar for the city of Rome, written by Furius Dionysius Filocalus in 354 A.D., and containing a series of drawings by his hand showing the symbolical figures of the months of the year. Though the original manuscript is lost, several apparently faithful copies exist, one of which is in the Imperial Library in Vienna. Much of this work deals with matters referring to the Roman calendar, but perhaps its most valuable part is a list of the early Christian saints and martyrs. As this is the earliest list of the kind, of even earlier date than the rest of the work, we give it here unabridged, as a most interesting documentary proof of the veneration in which the saints were held in the fourth, or, we should probably say, in the third century.

ITEM DEPOSITIO MARTIRUM [15]

VIII kal. Jan. natus Christum in Betleem Judeæ.
mense Januario.
XIII kal. Feb. Fabiani in Callisti
et Sebastiani in Catacumbas.
XII kal. Feb. Agnetis in Nomentana.
mense Februario.
VIII kal. Martias natale Petri de cathedra.
mense Martio.
non. Martias. Perpetuæ et Felicitatis, Africæ.
mense Maio.
XIIII kal. Jun. Partheni et Caloceri in Callisti,
Diocletiano VIIII et Maximiano VIII
[304].
mense Junio.
III kal. Jul. Petri in Catacumbas
et Pauli Ostense, Tusco et Basso cons.
[258].
mense Julio.

[15] Achelis, "Die Martyrologien," p. 8.

VI idus Felicis et Filippi in Priscillæ
et in Jordanorum, Martialis Vitalis Alexandri
et in Maximi Silani. hunc Silanum martirem
Nouati furati sunt.
et in Praetextatæ, Januari.
III kal. Aug. Abdos et Semnes in Pontiani, quod est
ad ursum piliatum.
mense Augusto.
VIII idus Aug. Xysti in Callisti
et in Praetextati Agapiti et Felicissimi.
VI idus Aug. Secundi Carpofori Victorini, et Seueriani
Albano.
et Ostense VII ballisteria Cyriaci
Largi Crescentiani Memmiæ Julianetis
et Ixmaracdi.
IIII idus Aug. Laurenti in Tiburtina.
idus Aug. Ypoliti in Tiburtina.
et Pontiani in Callisti.
XI kal. Septemb. Timotei, Ostense
V kal. Sept. Hermetis in Basillæ Salaria uetere.
mense Septembre.
non. Sept. Aconti, in Porto, et Nonni et Herculani
et Taurini.
V idus Sept. Gorgoni in Lauicana.
III idus Sept. Proti et Jacinti, in Basillæ.
XVIII kal. Octob. Cypriani, Africæ. Romæ celebratur
in Callisti.
X kal. Octob. Basillæ, Salaria uetere, Diocletiano
IX et Maximiano VIII consul. (304)
mense Octobre.
pri. idus Octob. Callisti in via Aurelia. miliario III.
mense Nouembre.
V idus Nou. Clementis Semproniani Claui Nicostrati
in comitatum.
III kal. Dec. Saturnini in Trasonis.
mense Decembre.
idus Decem. Ariston in pontum.

This list, which begins with the great Christian festival of Christmas, enumerates the days on which Roman martyrs died and were buried. The months are given in their order and below their names appears a very brief record, giving the day and place of burial and the name of each of the martyrs. The first entry, for instance, reads: "January 20, interment of Fabianus in the cemetery of Callistus." The earliest martyrs mentioned are SS. Perpetua and Felicitas who died in 202 A.D.; thus all definite memory of the many martyrs of the first and second centuries seems to have been lost. Even heretics do not appear to have been excluded, for as it is stated that the Novatians carried away the body of Silanus, it seems more than probable that he himself belonged to this heretical sect. As martyrs, all are regarded as equally entitled to the highest veneration, regardless of what they may have passed through on earth. Other communities than the Roman one possessed similar lists, as is clearly indicated by the words of Cyprian, in his thirty-ninth epistle, where he says: "As you remember, we offered the sacrifice for them, just as we celebrated a commemoration of the sufferings of the martyrs and of their anniversary days."

To many of the saints curative powers are attributed, and these powers are usually specialized so that each of these saints is invoked for aid against a different disease or defect. With very few exceptions it will be found that some circumstance in the history or legend of the saint is the origin of these beliefs. An exception may perhaps be made in the case of the two saints to whom recourse is most frequent at the present day, namely, St. Anthony of Padua (June 13) and St. Anne, the mother of the Virgin Mary (July 26). Relics of the latter saint, preserved in many parts of Europe and also in America, are regarded as endowed with wonderful therapeutic powers. Recently, in New York City, at the church of St. Jean Baptiste, a relic of St. Anne was shown to many thousands of the faithful, and some wonderful cures are said to have been accomplished by its aid. Sceptics will be inclined to attribute such cures to the influence of suggestion, while Catholics will see in them a proof of the power of the saint's intercession on behalf of those who repose their trust in her. St. Anthony is usually appealed to for success in difficult enterprises, and more particularly for the discovery of lost articles. Here the belief in the successful intervention of the respective saints is more generalized and appears to have grown up independently of any event chronicled in the legends, but these instances are quite exceptional.

An exceedingly beautiful jewelled medallion said to have been given by Pope Paul V, in 1614, to the Archbishop of Lisbon, Don Miguel de Castro, shows in the centre the figures of the Virgin and Child, surrounded by a setting of old Indian, table-cut diamonds. The archbishop donated this to the Church of St. Antonia da Se, sometimes called the "Royal House of St. Antonio," for this church was built on the site of the house in which dwelt the parents of St. Anthony, Don Martin de Bulhoes and Dona Teresa de Azavedo, and in which the saint was born on February 6, 1195. At his baptism he was given the name Fernando, but later he changed this to Antonio. The great Lisbon earthquake of 1755 completely wrecked this church, but the high altar wherein the medallion had been placed escaped comparatively unharmed, and the jewel was found by some peasants, who later sold it to the family of Machados e Silvas, in whose private chapel it reposed until within a few years.

The shrine of St. Anne de Beaupré may be seen in the Basilica of Beaupré, about 20 miles distant from Quebec. It stands on the site of a small wooden sanctuary erected about the middle of the seventeenth century by some Breton mariners who, when in imminent danger of shipwreck while navigating the St. Lawrence, made a vow to build a chapel to

THE ANGEL RAPHAEL REFUSING THE GIFTS OFFERED BY TOBIT
By Giovanni Biliverti. Pitti Palace, Florence.

JEWELLED MEDALLION SAID TO HAVE BEEN DONATED BY POPE PAUL V TO THE CHURCH IN LISBON BUILT ON THE SITE OF THE HOUSE WHERE ST. ANTHONY OF PADUA WAS BORN, FEBRUARY 6, 1195.

St. Anne, the dearly-loved patron saint of their native province, at the spot where they should first come to land. St. Anne was regarded in French Canada as the patroness of seafarers and hence a large number of those who frequented her shrine were seafaring people. However, even more were attracted by the report of the marvellous cures of all kinds of diseases which were said to have taken place there. Pilgrimages to this shrine continue to be made at the present time; indeed, the number of those who thus testify to their belief in the power of the saint has increased rapidly during the past thirty years. In 1880 the pilgrims numbered 36,000; in 1900 the record showed 135,000, and in 1910 the number had increased to 188,266, a proof that the devotees are more and more convinced that St. Anne's relics are the sources of great healing virtue.

All of the numerous relics of St. Anne exhibited in Canada and elsewhere are said to have come originally from the town of Apt in France, where, according to Catholic tradition, her body was found by the Emperor Charlemagne in 792, and it is related that when the reliquary covering the holy body was opened a fragrance as of balsam emanated from the interior. How the body was transferred to Apt from its resting place in Palestine is a mystery not solved even in tradition, although some believe that it was brought thither by St. Auspicius, known as the Apostle of Apt. The Basilica of Beaupré contains five of these precious relics; one of them was brought to Canada from the Cathedral of Carcasonne, in France, about the year 1662, at the instance of Monseigneur de Laval, first bishop of Quebec, and founder of Laval University. This is the first joint of the middle finger of the saint. The devotees at the shrine first saw this precious gift March 12, 1670; it is adorned with two intersecting rows of pearls, forming a cross. Another relic of peculiar importance is that given in 1892 by the late Cardinal Taschereau. This is a bone from St. Anne's wrist measuring four inches in length. It is enclosed in a reliquary made of massive gold and studded with precious stones, the gifts of those whose prayers to the saint had been answered. In the ornamentation appear eight diamonds, four amethysts, a fire opal, etc. At the bottom of the reliquary there is a gold plate with the inscription: "Ex brachio S. Annae," and a gold ring set with twenty-eight diamonds. This jealously-guarded treasure is exhibited in the shrine but once a year, from July 26 to August 2, a period comprising St. Anne's Day and the week following it; at other times the reliquary is kept in the Sacristy, but may be seen on special request.

A remarkable jewel in the treasury of the Basilica is the seal of Santa Anna, elected president of Mexico in 1832. A golden eagle, with eyes formed of two rubies, stands on a rock of lapis lazuli and bears the stamp of the seal; resting on his spread wings is a sphere of lapis lazuli in which the words "Diaz, Mexico," are inlaid in letters of gold. The seal is engraved with the initials of the president's name, surrounded by a design embodying the insignia of his office.

At the feast of St. Blaise, Bishop of Sebaste, in Armenia (d. circa 316), which occurs on February 3d in the Roman Church, the wick of a candle is sometimes dipped in a vessel containing consecrated oil, the throats of the faithful being then touched with this wick, to preserve them from diseases of the throat. At other times the ceremony is performed in a different way. The priest holds two candles, adjusted so as to form a cross, above the heads of those who come to seek the saint's aid, and the following prayer is recited: "Through the intercession of St. Blaise may God free thee from diseases of the throat, and from every other disease. (Per intercessionem S. Blasii liberet te Deus a malo gutteris et a quovis alio malo.)

It is related that this saint in his travels, once meeting a poor woman whose only child had swallowed a fish-bone, relieved the child of its trouble by offering up a prayer and laying his hand upon its throat. In the prayer he adjures all who may suffer from a like trouble to seek his intercession with God.

St. Apollonia of Alexandria (February 9) is said to cure toothache and all diseases of the teeth, the reason for this being that at her martyrdom all her beautiful teeth were pulled out. In a similar way St. Agatha, of Catania or Palermo, in Sicily, is endowed with the power to cure diseases of the breast, because it is related that before her martyrdom her breasts were cruelly torn and mutilated.

To recite the formula of St. Apollonia was considered by the Spaniards of three centuries ago to be a cure for toothache. This fact is brought out by a passage in Don Quixote, when the knight's housekeeper is urged to recite it for her master's benefit when he is ailing. To this request the woman quickly answers: "That might do something if my master's distemper lay in his teeth, but, alas! it lies in his brain." This formula was probably used before the age of Cervantes, and has persisted to our own time. It is in verse and has been literally translated into English as follows:[16]

> Apollonia was at the gate of Heaven and the Virgin Mary passed that way. "Say, Apollonia, what are you about?" "My Lady, I neither sleep nor watch, I am dying with a pain in my teeth." "By the star of Venus and the setting sun, by the Most Holy Sacrament, which I bore in my womb, may no pain in your tooth, neither front nor back, afflict you from this time henceforward."

Of Santa Lucia (December 13), born in Syracuse on the island of Sicily, a strange legend is told. A young man fell

---

[16] Parmele, "Tothe-Lore," reprint from the International Dental Journal, January, 1899, p. 14.

passionately in love with her, and wrote to her that her wonderful eyes pursued him even in his dreams. Moved by the Scripture text, "If thine eye offend thee, pluck it out," and longing to save the youth from sensual passion, Lucia cut out her beautiful eyes, placed them on a dish, and sent them to her lover with the following message: "Here thou hast what thou so ardently desirest; I beseech thee leave me in peace." Very naturally, this saint is believed to cure all diseases of the eye.

For protection against highway robbers and thieves, St. Nicholas (December 6), Bishop of Myra, in Lycia, was invoked. Legend relates of this saint that he restored to life three boys who had been murdered at an inn by the wicked innkeeper, a wretch who was in the habit of making away with his guests and then utilizing their bodies to enrich his menu. This tale accounts for the fact that, under the familiar name of Santa Claus, St. Nicholas is the patron-saint of children.

St. Barbara (December 4), born in Heliopolis, is appealed to for protection against lightning and injury by firearms. For this reason the gun-room on a ship is called in French the *sainte-barbe*. The legend, as usual, gives us the origin of the belief in the saint's special powers, for her heathen father is said to have been killed by a stroke of lightning, because of his having denounced his daughter, as a Christian, to the Roman authorities, and then executed judgment upon her with his own hands. Of St. Barbara the legend says: "She was a fair fruit from an evil tree."[17]

Beneath portraits or images of St. Christopher (July 25) there often appears a Latin verse to the effect that whoever gazes on the image will not suffer from faintness or exhaustion on that day. As the saint is said to have been of great

---

[17] Symeonis Logothetæ, cognomento Metaphrastæ, "Opera Omnia," ed. Migne, Parisiis, 1864, vol. iii, col. 315.

SANTA BARBARA

French school, 1520. Leaf of a triptych in the Museum of Budapest.

size and strength, the worshipper at his shrine was believed to acquire some of his physical power.

The cure of diseases of the tongue was the province of St. Catherine of Alexandria (November 25), who was famed for her eloquence as well as for her devotion to the study of the Scriptures.

St. Roch, who was born in Montpelier toward the end of the thirteenth century (d. August 16, 1327), is regarded as the special guardian of those afflicted with plague or pestilence. In his lifetime he went from place to place ministering to those who suffered from the plague until finally he himself succumbed to this malady. So great was the repute of St. Roch's curative powers that the Venetians are said to have stolen his body from Montpelier, where it was interred, and transported it to Venice, that they might have ever-present help in the numerous pestilences from which this city suffered, because of the constant commercial intercourse with the East.

Another saint who was invoked for help in plague and pestilence was St. Sebastian (January 20), born in Narbonne in Gaul. In this case the story of the saint's martyrdom gave rise to the belief in his curative powers, for the legend tells us that he was transfixed with arrows, and these missiles were regarded as symbols of the plague. We have an illustration of this old belief in the first book of Homer's Iliad, where the pestilence that visited the army of the Greeks is represented as due to the shafts sped from Apollo's silver bow.

Although no curative powers are attributed to them, no one of English speech should forget SS. Crispin and Crispian, on whose day the battle of Agincourt was fought, in 1415. The old feud between France and England has been long forgotten, the rivalry between these nations has given place to a close friendship, and there is no trace of animosity in the glow that warms an Englishman's heart when he reads the ringing words put by Shakespeare into the mouth of Henry V:

> And Crispin Crispian shall ne'er go by
> From this day to the ending of the world,
> But we in it shall be remembered.

It is related by Metaphrastus that when St. George was condemned to death by burning, his executioners (fearing that the flames of the pyre might be extinguished because of his virtue) covered his body with a garment of amiantos (asbestos); for it was believed that when this material began to burn the flame could not be extinguished. But all precautions were vain, for as soon as the saint was placed in the flames the fire went out, contrary to the laws of nature, and not a hair of his head was injured. This tale illustrates a curious but not unnatural misunderstanding of the name asbestos, which really signifies inextinguishable, but was intended to mean that the substance would not burn, and hence that no flame could be extinguished in it.[18]

In an unpublished manuscript written by Aubrey are quoted the following curious lines on the legend of St. George and the Dragon:[19]

> To save a mayd, St. George the Dragon slew,
> A pretty tale if all is told be true;
> Most say there are no Dragons, and 'tis sayd,
> There was no George; pray God there was a mayd.

The St. George thalers, coined by the counts of Mansfeld (Thüringen), enjoyed in bygone times a reputation as amulets for soldiers. This belief is said to have originated from the actual preservation of a soldier's life by one of these coins, which he had sewed up in the lining of his coat just

[18] Aldrovandi, "Museum metallicum, Bononiæ," 1648, p. 653.

[19] Thoms, "Anecdotes and Traditions," London, 1839, p. 103 (Camden Soc. Pub.).

over his heart for safekeeping. A bullet which struck him here and would otherwise have killed him, was diverted by coming in contact with the thaler. Hungarian St. George thalers were regarded as amulets for sailors as well as soldiers. These coins derived their name from bearing the design of St. George and the Dragon.

Among the wonder-working saints none enjoyed greater repute in medieval times than Sainte Foy, the virgin martyr whose remains were taken from Agen to the abbey-church at Conques, a village on the hills of Aveyron. Pilgrims came from far and near to the shrine of Sainte Foy, for she worked marvellous cures upon those who appealed to her for help, even giving sight to the blind. Her grace appears to have been bestowed upon animals as well as upon human beings, a fantastic legend relating that she had raised donkeys from the grave! Naturally the pilgrims must bring rich gifts, as otherwise the saint might turn a deaf ear to their prayers.

Many of these treasures may still be seen in this out-of-the-way church, wherein no one would suspect the existence of the rich specimens of early goldsmiths' work that are carefully preserved in the treasury. The most interesting of these treasures is a statuette supposed to represent the saint. This is a seated figure, about 33 inches high and encrusted with an immense number of precious stones, uncut emeralds, sapphires and amethysts, as well as with many cameos and pearls; all these having been offered at various times to the saint.

The figure—probably the representation of some ecclesiastic—is seated on an elaborate chair, originally surmounted by two golden doves. The saint is said to have appeared in a vision to the Bishop of Beaulieu and expressly directed this adornment; these doves have disappeared and have been replaced by crystal balls. The execution of the statuette—constructed of wood covered with gold plates—is stiff and conventional, but it is not unimpressive and gives evidence of considerable skill on the part of the artist. Nevertheless, it certainly has nothing of the youthful grace we would associate with a virgin martyr.[20]

The offering of precious stones to attract the favor of gods or saints is really a talismanic use of such gems and is intimately connected with the wearing of gems for their talismanic or therapeutic effect. The gift established a sort of relation between the being whose help was desired and the petitioner, and the gem was the medium through which the favor was bestowed.

The legend of the royal princess who was canonized by the Church as St. Enimie (d. 628 or 630 A.D.) contains an account of a miraculous spring and also enshrines the popular view of the cause of the strange outlines of an extensive mass of heaped-up boulders. This saint was a daughter of the French king Clotaire II (d. 628). Her most ardent wish was to devote herself exclusively to the service of Christ, but her royal parent insisted upon a marriage with one of the great nobles. The princess, who was the fairest of the fair, put up an earnest prayer that the Lord would destroy her beauty, even at the expense of some dreadful malady, so that she might cease to be an object of desire for men. Her prayer was heard and she was stricken with leprosy which entirely blotted out her charms. Not long after this an angel appeared to her in a dream and directed her to bathe in the Fountain of Boule, in the region of Gévaudan. On doing so she was immediately cured of her leprosy, but as soon as she went away from the spring to return to the royal residence, the malady returned. A second attempt had the same favorable and unfavorable results, and she

[20] See plate in the present writer's "Curious Lore of Precious Stones," J. B. Lippincott Company, 1913, opp. p. 356.

now recognized that she must remain near the spring. So after bathing there a third time and being again completely cured, she erected a monastery on the spot and became the prioress. The institution flourished, but a few years later the saintly prioress was horrified to see that the Devil was busy with her nuns. Once more she sought for divine aid, and she was given authority to imprison the Evil One should she catch him in the monastery. This she did, but the Devil was crafty enough to make his escape. Near the spot where the monastery stood was a mass of heaped-up boulders, through which led a way called the Chasm Road which led to a rocky aperture of unknown depth. This was fabled to afford egress and ingress to the Devil in his passage out of and back to the infernal regions. Along this road he fled when he escaped from the monastery; St. Enimie fearlessly pursued, but the agile demon was on the point of slipping back again into his own realm, when the saint made a supreme appeal and called upon the rocks to help her. As she raised her arms in supplication, one of the largest boulders, called "La Sourde," moved of its own accord and fell upon the Devil, pinning him fast to the ground beneath its ponderous weight. In his rage and despair he made frantic efforts to free himself and his bloody claws left an imprint on the rock. This mark, still observable a half-century ago, though it has now disappeared, was prosaically explained by scientists as a stain of iron-oxide. The other boulders were in motion to assist in the good work, but when the Devil had been caught they stopped short in their downward course, and this is supposed to account for the strange angles at which they stand.[21] It would be pleasant to fancy that His Satanic Majesty eventually failed

[21] Mlle. Marie König, "Poupées et légendes de France," Paris, n. d., pp. 77–80.

to make his escape, but unfortunately the ever-recurring instances of his activity from the age of St. Enimie down to our own time preclude this belief.

An heirloom in the family of Dom Pedro of Brazil is said to have been loaned to one of the pioneer aviators, Santos-Dumont, by Dom Pedro's daughter, the Comtesse d'Eu. This was a medal of St. Benedict and had been long regarded as a powerful talisman in the Braganza family. One of its princely members had a striking proof of this virtue in 1705, when, after having worn the medal but two weeks, he was saved from deadly peril by the timely discovery and consequent defeat of a plot. Santos-Dumont had just experienced a terrible fall while experimenting with his new airship in the Rothschild park near Paris, and this it was that induced the Comtesse d'Eu to loan him the talismanic medal, with the injunction that he should always wear it on his person, and the assurance that if he did so no further harm could befall him. The talisman seemed to do its work well, for although the aviator had many narrow escapes, he was always saved from serious injury. Unfortunately, however, a thief picked it from the pocket of his coat while he was busily engaged in work on an airship in a Paris machine-shop.[22]

While it was customary to close the shops of the goldsmiths on Sundays and feast-days, a special exception permitted the "Confrérie de St. Eloi," the goldsmiths' guild, to open a single shop (not always the same one) on each Sunday and feast-day, the profits of the sales being devoted to providing a dinner on Easter Day for the poor of the Hôtel Dieu.[23] This combination of commercialism and philanthropy has illustrations in our own day, and, whatever

---

[22] St. Louis Democrat, 1905.

[23] De Lespinasse, "Les métiers et corporations de la ville de Paris," Paris, 1892, p. 11.

may be the ulterior motives, some good results are certainly attained.

The Well of St. Cuthbert, near Cranstock, Newquay, England, long enjoyed the repute of miraculously curing the ailments of infants. Not only were curative powers attributed to the waters of the well, but also to a perforated stone alongside of it. As recently as 1868 a puny infant is said to have been passed through the orifice of this stone with the firm expectation that this act would strengthen the infant and bring good luck to it.[24]

In the region of the Abruzzi, in Italy, more especially in the province of Teramo, wonderful virtues are attributed to the intercession of St. Donato. So great is thought to be his power to cure those afflicted with epilepsy that in this region the disease is called the malady of St. Donato. This saint, however, is credited with much more extensive powers, for he is believed to cure hydrophobia, to prevent the ill effects of the Evil Eye, and in general to bring to naught the enchantments of witches. Such being his powers, it is not surprising that his image was added to many amulets, those figuring the lunar crescent being frequently surmounted with the bust of the saint. This type of amulet owes its supposed efficacy to the horn-like shape of the crescent, horns or substances having a likeness to a horn, like certain branches of coral, being regarded as a sure protection against the Evil Eye. A curious amulet bears the bust of St. Donato surmounting a crescent moon within which is the dreaded number thirteen. This fateful number is considered to be a source of misfortune for those who do not wear it inscribed on an amulet; but it becomes a source of good fortune and a happy life for those who possess such an amulet.[25]

---

[24] Nature, vol. lxxxvi, p. 429; Oct. 6, 1910.

[25] Bellucci, "Il feticismo in Italia," Perugia, 1907, pp. 113–119. Figures.

A notable instance of the use of a saint's name to facilitate the perpetration of a crime is afforded in the case of the poison known as Aqua Tofana. This appears to have been a preparation of arsenic and was concocted by a woman named Tofana, a native of Palermo, in Sicily, who eventually took up her abode in Naples and devoted herself to the preparation and sale of her poison in Naples, Rome and elsewhere. To divert suspicion she used vials marked "Manna of St. Nicholas of Bari," and bearing the image of this saint. Most of her clients are said to have been women who were anxious to rid themselves of their husbands, and she must have had a large practice in this specialty, for so many husbands died in Rome in a mysterious manner that in 1659 the authorities finally took cognizance of the matter and instituted a searching investigation. This revealed the fact that there existed in Rome a secret society entirely composed of women who wished to "remove" their husbands by poison. The leader of this society and many of the members were duly executed, but Tofana does not seem to have been molested.

Many strange superstitions as to the saints prevail among the Spanish-speaking inhabitants of New Mexico. If a saint whose aid has been invoked fails to respond to the appeal, his image is shut up in some receptacle until he vouchsafes to render the service desired. On the other hand, if the image of a saint falls to the ground, this is interpreted as a sign that the saint has performed a miracle. One means of forcing a saint to perform a miracle was to hang the image head downward; this was especially recommended in the case of St. Anthony. All strangers who presented themselves on St. Anthony's day or St. Joseph's day were to be hospitably received and entertained, for one of them might be the saint himself. Those who wished to read the future were instructed to put the white of an egg in a glass of water

BLOODSTONE MEDALLION, SHOWING THE SANTA CASA OF LORETO CARRIED BY ANGELS TO DALMATIA FROM GALILEE

on the eve of St. John's day; on examining the contents of the glass the next morning they would see written in black characters on the white background a prophecy of what was to happen. On this saint's day women were assured that if they cut the tip of their hair with an axe, or merely washed it, they would be blessed with an abundant growth of hair.

A strange legend of angelic activity is that touching the miraculous transportation through the air (from Galilee to Dalmatia) of the "Santa Casa," the house wherein the Virgin Mary dwelt. This event is placed in 1295, and the reverse of an Italian medallion engraved in 1508, during the pontificate of Julius II, gives a representation of the journey to Dalmatia, two angels sufficing to bear the little edifice. The sea, over which the house is being borne, is conventionally indicated by waves; but the fact that the medallist has seen fit to show a relatively large figure of the Virgin seated on the roof of the little structure and holding the Infant Jesus in her arms, scarcely adds to the realism of the effect.

Quite naturally Catholicism could not be satisfied with the pagan idea that the constellations held sway over the different parts of the human body, and the saints were substituted for the stars.

> The saints of the Romanists have usurped the place of the zodiacal constellations in their government of the parts of man's body, and so for every limbe they have a saint. Thus, St. Otilia keepes the head instead of Aries; St. Blasius is appointed to govern the necke instead of Taurus; St. Lawrence keepes the backe and shoulders instead of Gemini, Cancer and Leo; St. Erasmus rules the belly with the entrayls, in the place of Libra and Scorpius; in the stead of Sagittarius, Capricornus, Aquarius and Pisces, the holy church of Rome hath elected St. Burgarde, St. Rochus, St. Quirinius, St. John, and many others, which govern the thighes, feet, shinnes and knees.[26]

[26] Pettigrew, "On Superstitions Connected with the History and Practice of Medicine and Surgery," p. 36. (Quotation from Melton, "Astrologaster," p. 20.)

When we consider how many beautiful and symbolic rites and observances have marked the celebration of saint's days and holidays in the Old World, and how few of these have been preserved by the inhabitants of our own country, we must find this most regrettable. Of late years there has been a marked tendency to increase the number of holidays, and in a few cases to revive the celebration of old holidays, but the popular idea of the best way to celebrate these occasions seems to be confined to making them carnivals of noise and disorder. This is largely owing to a lack of intelligent guidance, for it is too much to expect that any people, above all those so practical as our American people, can spontaneously evolve, at short notice, an emblematic expression of the idea underlying the festival. If, however, a beautiful and adequate symbolism were presented in a concrete form, the masses of the people would grasp its significance quickly enough, and would thus gain a higher and better conception of the historic anniversary or the time-honored festival they were called upon to celebrate.

The saint's days on which the summer and winter solstices fell were memorized by distichs. For instance:

> St. Barnaby bright! St. Barnaby bright!
> The longest day and the shortest night.
>
> St. Thomas gray! St. Thomas gray!
> The longest night and the shortest day.

The former of the verses is probably the earlier, as St. Barnabas' Day is June 11, the day on which the summer solstice fell in England for some time before the reform of the "Old Style" calendar, in 1752, replaced this date; while St. Thomas' Day is December 21, the date of the winter solstice in our modern calendar.[27]

Writing of the origin of the rural superstitions in re-

---

[27] Notes and Queries, 2d Series, vol. viii, London, 1859, p. 242.

gard to the weather on certain saint's days, Wehrenfels quotes the distich:

If Paul's Day be fair and clear
It foreshows an happy Year.

and continues:

The contrary has happened a thousand Times, but however this cannot destroy the Rule. It once happened; certainly, say they, these Rules of the Husbandmen are not to be despised; see how exactly they are made good by Experience. Thus a great Part of Mankind reasons; which if one consider, he will neither depend much upon the Content of the common People in these Things, nor wonder at so great a Number of most silly Opinions.[28]

VERSES ON SAINTS' DAYS AT VARIOUS SEASONS OF THE YEAR.[29]

January 25. Saint Paul's Day:

If the clouds make dark the sky,
Great store of people then will die;
If there be either snow or rain,
Then will be dear all kinds of grain.
(Robin Forby, "Vocabulary of East Anglia," London, 1830.)

Somewhat different in a Latin form:

Clara dies Pauli multas segetes nitant amni,
Si fuerint nebulæ, aut venti, erunt proelia genti.

February 2. Candlemas Day:

If Candlemas day be fair and bright,
Winter will have another flight;
If on Candlemas day it be shower and rain,
Winter is gone and will not come again.
(John Ray, "A Collection of English Proverbs," 2d ed., Cambridge, 1678.)

February 12. St. Eulalia's Day:

If the sun shines on St. Eulalie's day,
It is good for apples and cider they say.

[28] Wehrenfels, "A Dissertation on Superstition," p. 36; prefixed to "Occasional Thoughts on the Power of Curing the King's-Evil," London, 1748.

[29] Lean's Collectanea, vol. i, Bristol, 1902, pp. 373–384.

February 14. St. Valentine's Day:

On St. Valentine's day
Cast beans in clay
But on St. Chad
Sow good or bad.

(Seed time of this Lenten crop limited between February 14 and March 2.)

February 24. St. Matthias' Day:

Saint Matthew (Sept. 21)
Get candlesticks new;
St. Mattheg
Lay candlesticks by

March 1. St. David's Day:

Quoth Saint David, " I'll have a flood."
Saith our Lady [Mch. 25] " I'll have as good."

(Referring to spring tides in Wales, from Poor Robin's Almanack, 1684.)

June 15. St. Vitus' Day:

If Saint Vitus' day be rainy weather,
It will rain for thirty days together.

(M. A. Denham, " Proverbs and Popular Sayings Relating to the Seasons," Percy Soc., 1846.)

July 15. St. Swithin's Day:

St. Swithin's day, if thou dost rain,
For forty days it will remain;
St. Swithin's day, if thou be fair,
For forty days t'will rain nae mair.

(M. A. Denham, " Proverbs and Popular Sayings Relating to the Seasons," Percy Soc., 1846.)

July 15: All the tears that St. Swithin can cry
Aug. 24: Saint Bartholomew's dusty mantle wipes dry.

(R. Inwards, " Weather Lore," London, 1893.)

July 20. St. Margaret's Day:

" Margaret's floods " (heavy rains).

July 25. St. James' Day:

"Whoever eats oysters on St. James' day will never want money."

(M. A. Denham, "Proverbs and Popular Sayings Relating to the Seasons," Percy Soc., 1846.)

August 24. St. Bartholomew's Day:

St. Bartholomew
Brings cold dew.

(John Ray, "A Collection of English Proverbs," 2d ed., Cambridge, 1678.)

October 28. St. Simon and St. Jude:

Simon and Jude
All the ships on the sea home they do crowd.

Dost thou know her then?
Trap. As well as I know 'twill rain upon
Simon and Jude's day next.

(Middleton, "The Roaring Girl," Act 5, Sc. 1.)

Now a continual Simon and Jude's rain beat all your feathers as flat down as pancakes!

(Idem, Act II, Sc. 1.)

November 11. St. Martin's Day:

Expect St. Martin's summer, halcyon days.

(Shakespeare, "I Henry VI," Act 1, Sc. 2.)

December 13. St. Lucy's Day:

Lucy [bright] light
The shortest day and the longest night

(For a long time, before the change of the calendar, St. Lucy's Day corresponded to our 21st of December.)

December 21. St. Thomas' Day:

St. Thomas gray, St. Thomas gray
The longest night and the shortest day.

December 27. St. John the Evangelist's Day:

Never rued the man
That lead in his fuel before St. John.

(Robin Forby, "Vocabulary of East Anglia," London, 1830.)

Additional verses on Candlemas Day (Purification of the Blessed Virgin):

If the sun shines bright on Candlemas Day,
The half of the winter's not yet away.

In Latin:

Si sol splendescat Maria purificante,
Major erit glacies post festum quam ante.

SAINTS' DAYS

ADRIAN. September 8. As also of his wife, Natalia. Anniversary of translation of his relics to Rome; anciently his festival on day of his martyrdom, March 4, 306. Patron of soldiers in Flanders, Germany, and northern France; also against the plague. Relics in Abbey of St. Adrian, Gearsburg, Belgium; and elsewhere.

AFRA. August 5. Especially celebrated in Augsburg, of which city (her native one) she is patroness. Martyred Aug. 7, 304.

AGATHA. February 5. Patroness of Malta, and Catania, Sicily. Died February 5, 251.

AGNES. January 21. Supposed anniversary of martyrdom in 304.

ALBAN. June 22. First English saint and martyr, died June 22, 303. Present town of St. Albans upon site of martyrdom.

AMABLE. June 11. Patron of Riom, France. Died 475.

AMBROSE. December 7. Patron of Milan. Died April 4, 397. Founder of church, now Sant' Ambrogio basilica Maggiore, Milan, in 387. One of four Latin Fathers.

ANDREW. November 30. Apostle, patron of Scotland and Russia.

ANNE. July 26. Supposed anniversary of her death. Mother of the Virgin Mary. Patroness of Canada.

ANSELM. April 21. Archbishop of Canterbury (1033–1109).

ANTHONY. January 17. Hermit (251–356).

ANTHONY OF PADUA. June 13. Died June 13, 1231.

APOLLONIA. February 9. Martyred February 9, 250. Patroness of those suffering from toothache.

ATHANASIUS. May 2. One of four Greek Fathers. Died May 2, 373.

AUGUSTINE. August 28. Died 430. Patron of theologians and learning. Bishop of Hippo in Africa. One of four Latin Fathers.

AUGUSTINE. May 26. Apostle to England in 596. Died May 26, 604.

BABYLAS. September 1 (14) in Eastern Church; January 24 in Western Church (237–250). Bishop of Antioch. Relics said to have silenced the revived oracle of Apollo at Delphi, during reign of Julian the Apostate.

BARBARA. December 4. Patroness of Ferrara, Mantua and Guastalla, Italy, and of armourers and gunsmiths. Died December 4, 235 (?).

BARNABAS. June 11. His birthday. One of the patrons of Milan. Apostle.

BARTHOLOMEW. August 24. Apostle.

BASIL THE GREAT. January 1, Eastern Church; June 14, Western Church (328–380).

BATHILDA. January 30 in France; January 26 in Roman Martyrology (died ca. 680).

BAYO OR BAVON. October 1. Patron of Ghent (589–653).

BENEDICT. March 21. Founder of Benedictine Order (480–543).

BERNARD OF CLAIRVAUX. August 20. Founder of Abbey of Clairvaux, one of the Fathers of the Church (1091–1153).

BERNARD OF MENTHON. June 15. Founder of hospices in the Alps, "Great St. Bernard" and "Little St. Bernard" (923–1008 ?).

BLAISE. February 3. Patron of Ragusa, and of those afflicted with throat diseases. Bishop of Sebaste, Cappadocia (died 316).

BONIFACE. June 5. Apostle of Germany (680–755).

BRIDGET OR BRIDE. February 1. Patroness of Ireland (450–521).

BRUNO. October 6. Founder of Carthusian Order (1035–1101).

CATHERINE. November 25. Patroness of Venice and appealed to against diseases of the tongue.

CATHERINE OF SIENA. Patroness of Siena; lived in fourteenth century.

CECILIA. November 22. Patroness of sacred music (died 100).

CLEMENT. November 23. Patron of farriers and blacksmiths (died 100).

COLUMBAN. November 21. Irish saint (543–615).

CRISPIN AND CRISPINIAN. October 25. Patrons of shoemakers (died 284).

CUTHBERT. March 20. Patron saint of Durham, England (died 687).

DAVID. March 1. Patron saint of Wales (446–549).

DECLAN. July 24. First bishop of Ardmore, Ireland.

DENIS. October 9. Patron of France. Living in 250.

DOMENIC. August 4. Founder of Dominican Order (1170–1221).

EDMUND. November 20. King of East Anglia and martyr (died 870).

EDWARD. March 18. King of England and martyr (962–978).

EDWARD THE CONFESSOR. October 13. King of England (1004–1066).

ELIZABETH OF HUNGARY. November 19. Daughter of Alexander II, King of Hungary (1207–1231).

ELMO (ERASMUS). June 2 (died 304).

ELOY (ELIGIUS). December 1. Patron of goldsmiths (588–659).

EMERIC. November 4. Eldest son of St. Stephen of Hungary.

ENGRACIA.

ERIC (OR HENRY). May 18. Patron of Sweden (died 1151).

ETHELREDA (AUDREY). October 17. Princess of East Anglia (died 679).

EUPHEMIA. September 16. Patroness of Chalcedon (died ca. 307).

FELICITAS. November 23. Patroness of male heirs (died 173).

FILLAN. January 9. Scotch saint (died ca. 649).

FILOMENA (FILUMINA, PHILOMENA). August 10. Supposititious saint.

FRANCIS OF ASSISI. October 4. Founder of Franciscan Order (1182–1226).

FRANCIS XAVIER. December 3. Patron and Apostle of India (1506–1552).

FRIDESWIDE. October 19. Patroness of city and university of Oxford, daughter of Sidan, Prince of Oxford (died ca. 740).

GENEVIEVE. January 3. Patroness of Paris.

GEORGE. April 23. Patron of England, of Germany and Venice, of soldiers and armourers (born third century).

GILES. September 1. Patron of Edinburgh (ca. 640–).

GREGORY THE GREAT. March 12 (born 540).

GUDULA. January 8. Patron of Brussels (born middle of seventh century).

HELENA. August 18. Wife of Constantius, mother of Constantine the Great (died 328).

HENRY OF BAVARIA. July 15. Patron of Bavaria. Emperor (Henry II) of Germany (972–1024).

HILARY. January 14 (died 368).

HONORATUS. Bishop of Arles. Died January 6, 429.

HONORATUS (HONORÉ). May 16. Patron of bakers. Bishop of Amiens. (Died 690.)

HUBERT OF LIEGE. November 3. Patron of the chase and of dogs (died 727).

IGNATIUS LOYOLA. July 3. Founder of Jesuit Order (1491–1556).

ISIDORE THE PLOUGHMAN (Isidro el Labrador). May 15. Patron of Madrid and of farmers (born ca. 1110–1170).

JAMES THE GREAT. July 25. Apostle; patron of Spain and of pilgrims to Jerusalem (died 42).

JANUARIUS. September 19. Patron of Naples (died 305).

JEROME. September 30. Patron of scholars. One of the four Latin Fathers (342–420).

JOHN THE BAPTIST. June 24, or Midsummer Day.

JOHN THE EVANGELIST. December 27 (died 101).

JOSEPH. March 19.

JULIAN HOSPITATOR. January 9. Patron of hospitals (died 313).

JUSTINA OF PADUA. October 7. One of the patrons of Padua and Venice (died 303).

KENELM. December 13 and July 17. Son of Kenulph, King of Murcia (812–820).

KEYNE (KEYNA). Cornish saint (died 689).

KILIAN. July 8. Irish saint (died 689).

LAWRENCE. August 10. Patron of Nuremberg, Genoa, and of the Escorial.

LEONHARDT. November 6. Patron of prisoners and slaves; in Bavaria, of cattle (died ca. 560).

LUCY (LUCIA). December 13. Patron of Syracuse, and against eye-diseases.

LUDMILLA. September 16. Patron of Bohemia. Queen of that country (died ca. 920).

LUKE. October 18. Patron of painters.

MACAIRE THE ELDER. January 15. (Fourth century.)

MACAIRE THE YOUNGER. January 2. (Fourth century.)

MALO (MACLOU). November 15. Patron of St. Malo, France (died 627).

MARGARET. July 20. One of the patrons of Cremona and of women in childbirth (died fourth century).

MARK. April 25. Evangelist (died 68).

MARTHA OF BETHANY. July 29. Patroness of cooks and housewives (died 84).

MARTIN OF TOURS. November 11, Martinmas. Patron of Tours and of beggars, tavern-keepers and wine-growers (316–397).

MARY MAGDALENE. July 22. Patroness of Provence and of Marseilles as well as of penitent fallen women.

MATTHIAS. February 24.

MAURICE. September 22. Patron of Austria, Savoy, Mantua, and of foot-soldiers (fourth century).

MICHAEL. September 29. Archangel.

NICHOLAS. December 6. Archbishop of Myra in Lycia, patron of Russia, and especially of serfs and serfdom (died 342).

OLAF. July 29. Patron of Norway. Not canonized but informally accepted.

OUEN (OUINE). August 24. Patron of Rouen (595–683).

PANTALEONE. June 27. Patron of physicians (fourth century).

PATRICK. March 17. Patron of Ireland (born ca. 386).

PAUL. June 29 (with St. Peter), and January 25.

PETER. June 29; also August 1, St. Peter's Chains, and January 18, Chair of St. Peter.

PHILIP. May 1. Patron of Brabant and Luxemburg.

PHILIP NERI. May 26. Founder of Oratorian Order (1515–1595).

POLYCARP. January 26. Bishop of Smyrna (died 167).

QUIETUS. (No day.) Bones in church of Our Lady of Grau, Hoboken, enshrined June 1, 1856, Archbishop Bailey officiating.

ROCHE (ROCH, ROQUE). August 16. Patron of prisoners and the sick, especially the plague-stricken (born ca. 1280–1327).

ROMAIN. October 23. Patron of Rouen (died 639).

ROMUALD. February 7 (956–1027).

ROSALIA. September 4. Patroness of Palermo (died 1160).

RUMALD (RUMBALD). November 3. Patron of Brackley and Buckingham, England. Son of King of Northumbria.

SCHOLASTICA. February 10. Sister of St. Benedict (died ca. 543).

SEBALD. Son of a Danish king (eighth century).

SEBASTIAN. January 20. Patron of Chiemsee, Mannheim, Oetting, Palma, Rome, Soissons, and of archers (fourth century).

SECUNDUS. March 30. Patron of Asti (died 119).

STEPHEN. December 26. Patron of horses.

SWITHIN (SWITHUN). July 15. Patron of Winchester (died 862).

SYMPHOROSA. July 18. Only in Greek Church. A Jewish martyr, the mother of the Maccabees (second century B.C.).

THERESA. October 15. Patron of Spain (1515–1582).

THOMAS À BECKET. July 7 (1117–1170).

THOMAS DIDYMUS. December 21. Apostle, patron of Portugal and Palma.

URBAN. May 25. Pope and martyr (died 236).

URSULA. October 21. Patroness of young girls, and of educational institutions (died 383).

VALENTINE. February 14 (first century).

VERONICA. Shrove Tuesday (first century).

VICTOR. Patron of Marseilles (fourth century).

VINCENT. January 22. Patron of Lisbon, Valencia, Saragossa, Milan, and Châlons.

VINCENT DE PAUL. July 19. Founder of Order of the Sisters of Charity.

VITUS. June 15. Patron of Bohemia, Saxony, Sicily, and of dancers and actors (third century).

WALBURGA. February 25 (died ca. 778).

WILLIAM. January 10. Patron of Bruges (died 1209).

WINIFRED. November 3. British maiden of seventh century.

VII

On the Religious Use of Various Stones

THE precious stone mentioned in the earliest biblical reference, Gen. ii, 12, and there translated onyx, is rendered chrysoprase in the Septuagint version, and is by others referred to the emerald on the ground that the land of Havilah, where it is there said to occur, is thought to have been a part of what was later called Scythia, and as such would include the emerald region of the Urals. But the ancient emeralds are now known to have come largely from Upper Egypt, and such vague conjectures are of little use in determining what stone was really meant in this most ancient allusion. Professor Haupt has even suggested that we might translate the Hebrew word *shoham* used in this passage by "pearl," since he conjectures that one of the four "rivers" surrounding the land of Havilah was the Persian Gulf.

For all attempted identifications of the stones mentioned in the Old Testament, we are principally dependent upon the Greek version of the Seventy. As this was made in the Alexandrian period, not far from the time of Theophrastus, whose work on gems we shall presently mention, the names at that time adopted by the Greek translators may be regarded as fairly correct equivalents of the Hebrew. The difficulty lies more in the translation of the classical names into the English, and arises largely from the unscientific nomenclature of the ancients; the same name being employed for stones that resemble each other to the eye, but which are now well distinguished by chemical and physical differences formerly unknown.

There are some traces in the Bible of the use of precious stones as amulets. In Proverbs xvii, 8, we read that "a gift is like a precious stone in the eyes of the owner; whithersoever he turneth he prospereth." This passage is rendered somewhat differently in the Authorized Version, but the above translation is evidently more correct. The stones of the breastplate were of course amulets in a certain sense, and possibly oracles also, and it is therefore quite probable that the Hebrews shared in the belief common to all the peoples around them, although opposition of the orthodox to all magical practices prevented them from going into particulars in regard to such superstitious fancies.

In support of his theory that the Urim and Thummim of the Hebrew high-priest signified the stones of the breastplate worn on the sacred ephod, and should be rendered "perfectly brilliant," Bellermann cites the passage in Ezekiel (chap. xxviii, verse 14), where he writes of "fiery stones" in treating of the royal splendors of the ruler of the great commercial city of Tyre. As to the oracular utterances of the high-priest when, clad in the ephod and wearing the glittering breastplate, he sought for the counsel of the Almighty, this author rejects the idea that the divine will was revealed by changes in the brilliancy of the stones, by casting of lots, or by a mysterious use of the ineffable name, the Tetragrammaton, J h w h (Jahweh), but believes that the answer to the questions was communicated to the high-priest by an inner voice, an inspiration similar to that vouchsafed to the great prophets of Israel.[1]

A curious analogy to the use by Christians of fragments supposed to have come from the True Cross as amulets, was the employment by the Talmudic Jews of chips from an

[1] Johann Joachim Bellermann, "Die Urim und Thummim, die altesten Gemmen," Berlin, 1824, pp. 21, 22. For a full account of the breastplate see the present writer's "The Curious Lore of Precious Stones," Philadelphia and London, 1913, chap. viii, pp. 275–306.

idol or from something that had been offered to an idol, for the same purpose. It is needless to say that this was severely condemned by the Rabbis.

It is interesting to note the statements of Arab historians that the mummy of Cheops, the Pharaoh of the Great Pyramid, was decorated with a pectoral of precious stones. As the regal and priestly functions were united in the monarch, we may have here the first form of the high-priest's breastplate.

The Arab historian Abd er-Rahmân, writing in 829 A.D., states that Al Mamoun(813–833), son of Haroun-al-Raschid, entered the great pyramid and found the body of Cheops:

> In a stone sarcophagus was a green stone statue of a man, like an emerald, containing a human body, covered with a sheet of fine gold ornamented with a great quantity of precious stones; on the breast was a priceless sword, on the head a ruby as large as a hen's egg, brilliant as a flame. I have seen the statue which contained the body; it was near the palace of Fôstat.

Essentially the same account is given by Ebub Abd el-Holem, another Arab, who says:

> One saw beneath the summit of the pyramid a chamber with a hollow prison, in which was a statue of stone enclosing the body of a man, who had on the breast a pectoral of gold enriched by fine stones, and a sword of inestimable price, on the head a carbuncle the size of an egg, brilliant as the sun, on which were characters no man could read.

In the opinion of Mariette Bey these details are so circumstantial as to leave little doubt that the mummy of Cheops was found by Mamoun, but he believes that the body was covered with a gilt wrapper and that the stones were paste imitations. The ruby was probably the "uræus," the sacred asp, emblem of royalty, and the wonderful sword may have been a sceptre or a poniard similar to those found in tombs of the eleventh dynasty and in that of Queen Aah-Hotep; the statue of green serpentine often occurs in later tombs. Should this view be correct, precious stones were imitated in glass at a very remote period.[1a]

An exceedingly fine specimen of ancient Egyptian goldsmith's work, now in the Louvre Museum, Paris, is a pendant terminating in a bull's head, each of the horns being tipped with a little ball. Above the double reins are four rondelles, one of gold, two of a material still undetermined, and one of lapis lazuli; the different parts of the pendant are connected by gold wire. Its most interesting and attractive feature, however, is a polished hexagonal amethyst, engraved on both faces. In each case the form of a priest is figured; in one he appears with his official staff or wand, and in the other he is represented as bearing an incense-burner and offering the mineral and vegetable sacrifices; an Oriental pearl is set above the engraved amethyst. The religious and sacrificial significance of this ornament, coupled with the costliness of the materials and the superior excellence of the workmanship, make it likely that we have here an amulet or talisman made for some Egyptian of very high rank.[2]

St. Jerome (346?–420 A.D.), in his commentary on Isaiah (liv, 11, 12), alludes to the verses of Ezekiel describing the glories of the King of Tyre and the precious stones with which he was adorned. Evidently Jerome believed that this passage was to be taken symbolically, for he asks:

> Who could have so little judgment and intelligence as to think that any Prince of Tyre whatever should be set in the Paradise of God, and have his place among the Cherubim, or could fancy that he dwelt with the glowing stones, which we should without doubt understand as the angels and the celestial virtues.[3]

[1a] Wallace-Dunlop, "Glass in the Old World," London, n. d., p. 6.

[2] From "Jewellers' Circular Weekly," Nov. 12, 1913.

[3] Sanctii Eusebii Hieronymi "Opera Omnia," ed. Migne, vol. iv, Parisiis, 1865, cols 543, 544.

It would be both curious and interesting if we could trace a connection between the significance of the names of the Hebrew tribes and those of the breastplate gems assigned to the tribes. In ancient times names were much more significant than they are to-day, and the tribal names in particular possessed for the Hebrews a symbolic meaning, but this does not appear to have induced any marked tendency to connect the colors or the symbolic meanings of the different stones with the fame, or with the characteristics or fortunes of the several tribes. On the other hand, the foundation stones, as symbols of the Apostles, became a favorite theme with the early Christian writers. Possibly the neglect of ancient Hebrew writers to perform a similar task in connection with the breastplate stones might still be made good, even at this late date, and an effort in this direction might result in giving a wider range to the symbolic value of certain well-known gems.

The name Reuben signifies "Behold a Son," and this has been given a Messianic meaning by some commentators. In Jacob's enigmatic blessing, "excellency of dignity" and "excellency of power" are attributed to Reuben, but this birthright is taken from him because of a heinous sin he has committed. Still we might see in the carnelian, the gem of Reuben, a symbol of "dignity" and "power."

Simeon has been variously rendered "Hearing" or "Hearkener." The blessing accuses him of an act of cruelty in which he was aided by his brother Levi. To the peridot, or chrysolite, dedicated to Simeon, could be appropriately assigned the meaning "good tidings."

The priestly functions of the tribe of Levi are expressed by the name itself which means "attached" or "joined," that is, to the altar. Hence in the emerald we should see the symbol of "dedication" or "ministration," in addition to its other and better known meanings, such as "hope," "faith," and "resurrection."

For the tribe of Judah we have the ruby, and here the meaning of the name, "praised," fits in well with the dignity of the rare and glowing ruby. This noble gem has always been a favorite adornment for royal crowns and from Judah sprang the royalty of Israel. The blessing given to this tribe declares that "the sceptre shall not depart from Judah, nor a lawgiver from between his feet, until Shiloh come." This is often taken to signify the consummation of the Kingdom of Israel in the Kingdom of Heaven.

Issachar, signifying "reward," or "the rewarded," suggests as symbolic meanings of the tribal stone lapis lazuli, "success" and "fruition." This stone, the sapphire of the ancients, was typical of heaven, probably owing to the appearance of the specimens most highly valued in olden times, those in which a number of golden spots are scattered over the blue surface of the stone, which thus figure both the blue of heaven and the hosts of the stars.

The tribal name Zebulon signifies "exaltation," and to this tribe is assigned a dwelling-place by the sea bordering on the domains of the rich Phenician seaport, Sidon. We could thus see in the gem of Zebulon, the onyx, a symbol of dominion and authority. This could serve to offset some of the old superstitions regarding the onyx, which was sometimes charged with bringing discord and dissension.

Of the tribe Joseph, we are told that it was to be increased, and this meaning is contained in the name itself, which is rendered: "May God add." To Joseph were promised "blessings of heaven above," and "blessings of the deep that lieth under." The sapphire, probably the tribal stone of Joseph, was known in ancient times by the name hyacinth and was a stone of good omen, bringing increase

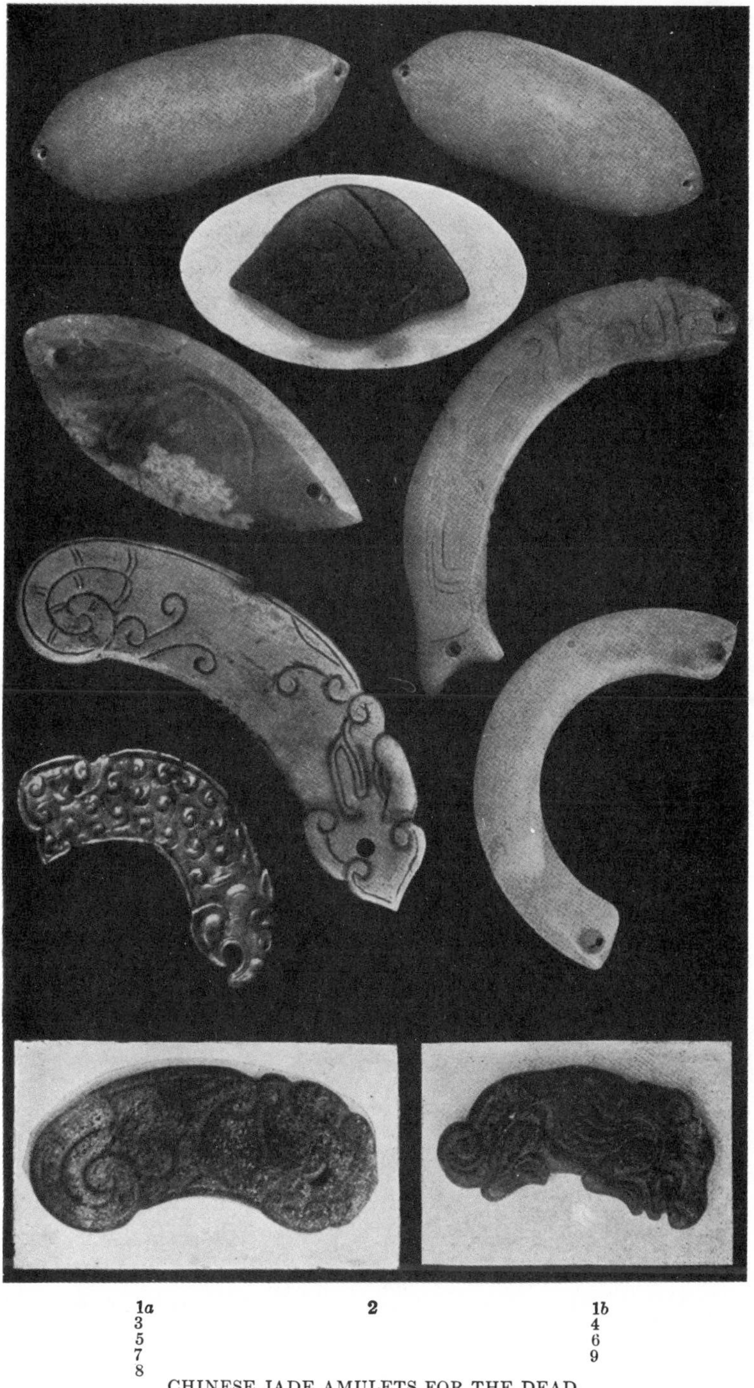

1*a*	2	1*b*
3		4
5		6
7		9
8		

CHINESE JADE AMULETS FOR THE DEAD

Figs. 1*a* and *b*, pair of eye-protecting amulets ; Fig. 2, presumably eye-amulets ; Fig. 3, eye-amulet with design of fish ; Figs 4-7, lip amulets, 4 and 7 in shape of fish ; Figs. 8-9, amulets in the shape of monsters. From "Jade," by Berthold Laufer.

By courtesy of the author and Field Museum of Natural History, Chicago.

LA MADONNA DELLA SALUTE, BY OTTAVIANO NELLI

In the Basilica of S. Francesco at Assisi.

of health and wealth; therefore its significance as a tribal gem does not differ essentially from the traditional one.

Benjamin signifies "son of the right hand," hence this name denotes strength and power. This meaning accords well with what is said in Jacob's blessing: "Benjamin shall raven as a wolf; in the morning he shall devour the prey and at night he shall divide the spoil." The banded agate symbolizing this tribe would have the meaning "strength" and "mastery"; indeed, according to other sources the agate was reputed to bring victory to the wearer.

Dan is the "judge" among the tribes, according to the meaning of the name. In Jacob's blessing Dan is said to be "a serpent by the way," and "an adder in the path." These metaphors, which may not strike us as commendatory of the tribe, probably indicated the craft and courage of the tribesmen in attacking and defeating their foes, and enriching themselves with the spoils of war. The amethyst, as the tribal stone of Dan, could thus signify both "judgment" and "craft."

To the tribe of Gad was given the beryl, and the fact that spheres made from this stone were believed to be best adapted for use in crystal-gazing makes it an especially appropriate gem for the tribe of "good fortune," this being the most probable signification of the name "Gad," although in the Bible the interpretation "a troop," is given. The beryl would therefore signify "good luck" and perhaps also "coöperation."

The twelfth and last tribe, Asher, has the jasper for its gem. This would also gain an auspicious significance from its association with Asher, which means "happy." To the other meanings assigned to jasper might be added that of "happiness." As we have elsewhere remarked, there seems good reason to suppose that jade was frequently designated jasper in ancient times, and this stone was everywhere believed to possess wonderful magic powers.

The jasper [4] as an emblem of strength and fortitude is noted by St. Jerome in his commentary on Isaiah (liv, 11, 12), where he writes that the bulwarks or walls of the Holy City were strengthened by jasper. These bulwarks served "to overthrow and refute every proud attack against the knowledge of God, and to subject falsehood to truth. Whoever, therefore, is most convincing in debate and best fortified with texts of Holy Scripture is a bulwark of the Church." [5] Jerome also alludes to the variety of jasper called *grammatias,* because of the peculiar markings, suggesting letters of the alphabet. This was believed to possess great talismanic virtue, especially in putting to flight phantoms and apparitions, since the markings were thought to signify some potent spell, written on the stone by nature's hand. Of another kind of jasper, "white as snow or sea-foam," [6] and having reddish stains, we are told that it symbolizes the spiritual graces, which preserve those endowed with them from vain terrors; and the learned Father quotes as descriptive of this stone the words of Solomon's Song (v, 10): "My beloved is white and ruddy." [7]

Writing of the sapphire (lapis lazuli), one of the foundation stones of the Holy City, St. Jerome likens it to heaven and to the air above us, adding, somewhat fancifully, that we might apply to the sapphire the words of Socrates in the "Clouds" of Aristophanes: "I walk upon air and look down upon the Sun." Turning then to Holy Scripture, Jerome notes the well-known passage in Ezekiel (i, 26) where the

[4] Sometimes believed to be rock crystal.

[5] Sancti Eusebii Hieronymi "Opera Omnia," ed. Migne, vol. iv, Parisiis, 1865, col. 544.

[6] A stained or colored massive quartz.

[7] Sancti Eusebii Hieronymi "Opera Omnia," ed. Migne, vol. iv, Parisiis, 1865, col. 545.

Throne of God is said to have "the appearance of a sapphire stone," and finds in this text a proof that blue denoted the glory of God.[8] The ingenuity of the ancient commentators in finding hidden meanings in the simplest things is well shown by the assertion of Thomas de Cantimpré that St. John placed the emerald fourth in the list of foundation stones, because the *four* evangelists are constant in their praise of chastity.[9]

Certain gems and stones have a definite relation and appropriateness to the various religious holidays and festivals. Notable among these is the rhodonite, a silicate of magnesia, named from the Greek word *rhodon*, "a rose," because of its beautiful rose-pink hue. This is found more especially in the Ural Mountains, and in Massachusetts, but in a number of other places as well. In the Ural Mountains one single mass was so immense that ninety horses were needed to move the 22-ton weight a distance of thirty miles to the Imperial Lapidary Works at Ekaterineburg; here the material was cut up into smaller masses to be finally worked up in the Imperial Lapidary Works at Peterhof into a sarcophagus and tomb for the Emperor Nicholas I.

This stone is a great favorite in Russia, and is frequently cut into egg-shaped ornaments, either in the form of a simple egg, or of one with a halo and a moonstone effect at one end. It may well be termed the "Easter Stone." For those unable to afford such an egg-shaped piece of rhodonite, a yellow fibrous gypsum or satinspar cut into a similar form may be substituted. Jade cut in the same way is also sometimes favored, as well as many varieties of rock-crystal.

In marked contrast with the joyful festival of Easter stands the most solemn day of the Christian year, Good

---

[8] Ibid. col. 544.

[9] Konrad von Megenberg's version, "Buch der Natur," ed. by Dr. Franz Pfeiffer, Stuttgart, 1861, p. 459.

Friday, and for this day also we have a singularly appropriate stone, the variety of jasper known as the bloodstone. Here the red markings can be regarded as symbolical of the blood of Our Lord, shed for the salvation of mankind in the supreme sacrifice of the Passion. When the head of the Christ is cut in this stone it is often possible to utilize the red spots to figure the drops of blood flowing from the wounds inflicted by the Crown of Thorns.

With the glad tidings of Christmas Day is intimately associated the memory of the Star of Bethlehem, which served as a beacon light to guide the three wise men of the East to the humble manger wherein reposed the newly-born Saviour of the World. Hence for this great Christian festival no gem can equal the star-sapphire, combining as it does the pure sapphire-hue, always looked upon as symbolic of the highest moral, spiritual, and religious sentiments, and the mysterious moving star, which, shifting its apparent place with the slightest movement of the stone, seems endowed with a wonderful independent life, just as the phenomenal star of Bethlehem, unlike the fixed and changeless stars of the firmament, glided through the heavenly expanse, by a miraculous motion, due indeed to some supernatural law, but differing in kind and degree from all the usual, every-day aspects of nature.

The symbolism of precious stones presented in so many different ways by the early ecclesiastical writers appears in the prayer offered by the Archbishop of Canterbury at the coronation of the kings and queens of England. While the king kneels upon a footstool, the archbishop takes St. Edward's Crown and lays it upon the altar; whereupon he pronounces the following words:

O, God, the crown of the faithful, who on the heads of Thy saints placed crowns of glory, bless and sanctify this crown, that as the same is adorned with divers precious stones, so this Thy servant, wearing it, may be replenished of Thy grace, with the manifold gifts of all precious virtues, through the King eternal, Thy Son our Lord. Amen.[10]

In a tractate "Of the Crown of the Virgin," ascribed to Saint Ildefonso (607–669), the writer describes this wondrous gold crown as adorned with twelve precious stones, six splendid stars, and six beautiful and fragrant flowers, thus uniting the fairest treasures of earth and sky in honor of the Queen of Heaven.[11]

The gems, stars and flowers are given in the following order: Topaz, Sirius, sard, lily, chalcedony, Arcturus, sapphire, crocus, agate, the evening star, jasper, the rose, carbuncle, the Sun, emerald, the violet, amethyst, the Moon, chrysolite, sun-flower, chrysoprase, Orion, beryl, camomile. "That thus," the writer concludes, "with precious stones, radiant luminaries, and fair flowers, a splendid crown may be ennobled, beautified and adorned, and may be the more willingly and gladly accepted by Our Lady."

In a private collection in Smyrna there is a black hematite engraved somewhat in the style of an Abraxas gem; and certainly not Christian. On it is represented a galloping horseman, beneath whose steed is a crouching man; above the rider's head appears a star. The reverse bears the inscription: *σφραγίς θεοῦ*, "seal of God." In contrast with this is an intaglio carnelian of the Munich Royal Collection, with the figures of the Virgin Mary and the Infant Jesus, and the Greek words *ἡ εἰκὼν τῆς ἁγίας Μαρίας*, "the image of the Holy Mary." This is one of the best examples of Byzantine work in gem-cutting.[12]

---

[10] The Complete Ceremonies and Procedures Observed at the Coronation of the Kings and Queens of England, London, n. d., p. 28.

[11] Sanctorum Hildefonsi, Leodegarii, Juliani, "Opera Omnia," ed. Migne, Parisiis, 1882, coll. 283–318.

[12] Adolf Furtwängler, "Die Antiken Gemmen," Berlin, 1900; vol. i, Plate LXVII, Nos. 5, 2; described in vol. ii, p. 309.

One of the very curious cases of the employment of a purely secular Roman gem for ecclesiastical uses is offered by the exceedingly beautiful convex blue aquamarine engraved with the head of Julia, daughter of Titus, a fine work of the Augustan Age, now in the French Cabinet des Médailles in Paris. This was donated in the ninth century by the Carolingian emperor, Charles the Bald, to the Treasury of St. Denis, after it had been given a setting of pearls and precious stones. In St. Denis it was placed at the apex of a reliquary, which became known as the Oratorium of Charlemagne, and the head of the vain and worldly princess is said to have been venerated by the pious monks and priests as that of the Virgin Mary. As a work of portrait art this gem is one of the finest examples from classic times.[13]

The strange decadence and the conventionalized but profoundly earnest quality of Early Christian art is shown in an intaglio gem of the Royal Numismatic Museum in Munich. This is a dark-hued sardonyx of two layers, and the engraving depicts a bearded Christ, enthroned and accompanied by the twelve apostles, six on either side, four of them beardless while the remainder are represented with beards; they are all gazing reverently upon the central figure, behind whose head appear the arms of the cross and above them the letters $\overline{IC}$ $\overline{XC}$ *Ἰησοῦς Χριστός*.[14] Another somewhat similar Early Christian gem is a cameo cut in a sardonyx of three layers, the groundwork being a brownish-black, and the figures of a light-bluish hue, the upper parts yellowish-brown. Here also we have an enshrined Christ; above his head two angels hold a diadem. This is of superior workmanship to the intaglio gem just described.[15] There is a sardonyx cameo showing a rude figure of the Prophet

[13] Ibid., vol. i, Plate LXVIII, fig. 8; described in vol. ii, p. 307.
[14] Op. cit., vol. i, Plate LXVII, in No. 7; described in vol. ii, p. 307.
[15] Op. cit., vol. i, Plate LXVII, No. 3; described in vol. ii, p. 307.

Daniel, a lion on either side of him, and inscribed with his name in Greek letters. This is of Byzantine workmanship.[16]

The reliquarium of Wittekind, now in the Kunstgewerbe Museum at Berlin, is considered to be probably the most important specimen of early Frankish goldsmith-work that has been preserved, and is richly set with precious stones, some of these being ancient gems. This is one of a number of cases where engraved stones of Pagan times were used in the adornment of ornamental objects destined for Christian religious use. The upper edge shows a row of entwined animal figures, and the front side has medallions with primitive bird forms in cloisonné enamel; on the reverse side are very rudely executed repoussé figures of saints. This work is assigned to the latter part of the eighth century A.D., and is conjectured to have been a gift from Charlemagne to the Saxon King Wittekind, on the occasion of the latter's conversion to Christianity in the year 807. It was long preserved in Wittekind's foundation at Enger near Herford, to which he had bequeathed his treasures; in 1414 it was removed for safe-keeping to the Johanniskirche at Herford, where it remained until 1888, when it came into the possession of the Berlin Kunstgewerbe Museum. This precious example of the earliest German work has the form of a small portable satchel, in which could be placed those sacred relics the owner might wish to bear around with him because of the protection they were assumed to afford.[16a]

One of the most notable and valuable objects in the famous Guelph treasure that has recently been brought back to the city of Brunswick as a result of the marriage of the Duke of Cumberland's son, Ernest Augustus, with the daughter of Emperor William II, is an elaborately designed

---

[16] Op. cit., vol. i, Plate LXVII, No. 1; described in vol. ii, p. 307.

[16a] Handbuch der Königlichen Museum zu Berlin, Kunstgewerbe Museum, by Julius Lessing, Berlin, 1892, p. 14.

cross, a very fine specimen of the goldsmith's art of the twelfth century. This with the other treasures was taken by the Duke of Cumberland to Vienna for safe-keeping, at the time he gave up, in 1884, his title as Duke of Brunswick, rather than acknowledge Prussian supremacy. The cross, which has the form of a so-called "crutch-cross," with rectangular projecting plates at the ends of the arms, was designed to serve as a reliquary, the relic shrine being in a cruciform capsule behind a small, round-edged golden cross set in the midst of the cross proper. The precious relics reposing here were said to be bones of John the Baptist, St. Peter, St. Mark the Evangelist, and St. Sebastian. On the reverse side of the cross are set four large and beautiful sapphires and in the centre is a remarkably brilliant topaz.

While nothing definite is known as to the goldsmith who executed this work, its style and general character suggest the conjecture that it may have been produced by the artist who made the "Crown of Charlemagne" in Vienna, really a crown executed for Conrad III, King of the Germans (1093–1152), the first Hohenstaufen, and also several regal ornaments for the latter's consort, Queen Gisela. In addition to the jewelled decoration of its reverse, the front of the cross is set with many pearls, and the form of these settings is one of the chief arguments adduced in favor of attributing it to the maker of the so-called "Crown of Charlemagne."[16b]

An ecclesiastical jewel of great beauty and remarkable historic interest is known as the Cross of Zaccaria. It was secured in 1308 by Ticino Zaccaria at the capture of the ancient Greek colonial city Phocæa, in Asia Minor, and was donated to the Cathedral of San Lorenzo in Genoa. This

---

[16b] The Jewellers' Circular, Wednesday, December 16, 1914, vol. lxix, No. 20, p. 43.

cross is of silver gilt, measuring 64 cm. in height and 40 cm. in width, and within it behind a crystal is set a piece of the Holy Cross. It is profusely adorned with precious and semi-precious stones, there being 57 good-sized rubies, emeralds, sapphires, carnelians, malachites and amethysts, besides 44 smaller stones and 299 of still lesser size. The jewel is now preserved in the Palazzo Bianco, Genoa.

The greatest treasure in the Cathedral of Chartres was the "Sacred Shrine." It was made of cedar-wood covered with gold plates and was adorned with an immense number of precious stones including diamonds, rubies, emeralds, sapphires, jacinths, agates, turquoises, opals, topazes, onyxes, chrysolites, amethysts, garnets, girasols, sardonyxes, asterias, chalcedonies, heliotropes, etc. These had been presented by many different donors during a long period of time. In front of this shrine was a cross composed entirely of precious stones, comprising 56 rubies and garnets, 18 sapphires, 22 pearls, 8 emeralds, 8 onyxes and 4 jacinths. When this was first placed in the cathedral is not known, but it was there in 1353, as it is noted in an inventory made at that time. An uncut diamond weighing about 45 carats, and constituting one of the adornments of the shrine in 1682, was said to have been the gift of a marshal of France; another ornament, an oval agate engraved with the Virgin and Child, may now be seen in the Louvre where it forms part of the Sauvageot Collection.[17]

That all trace has been lost of an emerald engraved with the head of Christ and given to Pope Innocent VIII by Sultan Bajazet II about the year 1488, is greatly to be deplored, even though there be no truth in the legend or report that it had been engraved in the time of Christ by the order of Tiberius Cæsar. The evidence of two medals with Latin legends and of certain old paintings with English inscrip-

[17] F. de Mély, "Le Trésor de Chartres 1314–1793," Paris, 1886, pp. 16–21, 30.

tions of the sixteenth century seems to prove the existence of the gem in the Vatican treasury about the time specified, and it has been conjectured, with some probability, that the emerald had been engraved by a Byzantine artist at some time before 1453, when Constantinople fell into the hands of the Turks, and that this gem formed part of the booty they then secured. A print, often copied photographically and otherwise, purporting to be a representation of this emerald portrait of Christ, has no evidential value, and has either been freely worked up from the details of the spurious letter of Lentulus to Tiberius, giving a personal description of the Saviour, or still more probably from a Rafaelesque type of Christ's head.[18]

The beads of rosaries, when blessed by the Supreme Pontiff, or by one of the dignitaries of the Church, are considered to be endowed with a certain special virtue in favor of the individual for whom the blessing is imparted. However, should this person loan the beads to another with the intention of making him a partaker of this special blessing, or indulgencing, they lose their virtue. It is prescribed that these beads should be made of stone, glass, or some other durable material not easily broken, in order that the effects of the blessing should not be lost, or perhaps that the object so blessed should be less liable to injury. Various precious stones as well as pearls are used for this purpose, there being generally groups of ten small spheres, each group separated from the other by a larger sphere, the ten smaller beads serving to numerate the paternosters while the large bead is passed through the fingers when a credo has been recited.

A legend very popular in the Middle Ages has been conjectured to be the source of the word "rosary" as applied

[18] See C. W. King, "Early Christian Numismatics," London, 1873, pp. 95–112; "The Emerald Vernicle of the Vatican."

to a chaplet of beads for counting prayers. This legend tells of a pious youth, who on each and every day wove a garland of roses for the statue of the Virgin in the parish church. His religious zeal soon induced him to become a monk, and as the restrictions and duties of monastic life forced him to discontinue his floral offerings, he was much troubled in conscience, and was only relieved when the abbot told him that by reciting 150 aves at the close of each day, he would please the Virgin as much as by the gift of flowers. The prayers were faithfully said and they eventually became the occasion of a miracle. One evening, as the young monk was traversing a dense forest, it suddenly occurred to him that he had forgotten to recite his aves. He knelt down quickly and began to pray; all at once he saw a radiant and beautiful figure standing before him, and he immediately recognized in it the Blessed Virgin. Graciously she bent over him and drew from his lips one rose after the other, until fifty roses of supernatural beauty lay upon the ground. Of these she then made a garland and placed it upon the head of her faithful servant.[19]

The first literary allusion to rosaries in India is in a Jain treatise written about the beginning of our era. The Prakrit name here employed, *ganettiya,* is equivalent to the sanscrit *ganayitrika,* or "counter," and it is enumerated among the ten utensils of a Brahman ascetic. The other nine are the tridaṇda-stick, the water jar, the Bramanical thread, the earthen vessel named karotikâ, the bundle of straw used as a seat, the clout, the six-knotted wood, the hook, and the finger-ring. It is said that no mention of rosaries has been found in Indian Buddhist literature.[20]

---

[19] Thurston, "History of the Rosary in all Countries," Journal of the Society of Arts, vol. 1, p. 271; London, 1902.

[20] Leumann, "Rosaries Mentioned in Indian Literature;" in Trans. of the Ninth Cong. of Orient; (1892), London, 1893, pp. 883–889.

A splendid ecclesiastical ornament is described in the inventory of the royal treasures in the Château de Fontainebleau made in 1560, on the accession of Charles IX. This was of gold and composed of a crucifix with the figures of the Virgin Mary and St. John. It was "enriched with 41 sapphires, 3 pointed diamonds and 12 balas-rubies," which served to mark the nails in the cross. The weight of the gold was 25 marks 5 ounces, and the value of the entire object, gold and precious stones, is given as 2720 écus, or about $6120. The intrinsic value of the gold alone would be about $4240.[21]

The most impressive of the ecclesiastical ornaments in the Spanish churches was the *custodia,* or monstrance, in which the Holy Eucharist was borne through the streets on Corpus Christi day; indeed, only at this time was the custodia publicly shown. It was in fact a large shrine, generally affecting the form of a church tower. The most ancient example now in existence is in the Cathedral of Gerona. It is of gold, is 1.85 m. (over 6 feet) high, and weighs nearly 66 pounds. This work, in which the architectural style is an ornate Gothic, was completed in 1458 by the goldsmith Francisco de Asís Artau. One of the finest specimens, however, was executed by Enrique d'Arphe for Charles V and is in the Cathedral of Toledo. This *custodia* measures no less than nine feet in height and is three feet wide. Here also the form is that of a Gothic tower; the cross at the apex was made by the goldsmith Lainez, and is adorned with 86 pearls and 4 large emeralds.

The shrine itself contains 795 marks' weight of silver (about 600 pounds), the gold in its composition weighing

---

[21] Inventory of royal treasures in the Château de Fontainebleau, Bibl. Nat. MS. franc. 4732; fol. 3 of transcript in author's library from the collection of M. E. Molinier.

57 marks, or about 38 pounds. The Venetian Navagero estimated its worth to be 30,000 ducats.[22]

The wife of Marshal Junot, the celebrated Duchesse d'Abrantès, seeks to exonerate her husband and to refute the many charges of spoliation brought against him during and after the French occupation of Spain in 1808 and the succeeding years. For her, Marshal Lannes was a much worse offender, and she asserts that after the siege of Saragossa in 1809, Lannes secured possession of the immensely valuable treasures of the church of Nuestra Señora del Pilar, treasures valued at nearly $1,000,000. On his arrival in Paris, Lannes informed Napoleon that he had brought with him from Spain "a few colored stones of little value," and was graciously told that he could keep them for himself. The finest jewel of this collection contained 1300 diamonds, nine of which were of great magnitude and value; the jewel was heart-shaped, and had in the centre a dove, typifying the Holy Spirit, with wings extended. It had been given to the church by Doña Barbara de Portugal, Queen of Spain.[23]

About the year 1630 there could be seen in Paris a crucifix a foot and a half high, all of a single piece of yellow amber; on either side were the figures of the Virgin Mary and of St. John respectively, each carved in most excellent style. The writer who gives this information, a lineal descendant of Lodowyk van Berghem, commonly regarded as the first diamond-cutter, tells from hearsay evidence of a marvellous emerald which six hundred years before his time, or about 1060, hung suspended from the top of the nave of the Cathedral of Mainz. It was "as large as half-a-melon," and was of exceeding brilliance.[24]

---

[22] Carlos Justi, "Los Arfe"; in España Moderna, vol. 299, November, 1913, pp. 83, 87.

[23] Mémoires de Madame la Duchesse d'Abrantès, Paris, n. d., vol. 7, p. 447.

[24] Robert de Berquen, "Les Merveilles des Indes," Paris, 1661, pp. 87, 32.

The writer of a Bohemian poem on the legend of St. Catherine's betrothal to Christ, written about 1355, appears to have been, in one part, inspired by the glowing adornment of the Wenceslaus chapel in the cathedral of St. Veit. The poet gives an enthusiastic description of the gorgeous ornamentation of the mystic, imaginary temple in which the betrothal takes place. The pavement is of aquamarine beryl, the walls are studded with diamonds in golden settings, the framework of the windows is alternately of emerald or of sapphire, and the window-panes are not of stained glass, but of precious or semi-precious stones. Some of these are not ill fitted for this use, the transparency of rubies, amethysts, spinels, jacinths, garnets, and similar stones, admitting quite sufficient light; but others mentioned here, such as turquoises, chalcedonys and jaspers, would permit but a dim ray of light to traverse their opaque or semi-opaque substance. It has been conjectured by some that the poet drew his material from the account of the temple of the Holy Grail in the old German legend, probably through a Bohemian version; but as he omits in his enumeration twelve of the stones given in the Grail legend, and adds a number of others, diamond, turquoise, chalcedony, garnet, etc., this literary source is not fully satisfactory. Rather might it be believed that the splendid decoration of the Wenceslaus chapel and of the Karlstein Castle suggested the vision wrought out by the Bohemian poet, especially as among the stones he mentions which are not in the Grail legend, we have the garnet, so eminently a product of Bohemia.[24a]

A peculiar and very interesting facetted diamond of $6\frac{3}{32}$ carats displays alternate black and white facets and presents the appearance of a clearly defined Greek cross in

[24a] Dr. B. Ježek, "Aus dem Reiche der Edelsteinen," Prag, 1913, pp. 128–131.

black outline when viewed by transmitted light. The original crystal, which came from Brazil and weighed 10½ carats, was an octahedron and was of a jet black hue. The expectation was that the result of its cutting would be the production of a black brilliant, but when one of the points of the octahedron had been removed to form the table, it became evident that the black tint was only superficial, the body of the crystal being white. This peculiarity was then utilized by leaving some of the natural black faces of the crystal. This diamond was found to be of excessive hardness, rendering the task of cutting it an exceedingly arduous one. It is now in the possession of one of the Royal Household of Siam.[25]

Among the Buddhist legends current in India in the seventh century A.D. is one referring to the vases offered by the "four kings of heaven" to the Buddha. They first brought four gold vases, but the Buddha declared that one who had renounced the world could not use such costly vases. Silver vessels were then substituted, and were also refused, as were successively vases made of rock-crystal, lapis lazuli, carnelian, amber, ruby and other precious materials. Finally, four stone vases were proffered. These were of violet color and transparent, but the fact that they were not of precious material rendered them acceptable to the Buddha.[26]

The images of Buddha usually bear as adornment a small gem. This is most frequently a moonstone, but occasionally a ruby or some other gem will be used. The reason for this religious use of gems must not be sought only in the idea that precious and costly objects are most fitting as decora-

---

[25] See G. F. Kunz, "Five Brazilian Diamonds," Science, vol. iii, p. 649, No. 69, May 30, 1884.

[26] Heuen Tsang, "Mémoires sur les contrées occidentales," French trans. by Stanislas Julien, Paris, 1857, vol. i, p. 482.

tions of the sacred images, but it also implies a certain belief in the magic or quasi-sacred character of the gem itself.

The Saddharma Pundarîka, one of the nine most sacred books of the Buddhists, composed perhaps as early as the beginning of our era, gives the following description of a celestial stûpra, a sort of shrine containing a celestial being: [27]

> It [the *stûpra*] consisted of seven precious substances, *viz.*, gold, silver, lapis lazuli, musaragalva, emerald, red coral, and Karketana stone.
>
> This *stûpra* of precious substances once formed, the gods of paradise strewed and covered it with *mandârava* and great mandâra flowers. And from that stûpra of precious substances there issued the voice: "Excellent, excellent, Lord Sâkyamuni! thou hast well expounded the Dharmapayârya of the Lotus of the True Law. So is it, Lord; so is it, *sugata*."

Some of the most valuable temple treasures in the Island of Ceylon were preserved in a pagoda near the frontiers of the realm of Saula. The report of the gold and jewels accumulated here excited the avidity of the Portuguese, then in control of a considerable part of the island, and finally an energetic attempt was made to gain possession of them. Although the existence of the pagoda was well attested, the Portuguese were ignorant of its exact location in the tract of forest land wherein it stood. The expeditionary force consisted of 150 Portuguese and 2000 Lascars. On nearing the forest they placed themselves under the guidance of a native captured in the neighborhood. He led them through the woodland, traversing it hither and thither, but no pagoda appeared. Suddenly the native exhibited signs of madness, which were at first believed to be simulated, but were later regarded as genuine, on which he was made away with and another native substituted, however, with the same result. One after another five natives showed the same symptoms

[27] "The Saddharma-Pundarîka, or the Lotus of the True Law," trans. by H. Kern, Oxford, 1884, p. 228.

and were successively put to death, and at last the Portuguese were compelled to abandon this unsuccessful quest. We have here either a remarkable example of fidelity to the temple, or else an instance of the psychic influence of the terror inspired by the risk of violating it. Undoubtedly the priests represented the result as due to supernatural influence, and perhaps really felt justified in doing so.[28]

An official account of the embassy of the Cinghalese monarch Kirti Sri to Siam, in 1750, offers a description of the magnificent pagoda erected over the Sacred Footprint of Buddha, at Swarna Panchatha Maha Pahath. The free use of sapphires and rubies is quite natural, when we consider that some of the finest specimens of these stones are still found in this region: [29]

> Above the sacred footstep and made of solid gold was a pagoda supported on suitable pillars, forming a shrine. At the four corners were placed four golden *sésat,* and from above hung four bunches of precious stones like bunches of ripe areca-nuts in size. On the edge of the roof hung ropes of pearls, and on the point of the spire was set a sapphire the size of a lime fruit. Within and overshadowing the footprint like a canopy, there hung from the middle of the spire a full-blown lotus of gold, in the middle of which was set a ruby of similar size. Chariots, ships, elephants, and horses with their riders, all made of gold, and of a suitable size, were placed on a golden support above the silver pavement. This was hung on wires of gold, to which were hung ornaments set with pearls the size of the *nelli* fruit, as well as other jewelled ornaments, rings and chains. By some skilful device all this could be moved along the silver pavement.

Recent excavations made by Dr. J. H. Marshall in the Punjab, India, on the site of the ancient city of Taxila, captured by Alexander the Great during his Indian campaign, have brought to light many valuable Buddhist remains, dat-

---

[28] See J. Ribeyro, " Histoire de l'Isle de Ceylon," French trans. of Abbé le Grand, Amsterdam, 1701, pp. 184, 185.

[29] An account of King Kirti Sri's embassy to Siam in 1672, Saka (1750 A.D.), trans. from Sinhalese by P. E. Pieris. Extract from Jour. Roy. As. Soc., vol. xviii, No. 54 (1903).

ing from about 2000 years ago. One of the most striking of these is a relic casket taken from a *tope* of the type called *dagoba,* this name designating that class of those Buddhist structures designed especially for the reception of relics. This relic casket is of steatite, and contained a golden box within which was a fragment of bone, presumably regarded as a relic of the Buddha; around it were many pearls as well as engraved carnelians and also a number of other precious stones.

A carved sapphire, once in the collection of the Marquess of Northampton, shows a representation of the Hindu divinity, Siva. It is of Indian workmanship and the stone measures 1½ inches in length, 1½ inches in width and ¾ inch in thickness.[30]

One of the writers most familiar with Indian gem-lore recognizes that while the rich and educated Hindus of our day wear diamonds and other gems chiefly as ornaments, in ancient times these brilliant objects were more largely employed in India to enrich the images of the gods, thus rendering the idols more impressive and causing them to be worshipped with more intense fervor. In ancient India gemmed ornaments were believed to bring to the wearer "respect, fame, longevity, wealth, happiness, strength, and fruition"; a list of benefits long enough to satisfy the most exigent. However, as though this were not enough, we are further assured that these gems "ward off evil astral influences, make the body healthy, remove misery and ill-fortune, and wash away sin." [31]

The oldest jewel offered to a shrine by an Indian potentate, of which we have certain knowledge, was a magnificent pendant containing a number of precious stones, the gift of

[30] Proceedings of the Society of Antiquaries of London, vol. xvii, p. 168, illustration.

[31] Surindro Mohun Tagore, "Mani Mala," Pt. II, Calcutta, 1881, pp. 573, 601, 703.

Sundara Pandiyan, at a date prior to 1310 A.D. Another magnificent gift was a gorgeous jewelled turban adorned with diamonds, rubies, emeralds and pearls, bestowed in 1623 by Trimal Nayakkan.[32] These gifts or dedications show the prevailing tendency to propitiate the higher powers and insure success in royal enterprises.

The English ambassador, Sir Thomas Roe, sent to the court of Shah Jehangir by King James I, saw the Shah on the day of his great birthday festival when he was weighed against a great variety of objects, jewels, gold, silver, stuffs of gold and silver, silk, butter, rice, fruits, etc. All these things, heaped up on the scale balancing the one in which stood the Shah, were distributed as imperial gifts after the conclusion of the ceremony. Sir Thomas Roe declares that on this occasion (he missed seeing the actual weighing) the monarch was adorned with a great array of jewels, and he adds: "I must confess I never saw at one time such unspeakable wealth," a testimony of considerable value, for the English Court in the time of James I was one by no means poor in jewels, that sovereign having a great fondness for them. After the ceremony of weighing had been completed, Jehangir enjoyed the spectacle of a procession of twelve troupes of his choicest elephants, each troupe led by a "lord elephant of exceptional stature." The finest of these had all the plates on his head and breast set with rubies and emeralds, and all the elephants as they neared the Shah saluted him with their trunks.[33]

In Persia the pink and red coral was believed to have acquired its beautiful color after removal from the water, and the odor of the material was said to be a trustworthy

[32] Hendley, "Indian Jewellery," London, 1909, p. 106; see Major H. H. Cole, "Preservation of the Natural Monuments of India," Pl. 52.

[33] "Journal of Sir Thomas Roe, Ambassador of James I to Shah Jehangir, Mogul Emperor of Hindoostan"; in Kerr's Collection of Voyages and Travels, Edinburgh, 1824, vol. ix, p. 288.

means of discriminating between genuine and imitation coral; genuine coral had the smell of sea-water. The Chinese and the Hindus prized this substance very highly, because among them it was used to adorn the images of the gods.[34]

The perforated jade disk called *ts'ang pi* is still used as the symbol of the deity Heaven (T'ien) in the temple of that divinity at Peking. By a regulation of Emperor K'ien-lung, the proper dimensions of this ceremonial disk were rigidly established; the diameter of the disk proper was set at 6.1 inches, and its thickness at 7/10 of an inch; the perforation was to have a diameter of 4/10 of an inch. While the quality of the jade to be employed is not especially determined, the name *ts'ang* implies jade of a bluish shade. The veined type of stone is regarded as peculiarly adapted for this purpose.[35]

We are apt to regard Tibet as the land least accessible to modern influence of any kind, and that least in touch with any aspect of European civilization. It seems, therefore, not a little strange that at the chief altar of the Royal Chapel in the Dalai Lama's palace on Potala Hill, Lhasa, the elaborate *tse-boum* (incense vase or vessel), used by the Buddhist priests in their services, is a product of modern Parisian art, having been made in Paris about ten years ago. The vessel proper, which is carved from several exceptionally large pieces of coral, rests upon a flat, silver-gilt base, ornamented with two dragons, and is crowned with an oval framework of lapis lazuli leaves; upon this framework is a coral statuette of Amitabha, the "Lord of Boundless Light," revered as the emanation of Adi-Buddha, supported by a lotus flower of

[34] Von Hammer, " Auszüge aus dem persischen Werke, Buch der Edelsteine, von Mohammed Ben Manssur "; in Fundgruben des Orients, vol. vi, p. 138; Wien, 1818.

[35] Berthold Laufer, " Jade, a Study in Chinese Archæology and Religion," Chicago, 1912, p. 157.

Ceremony annually observed in the Mogul Empire of weighing the sovereign against precious metals, jewels and other valuable objects, which were distributed as gifts. From "Histoire générale des cérémonies religieuses de tous les peuples du monde," by Abbé Banier and Abbé Mascrier, Paris, 1741.

PERFORATED JADE DISK CALLED *TS'ANG PI*, A CHINESE SYMBOL OF THE DEITY HEAVEN (T'IEN)

From Berthold Laufer, "Jade, a Study in Chinese Archæology and Religion," Chicago, 1912, p. 157.

By courtesy of the author and Field Museum of Natural History, Chicago.

white chalcedony. At the apex of the leafy oval rests a representation in white chalcedony of a crescent moon, above is a sun in yellow stone from which springs a coral flame, symbolizing the radiance of wisdom (*nada*). Although the Dalai Lama was anxious to avail himself of the aid of French art for the embellishment of his altar, he took due precautions that the religious character of the vessel should be properly conceived and maintained, and therefore sent one of his high-priests to Europe to choose the artists best fitted for the execution of the vessel, and this priest took the pains to make a special trip to Leghorn in order to select the coral appropriate for the sacred utensil. As will be noted, this material, so greatly prized by the Tibetans, is that most prominent in this temple incense-vase. The dragons attached to the silver-gilt platter have been placed there to honor the Chinese, and are so affixed that they can be removed when no Chinese representatives are present at the ceremonies. In the older *tse-boum*, to take the place of which this Paris product was executed, the red-tinted ivory was used where coral appears in the newer vessel. The employment of this color is due to the fact that it is the sacred color of Amitabha.[36]

Within the sacred precincts of the temple of Cho Kang, in Tibet, is a splendid, life-size image of the Buddha formed of solid gold. The priests teach that it is of supernatural origin, and ascribe its execution to the creative energy of Visvakarma, a personification of the formative energy in the cosmos. The gold in this image is, however, not absolutely pure, but is alloyed with silver, copper, zinc and iron, the choice of these four metal alloys being dictated by the significance of the five metals in union as symbols of the world. The precious-stone adornment of this wonderful

[36] J. Deniker, "The Dalai Lama's new Tse-boum from Paris," Century Magazine, vol. lxvii, No. 4, Feb., 1904, pp. 582–583, with illustration.

idol consists of magnificent diamonds, rubies, emeralds and *indranila* or Indian sapphires. Pearl, turquoise and coral necklaces are twined around the figure's neck and crossed over its breast; on its head rests a golden coronet with a setting of turquoises, and rising from the rim of this coronet are five upright leaves within each of which is a small golden image of the Buddha; from one of these hangs as a pendant a remarkably fine, large and flawless piece of turquoise, measuring six inches in length and four inches in width. All these splendors lavished upon the image of the great apostle of the simple life show but a poor comprehension of the deep meanings and tendencies of his early career.

Treating of the religious associations of turquoise among the Tibetans, Dr. Berthold Laufer writes:[37]

> Turquoises, usually in connection with gold, belong to the most ancient propitiatory offerings to the gods and demons; in the enumeration, gold always precedes turquois as the more valuable gift. They also figure among the presents bestowed on saints and Lamas by kings and wealthy laymen. The thrones on which kings and Lamas take their place are usually described as adorned with gold and turquoises, and they wear cloaks ornamented with these stones. It may be inferred from traditions and epic stories that in ancient times arrowheads were made not only of common flint, but also occasionally of turquois to which a high value was attached. A powerful saint, by touching the bow and arrow of a blacksmith, transforms the bow into gold, and the arrowhead into turquois.

In the native languages of Mexico and Central America the name *chalchiḥuitl* most frequently designates jadeite, but it appears sometimes to have been applied to other stones of a green or greenish-blue color, such as the so-called amazon-stone from the region of the Amazon River, and even occasionally to the turquoise. Thus the talismanic value of the chalchihuitl seems to have depended rather upon its hue

---

[37] Berthold Laufer, "Notes on Turquois in the East," Field Museum of Natural History, Anthropological Series, vol. xiii, No. 1, Chicago, July, 1913, p. 11.

and its rarity, than upon its mineralogical character; indeed, among primitive peoples, stones of the same, or closely similar color, although of different composition, often bore the same name, and were conceived to have the same virtues whether talismanic or therapeutic. Writing of the rich gifts sent by Montezuma to Cortés upon the latter's arrival at San Juan de Ulúa (1519), Bernal Diaz de Castillo mentions[38] "four chalchiuites, a kind of green stone of great value, and much esteemed by them [the Indians], more highly, indeed, than we esteem the emerald. They are of a green color." And he proceeds to state that each one of these stones was said to be worth a great weight of gold.

The statue of the earth-goddess Couatlicue, found in the village of Cozcatlan, Mexico, and now preserved in the National Museum of Mexico, shows, inserted in the cheek, a disk of jadeite.[39] Green seems thus to have been the color sacred to this goddess, which may remind us of the attribution of the green emerald to Venus. Indeed, green as the color of foliage and plants must naturally have suggested itself as eminently appropriate for an earth-goddess, just as its significance as a symbol of life and generation connected it with the Goddess of Love.

The story of the emeralds brought from the New World by Hernan Cortés must have been quite familiar to sixteenth century writers, for we find Brantôme applying some details of this story to "a beautiful and incomparable pearl" said to have been brought from Mexico by Cortés on his return to Spain. This he later allowed to slip from his fingers into the sea while showing it to a friend on board

[38] "Verdadera historia de los sucesos de la conquista de la Nueva España," Bib. de Aut. Esp., vol. xxvi, Madrid, 1866, p. 35.

[39] Dr. Eduard Seler, "Similarity of Design of Some Teotihuacan Frescoes and Certain Mexican Pottery Objects," in Proceedings of the International Congress of Americanists, XVIII Session, London, 1912; Pt. II, London, 1913, p. 200.

the ship that was bearing him toward Algiers; it was lost in the sea, and in the words of Brantôme "vanished from the sight of mankind, unworthy to possess such a miracle of nature." The loss of this pearl is looked upon by the French writer as a punishment for the "inscription" Cortés had caused to be placed upon it: Inter natos mulierum non surrexit major;[40] this refers to John the Baptist and was, as we have seen, engraved upon one of the famous emeralds of Cortés. Brantôme believes that its application to a simple product of nature was sacrilegious and the cause of the object's loss; he also sees in this loss an omen of the death of the Emperor Charles which occurred shortly afterward, and he draws attention to the fact that the "Africans" called their kings "precious stones."[41]

The Aztec art-workers of the period immediately antedating the Spanish Conquest had attained a high order of skill in the difficult work of inlaying carefully cut and shaped bits of precious material so as to produce some form or design of symbolic or religious meaning. In judging the artistic merit of such work, we must always remember that the Aztec inlayers were only provided with rude and primitive tools and implements for the execution of their task, and extraordinary patience and application must have been necessary to complete some of the objects that have been preserved for us. This art seems only to have been cultivated in ancient Mexico and Central America, and perhaps Peru also; of the Mexican work some twenty-five examples have been saved. The Spaniards, shortly after their first landing, were given an opportunity to judge of the quality of this Aztec inlaying, for among the gifts sent by Montezuma to Cortés, were five such objects, a mask with incrusta-

---

[40] "Among them that are born of woman there hath not arisen a greater." Matt. xi, 11.

[41] "Œuvres du Seigneur de Brantôme," Londres, 1779, vol. v, pp. 35, 36.

By courtesy of Dr. Edward H. Thompson

THE SACRED WELL OF CHICHEN ITZA

Wherein, according to tradition, human victims and votive offerings of great value were cast.

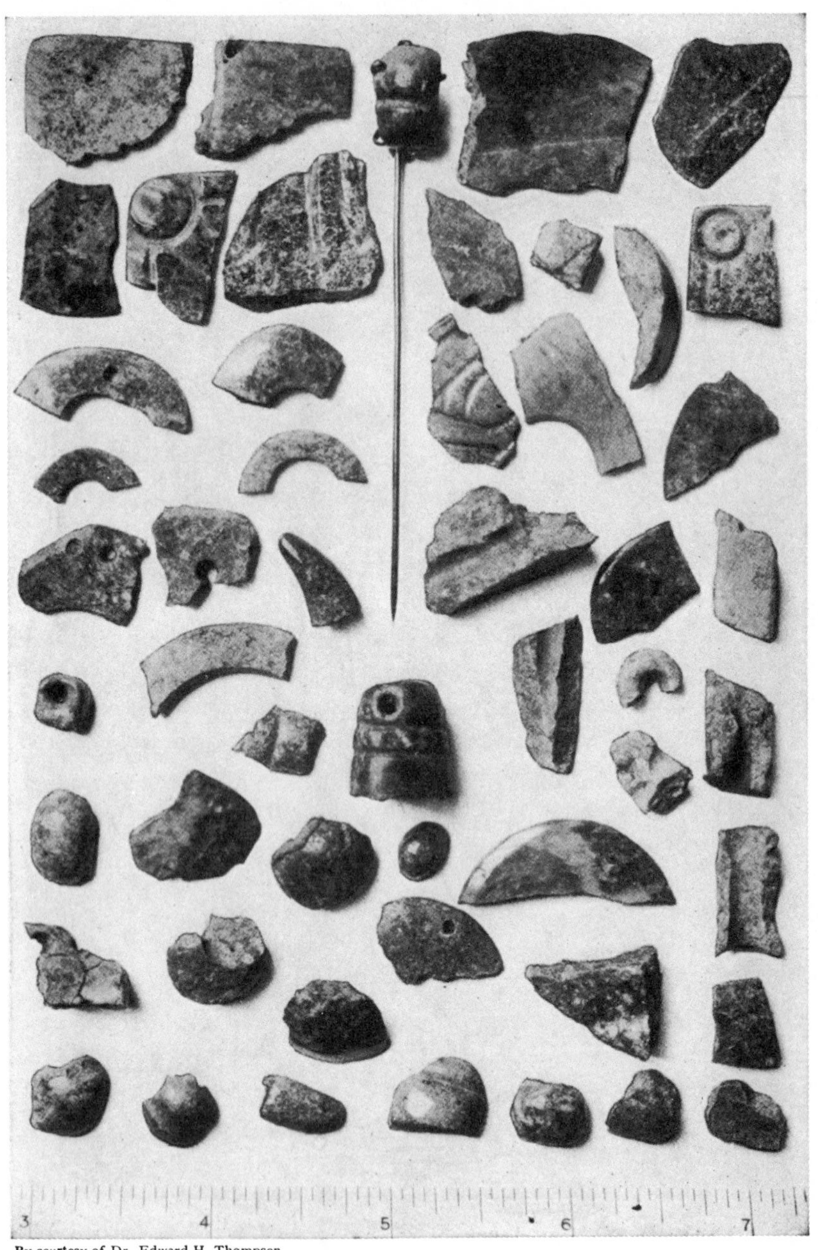

By courtesy of Dr. Edward H. Thompson.

CARVED AND WORKED STONES FROM THE SACRED WELL AT CHICHEN ITZÁ, YUCATAN, MEXICO

tions of turquoise, so disposed as to figure two intertwined serpents; a crozier, also with turquoise mosaic and ending in a serpent's head; a pair of large ear-rings of serpentine form decorated with the *chalchihuitl* stone (perhaps nephrite or jadeite); a mitre of ocelot skin, surmounted by a large *chalchihuitl,* and also decorated with turquoise mosaic, and a staff of office with similar inlays. A serpent-mask answering to the description of one of Montezuma's gifts is now in the British Museum and is in a fairly good state of preservation, although unfortunately the two serpent-heads have been lost. Evidently this mask was used in connection with the worship of Quetzalcoatl, the serpent-god, an incarnation of which deity the poor Aztecs at first believed Cortés to be.[41a]

Surpassing this mask in a certain strange and weird interest, and equalling it in artistic workmanship, is another most remarkable Aztec ceremonial mask, also in the British Museum Collection. The foundation of this is the front part of a human skull, and its outer surface has been covered with an incrustation of turquoise and jet mosaic in five alternate bands, the upper, middle and lower ones being of jet, while the two intermediate ones are of shaped pieces of turquoise; part of the nose has been removed and the space covered over by tablets of pink shell; protruding eyeballs are figured by convex disks of polished iron pyrites with a bordering of white shell; a number of the teeth have been broken out. Straps attached at the temples rendered it possible to bind this mask to the face of an idol, or for a priest of high rank to wear it on solemn ceremonial occasions.

Some three hundred yards or more from the great temple pyramid at Chichen Itzá, Yucatan, Mexico, at the termina-

---

[41a] W. H. Holmes, "Masterpieces of Aboriginal American Art," II, Mosaic Work; reprint from Art and Archæology, vol. i, no. 3, Nov., 1914; see pp. 96, 97, and Figs. 2 and 3, pp. 92, 93.

tion of the Sacred Way traversed in times of tribulation, of pestilence or famine, by processions of priests conveying sacrifices to be offered to the offended divinities, was the Sacred Well. Into this the priests would throw the ornaments and trinkets dedicated to the gods as peace-offerings. But such inanimate objects were regarded as insufficient, and even animal sacrifices were deemed to be inadequate, and hence it often happened that prisoners of war and fair maidens were cast into the deep, still waters of the Sacred Well.[42]

Many fragments of the carved stone ornaments have been recovered from the depths of this Sacred Well, and even in their present imperfect state, they testify to a considerable development of the lapidarian art among the ancient Mayas, and a high degree of artistic skill in the fashioning of such objects of adornment. Undoubtedly those used in this way as sacred offerings were considered to be amulets and therefore to be the more acceptable in the sight of the gods.

That lapis lazuli was as much favored for religious use by the aborigines of the New World as it was in ancient Egypt and in other parts of the Old World, is shown by the recent discovery of twenty-eight carefully formed cylindrical beads of lapis lazuli among some very ancient deposits in the island of La Plata, Ecuador. From the general character of these deposits it is evident that they did not belong to permanent dwellers on the island, and there is every reason to believe that they were left by visitors from the mainland, who came to the island for the performance of certain sacred rites and ceremonies.[43]

The ancient Mexicans held the turquoise in high esteem,

---

[42] Edward H. Thompson, "The Home of a Forgotten Race"; in The National Geographic Magazine, vol. xxv, No. 6, pp. 585–608; June, 1914.

[43] Fewkes, "Archæological Investigations on the Island of La Plata, Ecuador," Field Columbian Museum Pub. No. 56; Anthrop. Ser., vol. ii, No. 5, Chicago, 1901, pp. 266 sqq.

and that Los Cerrillos and other mines in Arizona and New Mexico were extensively worked prior to the discovery of America is proved by fragments of Aztec pottery-vases; by drinking, eating, and cooking utensils; by stone hammers, wedges, mauls, and idols which have been discovered in the débris found in many different localities.

While Major Hyde was exploring this neighborhood in 1880, he was visited by several Pueblo Indians from San Domingo, who stated that the turquoise he was taking from the old mine was sacred, and must not go into the hands of those whose Saviour was not a Montezuma, and these Indians offered, at the same time, to purchase all that might come from the mine in the future.

About ten miles from Tempe, Arizona, in ruins designated as Los Muertos, there was found enclosed in asbestos, in a decorated Zuñi jar, a sea-shell coated with black pitch, in which were incrusted turquoise and garnets, in the form of a toad, the sacred emblem of the Zuñi. Incrusted clam shells, representing toads, may be seen in the Brunswick Collection, the Christie Collection in the British Museum, and in the Pitorini Museum, Rome.

At the annual Fiesta which is attended by the San Felipe, the Navajo, the Isleta, the Acoma, the Jicorrilla, Apache and other Indians at the Pueblo of Santo Domingo, a place situated about three miles west by south of Wallace Station on the Atchison, Topeka and Santa Fé Railroad, a carved wooden image of the saint, about four feet in height, and said to date from the time of the conquest in 1692, is carried in procession through the principal streets to a small tent made of the finest Navajo blankets, where it is placed on an improvised altar. Here various offerings are made. Among them strings of turquoise beads, both round and flat, of the choicest color, are suspended from the ears of the figure, and from a string which encircles its neck. On the centre of the breast is one of the curious turquoise-encrusted marine clam-shells similar to the one found by Lieutenant F. H. Cushing in the excavations near Tempe, Arizona. The writer saw a fine example of this ornamental object suspended from the neck of the Virgin of Santo Domingo, at the Annual Fiesta, August 4, 1890. With the exception of a black band of obsidian running across the centre, the entire exterior of the shell is covered with a sort of miniature pavement of little squares of turquoise which are cemented to it with a black shellac-like substance obtained from "the grease-wood" plant common in New Mexico.[44]

It has been suggested that the types of ornamentation used by the aborigines of Central America may become fashionable at the time of the opening of the Panama Canal. In jewelry the crayfish model, as shown in a gold-plated ornament discovered in the Chiriqui district of Panama, offers a striking and peculiar form which might win favor; a curious frog pattern could also be used. If the local usage in ancient times is to be considered, the emerald and other green stones would be given the preference for decoration, as stones of this color were the most in favor among the primitive inhabitants of Central America because it symbolized the verdure of field and forest, and hence youth and vigor. When set in gold these stones gained in symbolic value, for gold, having the color of the sun, was regarded as typical of force, courage, and vitality.

The mystic lake of Guatavita, high up on the Andean plateau of Colombia, South America, was the chief holy place of the native Indians of this locality hundreds of years ago, at a time when gold and emeralds were plentiful among them, luxuries unknown to their impoverished descendants of our day. Legend had taught them to regard this lake as

[44] George F. Kunz, "Gems and Precious Stones of North America," New York, 1890, pp. 61, 62.

the abiding place of a powerful divinity or demon, whose good will must be secured at any price if dire disease were to be held aloof from the people. Four other sacred lakes on the plateau, Guasca, Siecha, Teusaca, and Ubaque, shared in a lesser degree with the principal one in the attribution of mysterious power. As early as 1534 word was brought to Sebastian de Belalcazar, founder of Quito, that in the course of the religious ceremonies held by the Indians at the Lake of Guatavita, they were wont to cast into its waters immense quantities of gold dust, emeralds and other precious stones. It was also related that at these semi-annual festivals the Caciques and the principal chiefs, bearing valuable gifts of gold-dust and emeralds, were paddled out in canoes (or on rafts) to the exact middle of the lake, this point being determined by the intersection of two ropes stretching from four temples erected at four equidistant points on its banks. Arrived at this spot the offerings were cast into the lake, and the Cacique of Guatavita, whose naked body had been coated with an adhesive clay, over which gold-dust was sprinkled in profusion, sprang into the water, and after washing off the gold-dust, swam to the shore. This resplendent living golden figure strongly appealed to the Spaniards' imagination, and the name they bestowed upon the Cacique, El Dorado ("The Golden," or "Gilded"), is used to our day as a designation of a region or a spot exceptionally rich in gold. At the moment the "Golden Cacique" made his plunge into the lake, the assembled people scattered along its banks turned their backs toward the water, shouted loudly, and threw their propitiatory offerings over their shoulders into the lake.

Attempts have often been made to secure the treasures by drawing off the waters of the lake, but only with very partial success so far. The first serious effort is said to have been made by Antonio de Sepulveda, a merchant of

Santa Fé, in United States of Colombia, who obtained a Spanish concession. In or about 1823 we have record of another unsuccessful venture on the part of José Ignacio Paris, in an account of Colombia written in 1824 by Captain Charles Stuart Cochrane, of the Royal Navy, who aided Paris in his efforts. The report that at the time of the Spanish Conquest, the Cacique of Guatavita caused gold-dust constituting the burdens of fifty men to be cast into the lake, greatly contributed to the zeal of the treasure-seekers in the vicinity. One of the early attempts at least resulted in the recovery of so much treasure that the Government's 3 per cent. share is said to have amounted to $170,000.

In none of these essays, however, was the lake really and effectually drained off, and that of Paris in 1823 or 1824 failed in the same way, because of inadequate capital. He had succeeded in persuading sixteen shareholders to club together, each one contributing $500 to a common fund, but after not only this $8,000, but $12,000 more supplied by himself had been expended, there still remained 33 feet of water in the lake.

Recently an English company has recognized that the treasure must be sought at or even beneath the true bottom, as this existed at the time of the Spanish Conquest, and thus at levels considerably lower than those of the bottom at the present time. The project is, after 30 feet of the present bottom has been removed, to set up a steam shovel and sink down 40 or 50 feet in search of the gold-dust, golden ornaments and emeralds believed to exist here.

VIII

Amulets: Ancient, Medieval, and Oriental

THE present and the following chapter are devoted to a study of the talismanic virtues attributed to precious stones and gems, as distinguished from the curative powers with which they were credited. It is sometimes difficult to establish a hard and fast dividing line between the two classes, as everything that conduces to the happiness and well-being of man also affects his bodily health, but a distinction, correct in the main, may be made by regarding the talismanic use as covering all cases except those in which the stone was used where to-day some really medicinal substance would be administered.

A modern German writer on amulets has proposed to apply the term "emanism" (Emanismus) to the virtue existing or supposed to exist in amulets and talismans, and gives as his opinion that their virtue is neither a spiritual nor a personal one, but the operation of forces, the latter not being special, mysterious vital forces, but impersonal physical components and qualities, and that these exercise their influence by means of emanation. Wundt has held that the very earliest amulets were parts of the human body, and almost always such parts as were believed to be the bearers of the soul.[1]

Radiation or emanation of energy, without observable loss of substance, is a fact familiar enough to us to-day, but this phenomenon was not so generally accepted centuries ago. Still the lodestone always offered a striking example

[1] Karutz, " Der Emanismus," in Zeitschrift für Ethnologie, 45th Jahrgang, 1913, Heft III, Berlin, 1913, pp. 559, 560.

with which all writers on such subjects were acquainted. A stranger argument in support of the truth of this property was adduced by the seventeenth century physician, Sir Thomas Browne (1605–1682), who writes: [2]

> If amulets do work by emanation from their bodies upon those parts whereunto they are appended and are not yet observed to abate their weight; if they produce visible and reall effects by imponderous and invisible emissions, it may be unjust to deny all efficacy to gold, in the non-emission of weight or deperdition of any ponderous articles.

While the learned doctor does not expressly state his belief in these "imponderous and invisible emissions" from amulets, he certainly does not attempt to deny their existence.

The Bolivian natives believe that the so-called mountain-sickness, the affection from which some travellers suffer at high altitudes, probably originates in subtle emanations from certain mineral veins. A confirmation of the fact that such a belief exists, though not of the truth of the theory, is found in the native name for this illness, *veta,* which signifies at once "mountain-sickness" and a vein or lode. The fact that at the pass of Livichuco, on the trail from Challapata to Sucre, there are considerable deposits of antimony, is regarded as substantiating this strange fancy.[3]

Among the Babylonians one of the most dreaded of the malign spiritual powers was the terrible female demon Labastu, and a long series of amulets are recommended, one or more of which should be worn to ward off her pernicious influence. For some of these amulets precious stones were used, and the effect of color, probably a determining circumstance in the selection of the particular stone, was to be strengthened by the color of the wrapping about the stone

---

[2] Browne, "Pseudodoxia Epidemica," London, 1650, Bk. II, chap. 5, p. 65.
[3] Scientific American, June 28, 1913, p. 575.

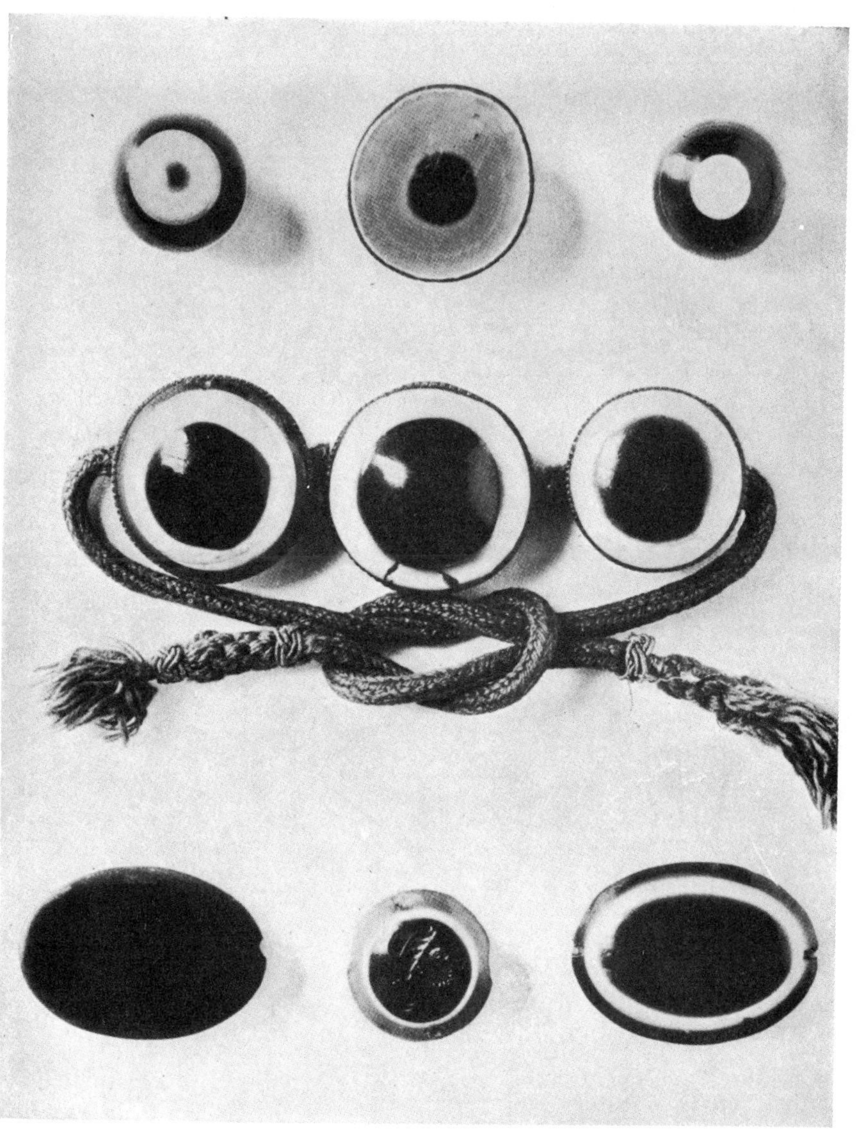

EYE AGATES
Used as charms against the Evil Eye. East Indian.

TYPES OF EGYPTIAN SEALS AND SCARABS IN THE MURCH COLLECTION, METROPOLITAN MUSEUM OF ART, NEW YORK

Royal names: Fig. 1, XII Dynasty (2000-1788 B.C.), Usertasen III; Fig. 2, XIII Dyn. (1788-1680, B.C.), Sebekhetep III; Fig. 3, Hyksos Kings (1680-1580 B.C.), Aamu; Fig. 4, XVIII Dyn. (1580-1350 B. C.), Amenhetep I; Fig. 5, XIX Dyn. (1350-1205 B.C.), Rameses II; Fig. 8, XXII Dyn. (945-745 B.C.) Sheshonk I; Fig. 9, XXV Dyn. (712-663 B.C.), Taharka; Fig. 10, XXVI Dyn. (663-525 B.C.), Psamtek I; Private names: Fig. 11, Shemses, "Attendant"; Fig 12, Rera, "Superintendent of the Storehouse of Offerings"; Fig. 13, Ankh, "Attendant." Figs. 14-16, scroll designs and ornamental groupings of hieroglyphs. Fig. 17, Goodluck amulet "May your name be established, may you have a son!" **Figs. 18-24, animal-back seals.**

and of the cord by means of which it was to be hung from the neck, or attached to the right or left hand or foot, or to other parts of the body. As this dreadful spirit was chiefly feared as the inducer of disease, the location of the amulet was perhaps in some cases determined by the presence of local pain or disorder; in this case it would be expected to act as a cure of disease rather than a mere preventive. The following passages refer to such stone amulets:[4]

Thou shalt wrap up a *shubu*-stone in white wool, and hang it on a white woollen cord, with four eye-stones (*enâti*) and four *parê*, and bind it to thy right hand.

A black *ka*-stone shalt thou enwrap in black wool, hang it on a black woollen cord, provide it with three eye-stones and three *parê*, and bind it to thy left hand.

Thou shalt wrap a white *ka*-stone in red wool, hang it on a red woollen cord, with four eye-stones and four *parê*, and bind it to the right foot.

An *appu*-stone shalt thou wrap up in blue wool, hang it on a blue woollen cord, furnish it with three eye-stones and three *parê*, and bind it to the left foot.

Seven eye-stones and seven *parê* shalt thou string on a black cord.

The *enâti* (eye-stones) here mentioned were most probably eye-agates similar to those still prized in the Mesapotamian region for their supposed magical virtues, and more especially for protection against the Evil Eye. There is, indeed, a bare possibility that some form of the cat's-eye (known by that name to the Arabs) or one of the star-stones may occasionally be signified by this Assyrian name. The word *parê*, as it is not preceded by the determinative character signifying stone, may refer to some other material.

An immediate association of an animal eye with a turquoise, an example of the sympathetic magic to which we have frequently alluded, comes from Persia. During the celebration of the imposing ceremonies attending the great

[4] Morris Jastrow, Jr., "Die Religion Babyloniens und Assyriens," vol. i, Giessen, 1905, pp. 335–339.

annual assemblage of pilgrims at the shrine of Mecca, it is customary to slaughter an immense number of sheep, and certain of the Persian pilgrims will secure possession of some of the eyes of their sacrificial victims, and will embed turquoises in them, firmly believing that in this way they have composed an infallible amulet against the Evil Eye.[4a]

A Persian manuscript of a work entitled "Nozhat Namah Ellaiy," written in the eleventh century by Schem Eddin, the transcription being dated 1304, asserts that the turquoise (piruzeh), though lacking in brilliancy, was esteemed to be a stone of good omen, and one that would bring good luck, since this was indicated by its name, signifying in Persian, "the Victorious."[5]

One of the Egyptian tales from the time of the early dynasties shows the value placed upon the turquoise in Egypt at that time. This recital occurs in Baufra's Tale. The reigning Pharaoh, to relieve a fit of mental depression, took a pleasure trip on the palace lake in a boat rowed by twenty beautiful and richly attired maidens. While bending over her oar, one of the maidens let fall into the water from her hair-adornment a fine turquoise (Egypt *mafkat,* thus rendered by Petrie) and was deeply chagrined at the loss. However, the court magician Zazamankh, who accompanied the sovereign, by his magic arts was able to provide a remedy, for on his reciting a charm of great power the turquoise rose up through the water so that it could be picked up from the surface and returned to its disconsolate owner.[5a]

The Egyptians believed that the different kinds of pre-

[4a] Pogue, "The Turquois," Washington, 1915, citing an article by Sikes, in "Folklore," vol. xii, p. 268, London, 1901.

[5] Cited by Joseph E. Pogue, in "The Turquois"; Memoirs of the National Academy of Sciences, vol. xii, pt. ii, Third Memoir, Washington, 1915, p. 13. From Ouseley, "Travels in Various Countries of the East, more Particularly Persia," London, 1819, vol. i, pp. 210–212.

[5a] Pogue, "The Turquois," Washington, 1915, citing Petrie "Egyptian Tales, First Series, Fourth to Twelfth Dynasty," London, 1895, pp. 16–22.

cious stones were endowed with certain special talismanic properties, and these stones were combined in their necklaces in a way supposed to afford protection from all manner of malign influences. The beads were of various forms, sometimes round or oval, and at others, rectangular or oblong; besides the stones in general use, such as the emerald, carnelian, agate, lapis lazuli, amethyst, rock-crystal, beryl, jasper and garnet, beads of gold, silver, glass, faience, and even of clay and straw, were employed. To complete the efficacy of the necklace, small images of the gods and of the sacred animals were added as pendants. Even on the mummies and mummy cases such ornaments are painted in imitation of necklaces or collars of precious stones, with flowers, etc., as pendants.[6]

One of the most artistic and beautiful specimens of ancient Egyptian goldsmiths' work was recently sent by Dr. Flinders Petrie, on behalf of the Egyptian Research Account Society, to the Boston Museum of Fine Arts. It is adorned with amethysts set in gold, the stones with their symbolic settings constituting a charm of powerful amulets for the protection of the wearer, who is believed to have been the Princess Sat-Hathor-Ant, of the Twelfth Dynasty, the wife of the heir to the throne. Dr. Petrie pronounces this to be one of the finest ancient Egyptian necklaces he has ever seen.

This splendid ornament came from tomb No. 154 at Haragh. It measures 26.3 inches in length and is composed of 88 amethyst beads varying in length from nearly a quarter-inch to about four-tenths of an inch (0.6 cm. to 1 cm.) and in diameter from a little over a quarter-inch to over four-tenths of an inch (0.7 cm. to 1.1 cm.). The beads are slightly flattened and the borings were made from both ends, meeting accurately in the centre in the majority of

[6] Budge, "The Mummy," Cambridge, 1894, pp. 330–331.

cases. In spite of small surface scars, they are generally of very clear and even color.[6a]

Special chapters from the great Egyptian collection of hymns and invocations known as the "Book of the Dead" were inscribed on certain particular stones, as in the following instances:

Chapter XXVI of the Book of the Dead to be inscribed on, or recited over, a figure in lapis lazuli.[7]

Chapter whereby the Heart is given to a person in the Netherworld.

He saith: Heart mine to me, in the place of Hearts! Whole Heart mine to me, in the place of Whole Hearts!

Let me have my Heart that it may rest within me; but I shall feed upon the food of Osiris, on the eastern side of the mead of amaranthine flowers.

Be mine a bark for descending the stream and another for ascending.

I go down into the bark where thou art.

Be there given to me my mouth wherewith to speak, and my feet for walking; and let me have my arms wherewith to overthrow my adversaries.

Let two hands from the Earth open my mouth: Let Seb, the Erpâ of the gods, part my two jaws; let him open my two eyes which are closed, and give motion to my two hands which are powerless; and let Anubis give vigor to my legs that I may raise myself upon them.

And may Sechit the divine one lift me up, so that I may arise in Heaven and issue my behest in Memphis.

I am in possession of my Heart, I am in possession of my Whole Heart, I am in possession of my arms and I have possession of my legs.

[I do whatsoever my Genius willeth, and my Soul is not bound to my body at the gates of Amenta.]

Chapter XXVII of the Book of the Dead to be inscribed on, or recited over, a figure in green feldspar.[7a]

Chapter whereby the Heart of a person is not taken from him in the Netherworld.

[6a] Communicated by Dr. Arthur Fairbanks, Director of the Boston Museum of Fine Arts.

[7] "Life Work of Sir Peter Le Page Renouf," vol. vi, Paris, 1907.

[7a] "The Life Work of Sir Peter Le Page Renouf," vol. iv, Paris, 1907, p. 71.

O ye gods who seize upon Hearts, and who pluck out the Whole Heart; and whose hands fashion anew the Heart of a person according to what he hath done; lo now, let that be forgiven to him by you.

Hail to you, O ye Lords of Everlasting Time and Eternity!

Let not my Heart be torn from me by your fingers.

Let not my Heart be fashioned anew according to all the evil things said against me.

For this Heart of mine is the Heart of the god of mighty names [Thoth], of the great god whose words are in his members, and who giveth free course to his Heart which is within him.

And most keen of insight is his heart among the gods. Ho to me! Heart of mine: I am in possession of thee, I am thy master, and thou art by me; fall not away from me; I am the dictator to whom thou shalt obey in the Netherworld.

Were there sufficient evidence as to the use of jade by the ancient Egyptians, we might be justified in finding an allusion to this substance in the 160th chapter of the Book of the Dead. This chapter was to be inscribed upon a small column made of a green stone (Renouf translates "green feldspar"), as appears in the text, which reads, in part, as follows:

I am the column of green feldspar which cannot be crushed, and which is raised by the hand of Thoth.

Injury is an abomination for it. If it is safe, I am safe; if it is not injured, I am not injured; if it receives no cut, I receive no cut.

Said by Thoth: arise, come in peace, lord of Heliopolis, lord who resides at Pu.

The text is accompanied by a vignette in which Thoth is represented bringing the column enclosed in a box or casket. This is one of the forms of the *neshem*-stone, a name used in Egyptian as widely and vaguely as was *smaragdus* in Latin. One thing is, however, quite evident, the material designated here must have been of exceptional hardness and toughness, for the special virtue of the column-amulet was to make the body as hard and indestructible as itself. Incidentally we may recall that the hermetic work of Thoth, named by the later Greeks Trismegistos, the Thrice Mighty One, which was said to have been unearthed in a tomb, was inscribed upon *smaragdus*.

The larger part of the amulets used in ancient Egypt represented some living creature. The most usual type is the bull's head, which was cut from carnelian, hematite, amazon stone, lapis lazuli, or quartz. Prehistoric Egyptian amulets representing the fly have been found; these were of slate, lapis lazuli and serpentine. In historic times gold was employed as the material. Other types occurring in prehistoric times are the hawk, of quartz or limestone; the serpent, of lapis lazuli or limestone; the crocodile and the frog. Carnelian was freely used as the material for amulets in the earlier historic times, among the prevailing forms were the hand, the fist, and the eye; amulets figuring the lion, the jackal-head, the frog, and the bee, also appear. Silver or electrum was substituted for carnelian in the Middle Kingdom. At a later period amulets were used less and less frequently.[8]

The mysterious virtues of the scarab are not yet forgotten in the East, in Syria at least, for we are told that this beetle is an object of much veneration among the Syrian peasants as an amulet. One use of it in this way is to enclose a specimen in a box and lay this upon the breast of a babe in its cradle as a sure protection against the greatly-dreaded Evil Eye. There is also a superstition in this region that if a "scarab" is found lying helplessly on its back, anyone who charitably relieves it of its embarrassment by setting it on its feet, will be relieved of the guilt of a number of sins.[9]

---

[8] Flinders Petrie, "The Arts and Crafts of Ancient Egypt," Edinburgh and London, 1909, p. 79.

[9] Carlo Landberg, "Proverbes et dictons de la province de Syrie, Section de Sayda," Leyden, 1883, pp. 313, 314.

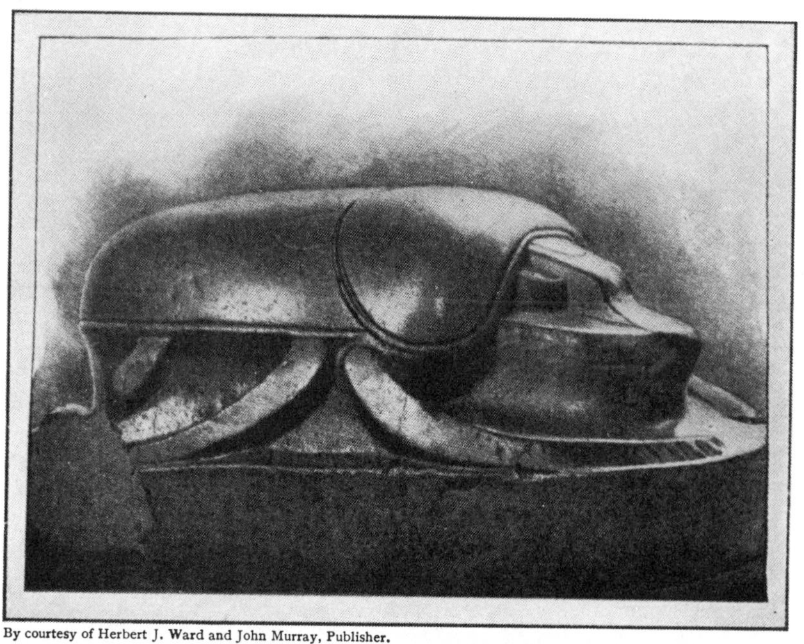

By courtesy of Herbert J. Ward and John Murray, Publisher.

COLOSSAL SCARAB IN BLACK GRANITE, BRITISH MUSEUM

Length 60 in., by 33 in. high. From "The Sacred Beetle" by John Ward, F.S.A.

It is difficult to see any other origin for the scaraboid, or imperfect scarab form, than that afforded by the Egyptian scarabs, some of which date back to about 4000 B.C. Whether we can literally say that the scaraboid was introduced into Babylon by the Egyptians may be open to question, as the form itself appears to have been evolved by Etruscans and Greeks. Unquestionably the scaraboid was much more easily shaped than the scarab proper, and for those traders who wished large supplies for commercial purposes at a low cost, this was by no means a negligible quality.

The evolution of the ring from the cylindrical seal is of course purely a matter of conjecture. Here, as is often the case in a chain or series of fossil remains, we have a succession of types which *may* be connected with one another genetically, but which *must* not be so connected. That is to say, we cannot prove the affirmative and can only point to a probability.

Many cut and engraved stones, some of which had evidently been used as talismans, have been washed up on the shore at Alexandria, Egypt. Not all of these are completed, some being only half worked, as though the engraver had become dissatisfied with his design, or had found a flaw in the material, or that they had been lost from boats or ships. It has been conjectured that these half-completed gems were the work of household jewellers employed in the palaces of Alexandria.[10] In Mas'ûdi's "Meadows of Gold" we read that in his time, in the tenth century A.D., there was what he terms "a fishery for precious stones" on the seacoast near Alexandria, Egypt. To account for this he relates two bits

[10] Oskar Schneider, "Ueber Anschwemmung von antiken Arbeitsmaterial an der Alexandriner Küste," in "Naturwissenschaftliche Beiträge zur Geographie und Kulturgeschichte," Dresden, 1883, pp. 4, 5, 6.

of legend. One of them represents these fragments of precious stones as having originally adorned the richly decorated vases and vessels of Alexander the Great, which were broken up and cast into the sea by Alexander's mother after his death. The other tale was to the effect that Alexander himself had gathered together a mass of jewels and ordered them to be thrown into the sea near the Pharos, so that its neighborhood should never be deserted; for, Mas'ûdi remarks, wherever precious stones are to be found, whether in mines or in the depths of the sea, men are sure to assemble to seek for them.[11]

The prophet Isaiah in his third chapter, where he scores the wantonness and vanity of the Daughters of Zion (vs. 16–26), enumerates in detail the various adornments of a Hebrew *mondaine* toward the end of the eighth century before Christ. Among the jewels and trinkets, amulets (*lehâshîm;* v. 20) are expressly mentioned, and also "crescents," these being probably of gold. While it is not possible to determine the material of the amulets, the fact that they are named together with rich ornaments of various kinds, rings, nose-jewels, bracelets, anklets, etc., indicates that they were of precious material, and were possibly engraved precious stones or seals of some sort.[12] In the Song of Songs, which can scarcely be assigned to a later date than Isaiah, and may have been written earlier, the seal is named in what is perhaps the most beautiful passage of this unique poem, Chapter VII, verse 6:

---

[11] Maçoudi, "Les Prairies d'Or," text and French trans. by Barbier de Meynard and Pavet de Courteille, vol. ii, Paris, 1863, pp. 436, 437, chap. xxxii.

[12] Gesenius in his Hebrew Dictionary even conjectures that the leḥâshîm may have been shells, which when held to the ear gave forth sounds believed to have an ominous significance.

Set me as a seal upon thine heart;
as a seal upon thine arm.
For love is strong as death;
passion is unyielding as Hades,
The flashes thereof are flashes of fire;
an all-consuming flame.

The golden "crescents" were used as amulets by the Midianites for suspension on the necks of their camels, at the period of the Hebrew conquest of Canaan, as appears from the eighth chapter of Judges (v. 21).

The burying in a grave of valuable gems and ornaments worn by the deceased during life must have been originally due to a belief that they served as talismans to guard the remains from the malign influence of evil spirits, or perhaps even to afford protection and aid, by some strange occult power, to the soul of the departed in the under or upper world whither it had journeyed. In the New World, among the more highly civilized and wealthy Indian tribes of the south, this custom was very general, and rich spoils have been taken from their graves by the unsentimental settlers from Europe. In the Old World also this usage was quite common; Egyptian tombs have afforded jewels of gold and gems worth large sums intrinsically, apart from their archæological value, and only to note one among many instances, we may recall the treasures unearthed by the indefatigable Schliemann in the old Greek tombs of Mycenæ. However, of all these finds none surpasses in interest that made by M. Henry de Morgan near Susa on February 10, 1901, when there was brought to light, from a depth of some six metres below the surface, a bronze sarcophagus containing the skeleton of a woman. Heaped upon the breast of the skeleton and strewn about the head and neck was a mass of finely-wrought and artistic gems and jewels, including several detached amulets. From coins found in the burial and also from the general character of these relics, M. de Morgan believes that the interment must have been made at some date between 350 and 330 B.C., just before Alexander's invasion of Persia.[13]

The jewels embrace a beautiful gold torque weighing 385 grams (something over one pound Troy). The hoop terminates in two lions' heads having cheeks of turquoise, while on the muzzle is a lapis lazuli flanked by two turquoises; on the top of the head is a plate of mother-of-pearl. Bracelets similar in design and decoration to the torque go to complete the parure. Of even greater interest than the gold torque was a three-row pearl necklace, 238 of the pearls being still more or less well preserved; originally there must have been from 400 to 500 of them. Still another valuable necklace consists of 400 beads of precious or ornamental stone material and 400 gold beads. The stones represented are turquoise, lapis lazuli, emerald, agate, various jaspers, red and blond carnelian, feldspar, jade (?), hyaline and milky quartz, amethyst of a pale violet hue, hematite, several marbles and breccia. A fourth necklace had a row of beads and pendants incrusted with carnelian, lapis lazuli and turquoise; here the sharp contrast of the bright red carnelian disturbs the harmonious effect produced by the combination of the dark blue lapis lazuli and the light blue turquoise.

The detached amulets are of various forms, one figuring a sphinx with a ram's head; this was in white paste with green enamel. Another, of gold, was rudely fashioned in the form of a lion or a cat, and there was also a dove of lapis lazuli, poorly executed, the amulets (mainly of Egyptian type) being of very inferior workmanship as compared with the jewels. Still they serve to confirm the belief that this heaping up in the tomb of all the dearest treasures cherished

[13] Delegation en Perse, vol. viii, Recherches Archéoligiques 3 ème Série, Paris, 1905, pp. 36–58.

in life, was intended to exert a post-mortem influence upon the after-life of the dead woman.

That some of the Hebrew patriots who fought under the banner of Judas Maccabæus toward the middle of the second century B.C. were tinged with the prevailing superstition regarding amulets, appears in a passage of the second book of Maccabees, where it is stated that when Judas collected together for burial the bodies of those patriots who had fallen in battle before Odolla, they were found to have worn beneath their tunics certain idolatrous amulets, a custom strictly forbidden to the Jews. Their death was then looked upon as a signal instance of divine justice, which "had made hidden things manifest," and Judas exhorted the people to take this lesson to heart and guard themselves from sin.

The wealth of books on magic and divination produced in the ancient city of Ephesus, in Asia Minor, was so great that the designation "Ephesian writings" was quite generally given to writings of this kind, more especially to denote short texts that could be worn as amulets or charms. We read in the Acts of the Apostles (xix, 19) that after hearing the fervent discourses of St. Paul, in which he eloquently attacked the superstitions of the Ephesians, many of those who owned books of this description were so deeply moved that they burned up all such books in their possession, to the value of 50,000 pieces of silver, that is to say $9000, equivalent perhaps to $90,000, if we make due allowance for the greater purchasing power of money nearly two thousand years ago. The small literary value of the writings of this sort that have been preserved for us indicates that the loss to posterity by this auto-da-fé was not very considerable, and yet many queer superstitions and strange usages of which we now lack information must have been noted in these magic rolls and sheets.

The following lines may serve to show how highly the

jasper was esteemed in ancient times, this designation covering jade as well:[14]

Auro, quid melius? Jaspis. Quid Jaspite? Virtus. Quid virtute? DEUS. Quid deitate? Nihil.

What is better than Gold? Jasper.
What is better than Jasper? Virtue.
What is better than Virtue? GOD.
What is better than the deity? Nothing.

The first mention of the famous charm Abracadabra, which so often appears engraved on Gnostic gems, occurs in a Latin medical poem written by Serenus Sammonicus who lived in the third century and is said to have bequeathed his library consisting of sixty-two thousand volumes to the Emperor Gordian the Younger. The poem recommends this mystic word, or name, as a sovereign remedy for the "demi-tertian" fever, if it were written on a piece of paper and suspended by a linen thread from the neck of the patient. To have its full efficacy the word should be written as many times as there are letters in it, but taking away one letter each time, so that the inscription assumed the form of an inverted cone.[15]

It is interesting to note that De Foe, writing in the seventeenth century of the Great Plague in London (1665), alludes to this strange talisman as still in use.[16] Treating of the curious prophylactics employed at that time, he reproaches those who employed such methods, and acted "as if the plague was not the hand of God, but a kind of possession of an evil spirit, and that it was to be kept off with crossings, signs of the zodiac, papers tied up with so many

---

[14] "Curieuse Kunst und Werck-Schul," Nürnberg, 1705, p. 994.

[15] Préceptes Médicaux de Serenus Sammonicus, text and trans. by L. Baudet, Paris, 1845, pp. 74–77.

[16] De Foe, "A Journal of the Plague Year," London, 1895, p. 38 (vol. ix of Works ed. by Aitken).

knots, and certain words or figures, as particularly the word Abracadabra formed in triangle or pyramid, thus:

A B R A C A D A B R A
A B R A C A D A B R
A B R A C A D A B
A B R A C A D A
A B R A C A D
A B R A C A
A B R A C
A B R A
A B R
A B
A

A curious charm which was extensively used as an amulet in medieval times consists of five Latin words so arranged that they can be read backwards or forwards and also upwards or downwards. The disposition of the letters is as follows:

s a t o r
a r e p o
t e n e t
o p e r a
r o t a s

This charm has been preserved for us in Greek and Coptic as well as in Roman characters, and examples of it have been found cut in a marble slab above the chapel of St. Laurent at Rochemaur (Ardèche), France, and also in the plaster wall of an old Roman house at Cirncester, Gloucestershire, England. In a Greek manuscript in the Bibliothèque Nationale, in Paris,[17] the Latin words are transliterated and translated as follows:

σάτορ, the sower
ἀρεπο, the plough
τένετ, holds
ὄπερα, works
ρόταϛ, wheels

[17] Ms. Gr. No. 2411, fol. 60. See C. Werscher, Bull. de la Soc. Nat. des antiq. de la France, 1874, vol. xxxv, pp. 153 sqq.

Another and more ingenious explanation of this puzzle has, however, been given.[18] Beginning with the last word "rotas," and taking the other words in their order, it is proposed to read as follows: "The plough-wheels (rotas), the laborer (opera), holds (tenet), creep after him (arepo), I, the sower (sator)." The chief defect in this version appears to be the assumption that "opera" can be rendered "laborer," an interpretation which is, at best, supported by a doubtful use of the word in that sense by Horace. This charm appears in an Italian manuscript of the fourteenth century,[19] where it is recommended to be used for the assurance of a speedy delivery.

Touching the wonderful and mystic power attributed to the seven vowels of the Greek alphabet by the Gnostics, C. W. King cites the following words from the Pistis Sophia of Valentinus: [20]

> Nothing therefore is more excellent than the mysteries which ye seek after, saving only the mystery of the Seven Vowels and their forty and nine Powers, and the Numbers thereof. And no name is more excellent than all these [Vowels], a Name wherein be contained all Names and all Lights and all Powers.

The last sentence probably refers to the arrangement of these vowels often met with in inscribed Gnostic talismans, the so-called Abraxas gems. Here we often find them in the following order *Ι Ε Η Ω Ο Υ Α*, and the sound of these vowels really suggests the conventional pronunciation of the Hebrew name Jehovah (yehowah). The words quoted from the Pistis Sophia are placed in the mouth of Jesus, and King calls attention to the fact that in Greek the same word is used for voice and vowel (*φώνη*). He therefore believes that

---

[18] King, "Early Christian Numismatics," London, 1873, p. 187.
[19] In the author's library.
[20] King, "Early Christian Numismatics," London, 1873, pp. 229, 230.

s	a	t	o	r
a	r	e	p	o
t	e	n	e	t
o	p	e	r	a
r	o	t	a	s

A MEDIEVAL SPELL

From a XIV century Italian MS. in the author's library. The efficacy of the spell is to be insured by reciting the accompanying invocation thrice.

the passage in Revelations (x, 3–4): "The seven thunders uttered their voices," signifies that the sound of the seven vowels "echoed through the vault of heaven, and composed that mystic utterance which the sainted seer was forbidden to reveal unto mortals."

Certain talismans were supposed to afford protection not only to individuals but even to entire cities. Of this class were two talismans described by Gregory of Tours. He relates that Paris had enjoyed from ancient times a surprising immunity from serpents and rats, as well as from fires. However, in clearing out the channel beneath a bridge across the Seine, the workmen found, embedded in the mud, two brazen images, one of a serpent and the other of a rat; after these had been removed from their resting place, serpents and rats appeared, and conflagrations became common.[21]

Of the many memorials of the Age of Charlemagne preserved in the Cathedral Treasury at Aachen, that popularly known as the Talisman of Charlemagne always exerted a peculiar fascination over the minds of those visiting the shrine, both because of its sacred character and on account of the mystic power ascribed to it.

The "Talisman" is composed of two large sapphires, cut *en cabochon,* one being of oval form and the other square, these constituting respectively the front and back of the relic; enclosed between them is a cross made from wood of the Holy Cross said to have been found in Palestine by St. Helena, mother of Constantine the Great. This is only visible when looking through the oval sapphire set in front of the medallion. The two sapphires are joined and framed by a band studded with precious stones, and various other gems are set above and below them. The oval sapphire is of

[21] Gregorii Episcopi Turonensis, "Historia Francorum," ed. Arndt, and Krusch, Pars I, Hannoveræ, 1884, p. 349, lib. viii, cap. 33.

a pale blue, and is furnished with a gold openwork bordering. At the top of the medallion, in a square space is set a lozenge-shaped garnet, and around the oval sapphire forming the front are placed successively, (1) an emerald, (2) a pearl, (3) a garnet, (4) a pearl, (5) an emerald, (6) a pearl, (7) a garnet, (8) a pearl, (9) an emerald, (10) a pearl, (11) a garnet, (12) a pearl, (13) an emerald, (14) a pearl, (15) a garnet, (16) a pearl.

The square sapphire at the back of the medallion is of poor quality and imperfect color; about it are sixteen settings, containing respectively, (1) (lacking), (2) a pearl, (3) a garnet, (4) a pearl, (5) an emerald, (6) a pearl, (7) a garnet, (8) a pearl, (9) an emerald, (10) a pearl, (11) a garnet, (12) a pearl, (13) an emerald, (14) a pearl, (15) a garnet, (16) a pearl.

On the band are set the following stones: (1) a pearl, (2) a sapphire, (3) a pearl, (4) an amethyst, (5) a pearl, (6) a sapphire, (7) a pearl, (8) an amethyst, (9) a pearl, (10) an almost white sapphire, (11) a pearl, (12) an amethyst, (13) a pearl, (14) a white sapphire.

In the summer of 1804, Empress Josephine went to Aix-la-Chapelle (Aachen) to take the waters there, and during her stay, on August 1, she visited the tomb of Charlemagne in the Cathedral. We are told that Napoleon, who joined Josephine at Aix-le-Chapelle on September 3, had already *authorized* the Cathedral chapter to part with certain of the relics and bestow them upon Josephine at the time of her visit to the tomb. This authorization, of course, was only a polite equivalent for a command, and was duly carried out, the most prized object secured by Josephine being precisely this famed talisman. It eventually came into the hands of Hortense, Josephine's daughter, the mother of Napoleon III, and was inherited by him. It is said to be now in a private collection in Paris.[22] Empress Eugénie is stated to have worn it at the time of the birth of the Prince Imperial, and to have further shown her belief in the mystic, or magic, virtues of the talisman by sending it several years later to Biarritz, that it might be kept for a time in the sick-room of M. Bacciochi, when he was prostrated by illness in that city.[23]

An Anglo-Saxon treatise on the medical art, from the beginning of the tenth century, the original manuscript of which was owned by an Anglo-Saxon leech named Bald, as testified to by an entry on the title-leaf, gives the agate a prominent place as a talismanic and curative agent. More especially is its power over the demon-world emphasized. Indeed it is asserted to serve as a sort of diagnostic of demoniacal possession, the words being: "The man who hath in him secretly the loathly fiend, if he taketh in liquid any portion of the shavings of this stone, then soon is exhibited manifestly in him that which before secretly lay hid." Less unfamiliar to those acquainted with the early literature on the subject are the statements that the wearers of agates were guarded against danger from lightning, and from venom. The liquid "extract of agate," taken internally, also produced smooth skin and rendered the partaker immune from the bites of snakes.[24]

An extremely strange type of amulets found occasionally in Gallic sepulchres are disks made from human skulls. It appears to be a well-ascertained fact that the operation of

---

[22] Dictionnaire d'Archéologie Chrétienne, ed. by Dom Fernand Cabrol and Dom H. Leclercq, Fasc. xxv, Paris, 1911, cols. 696–698, with cuts of the talisman taken from those given by E. Aus'm Weertht to illustrate a paper in the Jahrb. des Vereins der Alterthumsfreunde im Rheinlande, vols. xxxix–xl, p. 265–272, Plates IV, V, VI, Bonn, 1866. The original photographs were taken by express permission of Napoleon III.

[23] Emile Ollivier, " L'Empire Libérale," Paris, 1897, vol. ii, p. 55.

[24] Rev. Oswald Cockayne, " Leechdoms, Wortcunning and Starcraft of Early England," London, 1865, vol. ii, p. 299 (Bk. II, cap. 66 of the " Laece Boc ").

trephining was performed at this early date, almost if not quite exclusively in the case of infants, and it is believed principally for the cure of epilepsy. If the child survived the operation its skull was thought to have acquired a certain magic power. This idea had its rise in the belief that epilepsy was the result of an indwelling evil spirit, so that if the disease disappeared as a result or sequence of the operation, this evil spirit was believed to have made his way out through the aperture. On the eventual death of one whose skull had been successfully trephined, disks were sometimes cut just on the edge of the opening through which the possessing spirit had slipped out, leaving as a trace of his passage some of his diabolic but still potent virtue.[25] That the superstition regarding these cranial disks lasted well into the sixteenth century, even among some of the educated, is proven by the fact that on a bracelet which belonged to and was worn by Catherine de' Medici, one of the talismans was a piece of a human skull.

Attention was first called to the strange amulets taken from the human skull by the operation of trephining, by M. Prunetière, at a meeting of the French Association for the Advancement of Science, held in Lyons in 1873.[26] The specimen he then exhibited came from a sepulture in the department of Lozère. This particular example showed a break on the edge, and M. Paul Broca has conjectured that a small piece may have been chipped off, so that it might be pulverized and administered as a powder to persons suffering from disease of the brain, a treatment favored by those who doubted the generally-believed supernatural origin of

[25] Renel, "Les religions de la Gaule avant le Christianisme," Paris, 1906, p. 97.

[26] See Paul Broca, "Sur la trépanation du crâne et les amulettes crâniennes de l'époque néolitique," Revue d'Anthropologie, vol. vi, 1877, pp. 1–42, 193–225; and also his "Amulettes crâniennes et trépanation préhistorique" in the same Revue, vol. v, 1876, pp. 106, 107.

epilepsy, and suspected its source in some lesion of the brain or of the meninges. For this, of course, no more efficient remedy could suggest itself, according to the old sympathetic theory of medicines, than a powder made from the skull of one who had been an epileptic. These skull-amulets have been unearthed in neolithic burials in various parts of France, a considerable number having been found by M. de Baye and others in the department of Marne; a specimen was also found in an Algerian sepulture by General Faidherbe.

The great Greek physician Hippocrates of Cos, a contemporary of Plato, advised that resort should be had to the operation of trephining in many cases of injury to the head, and that the ancient Hindus were to a certain extent familiar with it as a method of treating diseases of the brain appears in one of the Buddhist recitals from a Tibetan source. Here it is related that Atreya, master of the King of Physicians, Jîvaka, when appealed to for help by a man suffering from a distressful cerebral disorder, directed the man to dig a pit and fill it up with dung; he then thrust the man into this soft and savory mass until nothing but his head and neck protruded, and opened his skull. From it was drawn out a reptile whose presence had caused the malady. Jîvaka seems to have been in consultation with his master in this interesting operation, and is said to have later extracted a centipede from a man's skull after making an aperture therein with a golden knife.[27] In neither of these cases, however, do we have any hint that disks or fragments from the human skull were used as amulets.

A ghastly object much favored in France in the Middle Ages, as it was believed to give the owner the power to dis-

[27] Kumagusu Minakata, "Trepanning among Ancient Peoples," Nature, Jan. 15, 1914, pp. 555, 556; citing Encyclopædia Britannica, 1910, vol. xiii, p. 518, and E. A. Schiefner, "Tibetan Tales," trans. Ralston, 1906, p. 98.

cover hidden treasures, was the so-called *main-de-gloire,* or "hand of glory," which was the desiccated hand of one who had met his death by hanging.[28]

A remarkable talismanic bracelet owned by Catherine de' Medici was set with a skull-fragment and with a representation of a "*main-de-gloire.*" This is described in the catalogue made in 1786 of M. d'Ennery's collection. The settings of the bracelet, ten in number, comprised the following objects, to each of which was probably ascribed some special significance and virtue.[29]

An oval "eagle-stone" (ætites), on which was graven in intaglio a winged dragon; above this figure was the date 1559, the year in which the bracelet was composed and that of the death of Catherine's husband, Henri II.

An octagonal agate, traversed by a number of tubular apertures, the orifices of which could be seen on either side of the stone.

A very fine oval onyx of three colors, bearing graven on its edge the following names of angels: Gabriel, Raphael, Michael, Uriel.

A large oval turquoise with a gold band.

A piece of black and white marble.

An oval brown agate, with a caduceus, a star and a crescent engraved in intaglio on one of its faces, and on its edge the name Jehovah and certain talismanic characters; on the other face were figured the constellation Serpens, the zodiacal sign Scorpio and the Sun, around which were the six planets.

An oblong section of a human skull.

A rounded piece of gold on the convex side of which was

[28] Pierre Lacroix, "Sciences et Lettres au Moyen Age," Paris, 1877, p. 250.

[29] Martin, "Histoire de France," vol. x, Paris, 1844, p. 451, note. From a communication of Pierre Lacroix, citing as authority: "Catalogue des tableaux, antiquités, pierres gravées, etc., etc., du cabinet de feu M. d'Ennery, écuyer," by Remi and Miliotti, Paris, 1786.

Courtesy of Ernest Leroux, Paris.

SKELETON OF AN ACHEMENID NOBLEWOMAN, PERHAPS A ROYAL PERSONAGE, AS FOUND ENTOMBED WITH A WEALTH OF JEWELED ORNAMENTS AT SUSA IN PERSIA, BY M. HENRY DE MORGAN, IN 1904.

FROM A PORTRAIT OF QUEEN ELIZABETH

In the possession of the Duke of Devonshire, K. G., Hardwick Hall. The queen has jewels in her hair, a pearl eardrop, and two necklaces, one fitting close to the neck, the other falling over the breast. The stiff brocade skirt is embroidered with a wonderful array of aquatic birds and animals. On the left, the cushion of the chair of state is embroidered with the queen's monogram. Surmounting the chair is a crystal ball. The original canvas measures 90 x 66 inches.

graven in relief the "hand of glory" (*main-de-gloire*); on the concave side appeared the Sun and Moon done in repoussé work.

A perfectly round onyx, bearing graven in the centre the name or word "Publeni"; this possibly designated the original Roman owner of the stone.

In the opinion of a German writer of the eleventh or twelfth century, the amethyst, if worn by a man, attracted to him the love of noble women, and also protected him from the attacks of thieves.[30] This stone was always prized because of its beautiful color, even though it was never so rare or costly as some others. Some authorities assert that the amethyst induces sleep.[31] Perhaps this was one of the means by which the stone cured inebriety, as it enabled its votaries to sleep off the effects of their potations.

As testimony of the belief in the efficiency, remedial or talismanic, of precious stones prevalent at the opening of the fifteenth century, may be noted the presence among the manuscript books of Marguerite de Flandres, Duchesse de Bourgogne, of a work listed as follows: "The book of the properties of certain stones." It was carefully enclosed in a crimson velvet covering.[32] Incidentally it is a rather interesting fact that at this early date, 1405, we find in Duchess Margaret's little library two Bibles in French and a separate copy of the Gospels also in that language. This serves to disprove the popular idea that translations of the Bible into the vernacular were in distinct disfavor with Roman Catholics before the era of the Reformation. Of course until the

[30] Birlinger, "Kleinere deutsche Sprachdenkmäler"; in Germania, vol. iii (1863), p. 303.

[31] Cardani, "De subtilitate," lib. vii, Basileæ, 1560, p. 473.

[32] Inventaire des biens de Marguerite de Flandres Duchesse de Bourgogne, Bibl. Nat., coll. Moreau, 1727; on fol. 96 of transcription in author's library, from the collection of M. E. Molinier.

invention and use of the art of printing there could be no wide diffusion of such translations.

The jacinth is described by Thomas de Cantimpré as being a stone of a yellow color. "It is very hard and difficult to cleave, or cut; it can, however, be worked with diamond dust. It is very cold, especially when held in the mouth." Among many other virtues, it protects from melancholia and poison, and makes the wearer beloved of God and men. It also acts as a sort of barometer, since it grows dark and dull in bad weather and becomes clear and bright in fine weather.[33] Cardano says that when the weather was fine the stone became obscure and dull, but when a tempest was impending, it assumed the ruddy hue of a burning coal. It also lost its color when in contact with any one suffering from disease, more especially from the plague.[34]

As a result of his study of precious stones, Cardano was induced to affirm that they had life, but he gravely states that he had never noted that they possessed sex (a common belief in his day), although "as nature delights as much in miracle as we do, some may be so constituted that they are almost distinguished by sex."[35]

The beautiful sapphire has always been a great favorite with lovers of precious stones and to it has been attributed a chastening, purifying influence upon the soul. Even Burton, in his Anatomy of Melancholy, wherein precious stones are rarely mentioned, takes occasion to write as follows of the sapphire: "It is the fairest of all precious stones of sky colour, and a great enemy to black choler, frees the mind, mends manners."[36]

---

[33] Konrad von Megenberg's old German version "Buch der Natur," ed. by Dr. Franz Pfeiffer, Stuttgart, 1861, p. 449.

[34] Cardani, "De rerum varietate," lib. v, Basileæ, 1557, p. 100.

[35] Cardani, "Philosophi opera quædam," Basileæ, 1585, p. 330.

[36] "Anatomy of Melancholy," Bk. II, § 4, i, 4.

The poets have sung the praises of the turquoise. In Shakespeare's Merchant of Venice, when the "amorous Jessica" made off with her father's jewels, Shylock particularly bewails the disappearance of his turquoise, crying out that he would not have lost it for "a wilderness of monkeys." The poet Donne, also, writes of this stone and draws attention to its sympathetic quality in these words:

> As a compassionate turquoise that doth tell,
> By looking pale, the wearer is not well.

That Queen Elizabeth clung fondly to life is well known, and it is said that she trusted much in the virtues of a talisman which she wore round her neck. This was a piece of gold engraved with certain mystic characters. The statement has also been made that at the bottom of a chair in which she often sat, was the queen of hearts from a pack of cards, having a nail driven through the forehead of the figure.[37] Could this have been a spell of witchcraft used against her hated rival, Mary of Scotland?

The belief that turquoise changes its hue with the changing health of the wearer leads an early seventeenth century author to offer it as a symbol of wifely devotion, saying that "a true wife should be like a turquoise stone, clear in heart in her husband's health, and cloudy in his sickness." Although a more prosaic explanation than that of occult sympathy has been proposed for this asserted change of hue, we need not therefore reject the more poetic fancy.[38]

Among the believers in the virtue of amulets must be counted the French religious philosopher, Pascal. After his death in 1662 there was found, sewed up in his pourpoint, a piece of paper bearing a long and very strange inscription.

---

[37] Agnes Strickland, "Lives of the Queens of England," vol. vii, pp. 770, 778.

[38] Alex. Nicholes, "A Discourse of Marriage and Wiveing," 1615, Hasl. Misc. II, 180; cited in Lean's Collectanea, vol. ii, Pt. II, Bristol, 1903, p. 641.

At the top was a cross with rays, a similar cross being drawn at the bottom of the text. This began with the following words:

> Monday, November 23, the day of St. Clement, pope and martyr, and of others in the martyrology.
>
> The Eve of St. Chrysogone, martyr, and of others. From about half-past ten in the evening until about a half-hour after midnight,
>
> FIRE

Then follow a series of ejaculations and short religious sentences, and toward the end, after the name of Christ, thrice repeated, the words:

> I have separated myself from Him, I have fled from Him, denied Him.

and finally the prayer that this separation might henceforth cease. The original text is said to be in the Bibliothèque Nationale in Paris with the MS. of the "Pensées."

Pascal is stated to have always kept this amulet on his person, removing it carefully from the lining of an old garment and putting in a new one, when this was assumed. The strange introduction referred to a vision of fire which he had had on the night in question, and this has been explained as resulting from a severe nervous shock he had experienced six months before, when driving along the banks of the Seine. As the vehicle neared Neuilly the horses took fright and ran away, dashing toward the edge of the bank; just on the brink the reins broke and the horses plunged down into the river, leaving the carriage in which Pascal was sitting on the edge of the precipice. This shock impressed him so vividly that he would often see the precipice before him as distinctly as though it were a reality. In any case the matter is of interest as showing that one of the most gifted men of the seventeenth century was a believer in amulets.[39]

[39] F. Lalut, "L'amulet de Pascal," in Annales méd. psych., I ser., vol. v, pp. 157–180; and P. E. Littré, "Médecine et médecins," Paris, 1872, pp. 95–97.

The giving of corals to new-born infants was expressly forbidden in 1708 in the bishopric of Bamberg, because of the superstition connected therewith, although Christian painters of the fourteenth century often represented the child Jesus as holding corals in his hand. The persistence of the superstition as to the Evil Eye and the belief that coral safeguarded the wearer therefrom, have impressed many cultured Italians of our day, and even so able and clear-headed a statesman as prime minister Crispi is said never to have gone to a parliamentary sitting without having with him a coral amulet.[40]

Some characteristic Hindu amulets figure the god Jagannath (Lord of the World), or associated divinities, and also symbols related to the worship of this form of Krishna.[41] In the month Joyestha (May–June) his world-renowned temple at Puri in Orissa is thronged with pilgrims from all parts of India, and on the great festival day his image and those of his brother Balarana and of his sister Subhadra are taken out of the sanctuary and placed in an elaborately decorated car, which is drawn through the streets of the city. The readiness of fanatical believers to sacrifice their lives by casting themselves beneath the wheels of this ponderous car, has made the expression "Car of Jagannáth" almost a household word, freely used by those who know little or nothing about Hindu religion. The English Government has long since put a stop to these reckless and useless martyrdoms.

Many of these amulets are made of a black steatite. One represents Krishna (Jagannath) standing and playing on a flute, another figures this avatar of Vishnu with his wife

[40] "Die Religion in Geschichte und Gegenwart," ed. by Friedrich Michael Schiele, vol. i, Tübingen, 1909, col. 455.

[41] Enrico H. Giglioli, "Di alcuni ex-voto amuleti, ed altri oggetti litici adoperati nel culto di Krishna, sotto la forma di Jagan-natha a Puri in Orissa," Archivio per l'Antropologia, vol. xxiii, pp. 87–89; Firanzi, 1893.

Radha. A curious series presents Jagannath, Balarana and Subhadra; the unnaturally large heads of the figures and the truncated crowns and legs are explained by the fact that the group was carved from the trisala of a tope of a Buddhist temple erected at Puri in the third century B.C., the Hindus of a later time having utilized this relic of a former faith for gods of their ethnic religion. There are also a number of stamps, incised with emblematic figures such as a shell, a *sankha* wheel, a serpent, two footprints, etc., so that the corresponding seal may be impressed in colored clay upon the arms of the faithful in the sanctuary of Jagannath. Many of the amulets bearing the double footprint, emblematic of Vishnu (Krishna-Jagannath), are arranged in groups of five, all being perforated so that a group can be suspended on the person.

The footprints are explained by a curious legend to the effect that when a dispute as to superiority arose between the gods of the Trimurti, Brahma, Siva and Vishnu, the selection of a test to decide this was left to Bhrigu, one of the ten patriarchs. He approached Brahma without saluting him; this infuriated the god, but he restrained himself. Approaching Siva in turn, Bhrigu failed to return the god's salutation, which so enraged him that he raised his trident to slay the insulter, and was only prevented from doing this by the timely intervention of the goddess Parvati. Nothing daunted Bhrigu pursued his test, and, finding Vishnu reposing with his head in Lakshmi's lap, he kicked the divinity to arouse him. Vishnu, however, instead of losing his temper, quietly arose; saluted the rash patriarch, and even thanked him for the reminder, and craved his pardon that he had not immediately greeted him, asserting that the kick (which must have been most vigorously administered if it left *two* footprints) had left on his breast a mark of good augury.

A fine presentation of the style of jewels worn by the

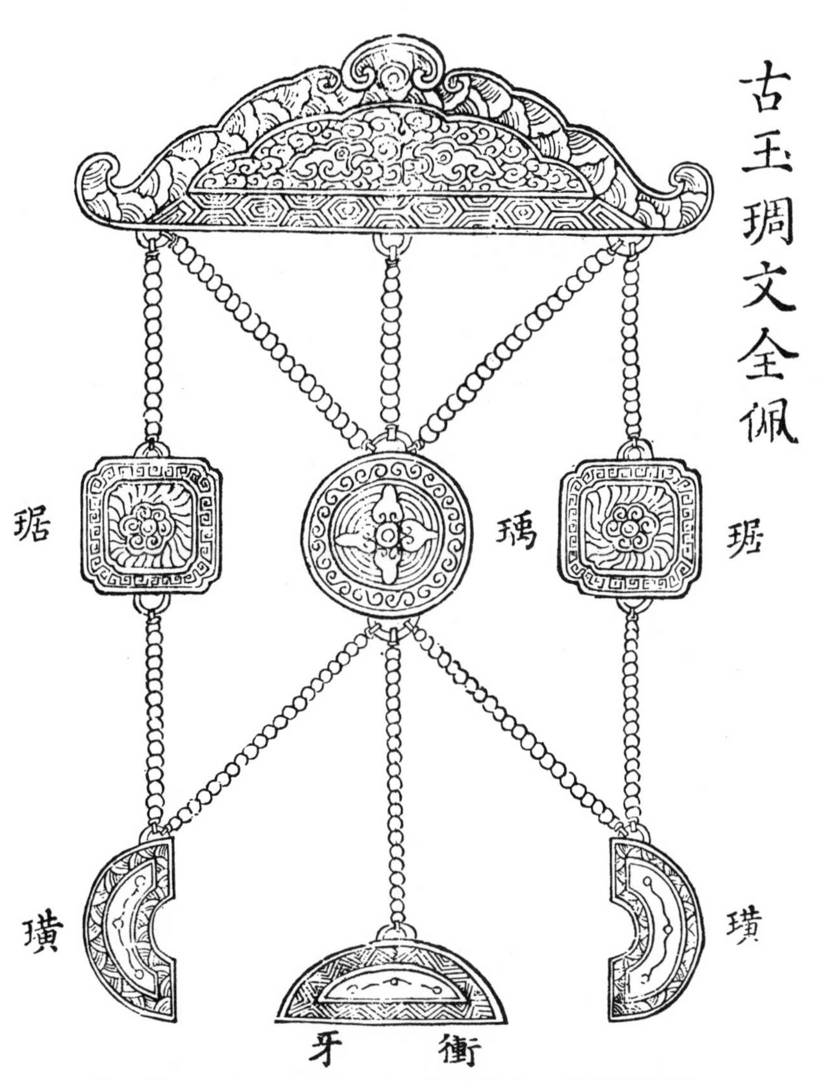

COMPLETE VIEW OF THE ANCIENT JADE GIRDLE-PENDANT
(FROM, KU YÜ T'U P'U)

From "Jade," by Berthold Laufer.

By courtesy of the author and Field Museum of Natural History, Chicago.

Mahârânî of Sikkim, a full-blooded Tibetan by birth, is offered by a portrait of this queen done in oil by Damodar Dutt, a Bengali artist, in 1908, while the Mahârânî was sharing the captivity of her husband at Darjeeling, where they had been sequestrated by the British authorities for many years. The elaborate and rather oppressive headdress is a typical adornment of the queens of Sikkim; the broad bandeaux are composed of pearls, and a brilliant color effect is produced by the rows of alternating corals and turquoises. The gold ear-rings have a turquoise-inlay, in concentric rings, and from the queen's neck hangs a long necklace of coral beads, separated at intervals by large spheres of amber; a coral bracelet and two rings, with coral and turquoise setting respectively, complete the very effective, if not especially costly, jewelry.[42]

Jade girdle pendants having a talismanic quality were in great favor during the period of the Chou dynasty (1122–249 B.C.). The typical girdle pendant of that time was a seven-jewelled one, each of the combined ornaments being made of some one of the choice varieties of jade. These adornments consisted of a top-piece or brooch, whence depended a circular central plaque (yü), flanked by two square ornaments (kü); below followed a centre-ornament of segment form, on either side of which was a bow-shaped jewel. The girdle ornaments were rich in symbolic significance, the rhythmic swinging of the jades caused a musical note whenever they came in contact with one another, or with any metallic object; as love-trinkets they had the most fortunate meaning; as indications of office they gained consideration and respect for the wearers of high rank, while for those of

[42] Berthold Laufer, "Notes on Turquois in the East," Field Museum of Natural History, Publication 169; Anthropological Series, vol. xiii, No. 1. Chicago, July, 1913; see text opposite frontispiece plate.

less distinction they were so differentiated as to become marks of the respective craft or vocation.[43]

In Siam the girls' heads are shaved, with the exception of the top of the head, where a knot of hair is allowed to grow. On the fourteenth anniversary of the girl's birthday this "top-knot" is cut off, the operation being accompanied by a solemn religious ceremony, to mark and consecrate the event, which denotes the passing of the girl into womanhood. On this occasion, the members of the family gather together all the jewels they can secure for the adornment of the "new woman," and where they are not wealthy enough to provide brilliant and rich ornaments from their own possessions kind friends will always be found ready to supply the deficiency. In the case of the Siamese girl figured in our plate, and of a girl companion, the Queen of Siam herself acted as fairy godmother to the extent of furnishing from her own private treasures a costly and suitable decoration. The gems and ornaments worn were worth $20,000 and are said to have filled a small steamer-trunk.[44]

In a favorite form of white jade amulet, the stone is cut flat and is then inlaid with rubies in gold settings, so disposed as to indicate a flower-form. Jade amulets of this type are found in China and in various parts of northern Asia, and are believed to guard or free the wearer from palpitation of the heart.[45]

Flowers fashioned from precious stones make most attractive ornaments, and by their variety of coloring can be worn with almost any costume. A celebrated beauty of London society has a number of pansies of different colors,

[43] Berthold Laufer, "Jade, a Study in Chinese Archæology and Religion," Chicago, 1912, pp. 194 sqq.

[44] Communicated by Dr. Charles S. Braddock, formerly physician to the court of Siam, under date of February 13, 1903.

[45] Hendley, "Indian Jewellerv," London, 1909, p. 27; Plate XV, Figs. 112, 113.

TIBETAN WOMAN WITH COMPLETE JEWELRY

From "Notes on Turquois in the East," by Berthold Laufer.

By courtesy of the author and Field Museum of Natural History, Chicago.

"THE LIGHT OF THE EAST"

Mural fresco painting by Albert Herter, in the Hotel St. Francis, San Francisco, California. The crystal ball upheld by the female figure is more highly esteemed in Japan than any other jewel. Note the fine contrast afforded by the black armor of the Japanese warrior to the white arm and pure crystal sphere.

By Courtesy of the Artist and Hotel St. Francis, San Francisco.

one made of rubies, another of sapphires, still another of emeralds, and so on through the range of colors. In this way she always had a pansy according in color with that of her gown. As bridal gifts these jewel-flowers are most appropriate, more especially when the lady-love bears a "floral name" such as Violet or Rose.

Coral ornaments of all sorts are in great demand in Tibet, and a fine piece of this material will bring about $20 an ounce, and is therefore literally worth its weight in gold. The Venetian traveller, Marco Polo, who visited Tibet in the latter half of the thirteenth century, already noted that coral was in high favor there and that coral necklaces adorned the necks of the women and also those of the idols in their temples. The love of personal adornment is very strong among the Tibetan women, and those in any way well-to-do load themselves with a mass of jewelled ornaments, great pieces of amber, coral and turquoise constituting the principal gem-material. The favor extended to coral, apart from the religious significance of red as symbolical of one of the incarnations of Buddha, may perhaps have an esthetic basis as well, for red or pink affords a pleasant contrast to the dark complexions and hair of the Tibetans.[46]

Much more prized, however, than coral is the beautiful blue turquoise, which not only serves for purely ornamental use but is freely employed in the decoration of religious objects, such as the curious "prayer wheels" so indispensable a part of Tibetan ritual.

The talismanic quality of this stone is an important element in its popularity, as it is supposed to bring good fortune and physical well-being to the wearer and to afford protection against contagion. The Tibetans share in the quite general belief that the turquoise will grow pale in

[46] L. Austine Waddell, "Lhasa and its Mysteries, with a Record of the Expedition of 1903–1904," London, 1905, pp. 347, 348.

sympathy with the present or prospective fortune and health of the person wearing it, and as a loss of color is considered portentous of coming evil, such stones are gotten rid of as soon as possible to be replaced by those of a brighter hue. The dealers who buy up for a trifling sum these discolored turquoises often treat them with a dose of blue dyestuff which superficially restores the color, and it is stated that many of the soldiers of the British expeditionary force to Tibet in 1904 were at first deceived into buying these vamped-up stones, but they soon discovered the deception and were more careful later on. Turquoises are also believed to guard against the Evil Eye, and a quasi-sacred character is lent to some especially fine specimens by setting them in the foreheads of statues of the Buddha or other religious images.[47]

The women of Tibet are said to prize most highly as amulets pieces of cloth adorned with turquoise or coral, which they have acquired from the Lamas, who by the imposition of their priestly blessing have endowed these objects with a peculiar sanctity in the eyes of the Tibetan devotees. Another amulet favored in this far-off land is a small metal box of gold, silver, or copper, and encrusted with turquoise. Within are enclosed little scrolls inscribed with mystic characters to conjure evil spirits and thwart their malevolent schemes for the tribulation of mankind.

An ingenious, if rather far-fetched explanation of the supposed power of coral to avert lightning and hail is given by Fortunio Liceti. In his opinion, coral, being of a warm quality, overcomes the coldness of the atmosphere, which produces lightning by the attraction of contraries, and hail by its own quality. This is a specimen of the attempts to find a plausible physiological reason for the powers of gems, the

---

[47] Ibid., pp. 348, 349.

writers never for a moment hesitating to accept the popular beliefs in this respect.[48]

Among the Bhots of Landakh in the western part of Tibet, a large piece of amber or agate is often worn by the men suspended from the neck as an amulet. Here as in so many other parts of the world, the amulet is believed to acquire especial efficacy when worn in this way, as it comes in immediate contact with the person of the wearer.[49]

A very singular manner of using precious stones as talismans is noted in Burma.[50] There are certain talismans called *hkoung-beht-set,* which are inserted in the flesh beneath the skin. They are usually of gold, silver, or lead, or else of tortoise shell, horn, etc., but sometimes they are rolled pebbles and occasionally precious stones. We are told that when a prisoner is found to have such talismans on, or rather *in* his person, the jailer cuts them out lest they should be used to bribe the guards. The talismans owe much of their supposed power to inscriptions in mystic characters, and they are so highly favored that some of the natives wear one or more rows of them across the chest.

For the Japanese, rock-crystal is the "perfect jewel," *tama;* it is at once a symbol of purity and of the infinity of space, and also of patience and perseverance. This latter significance probably originated from an observation of the patience and skill required for the production of the splendid crystal balls made by the accurate and painstaking Japanese cutters and polishers.

The belief of Mohammedans in the Evil Eye claims the authority of the Prophet to the effect that "the áïn (eye) is a reality." The Arabs also designate the Evil Eye as

[48] Fortunio Liceti, De annulis, cap. 19.

[49] Hendley, " Indian Jewellery," London, 1909, p. 59.

[50] H. Shway Yoe, "The Burman: His Life and Nations," in " Indian Jewellery," by T. H. Hendley. The Journal of Indian Art and Industry, Jan., 1909, vol. xii, No. 105, p. 143.

nuzra, "the look," and *nafs,* "breath or spirit." It is not commonly regarded as the result of a definite malevolent intention, but rather as an effect engendered by envy at the sight of anything especially beautiful or attractive. Indeed, sometimes the bare expression of great admiration is supposed to produce evil results, as is illustrated by the assertion that when a man, on seeing an exceptionally large and fine stone, exclaimed, "What a large stone!" it immediately broke into three pieces.

In the Sahara, the horns of oxen, and sometimes their skulls with the horns attached, are set over the entrances of dwellings to protect the residents from this dreaded influence; in Tunis and Algiers, boars' tusks are also used in this way. However, the most favored weapons of defence are the outstretched fingers of the hand, sometimes but two fingers, but more often all five. The gesture of holding out the fingers toward the envious person is frequently accompanied by the utterance of the words: *Khamsa fi äïnek,* "five (fingers) in your eye!" The number five has thus acquired such a special significance that Thursday, as the *fifth* day of the week, is looked upon as the appropriate day for pilgrimages to the shrines of those saints whose protection against the Evil Eye is believed to be most potent.[51]

The Arabs of Arabia Petræa believe that when anyone casts longing and covetous eyes upon any animal belonging to another, part of his soul enters the animal and the latter is doomed to destruction if it remains in the possession of the rightful owner. The same idea prevails in the case of a child whose possession is envied, or who is unduly admired. Where the identity of the one who has cast the spell is known, there is a fair chance of rendering it harmless if a piece of the guilty one's garment can be stolen and the animal or child rubbed with it. The virtue of coral as a protection

[51] Edmond Doutté, "Magie et Religion," Alger, 1909, pp. 320 sqq.

from such dangers is generally believed, and almost every woman, child, mare and camel, wears or bears a coral amulet of some kind. A special variety of amulets against the Evil Eye, worn by equestrians, are small, smooth flint-stones, gathered at a spot where two valleys unite; and, for horses, protection is believed to be afforded by a ring of blue glass or blue porcelain, suspended from the neck. Another queer superstition among these Arabs regarding the Evil Eye is that if a child yawns, this is supposed to be a sign that he has been smitten by the evil spell, and the mother is advised to place glowing coals on a plate, strew alum over the coals, and bear the plate around the child.[52]

Over the entrance gate of the Alhambra in Granada, Spain, may be seen the representation of a hand, and this is regarded as having been figured there to serve for a talisman against the Evil Eye,[53] just as some of the Arabs are still wont to paint or figure a so-called "Fatima's Hand" on doors or door-posts for a similar purpose. The idea which has been advanced that the "horse-shoe arch" had some connection with the belief in the luck-bringing quality of the horse-shoe, is, however, scarcely to be admitted as an explanation of this most characteristic feature of Moorish architecture.

---

[52] Alois Musil, " Arabia Petræa," Wien, 1908, vol. iii, pp. 314, 315.

[53] Lean's Collectanea (by Vincent Stuckey Lean), vol. ii, Pt. I, Bristol, 1903, p. 468.

IX

Amulets of Primitive Peoples and of Modern Times

THE folk-lore tales of the settlement called Milpa Alta, in the Federal District, Mexico, not far from Mexico City, have preserved many legends from old Aztec times, as this community was originally settled by some noble Aztec families fortunate enough to escape with their goods from the Spaniards at the time of the conquest by Cortés. In several of these legends the chalchihuitl (a green stone, often nephrite or jadeite) is mentioned. Thus it is said that when some minor divinity sees fit to confer upon a man or woman the endowments of a *tlamátque* or "sage," he gave warning of this in a dream, and the truth of the vision was confirmed when, during the ensuing day, the dreamer found on the ground within his enclosure idols of *chalchihuitl,* or fragments of obsidian, which were believed to have fallen from the sky, this usually occurring during a rainstorm. Evidently the rain had washed them out of the earth or volcanic ash in which they had been buried. These objects were immediately picked up and preserved, as they signified that the person whose dream had thus been verified was admitted to the companionship of the gods. There appears to have followed some initiation ceremony to render definite the consecration of the chosen *tlamátque,* and this was to be connected with a fiery ordeal, the traces of which in scars or severe burns, and sometimes even in the loss of eyesight, served to recommend the "sage" to those seeking his aid. This was called for in cases of illness and also for the finding of hidden treasure and for predictions of the weather. In attempting to effect cures, the *tlamátque* made use of pieces of jade as talismans, fortified by elaborate exorcisms and prayers.[1]

Among the lower classes of the Mexican Indian population of Milpa Alta, to cure diseases the aid of a *tepo pohque* (one who purifies the disease) is sometimes called in. This once very general custom is, however, gradually falling into disuse. The progress of popular scepticism is illustrated by the half-apologetic tone in which this is explained in the words: "If he does no good, he will do no harm, and besides he is so cheap." The healer may be either a man or a woman. One of the most important helps is a chain of chalchihuitl beads. After invocations of the various appearances of Christ and of the Virgin chronicled in local tradition, and of the patron saints (for these Indians are devout Roman Catholics), the healer chooses out a chalchihuitl bead with which he pretends to extract the "air" from the sick person. He successively touches with it the patient's temples, the sides and top of the head, the stomach, and lastly the affected part, at the same time forcibly drawing in his own breath, producing thereby a peculiar noise. The use of the stone is sometimes supplemented by that of two eggs, one being held in each of the healer's hands. A different type or form of chalchihuitl is used for each different disease, and as a final operation the affected part is moistened with alcohol, and then "massaged" with the stone, bathing with a hot decoction of herbs being also resorted to in some cases.[2]

A characteristic object secured in the Province of Chiriqui, Republic of Panama, is a singular amulet of a fine quality of green translucent jade (jadeite). This is fashioned into a conventional representation of a parrot with a

---

[1] Professora Isabel Ramirez Castañeda, "El Folk-Lore de Milpa Alta, D. F., Mexico," in Proceedings of the International Congress of Americanists, XVIII Session, London, 1912, Pt. II, London, 1913, pp. 352–354.

[2] Ibid., pp. 356, 357.

disproportionately long beak. The details of the bird-form are but roughly indicated, what is supposed to represent the head and body being but a trifle larger than the beak. In the region of the neck, marked by a peripheral incision, there is a hole through which a cord for suspension was probably passed. The type resembles that of the Chiriquian gold parrots, and differs from that of the amulets of Las Guacas, Costa Rica. As a much larger number of jade objects have been found at this latter place than occur at Chiriqui, it has been conjectured that the common source was a deposit of jade somewhere in Costa Rica.[3] Chiriqui has also yielded a plain, highly-polished amulet of pale green jade; the front is convex and is traversed by a groove; a small hole has been pierced near the top to facilitate suspension.

The South American Indians had a class of stone love-amulets, representing more or less clearly two embracing figures. It was claimed by their magicians that these had not been cut or fashioned in any way, but were so formed by nature, and were endowed with the power of attracting to the wearer the love of the chosen object of affection. These special amulets bore in the native language the names of *huacanqui* and *cuyancarumi*. They were said to be found buried in the earth where a thunderbolt had descended, and were thus a particular class of the so-called "thunder-stones," and a high price could be obtained for one, more especially if the owner had to deal with a woman. A characteristic specimen, presumably from Ecuador, is of black serpentine.[4]

---

[3] George Grant McCurdy, Ph.D., "A Study of Chiriquian Antiquities," New Haven, Conn., 1911, p. 42, figs. 45 and 49; Mem. of the Conn. Acad. of Arts and Sciences, vol. iii, March, 1911.

[4] R. Verneau and P. Rivet, "Ethnologie ancienne de l'Equateur," Paris, 1912, vol. vi of Mission du service Géologique de l'armée pour la mesure d'un arc de méridien equatorial en Amérique du Sud, 1899–1906, pp. 222, 223, Plate XIII, fig. 4.

The Araucarian Indians of Chili and Argentina, who occupied a region 1000 miles in length, bordering on the Pacific Ocean, according to facts communicated by the Rev. Charles Sadleir, had their medicine *women,* instead of medicine men. These women carried with them a quartz crystal (as did many of the medicine men of the Indian tribes) or a rolled fragment of quartz found in the river beds. They affirmed that this crystal had been entered by a mighty spirit who dwelt in one of the great volcanoes which existed in that region (called *pillan* in the native tongue). This spirit inspired the medicine-woman with a knowledge of what she should tell those who came to her for advice or for forecasts of the future.

A medicine-woman will never show the crystal, because, as the abode of a spirit, it must not be seen. While it is to be supposed that the services of these "doctoresses" are not altogether gratuitous, the Araucarians as a general rule detest gold, although they willingly accept silver. This preference for the less valuable metal is due to the traditions handed down to them from the time the Spaniards persecuted their ancestors for the gold they owned, or were thought to own.

These Indians have a peculiar belief in regard to the nature of the soul, which they regard as a dual being formed of a superior essence, or spirit, which they call *pullu,* and an inferior essence, or soul, to which they give the name *am.*

An agate charm in the shape of a dog's head was found in the Valley of Mexico. The material used here was a banded agate with a rich stain in the centre. The great variety of markings presented by these stones rendered them especially attractive for use as amulets, since fancy could easily trace designs and figures of symbolic significance calculated to secure success or protection.

Of all quaint ideas in amulet making and naming, none

is stranger than that of employing for this purpose artificial eyes from Peruvian mummies. Originally eyes of the giant cuttlefish (*loligo gigas*), they were used by the ancient Peruvians to replace the natural eyes of the dead because these substitutes were more durable. Of course the rather grewsome source whence these mummy-eye amulets were secured, bringing them measurably in touch with a sort of necromancy, made them all the more sought after by the superstitious natives. An example from a mummy found at Cuzco, Peru, was exhibited by the writer in the Folk-Lore Collection at the Columbian Exhibition in Chicago in 1893.[5]

A strange animal figure from the Pueblo Bonito ruins, rudely carved out of stone and having a band composed of pieces of turquoise set about the neck, was undoubtedly an amulet. Two depressions in the stone where the eyes should be indicate that these were of inlaid turquoise. In spite of the imperfect form of this object, it gives evidence in some of its details to the skill of the native artist who executed it, especially in the care he has taken to protect the soft stone from the attrition of the cord used for its suspension, a piece of bird-bone having been introduced into the perforation near the neck, and the ends of the hole countersunk and filled with gum into which a piece of turquoise was set; one of these caps still remains in place. Frog forms, entirely of turquoise, also appear in Pueblo Bonito, several tadpoles and frogs of this material having been found in the burial-room explored by Mr. Pepper. Sometimes the form is barely indicated by the protuberant eyes and a slight incising which marks the place of the neck.[6]

The Pueblo Bonito ruins in New Mexico have furnished

---

[5] George Frederick Kunz, "Folk-lore of Precious Stones," Chicago, 1894; reprint from Memoirs of the International Congress of Anthropology; see p. 269.

[6] George H. Pepper, "The Exploration of a Burial-room in Pueblo Bonito, New Mexico," Putnam Anniversary Volume, New York, 1909, pp. 229, 230, 236, 237.

some very effective examples of turquoise inlaying by the Indians of an earlier time who dwelt in this region. The symbolic forms, the precious material used for the inlays, and the labor and skill expended in the execution of certain of these works, indicate that they must have been regarded as amulets. Perhaps the finest inlaying-work is shown in the turquoise decoration of a fragment of bone of peculiar shape, having alternate bands of jet with a chevron-decoration of interlaced triangular pieces of jet and turquoise. Another of these jet and turquoise amulets is a frog, the body being of jet and the protruding eyes of turquoise; about the creature's neck runs a band of turquoise mosaic. Still another of these relics is a square plaque of jet with an inlaid turquoise at each of the four corners; two of these inlays have fallen out.[6a]

The history of the turquoise, a stone which has been mined in Persia for thousands of years, and has long been prized as one of the most beautiful and attractive of the semi-precious stones, has been very fully and ably treated in an exceedingly comprehensive monograph recently published by Dr. Joseph E. Pogue.[7] This valuable and interesting work contains extracts from all the older and more modern writers on the subject, and also describes the stone fully from a mineralogical point of view, besides discussing it from the historic standpoints.

So highly was the turquoise esteemed among the Pima Indians of southern Arizona, that the loss of one was looked upon as a most ominous event, portending for the owner a serious illness or physical disability, which could only be cured by the magic rites of a medicine-man. When one of

[6a] George H. Pepper. The plate is from the "American Anthropologist," New Series, vol. vii, pl. xvii.

[7] "The Turquois. A Study of its History, Mineralogy, Geology, Ethnology, Archæology, Mythology, Folklore and Technology." By Joseph E. Pogue. Third Memoir, vol. xii, National Academy of Sciences, Washington, D. C., 1915, 162 p., plates 22, 4to.

those worthies is called in to avert the impending misfortune, his favorite remedy consists in placing a piece of slate, a turquoise and a crystal in a vessel filled with water, the liquid being administered in regular doses to the threatened victim. The threefold remedy, comprising a specimen of the lost stone, is supposed to outweigh and counteract the probable evil influences of the lost turquoise alone.[7a]

The magic power that dwelt in these Indian fetishes was named *oyaron* in the Iroquoian tongue, and each person or kindred was believed to have a special *oyaron* which exerted a controlling power over their good or evil fortune. The material object in which this entity would take up its abode was determined in a peculiar way. When a youth had attained maturity, he was intrusted to the charge of an old man who took him to a far-away lodge in the wilderness. Here he had his face, shoulders and breast blackened to symbolize his lack of spiritual or occult enlightenment. He was then compelled to fast for a considerable time and was instructed to carefully note his dreams, and if he should have an exceptionally vivid dream regarding any specific object, to tell his guardian of it. The fact was then duly reported to the wise men of the tribe, who decided whether the object was the chosen abiding place of his *oyaron*. This having been satisfactorily determined, an object of the kind was sought out and was preserved and treasured by the one to whom it had been assigned in the vision. Perhaps the familiar spirit might have elected to dwell in a calumet, a pipe or a knife, or else in some animal, plant, or mineral form.[8]

The Midêwiwin, or, as it is sometimes erroneously called, the "Grand Medicine Society" of the Ojibway Indians, is

---

[7a] Pogue, "The Turquois," citing Russell, "The Pima Indians," in 26th Annual Report of the Bureau of Amer. Ethnology, 1904–1905, p. 112.

[8] "Handbook of American Indians North of Mexico," ed. by Frederick Webb Hodge; Smithsonian Inst., Bur. of Am. Ethn., Bull. 30, Pt. II, p. 178; Washington, 1910.

INDIAN MEDICINE-MAN

From "Histoire Générale des Cérémonies Religieuses du tous les Peuples du Monde," by Abbé Banier and Abbé Mascrier, Paris, 1741.

an association composed of shamans, whose supposed powers are much in request among these Indians of the northwest. Two other classes of medicine-men exist among them to a very limited extent, the Wâbeno, "Men of the Dawn," and the Jessakid or "revealers of hidden things." The members of this latter class, who operate singly, are regarded as very dangerous and generally malevolent sorcerers, having the power to call evil spirits to their aid, and are even believed to practise the fearful art of drawing a man's soul out of his body, so that he either becomes insane or dies. The turtle is regarded by the Jessakids as the abode or symbol of the mightiest spirit. However, the Midês, members of the Midêwiwin, are far the most numerous, and it is to them that the Indian looks for help and health. While they usually "treat" their patients in their own abodes, when the disease fails to yield to the might of ordinary incantations and spells, the assistance of the great magic stone in the Medicine Lodge or Midêwigen must be resorted to. For this purpose the sick person is carried thither and is laid on the ground constituting the floor of the lodge, so that the diseased part of his body may touch the stone. In addition to this magic stone, which is set in the ground near the entrance, three magic wooden posts rise up, one behind the other, and at the end opposite the entrance is set a painted wooden cross, the base of which is cut four-square, each side having a different coloring, namely, white, for the East, the source of light; green, for the South, the source of rain which brings the verdure; red, for the West, where the red glow of the sunset appears and whither the spirits of the departed wend their way after death, and, lastly, black, for the cold and pitiless North, the origin of disease, famine and death.[9]

---

[9] W. J. Hoffman, "The Midêwiwin, or Grand Medicine Society of the Ojibway"; 7th Report of the Bureau of Ethnology, 1885–86, Washington, 1891, pp. 149–300, with many illustrations.

The various adjuncts of the sorcerer's trade are carefully preserved by the Midê or Jessakid in his medicine bag. A good specimen of this was made out of the skin of a mink, *Putorius vison*, Gapp., and adorned at one end with two fluffy white feathers.[10] Often a flat, black, water-worn pebble will be one of the great treasures in this sack. The virtues of a stone of this type are said to have been put to a curious test on the person of a Jessakid at Leech Lake, Minn., in 1858. The man offered to wager $100 that if he were securely tied up, hand and foot, with stout rope, but having his stone resting on his thigh, he could remove the bonds without assistance. The wager was taken up and the test duly applied; the Jessakid being left alone in his tent tightly and firmly bound. Before long he called out to those on the watch outside the tent that search should be made for the rope at a certain spot nearby. This was done and the rope was found with the knots undisturbed, while the Jessakid was to be seen calmly seated on the ground, smoking a pipe and still bearing his magic black stone on his thigh.[11]

French missionaries of the early part of the eighteenth century reported that the Indian wizards of some of the northwestern tribes would take a pebble the size of a pigeon's egg, and mutter over it certain conjurations. This, they assert, caused the formation of a like stone within the body of the person who was to be bewitched.[12] The medicine-men of certain Canadian tribes of this time were not content with muttered conjurations in treating their patients, but would not infrequently resort to the charm supposed to be exerted

[10] Loc. cit., Pl. XI, fig. 7, opp. 220.

[11] W. J. Hoffman, "The Midêwiwin, or Grand Medicine Society of the Ojibway"; 7th Report of the Bureau of Ethnology, 1885–86, Washington, 1891, p. 277.

[12] L'Abbé Banier and l'Abbé Mascrier, "Histoire générale des cérémonies, mœurs, et coutumes religieuses de tous les peuples du monde," Paris, 1741, p. 101.

Canadian Indian Medicine man. From "Histoire générale des cérémonies, mœurs, et coutumes religieuses de tous les peuples du monde," by Abbé Banier and Abbé Mascrier. Vol. VII. Paris, 1741.

by dancing and howling before the sick person. The nervous shock produced by a combination of such grotesque movements and discordant cries might well "rouse" the patient, and perhaps had sometimes good effects in restoring vitality.

An interesting use of the Röntgen rays to detect hidden amulets is noted by Stewart Culin. It was conjectured by Mr. Cushing that some pieces of turquoise, conceived to be the hearts of fetichistic birds, were concealed beneath the heavy wrapping of brown yarn that binds the finger-loops of the prehistoric throwing stick in the Museum of the University of Pennsylvania. This object was too valuable and too fragile to permit of its examination, and therefore the Röntgen rays were used, disclosing the presence of four stone beads, presumably of turquoise, as Mr. Cushing had indicated.[13]

As the Point Barrow Eskimos are so largely dependent on fishing, they especially favor amulets or talismans referring to this, and in many cases the peculiar power of the talisman is accentuated by giving it a specially significant form. Thus, from Utkiavwin was brought a piece of dark crimson jasper two inches long, rudely fashioned by chipping into the form of a whale, and also a similar figure made from a water-worn quartz pebble.[14] Another Point Barrow amulet consisted of three small fragments of amber, carefully wrapped up and placed in a cottonwood box 1½ inches in length. This box was cleverly made of two semicircular pieces of the wood, the flat faces having been hollowed out so as to leave space for the amber. They were then bound together by loosely knotted sinew braid.[15]

A black jade, adze-shaped, that may have served as a fisherman's talisman for the Point Barrow Eskimo, was brought from Utkiavwin. It measured 5.1 inches in length,

---

[13] Free Museum of Science and Art, Bulletin No. 4, Jan., 1898, p. 183 (with figures).

[14] John Murdoch, "The Point Barrow Eskimo," 9th Report of the Bureau of Ethnology, 1887–88, Washington, 1892, p. 435.

[15] Ibid., p. 439, fig. 426.

and was slung with a thong and whalebone, so that it could be suspended. Its weight is so considerable as to make it somewhat burdensome for wear on the person, but as one of these Eskimo wore a stone weighing two pounds suspended from a belt, the jade artefact may really have been worn in this way. The form suggests that of a sinker, as was also the case with the two-pound stone, and it may have earned its repute as a talisman from having been used in former times by some exceptionally fortunate or skilful fisherman, in the belief that it would transmit his good luck to anyone wearing it.[16] An artefact of somewhat similar form, 1.4 inches in length, and made of red jasper, came from the same locality; this was slung in a sinew band for suspension.[17]

The native Greenlanders of a couple of centuries ago had a great variety of amulets, and Hans Egede, in his Description of Greenland, notes these "Amulets or Pomanders" which the natives wore about the neck or arms, the materials being of the most heterogeneous kind, pieces of old wood, old fragments of stone, bones of various animals, the bill and claws of certain birds, and many other objects whose form or associations had suggested the possession of a magic potency.[18] A similar account of old Greenland amulets is given by David Crantz, another early author, who even asserts that some of the amulets were so grotesque that the natives themselves occasionally laughed at them. In the absence of any more definite talisman, recourse was sometimes had to the expedient of binding a leather strap over the forehead or around the arm.[19] Possibly, however, some

[16] Ibid., p. 438; see fig. 425.

[17] Ibid., p. 439.

[18] Hans Egede, "A Description of Greenland," London, 1745, p. 194 (Eng. trans.).

[19] David Crantz, "The History of Greenland," London, 1767, vol. i, p. 216 (Eng. trans.).

talisman was hidden beneath this strap, or else it may have been designed to serve as a point of support for an amulet that had been taken off at the time the traveller saw the strap.

Animal amulets, that is to say, amulets for animals, are in use in the Arctic regions, one class of these being stones that have fallen from a bird-rock. These the Eskimo attach to their dogs, proceeding upon the theory that as these pieces of rock in falling from a great height have traversed the air with tremendous rapidity, they will communicate the quality of fleetness to the dogs.[20] This transmission of an acquired quality of the stone to the person wearing it is shown in other instances, a favorite amulet with the Eskimos being a piece of an old hearth-stone. This is believed to give strength to the wearer, because the stone has so long endured the attacks of fire, the strongest and fiercest element. Such fragments of stone are often worn by Eskimo women, who wrap them up in pieces of seal-skin, making in this way a decoration to be worn on the neck.[21]

Not only does the medicine-bag of an Eskimo medicine-man serve to guard his trusted amulets and talismans, but some of these wonder-doctors claim to be able to draw within it the soul of a sick child, so as to keep this soul hidden away from all harm and danger. In fact, the opinion has been expressed that many personal amulets have owed their repute to their supposed power as soul-guardians, the owners' souls having been transferred to the material body of the amulet, which is more easily concealed and kept out of the way of injury than is the human body, the tabernacle of the spirit. A trace of this belief has been found by some in the term *battê ha-nephesh,* used by Isaiah (chap. iii, ver. 20). These feminine adornments are called "perfume boxes" in the

[20] Rasmussen, "The People of the Polar North," Philadelphia, 1908, p. 139.
[21] Ibid., p. 139.

Revised Version, but the literal meaning is "houses of the soul (or life)."[22]

The natives of southwestern Australia regard shining stones with so much veneration that only sorcerers or priests are believed to be worthy to handle them, and so great is the faith in the innate power of such objects that any ordinary native does not dare to touch them and cannot even be bribed so to do. For the preservation of the virtue of these stones it is considered essential that no woman shall be permitted to touch them, or even to look upon them. A particular form of talisman is made by winding lengths of opossum yarn about a fragment of quartz, of carnelian, of chalcedony, or some other attractive stone, and thus forming a round ball about the size of a crochet-ball; these are worn suspended from the girdle. Talismans of this type are very highly prized for their supposed power to cure diseases, and in case of illness a tribe which is not provided with one will borrow it from a more fortunate tribe.[23] White quartz is used by the natives in New South Wales, Australia, for the manufacture of a charm to cast a spell over an enemy. This charm is called *muli*, and consists of a fragment of white quartz to which a piece of opossum-fur has been gummed; it must then be smeared with the fat of a dead body and placed in a slow-burning fire. It is confidently believed that the person over whom the spell is cast wastes slowly away and dies.[24]

Jade carvings of an exceedingly peculiar type are the *hei-tikis* (neck-ornaments) greatly prized among the Maoris of New Zealand. The grotesque representation of the human form here realized by the native carvers, the association of

---

[22] J. G. Frazer, "Balder the Beautiful," London, 1913, vol. ii, p. 155. See also by the same writer, "Folk-lore in the Old-Testament," in Anthropological Essays, presented to E. B. Tyler, Oxford, 1907, pp. 148 sqq.

[23] Sir George Grey, "Journals of Two Expeditions of Discovery," London, 1841, vol. ii, pp. 340, 341.

[24] Bonney, Journ. of the Anthrop, Inst., vol. xiii, p. 130.

these objects, treasured up as heirlooms, with the personality of some renowned ancestor, the story that the special portraiture to be made was sometimes communicated in a dream or vision, all this induces the belief that in former times, though perhaps not at the present time, the Maoris looked upon their *hei-tikis* as amulets, or possibly even as fetiches.[25]

The Dowager Queen Alexandra is said to greatly value as a talisman a pendant consisting of a nugget of massive gold surmounted by a figure of a hunchback, executed in green enamel. The nugget is hollowed out and opens when a secret spring is touched; within appears a heart-shaped ornament made of New Zealand jade. The story runs that this jewel was given to his mother by the late Duke of Clarence, the elder brother of the present King George V.[26]

The popularity in England of these queer *hei-tiki* amulets, made from the *punamu* or "green-stone" (nephrite) of New Zealand, has been ascribed by many to the wearing by Queen Alexandra of ornaments made of New Zealand jade, and to the report that every member of the "All Blacks," an almost invincible English foot-ball team, carried some little trinket made from this material while he was engaged in play. The popular faith in "lucky jade" was further corroborated by the story that Lord Rosebery had on his person a jade amulet when his horse Cicero won the Derby and that Lord Rothschild was wearing such an amulet as his horse St. Amand carried his colors to victory.[27] When we consider to how great an extent popular enthusiasm is excited in England by her great and classic horse-races, we

[25] For further details concerning these strange ornaments, see the writer's "Curious Lore of Precious Stones," J. B. Lippincott Company, Philadelphia and London, 1913, pp. 87–90.

[26] Fernie, "Precious Stones for Curative Wear," Bristol, 1907, p. 39.

[27] A. E. Wright and E. Lovett, "Specimens of Modern Mascots and Ancient Amulets of the British Isles," Folk Lore, vol. xix, 1908, p. 293.

HEI-TIKI AMULETS OF NEW ZEALAND

Made of the jade found on the island, the *punamu*, or "green-stone." Illustrates the two types of this "neck-ornament," one with the eyes slanted to the left, the other to the right.

need not hesitate to believe that these reports did much to render jade amulets generally fashionable.

An old Polynesian legend recounts that jade was brought to New Zealand from a distant land by a certain Ngahue, who sought by this means to save the precious material from an enemy who coveted it. He settled at Arahua, on the west coast of the middle island, and in this region he found an eternal and safe resting place for his jade, which he valued above all things.[28] This legend has often been adduced as a proof that the New Zealand jade was brought from other countries, but as it proceeds to state that Ngahue made neck and ear ornaments of this material, there is at least as great probability that we have here the supposed origin of the *hei-tiki* ornaments, and that the legend testifies to the popular belief that the art of making these objects came to New Zealand from without.

The quasi-magic character of New Zealand jade (nephrite) in the eyes of Maoris of the olden time is proved by the fact that certain superstitious restrictions were established in regard to the cutting of nephrite, one of these being that no woman should be allowed to approach the jade-cutters while they were engaged in their task. For the drilling of holes in jade implements or amulets the cord-drill was employed, and the surface of the object received its polish by rubbing it with a piece of sandstone, after it had been roughly fashioned, by chipping, to the desired form. The toughness of jade is such that infinite patience and long-continued effort must have been necessary to complete any ornament or implement under these primitive conditions.[29]

A curious and characteristic jade artefact, known as *nbouet* or *koindien,* is found among the natives of New Cale-

---

[28] Grey, "Polynesian Mythology," London, 1855, p. 132.

[29] Elsdon Best, "The Stone Implements of the Maori," Dominion Museum Bulletin, No. 4, Wellington, New Zealand, 1912.

donia. This is a more or less circular disk of jade, with a cutting edge. In most cases this disk is attached through two perforations to a straight cylindrical handle, having a slit at the upper extremity into which the jade disk is introduced. The lower extremity has an ovoid termination, or else it is set in a cocoanut shell, usually covered with the integument of a pteropod. Attached are pendants of beautiful marine shells, and sometimes the cocoanut shell is filled with small pebbles so that it can be used as a rattle. These *nbouet* were originally used as cleavers to cut up the dead bodies for the cannibalistic orgies, and this use seems to have been thought to impart a kind of talismanic virtue to the objects, for they eventually became insignia of the chiefs of the native tribes.[30]

The ornament most highly prized by the natives of New Caledonia is a necklace of perforated jade beads. One of these necklaces, in the rich collection of Signor Giglioli, contains 122 jade beads, somewhat larger than peas; another necklace comprises eight beads alternating with small shells of the *oliva,* a species of mussel. As a pendant hangs an *oudip,* or slung-shot, of steatite.[31] Necklaces of this kind are called *peigha* by the natives, and the high esteem in which they are held probably arises from their supposed talismanic powers. The jade ornaments or artefacts found in the neighboring Loyalty Islands have all been brought from New Caledonia, and we are told that so great was the value placed upon them that the natives of the Loyalty Islands often traded their young girls in exchange for objects made from the greatly coveted jade.

From a Fijian mission teacher at Goodenough Island

---

[30] Giglioli, "Materiali per lo studio della Età della Pietra," Archivio per l'Antropologia e l'Etnologia, vol. xxxi, pp. 79, 80; Firenze, 1901.

[31] Ibid., pp. 82, 83.

comes a tale of a magic crystal. Many years ago some Europeans embarked in a boat manned by two Fijians to visit one of the smaller islands of the group. After they had landed and gone off to explore the island, one of the Fijians said to the other: "You look after the boat while I take a look around." He had not gone far when he saw two strange men, one of whom fled at his approach; the other he seized, holding on to him fast, although dragged along for a considerable distance until after scrambling up a hill the strange man finally loosed himself and disappeared in the hollow of a tree-trunk. For some time the Fijian lay in a trance, but awakening from this he found his way back to the boat. In the course of the afternoon the strange being appeared to him suddenly and told him "to go back to the tree, where he would find a small stone wrapped up in a piece of calico." This he duly sought and found; it proved to be a crystal, like glass. In the night time the man or spirit again appeared and strictly enjoined the Fijian not to let anyone see his crystal but told him that if he wished for anything he only had to look into the stone. The possession of this treasure earned a wonderful repute for the Fijian as a medicine-man, as when any sick person sought for help one look into the stone revealed the proper remedy for the disease. All this time, however, no one had been allowed to see his crystal, or to suspect the source of his wisdom. At last his fame reached the ears of some European doctors, who called him in to help them in their hospital work, and while he was at the hospital two young men came in and asked him to prescribe for a sick friend. The Fijian consented, but, unluckily for him, the men saw him take out his crystal and look into it before prescribing the treatment. They told this to the doctors and the man was locked up for two years, his crystal being taken away from him. The mission teacher who related the story believed that Sir J. Thurston, at this time governor of the islands, had secured possession of the confiscated crystal.[32] It is rather difficult to determine in what proportions truth and fiction are represented in this tale.

The doctrine of sympathy finds an echo among the natives of Melanesia. In the Banks Islands, for instance, if a native comes across a piece of coral to which the action of the waves has imparted the form of a loaf of bread, this will be taken to signify that such a coral has an affinity with the bread-fruit tree, and the native will bury it under such a tree in the confident expectation that its fruit-bearing quality will be enhanced thereby. Chance may perhaps seem to prove the truth of his belief, and in this case he will permit his neighbors to bury stones near his own, so that somewhat of its virtue may pass into them.[33]

To have one's life depend upon the safe preservation of a talisman may not always be a blessing, as appears in a Kalmuck story. A Khan who owned such a talisman thought that he had concealed it so effectively that no one could find it, and hence he did not hesitate to make the discovery of its hiding-place a crucial test of the skill of a wise man who came to visit his court. The sage proved equal to the emergency and found the talisman while its owner was asleep, but was so rejoiced at the successful accomplishment of the task that he very irreverently clapped a bladder on the sleeping Khan's head, who was so much enraged at the indignity that he ordered the wise man's immediate execution. However, the latter quickly made use of the magic power over the Khan's life that the possession of the talisman gave him, and cast it down so violently as to break it. No sooner

---

[32] "Folk Lore," vol. xxiv, No. 2, July, 1913, Story sent to R. R. Marett by Mr. D. Jenness of Baliol College, Oxford.

[33] Fraser, "The Golden Bough," Pt. I, "The Magic Art," London, 1911, vol. i, p. 164.

had this happened than blood spurted from the Khan's nostrils and death overtook him.[34]

Agate amulets still find favor in Spain, a number of interesting examples having recently been acquired in that country by Mr. W. L. Hildburgh, many of them being offered for sale in small stalls, both in the capital, Madrid, and in other of the Spanish cities.[35] In a number of cases these amulets are milky white agates, this hue recommending their use as lactation amulets. In one specimen, however, secured in Seville, the agate showed seven concentric white stripes, probably indicating that it had been used as a charm against the Evil Eye as well as to favor the secretion of milk.

For the latter purpose, in lieu of agate, white glass beads are often sold, a dealer in a small stall in Madrid having in his stock a string of fifty such beads which he sold one by one to the women who had faith in their efficacy; agate beads of combined grayish, reddish and white coloration are also to be found.

Quite an ambitious type of these popular amulets is figured by Mr. Hildburgh (Pl. i, p. 64, fig. 7). This is a triple pendant, with chain attached for suspension, the upper part being an agate grayish-white and reddish, probably rendering it at once a lactation amulet and one serving still another use as a woman's amulet. The middle of this pendant was of blue glass banded with other colors, and the terminal was of black glass, spotted blue, yellow and red; both of these glass objects are supposed to have served against the Evil Eye. Thus this particular amulet combined a number of virtues.

Coral is a favorite material for amulets in Spain as in many other lands, being shaped for this purpose as a "fig-

---

[34] J. G. Frazer, "Balder the Beautiful," London, 1913, vol. ii, p. 142; citing B. Julg, "Kalmückische Märchen," Leipzig, 1866, No. 12, pp. 58 sqq.

[35] W. L. Hildburgh, "Further Notes in Spanish Amulets," in Folk Lore, vol. xxiv, No. 1, March 31, 1913, pp. 63–74; 2 plates.

hand" or into some other of the diverse forms to which a certain symbolic significance has been given. One amulet of rock-crystal is reported, which may have been taken from some old reliquary; this was used against the Evil Eye. Amber also, in its way as generally popular as coral, is freely used in Spain by the makers of amulets; being generally given the form of beads. The wearing of these is regarded as very effective in the case of teething children. For some reason or other, a preference is given to facetted beads, in spite of the risk that the sharp edges may irritate the sensitive and delicate skin of an infant.[36]

Some of the "fig-hand" amulets made and sold in Madrid are of jet, the peculiar hand form being in many cases so highly conventionalized as to be barely indicated. These are believed to be efficacious not only against the Evil Eye, as the other amulets of this form, but also for the preservation of the hair. When worn for this purpose the women of Madrid are said to carry them upon any part of the person, but those of Toledo place them in the hair itself, so that the desired effect may be more immediate.[37]

In southern Russia amulets enjoy high power both among Jews and Christians. Especially are they valued for the protection of children and for the cure of their diseases. An imitation wolf's-tooth, made of bone, set in a ring, is one of these amulets; however, while such imitation teeth are used, the natural teeth are greatly preferred. As an amulet against the Evil Eye the wing-bones of a cock will be used. This malign influence is held in such awe by the common people that they do not even dare to use the word "evil" of it and call it "the *good* eye." Carnelian beads purporting

---

[36] W. L. Hildburgh, "Notes on Spanish Amulets," Folk Lore, vol. xvii, 1906, pp. 454–472. See Plate VIII, fig. 29, opp. p. 462.

[37] W. L. Hildburgh, "Further Notes on Spanish Amulets," in Folk Lore, vol. xxiv, No. 1, p. 66, March 31, 1913; one of those amulets is shown in Plate I, fig. 4, p. 64.

to have been brought from Palestine command what is regarded as a good price, three roubles being paid for a single one; these are great favorites with the Jews more especially, one of their supposed virtues being to prevent abortion.[38]

The religious fervor of the Russians is illustrated by the character of the amulet said to be constantly worn by the Czar as a protection against the dangers which hourly threaten him. This is a ring in which is set a piece of the True Cross, the sacred material which was believed to lend a mighty potency to the famous "Talisman of Charlemagne." A less venerable belief is said to render the Czar superstitiously careful to see that an ancestral watch in his possession is always kept wound up, for a family legend tells that should this watch ever stop the glory of the reigning house would pass away.[39]

Of bone amulets there is a great variety. Among those used in the British Isles may be noted a hammer-shaped type, fashioned out of a sheep's bone, worn by Whelby fishermen as protection from drowning; similarly shaped bone amulets find favor with some London laborers as preventives of rheumatism. This is the type of Thor's Hammer, still popular with the Manxmen. The strange resemblance of the os sacrum of the rabbit to a fox's head has recommended its use as a talisman, or luck-bringer, and a London solicitor is stated to have owned an example which he had mounted as a gold scarf-pin, the likeness to an animal head being brought out still more by the insertion of onyx eyes.[40]

The talismanic power of the turquoise is still credited in provincial England, for in the counties of Hampshire and Sussex it is believed that when two persons station them-

---

[38] S. Weissenberg, "Südrussische Amulette," in Zeitschrift für Ethnologie, 1897, pp. 367–369.

[39] From Jewellers' Circular Weekly, Feb. 5, 1913, p. 153.

[40] A. E. Wright and E. Lovett, "Specimens of Modern Mascots and Ancient Amulets of the British Isles," Folk Lore, vol. xix, p. 295, Plate V, fig. 1.

selves on opposite banks of a frozen stream or pond, on a Christmas Day, and each one slides a turquoise to the other over the ice, both of them will be blessed with good fortune for the following year and will prosper in all their undertakings. If the stream or pond were at all wide, the fact of having accomplished this feat successfully might indeed be taken as proof of considerable dexterity, and might perhaps indicate that one who could succeed in this little exploit had a chance of making his way in more important matters.

The natural markings on agate pebbles often present designs having some special symbolical significance, and could then be looked upon by the superstitious as amulets of notable power, much exceeding in efficacy those artificially formed. A strange instance in illustration of this is an agate pebble picked up not long since on Newport Beach, Rhode Island. This stone is clearly and definitely marked with the mystic Chinese monad, a device that is widely known in the United States from its adoption as a symbol by the Northern Pacific Railroad.

A limestone pebble with peculiar markings is in a private collection in New York. This somewhat resembles in shape the famous magatama jewel of the Japanese, and the markings suggest that, like the latter, it may have had a phallic significance, or at least one connected with the worship of the reproductive powers. The markings indicate an attempt to figure an undeveloped being, and possibly the object was intended for use as an amulet to facilitate parturition.

The prevailing reaction against the purely materialistic beliefs so generally accepted a score or more of years ago, finds expression in a marked tendency toward a renewal—in a greatly modified form, of course—of the old fancies or instinctive ideas touching the virtues of gems. Thus one modern writer at least was bold enough to suggest not long since that "the efficacy of charms and precious stones may be recognized and placed on a scientific basis before many years are passed."[41]

The belief in the hidden powers of precious stones was used as the theme of one of Hoffman's novels, "Das Fräulein von Scudéry." Here the hero, René Cardillac, is represented as a man for whom the possession of precious stones has become indispensable, and who is happy only when he can handle them and watch the play of light and color emanating from them. They exert a kind of hypnotic influence over him, and so intense and absorbing is his devotion to them that he even resorts to murder rather than part with one of his darling stones.

In the course of a meeting of the English Folk-Lore Society, one of the members expressed the opinion that the revival of interest in amulets and talismans and in all sorts and kinds of "mascots" was largely due to the articles printed about such things in certain of the daily and weekly papers. These items, put in a taking way and read with avidity, more especially by those who were already predisposed to a belief in the mythical or magical, served to spread these fancies far and wide throughout the land. The president of the society, Dr. Gaster, in closing the discussion, said that "from his experience the modern belief in amulets as aids to luck was genuine and widely spread."[42]

One of the latest Parisian oracles on mystic subjects, the Baroness d'Orchamps, says that emeralds should not be worn by women before their fiftieth year, although men may wear this gem without danger at any age. Sapphires, on the other hand, may be worn by both sexes at all times, since they have a potent influence for good luck. Hence

[41] See A. E. Wright and E. Lovett, "Specimens of Modern Mascots and Ancient Amulets of the British Isles," Folk Lore, vol. xix, 1904, pp. 288–303; citing Bratly, "The Power of Gems and Charms," London, 1907.

[42] A E. Wright and E. Lovett, "Specimens of Modern Mascots and Ancient Amulets of the British Isles," Folk Lore, vol. xix, p. 303.

speculators, and indeed all who hope for a favorable turn of Fortune's wheel, should look with favor on this stone. As medicinal gems, the ruby and the moon-stone are especially recommended; the former for chronic headaches and the latter for the manifold forms of nervousness. Lastly, the diamond, if worn on the left side, wards off evil influences and attracts good fortune. The unjustly maligned opal is asserted to be robbed of all power to harm if it be associated with diamonds and rubies.

Many of the members of the French nobility are the owners and wearers of talismanic ornaments of one kind or another. A powerful combination of such "life-preservers" is credited to the Duc de Guiche. On his right hand he wears three curiously chased rings, one on the first finger, the second on the middle finger, and the third on the "ring-finger." One of the rings is set with a sardonyx engraved with the figure of an eagle, the second ring bears a topaz on which has been graven a falcon, and the third ring shows a beautiful coral bearing the design of a man holding a drawn sword in his right hand. Both the stones and the special designs engraved on each one are in accord with the oldest traditional lore in regard to talismans, and the stones themselves are those indicated by the date of the duke's birth and by his baptismal name. While such an array of finger-rings would hardly appeal to the taste of an American man, the fashion of wearing an appropriate series of rings has met with considerable favor among our American mondaines, and certainly has the merit of lending an individual significance to the rings selected for wear.[43]

The magnificent star-sapphire set in the hilt of the richly chased and ornamented sword given by the Greeks of America to King Constantine of Greece, on Easter Day, 1913, just before the recipient succeeded to the royal dignity,

---

[43] St. Louis Democrat, 1905.

JEWELLED SWORD GIVEN BY THE GREEKS OF THE UNITED STATES, ON EASTER DAY, 1913, TO CROWN PRINCE CONSTANTINE, LATER KING CONSTANTINE XII OF GREECE

Top of scabbard, showing didrachm of Alexander the Great.

JEWELLED SWORD GIVEN BY THE GREEKS OF THE UNITED STATES, ON EASTER DAY, 1913, TO CROWN PRINCE CONSTANTINE, LATER KING CONSTANTINE XII OF GREECE

Side view of hilt.

may be looked upon as a talisman designed to assure good fortune and long life to the sovereign, as well as prosperity to the state over which he rules. This sword, which was made by Tiffany & Company, is even more noteworthy because of its artistic merit than on account of its intrinsic value. Another talismanic embellishment of the sword is an inlaid didrachm of Alexander the Great (356–323 B.C.); it is a well-known fact and one frequently recorded by ancient and medieval writers, that the coins of this monarch were often treasured up as amulets or talismans.[44] In the present instance, indeed, the charm, if charm there be, should work most effectively, as we can imagine no more appropriate guardian of the present ruler of Greece than the greatest hero and the mightiest conqueror the Greek race ever produced.

This sword was presented to His Majesty Constantine XII, King of the Hellenes, by the Greek residents of the United States, to commemorate his defeat of the Turks at Salonika and Janina. By these victories of the Greek armies under King Constantine, who was at that time the Crown Prince of Greece, the Greek people of Macedonia and Epirus were liberated from the Turkish yoke, and these rich provinces were added to the Greek crown. The Committee of Presentation consisted of Mr. Caftanzoglu, Chargé d'Affaires of Greece in Washington; Mr. D. Vlasto, editor of "Atlantis"; Dr. Breck Trowbridge, president, and Dr. T. Tileston Wells, vice-president of the Society of American Philhellenes, with the coöperation of Dr. George F. Kunz, a member of the council of the above society.

The green variety of microcline, a potash-feldspar, is known as the "amazon-stone." It is found at Amelia Court House, Virginia, at Pike's Peak, Colorado, at Rockport,

---

[44] See the writer's "The Curious Lore of Precious Stones," J. B. Lippincott Company, Philadelphia and London, 1913, p. 125; also pp. 68, 96.

Cape Ann, and in the Ural Mountains in Russia. It has recently been proposed as the stone for the Suffrage party. This amazon-stone could be cut in little beads of a beautiful pale green and after appropriate mounting they could be worn suspended by a ribbon from the button-hole. As the stone is inexpensive it ought to meet with favor among the hundreds of thousands who are aggressive in their advocacy of this cause.

Among the many persons of our day who still have or had a lingering faith in the efficacy of amulets, may be mentioned the late actress, Mrs. Annie Yeamans, who left special directions in her will that a little amulet attached to a gold chain which she constantly wore, should be left on her body and buried with her. We may call this superstition or sentiment, as we will, but there seems to be an almost invincible tendency to associate something of those dear to us and lost to us with inanimate objects that may have been theirs, and the memories called up by some simple trinket show that psychologically a certain power really does exist in such objects. The sentiment they awaken is only in ourselves, and the impression that awakes it as well, but the presence of the inanimate object actually conditions the awakening of the feeling. Thus we can scarcely deny to amulets a certain inherent quality in this respect.

Often some strange, quaint, or bizarre design seen in the shop of a dealer in antiques will make a peculiar and individual appeal to the observer, and will be chosen by him as his personal amulet, as though fate had destined the object for his special use. So we are told that Mr. Augustin Osman, the artist, secured possession of a singular gold ornament representing a human skull; upon it was figured in opals the word "Ave." On the first night after the acquisition of this object, the artist had a vivid dream, in which the impression was conveyed to him that he would always enjoy good fortune as long as the golden skull remained in his possession. Evidently the opals took nothing in his opinion from the luck-producing quality of this grewsome ornament; indeed, it seems more probable that they added to it.

A curious modern talisman is the work of M. Charles Rivaud, who has frequently exhibited splendid specimens of artistic jewelry at the Paris Salon; this talisman cleverly combines artistic merit with a dash of African magic. It is a slender bracelet composed of interlaced spirals of oxidized silver and gold; around the circlet is twined a hair taken from an elephant. Among the tribesmen of the Soudan the hairs of this animal are believed to be endowed with great talismanic virtue; indeed, they enjoyed a similar repute among the ancient Romans. Whether this belief was due to the idea that the wearer of the hair was assured a mighty protection, typified by the enormous strength of the elephant, or whether to the fact that the elephant was with some peoples a divine symbol, we cannot easily determine.

The opal has long since emerged from the slight cloud of disfavor due to a most erroneous fancy that it was in some way associated with ill-luck. This idea, possibly in its origin explainable by the comparative fragility of the gem, found a consistent and earnest opponent in the late Queen Victoria, whose influence did much to make opals fashionable. Of late years they have become favorite bridal gifts, the exceptional variety of color in the beautiful examples from the White Cliff mines in New South Wales, having also contributed to the renewed popularity of the stone. A parure of these opals was not long since bestowed upon the Empress Augusta by Emperor William of Germany, and one of the finest Australian opals is a treasured possession of the Duchess of Marlborough.

A very attractive example of symbolic jewelry has lately been made by a jeweler's firm of Besançon, France. This ornament is composed of three keys, to which are given the respective names, Key of Love, Key of Good Fortune, and Key of Heaven. They are to open up for the wearer the treasures of true love, of wedded bliss, and, finally, of paradise. A legend from the time of the Crusades suggested the form of this pretty jewel. Mourning the departure of a knight on the long and perilous journey to Palestine, a Provençal maiden wandered through the woodland, seeking peace and consolation in its quiet recesses. As she passed along the leafy pathways, she all unconsciously gave utterance to her longings and fears in softly spoken words. All at once a bright light beamed about her, and a radiant fairy advanced toward her and gave her an ivory casket in which lay three jewelled keys, masterpieces of the goldsmith's art. The first of these, the fairy assured her, would open the young knight's heart to receive her image; the second would open the church door to admit her, a happy bride; and the third, when life's journey was o'er, would unlock for her the gates of Paradise.

On the deservedly popular watch bracelets, things of beauty as well as utility, the precious stones used for decoration are sometimes selected for the significance of the first letters of their names when read in sequence. The following example may be noted:

D iamond
E merald
A methyst
R uby

S apphire
A gate
R uby
A methyst

In this way any name or endearing epithet can be prettily expressed.

X

Facts and Fancies about Precious Stones

MANY interesting facts about precious stones do not properly refer either to their talismanic or curative powers, and yet serve in not a few cases to indicate more or less clearly the reasons which have determined popular fancy or superstition in attributing particular virtues to a given stone.

As an instance of the strange vagaries of belief in the influence exerted by certain of these stones, we may take the statement that powdered agate dissolved in beer was used by the Bretons as a test of virginity. If a young girl were unable to retain this delectable mixture on her stomach, she was supposed to be impure.[1] The ability to stand this test seems rather to prove the possession of a strong stomach than a clear conscience.

Rainbow Agate is a name appropriately applied to agates showing a beautiful prismatic effect. These are composed of quartz and chalcedony in very fine layers. The writer secured a splendid specimen of this type of agate set in a jewel which had formed part of an old Saxon collection; it may possibly have come from India. The prismatic play of color differs from that observed in quartz iris, in that the iridescence is due to the minute interference lines and not, as with the iris, to internal fractures.

The greatest interest was manifested in the eighteenth century in these agates, one of which was described in a special pamphlet under the title, "Regenbogen Achat," and

[1] Wilhelmus Parisiensis, quoted in Pancirollus, "History of Many Memorable Things," London, 1715, vol. i, p. 42.

illustrated with a colored plate. The effect was that of a spectrum rather than the iris effect of the crystalline quartz. This iris was also highly valued, and great favor was set upon brilliant examples of what was in reality rock-crystal fractured, the small fracture-planes causing the breaking up of the light and producing the rainbow or iris effect. In fact it was a spectrum produced by the mixture of quartz between the chalcedonic layers.

Cellini has a marvellous story to tell of a luminous carbuncle. A certain Jacopo Cola, a vine-grower, going into his vineyard one night noticed what appeared to be a bit of glowing coal at the foot of one of the vines, but on reaching the spot he was unable to locate the source of this radiance. Very wisely he retraced his steps to the spot whence he had first observed the light, which became again apparent, and when he now very carefully approached the vine he found that the gleam proceeded from a rough little stone, which he joyfully picked up and carried off with him. He showed it to a number of his friends and among them chanced to be a Venetian envoy, an expert on precious stones, who immediately recognized that the find was a carbuncle. Thereupon taking a base advantage of the finder's ignorance, he succeeded in buying the stone for only ten scudi, and then hastened away from Rome, lest his deception should be discovered. Not long afterwards this same Venetian went to Constantinople and sold the stone to the Sultan of the time for 100,000 scudi, a profit of 10,000 per cent.[2] The fact that the vintner could only see the gleam from a given spot is in itself sufficient proof that what he noted was merely the reflection of some distant light striking a smooth surface of the stone at a certain angle.

Among the many virtues credited to carnelian by the

---

[2] Benvenuto Cellini, "Due trattati, uno intorno alle otto principali arti dell' oreficeria," etc., Fiorenzi, Valenti Panizzi & Marco Peri, 1568, fol. 10.

Mohammedans may be noted its power to preserve the equanimity and gravity of the wearer in the midst of disputes or inordinate laughter. A special and peculiar utilization of this material was to employ splinters of it as toothpicks. Their use not only whitened the teeth but also prevented bleeding of the gums. The Prophet, according to tradition, asserted that the wearer of a carnelian ring would never cease to be happy and blessed.[3]

The chrysolite is now regarded as a semi-precious stone only, yet Shakespeare presented this gem as the type of excellence in its kind when he wrote ("Othello," Act V, Scene 2):

> Nay, had she been true,
> If heaven would make me such another world
> Of one entire and perfect chrysolite,
> I'd not have sold her for it.

It is interesting to note that this appreciation of the beauty of the chrysolite is also shown in an old Greek glossary of alchemical terms, where occur the words: *Ιερὸς λίθος ἐστὶ Χρυσόλιθος*, "Sacred stone means the chrysolite."[4]

Such was the sacred quality ascribed to strings of coral beads in some parts of Africa, not long since, that they were regarded as the most precious gifts a ruler could bestow. If the favored recipient were so unfortunate as to lose this royal donation—which was a mark of high rank—he himself, as well as all involved in the theft, incurred the penalty of death. A writer of the seventeenth century, Palisot de Beauvais, relates that in Benin human victims were sacrificed at a "coral festival," when the corals of the king and royal family were dipped in the victim's blood, so as to placate the coral fetish and ensure a further supply of the precious

[3] Edmond Doutté, "Magie et Religion," Alger, 1909, pp. 83, 84.

[4] Berthelot, "Collection des anciens alchemistes grecs," Paris, 1888, 1889, vol. i, p. 9 of text.

material.[5] Possibly human blood was believed to strengthen the special virtue supposed to be inherent in this red substance.

There is a note of republican simplicity in the reported wearing of coral ornaments on ceremonial occasions by the present Queen of Italy. Indeed, the assertion that this is done to stimulate the coral industry in Italy may be true, as nothing would better tend to do this than such an example of royal favor for coral. Certainly this is in marked contrast with the almost exclusive use of pearl ornaments of all kinds so characteristic of Queen Margarita, whose devotion to the pearl, now perhaps the most costly of gems, had a poetic appropriateness for one bearing her name, and we can scarcely imagine the Pearl of Savoy without her splendid parures and necklaces of pearls. Still, undoubtedly this new departure renders it possible for all Italian women, rich or poor, to loyally follow the example set by their Queen Helena, and there is little danger that the rich will ever neglect to avail themselves of the exclusive privilege they possess of owning and wearing diamonds, pearls, rubies, sapphires and emeralds, which surpass coral as much in beauty as they do in price.

A comparatively recent attempt to use diamond dust as a poison is said to have been made in 1874 on Colonel Phayre, British Resident at the court of the then reigning Gaikwar of Baroda. The colonel was in the habit of refreshing himself after his morning walk with a glass of sugared water flavored with a little lime-juice. One day, on taking a sip of his customary beverage, he noted that it had a strange taste, and instead of drinking it he saved it up and had it analyzed. The analysis revealed the presence of arsenic in quantity sufficient to cause death, and of diamond dust as

[5] Roth, "Great Benin, Its Customs, Art and Horrors," Halifax, England, 1903, p. 95.

well. Here, as in the case of Sir Thomas Overbury, the really innocuous diamond material was accompanied by an actual poison. The current belief in the poisonous quality of the diamond is reflected in the words "mortal as diamond dust," used by Horace Walpole in one of his letters to the Countess of Ossory.[6]

A German writer of the seventeenth century quotes with admiration a wonderful tale told by Johannes Bustamantius to the effect that he had seen a marriage of two diamonds, the two crystals being so firmly drawn toward each other by mutual sympathy that when they were put in one place they would cling to one another, as with an "unending kiss," as though one were a man and the other a woman, and he asserts that the union was blessed with offspring. This curious idea has been repeatedly put forth by certain of the older writers as we have had occasion to note elsewhere.[7]

After expatiating on the mechanical skill displayed by the Indians of the New World, an early Spanish traveller gives the following details regarding their success as gem-cutters:[8]

> Yet all that we have said is surpassed by the ingenuity of the Indians in working emeralds, with which they are supplied from the coast of Manta and the countries dependent on the government of Atacames, Coaquis or Quaques. But these mines are now entirely lost, very probably through negligence. These curious emeralds are found in the tombs of the Indians of Manta and Atacames; and are, in beauty, size and hardness superior to those found in the district of Santa Fé; but what chiefly raises the admiration of the connoisseur is, to find them worked, some in spherical, some cylindrical, some conical, and of various other figures; and all with a perfect accuracy.

---

[6] See Wilt's "History of India," vol. ii, p. 197. Cited in Lean's Collectanea, vol. ii, Pt. II, Bristol, 1903, p. 641.

[7] C. G. Jentsch, "Dissertatio physico-historica de gemmis," Lipsiæ, 1706, p. 19. See also the present writer's "The Curious Lore of Precious Stones," Philadelphia and London, 1913, p. 41.

[8] Ulloa's Voyage to South America, trans. of John Adams, in Pinkerton's Voyages and Travels, vol. xiv, London, 1813, p. 546.

But the unsurmountable difficulty here is, to explain how they could work a stone of such hardness, it being evident that steel and iron were utterly unknown to them. They pierced emeralds and other gems, with all the delicacy of the present times, furnished with so many tools; and the direction of the hole is also very observable; in some it passes through the diameter, in others only to the centre of the stone, and coming out at its circumference they formed triangles at a small distance from one another, and thus the figure of the stone to give it relief was varied with the direction of the holes.

The existence of emeralds in the region near Berenice is vouched for by Ptolemy. The mines of emerald here were duly entered in the map of the patriarch and the Arabs are said to have dug for them; but, Pocock writes, "As all stones that may be found belong to the Grand Signior, the Arabs are very well satisfied that the presence of emeralds should not be suspected, because he would have the profit, and the inhabitants might be obliged to work in the mines for a very small consideration."[9]

The number of ancient hematite artefacts found in the United States indicates that this material was more largely used within its territorial limits for implements and ornaments than in any other part of the world;[10] indeed the somewhat sweeping statement has been ventured that it does not seem to have been used outside of this section of the New World; however, some exceptions to this rule must be admitted. That certain of these ornaments were used as amulets is highly probable, and they were undoubtedly regarded as objects of great value, since with the primitive tools at his command the Indian cutter must have found his task a very hard one, requiring the expenditure of much time and patience. In the Andover Collection there is an exceptionally fine specimen from Roos County, Ohio. It is

---

[9] Pocock's "Travels in Egypt," Pinkerton's "Voyages and Travels," vol. xv, London, 1814, p. 238.

[10] See Warren K. Moorehead, "Hematite Implements of the United States, Bulletin VI of the Department of Archæology, Phillips Academy, Andover, Mass., Andover, 1912.

of heavy pure hematite, which has been worked into the form of a pendant; notches have been made at both ends, as a form of decoration, and on the lower, broad end, fourteen lines have been incised; the edges are slightly beveled and the patina indicates the antiquity of the work. The lines have evidently been made by a flint cutting-implement.[11] Another probable hematite amulet is a rudely fashioned fish effigy. Here the appearances of eye and gill (only on one side) are evidently merely natural irregularities of surface, which it has been conjectured determined the cutter to add a mouth and round off the material so as to approximate a fish-form; the hematite is black and of fine quality. This relic comes from Cole Camp, Betnon County, Missouri.[12] The larger number of these hematite artefacts are from Missouri, southern Iowa, Illinois, Indiana, Ohio, West Virginia and Kentucky, and considerable numbers have been turned up in Tennessee, New York, Wisconsin, and parts of Arkansas. Only a relatively small number were taken out of burials or graves, the majority of specimens having been secured on or near the surface.

Shah Jehangir relates in his memoirs that Mûnis Khân, son of Mihtar Khân, presented him with a jug of jasper (jade), which had been made in the reign of Mîrzâ Ulugh Beg Gûrgân, in the honored name of that prince. It was a very delicate rarity and of a beautiful shape. Its stone was exceedingly white and pure. Around the neck of the jar were carved characters expressing the auspicious name of the Mîrzâ and the Hijra year. Jehangir ordered them to inscribe his name and the auspicious name of Akbar on the edge of the lip of the jar.[13]

---

[11] Ibid., p. 81, Fig. 41.

[12] Ibid., p. 91, Fig. 47.

[13] Note on jade copied from the Tûzuk-i-Jâhangîrî, or memoirs of Jahangir, trans. by Alexander Rogers, London, 1909, p. 146; Orient. Trans. Fund, N. S., vol. xix.

Jade ornaments of ancient workmanship have been found in Syria, and it is quite likely that in many cases where the designation plasma is used by ancient writers, true jade, or nephrite, was the material. As there was no specific designation for jade, the different varieties were assimilated to other stones of like color and appearance, so that, among others, the names jasper, plasma and even *smaragdus* were used to denote jade.

Mortuary tablets of jade have been used from time immemorial in China for the reception of historic inscriptions, the toughness and durability of the material making it especially desirable for this purpose. In the case of rulers, such tablets not only bore the names of the deceased sovereign but also an epitome of the leading events of his reign, and additions were made to this record from time to time so that in historic value they may be compared with the clay tablets of Babylonia and Assyria. One of these interesting monuments found its way to San Francisco, after the looting of the Forbidden City by the international army of relief in 1901. On it appeared a record of the treaty between the United States and China in 1868, and the other records went back to the death of Shun Chi in 1661. Probably owing to exposure to the weather the earlier inscriptions were not very legible.

At all important Chinese marriage ceremonies the priest carries what is known as a "marriage sword." This is usually about twelve or thirteen inches in length and the sheath is often studded with various pink stones, cut *en cabochon*. The stones most favored for this decoration are pink tourmaline, rubellite from the Shan Mountains, or rose-quartz, and the natural color of these gems is often intensified by placing a pink paste or foil beneath them; occasionally the coloration of the stones is enhanced by dipping them in a pink aniline solution. A piece of green jade is usually set as a boss at the hilt of this symbolical sword. In one remarkable specimen the guard consisted of a piece of white jade with the figure of a dragon carved in relief upon it; the sword-blade was of bronze. At the marriage ceremony the bridegroom is given the sword to hold, and the bride the sheath; as the wedding ring is placed upon the bride's finger, sword and sheath are brought together.

Among the innumerable forms of jade decoration or carving, produced by the indefatigable and painstaking Chinese artists, is a small curved wand often having a trefoil termination; sometimes the entire wand is of jade, and at other times it is of teakwood adorned with jade medallions, frequently showing birds and flowers. This wand was used as a kind of sceptre of office, and the official entitled to bear it would hold it in both hands when standing before the emperor. Its name, *ju-i,* means "may all be," and is to be taken as a wish that everything may turn out fortunately. In modern times the *ju-i* is carried as a lucky charm, although its official significance is not forgotten. This form of wand is said to have been introduced into China from India, at the time of the Buddhist propaganda, and in representations of Buddhist priests they are sometimes shown carrying one of them. In ancient India it was taught to be one of the seven precious objects, the *septa-ratna,* mentioned in the Vedas.[14] This Indian origin is, of course, highly probable, but it is strange that in ancient Egypt also, curved wands of a somewhat different type, made of ivory and embellished with symbolical figures, possessed the same blended significance of marks of official dignity and magic wands.

A large mass of lapis lazuli was found in one of the

---

[14] See The Morgan-Whitney Collection of Chinese Jades and other Hard Stones, donated to the Isaac Delgado Museum of Art, City Park, New Orleans, 1914, p. 32; plate opp. p. 33.

Inca graves of Peru by Señor Emilio Montés, and was exhibited by him in the Centennial Exhibition of 1913. With the exception of one corner that has been chipped off, the block is of symmetrical form, the dimensions being, in inches, 24 x 14 x 9, and the weight 312 pounds. The smoothed surface gives evidence of careful and fairly successful polishing by the native lapidaries. This exceptionally fine specimen of lapis lazuli is now in the Field Museum of Natural History in Chicago.[15] Evidently in ancient Peru as in the Old World the "celestial hue" of lapis lazuli was thought to render it most appropriate for use as a memorial offering to the dead or as a talisman by the aid of which their heavenward journey might be made easier.

The so-called "black onyx" has almost entirely replaced jet. This is a chalcedony impregnated with a carbonic matter, such as blood or a solution of sugar, the carbonate of which is charred by sulphuric acid, giving a rich, velvety, black hue to the stone, which takes a high polish. However, a certain limited amount of the old "Whitby Jet" once so highly favored is still mined and worked up into ornaments in the neighborhood of Whitby on the northeast coast of England, in the district of Leeds, although but fifty persons are now engaged in this industry which fifty years ago gave employment to 1500 workers. Some Spanish jet is also used, a material harder and more brittle than that found in England.

The story was current that Pope Leo X (1475–1521) had a precious stone, probably some type of "moonstone,"[15a] which grew brighter as the moon waxed, exhibiting the soft, silvery brilliance of our satellite, and then gradually lost its brightness as the moon waned, growing paler and dimmer

---

[15] Communicated by Dr. O. C. Farrington.

[15a] See in praise of the moonstone the poem autographed for this work by the poet, Edward Forrester Sutton.

The Legend of the Moonstone.

Published in the "Sentinel of the Blessed Sacrament" May. 1912.

I.

One dusk of eve, a drop of dew
Within a lily fell.
And nestling there, the essence drew
Forth from its silken bell
Of milky whiteness, clean and true
That in the flower doth dwell.

II.

This .... drawn to earth by souls in need
When the great moon was high ...
Our Lady saw, and said, "Indeed
Such beauty shall not die
All that the lily's heart doth bleed
Pearled in a gem shall lie".

III.

Thereat a moonbeam flew, and sought
Moth-like, the sleeping flower,
A clearness marvellously fraught
With strange and saintly power
And touched the dewdrop. Thus was wrought
The moonstone, in that hour.

IV.

"Moonrays and molten lily-white
In rainbow dew congealed,
This be the jewel of my might,
The symbol and the shield,"
She said, and all the winds of night
Whispered her will revealed.

V.

And the long grasses, to their head
Rippled like bending corn,
And leaves, low-drooped, that overspread
Grey waters, to the morn
Weaving grey veils, the whisper sped
That the snow-fires were born.

VI.

The stars of clear and stainless ray,
Of Faith and Purity,
Of white and maiden souls, and they
In Innocence that be
Of Childhood, or of Wisdom's way,
Who strive and so are free.

Written out for
Dr. George Frederick Kunz
Dec. 17. 1913.
Edward Forrester Sutton.

Autographed for this work by the author of the poem, Dr. Edward Forrester Sutton.

The birth – of the Opal.

The Sunbeam loved the Moonbeam
And followed her low and high,
But the Moonbeam fled and hid her head,
She was so shy, so shy:
The Sunbeam wooed with passion;
Ah he was a lover bold,
And his heart was afire ~~with~~ mad desire
For the Moonbeam pale and cold:
She fled like a dream before him;
Her hair was a shining sheen;
And oh that Fate would annihilate –
The space that lay between!

Just as the day lay panting
In the arms of the twilight dim,
The Sunbeam caught the one he sought

And drew her close to him.

But out of his warm arms startled
And stirred by love's first shock,
She sprang afraid like a trembling maid
And hid in the niche of a rock;
And the Sunbeam followed and found her,
And led her to Love's own feast;
And they were wed on that rocky bed
And the dying Day was their priest;
And lo! the beautiful Opal,
That rare and wondrous gem,
Where the moon and sun blend into one —
Is the child that was born to them.

Ella Wheeler Wilcox

THE BIRTH OF THE OPAL

Autographed for this work by the authoress, Ella Wheeler Wilcox

and becoming quite obscure as the moon's disk ceased to be illumined by the sun. As a mate to this, Pope Clement VII (1475–1534) was reputed to have in his possession a stone with a golden spot which moved across the surface in exact accord with the apparent motion of the sun across the heavens from sunrise to sunset.[16] These are undoubtedly fables that were circulated intentionally, or more probably through pure love of exaggeration, in order to enhance the merit of two exceptionally fine specimens of moonstone and sunstone in the papal treasury.

In the eighteenth century the collection of the Duke of Brunswick contained a magnificent ancient drinking-cup, of the kind used in sacrificial ceremonies, cut from a single piece of onyx; this cup was said to have formed part of the rich spoils taken from Mithridates by the Romans under Pompey. It was valued in the duke's inventory at 150,000 thalers, and Catherine II of Russia is stated to have offered four times that sum, or 600,000 thalers ($400,000) for this unique cup.[17]

In the symbolism of the Manichean sect, an early Christian heresy owing its origin to a direct and predominant influence of Persian ideas, pearls occupy a prominent place. A legendary or poetic pearl called "the bright moon" was the symbol of compassion, and one of the treatises ends with the words: "Our heart has received the majestic splendor of the pearl granting every wish." We are also told of "a diamond pillar" which sustains humanity, and the Messenger of Light is likened to a perfumed mountain entirely composed of a mass of jewels.[18]

---

[16] Petri Servii, "Dissertatio de unguento armario," Romæ, 1643, p. 43.

[17] Johann August Donndorf, "Natur und Kunst," Leipzig, 1790, vol. ii, p. 497.

[18] Berthold Laufer, "Notes on Turquois in the East," Chicago, 1913, p. 50, vol. xiii, No. 1, of Anthropological Series of Field Museum of Natural History; citing a translation by MM. Chavannes and Pelliot entitled: "Un traité manichéen retrouvé en Chine," pub. in Journal Asiatique, 1912.

The recital of two Arab travelers, Hasan ibn Vazid and Sulaiman, who visited India in the ninth century, contains a curious theory of the formation of pearls or rather of the pearl-oyster. The primal matter is assumed to be a gelatinous moss, analogous to that of a species of algæ. This floats upon the water and attaches itself to the keels of ships, where it hardens, develops a shell, and finally drops off to sink into the depths of the sea. The formation of the pearl itself is then discussed and the theory noted in Pliny's Natural History and so often repeated after his time, namely, that pearls are formed from the "dew of heaven," is cited; but the writer adds: "Others say that they [the pearls] are produced in the oysters themselves. This appears more probable and is confirmed by experience; for the greater part of those observed in the oysters are firmly attached there and are immovable. Those which are mobile are called by the merchants seed-pearls." As a true Mohammedan the writer concludes with the pious ejaculation: "God knows how the matter really stands!" [19]

The same travellers relate the story of the discovery of a pearl under very singular conditions. An Arab came to Bassora with a very fine pearl. He took it to a druggist whom he knew and asked the latter how much it was worth. The merchant estimated it at a hundred pieces of silver, to the great surprise of the Arab, who demanded whether anyone could be found willing to pay so much. Without hesitation the merchant declared that he was ready to give the price himself, and immediately paid over the money. He then took his purchase to Bagdad, where he secured a large profit on his investment. On concluding his sale the Arab told the Bassora druggist how he had secured his pearl. One day, while walking along the Bahrein coast, he saw on the

---

[19] "Ancient Accounts of India and China by Two Mohammedan Travellers," trans. by Abbé Renaudot, London, 1733, p. 96.

sands a dead fox, whose mouth was tightly compressed by a strange object. On closer observation this proved to be an enormous pearl-oyster shell. Evidently the fox had thrust his snout into the shell while the valves were open so that he might devour the soft contents, but the valves suddenly closed upon him and he had died of suffocation. On prying open the shell the Arab found therein the pearl which was destined to bring him what he regarded as a fabulous sum.[20]

The women of the Arab town occupying a site close to that on which stood the Babylon of ancient times, wore, as a favorite adornment, nose-rings of gold set with a pearl and a turquoise. The English traveller, John Eldred, who traversed Mesopotamia in 1583, found this custom so general that he writes: "This they doe be they never so poore." [21]

For years a statement has been going through the press that pearls are liable to become diseased and die, and that the famous necklace of pearls presented by President Thiers of France to his wife, and bequeathed by Mme. Thiers to the French Government, had lost their lustre and died, perhaps owing to the death of the owner. For there is an old belief that pearls, as well as opals and turquoises, lose some of their lustre when the owner or wearer becomes ill, and change to a dull and lifeless hue when the owner dies. An examination of the necklace by the writer showed that the pearls were in good condition, and to confirm his statement to this effect he had the director of the Louvre Museum write him a letter. In this official communication the director not only states that the pearls had not sickened and died, but that they were in as "healthy" a condition as they had ever been.

---

[20] "Ancient Accounts of India and China by Two Mohammedan Travellers," trans. by Abbé Renaudot, London, 1733, pp. 97, 98.

[21] See Hakluyt, "The Principal Navigations, Voyages and Discoveries of the English Nation," London, 1589.

The invariable experience of the writer has been that whenever pearls have been said to have suffered in this way, the true explanation has been that they were old and poor at the time of their purchase, and that this romance was started on its travels as an excuse to cover up the defect of such pearls and to arouse the belief that they had been remarkably beautiful and valuable when they were originally acquired.

As though to make amends to the Queen Gem for such disadvantageous rumors, considerable publicity has recently been given to a report that, in the Musée de Monaco, there was a luminous pearl whose beauties were revealed by an inner light, so that darkness had no power to dim its lustre. In a thoroughly impartial spirit, the writer went to the fountain-head for information in this matter, and received as answer from the director of the museum that there was no such pearl in the collection and that he had absolutely no faith in the luminosity of pearls.

As has been seen, both of these legends must be set aside as false, and we fear there is just as little truth in a report that a genuine "pearl-powder" is now used by the fair ladies of Paris and by their numerous imitators. The story goes that the Arab workmen engaged in pearl-piercing in India are noted for the clearness—we can hardly say, the lightness—of their complexions, and that this is supposed to be attributable to the fact that, when resting from their difficult task, they are in the habit of taking up some of the pearl-dust that has fallen on the floor and rubbing their faces with it. As the conditions under which these men work are eminently unsanitary, those who noted the clearness and smoothness of their complexions came to the conclusion that there must be something especially beneficial in pearl dust, and brought the matter to the notice of a French chemist. The latter proceeded to utilize the suggestion and compounded a new cosmetic. He did not, however, pin his faith to the pearl-dust alone, but wisely added a number of other ingredients.

Still another mythical tale in reference to pearls has to be refuted. For some time past numerous specimens of a so-called "cocoanut-pearl" have been brought from the East. These are very white pearls, resembling in hue the hard meat of the cocoanut, and said to have been produced in the cocoanut, just as other pearls are produced in certain species of mollusks. However, the writer has always found them to be pearls secreted by the gigantic mollusk *Ostrea Singapora.*

A strange poetic fancy regarding the transmutation of parts of the human form into gems of the sea appears in Ariel's song in Shakespeare's "Tempest":

> Full fathom five thy father lies,
> Of his bones are coral made;
> Those are pearls that were his eyes,
> Nothing of him that doth fade
> But doth suffer a sea-change
> Into something rare and strange.
> *Tempest,* Act I, Sc. ii.

Some natives of the Sulu Archipelago believe that the nautilus pearl is a most unlucky object to possess, for should a man engage in a fight while wearing such a pearl he would inevitably be killed. Hence, when a native by chance comes across one of them, he very quickly throws it away, as a probable bringer of ill-luck. Occasionally, however, such pearls fall into the hands of those who are less influenced by superstition, and one weighing 72 grains was given, in 1884, to an Australian gentleman, by Mohammed Beddreddin, brother-in-law of the Sultan of Sulu. This was a perfect, pear-shaped pearl of a creamy-white hue and somewhat translucent; it is composed of the porcelanous, not of the nacreous constituent of the shell.[22]

It has been stated that this Sulu superstition is not shared by the natives of Celebes Island, near Borneo, for here such pearls are kept as charms and talismans. One of an irregular pear-shape, weighing 27½ grains, has been found on the northern coast of the island.[23] The finding of a nautilus pearl by a Chinese woman in Borneo is noted by Rumphius, who describes it as being as large as a bean and

East Indian Baroque pearl. Weight over 1700 grains, Holland, 1775.

white as a piece of alabaster, hard and bright, but of very irregular shape. The finder put it in a closed box, and was not a little surprised to discover when she opened the box after a time that the original pearl had engendered another one the size of a lentil; later it had two other, smaller offspring. The woman carefully treasured her find as a lucky stone which would bring her good fortune in her search for mussels. Rumphius shrewdly conjectures that the smaller concretions had broken off the larger one while it was enclosed in the box.[24]

---

[22] H. Lyster Jameson, in "Nature," Oct. 7, 1912.
[23] See "Nature," Oct. 24, 1912, p. 220.
[24] Rumphius, "D'Amboinische Rariteitskamer," Amsterdam, 1741, p. 62.

The well-known lines in Shakespeare's "Othello":

> Of one whose hand, like the base Judean's,
> Cast away a pearl richer than all his tribe.

have been explained in many different ways by the commentators, one of whom (Steevens) saw in them a reference to the following story current in Venice in the sixteenth century. A Jew, after long and perilous wanderings in the East, succeeded in bringing with him to Venice a great number of fine pearls. These he disposed of there at satisfactory prices, with the exception of one pearl of immense size and extraordinary beauty, upon which he set a price so high that no one was willing to pay it. Finally, the Jew invited all the leading gem-dealers to meet him on the Rialto, and when as many of them as answered his call had assembled, he once more, and for the last time, offered his peerless pearl for sale, detailing all its perfections in eloquent terms. However, he made no concession in the price, and the dealers unanimously refused to purchase it, probably expecting that the Jew would at last be forced to make a reduction, but to their amazement, instead of doing this, he threw his pearl before their very eyes into the waters of the canal, preferring rather to lose it than to cheapen it.[25]

The belief that the growth of pearls in the pearl-oyster was due to rain-drops is perpetuated in the Arab proverb: "The rain of the month of Nisan brings forth pearls in the

---

[25] Schiller's "Werke," ed. by R. Boxberger, vol. iv, Berlin and Stuttgart, n. d., pp. 179, 180, note; from a communication to the editor by Dr. R. Köhler of Weimar, in illustration of the following lines of Schiller's "Don Karlos," Act II, Sc. 8:

> Dem grossen Kaufmann gleich
> Der, ungerührt von des Rialto's Gold,
> Und Königen zum Schimpfe, seine Perle
> Dem reichen Meere wiedergab, zu stoltz
> Sie unter ihrem Werte loszuschlagen.

sea and wheat on the land." [26] This spring month was, and is still, the period when pearl-fishing begins in the Orient. Another pearl proverb repeats the evangelical saying in this form: "Do not throw pearls under the feet of swine."

A Tonquinise legend of the origin of pearls represents them as springing from the blood of a young princess who was slain by the king, her father, because she had betrayed to her husband the secret of a magic bow, whose death-dealing arrows always flew to their mark. In his anger at his daughter's act, the father drew his scimitar and beheaded her, but with her last breath she prayed that her blood might be turned to pearls. Her prayer was heard and now the finest pearls of this land are found in the waters about the place where she died.[27]

From blue sapphires the color may be extracted so that they become white, in such sort that they excellently imitate the diamond, so well, indeed, that the fraud can only be detected by an expert jeweller. This art was known at an early period, and no doubt induced many writers to ascribe certain of the qualities of the diamond to the sapphire. As illustrating this, a Rabbinical author states that a certain man went to Rome to sell a sapphire. The purchaser said to him: "I will buy it provided I may first test it." He placed it on an anvil and struck it with a hammer; the anvil was split and the hammer was broken to pieces but the stone remained in its place uninjured.[28]

The virtues of the sapphire are enumerated at length by Bartolomæus Anglicus, the old scholastic philosopher, who flourished in the first half of the thirteenth century and

---

[26] G. W. Freytag, "Arabum proverbia," Bonnæ ad Rhenam, 1843, vol. iii, Pt. I, p. 495.

[27] Helvetius, "De l'esprit," vol. ii, p. 17.

[28] Johannis Braunii, "De Vestitu Sacerdotum Hebræorum," Amstelodami, 1680, p. 683.

CLEOPATRA DISSOLVING HER PRICELESS PEARL AT THE BANQUET TO MARK ANTONY

Tapestry. Eighteenth century.

taught theology in the famous University of Paris.[29] After noting the old dictum according to which the sapphire was the "gem of gems" and one worthy to adorn the fingers of kings, Bartolomæus proceeds to instruct his readers in regard to the wonderful curative powers of this beautiful gem. These appear always to be connected with its supposed calming and cooling influence. Thus it reduced the temperature in fevers and checked the flow of blood; for instance, if attached to the temples it stopped nose-bleed; if the heart were unduly excited, this agitation could be controlled by the power of the sapphire. Too profuse perspiration was also checked if a sapphire were worn. It shared with the diamond the virtue of reconciling discord. Its power as an antidote to poison was believed to be proved by an experiment in which a spider was placed in a box with a sapphire. After a short time the poor spider expired, done to death by the supreme virtue of the celestial stone. A like story was told by ancient writers in regard to the emerald. Of course, the chastening virtues of the sapphire are not forgotten, virtues which have caused it to be selected as especially appropriate for the rings of cardinals and high church dignitaries; this belief arose from the association of purity with the color of the heavens, the pure, unadulterated blue of the cloudless sky.

One of the rarest and most beautiful of the corundum gems of Ceylon is locally known there by the name *padparasham.* It is of a most rare and delicate orange-pink hue, the various specimens showing many different blendings of the pink and orange. The significance of the Cinghalese name seems to be somewhat obscure, but a probable conjecture explains it to mean "hidden ray of light"; another etymology

[29] From a XIII century MS. of his work, "De Proprietatibus Rerum," fol. clxi, recto and verso. This vellum MS. was originally in the possession of the Carthusian Monastery of the Holy Trinity at Dijon. Now the property of I. Martini of New York.

would see in the first syllable, *pad,* an abbreviation of *padma,* lotus, the petals of this flower often having a soft orange tint. In this case the meaning would be "hidden lotus," as though the very color-essence of the flower were enclosed within and shone through the gem.[30]

A Persian treatise on precious stones was composed by Mohammed Ben Mansur [31] in the thirteenth century of our era. This work was written for Sultan Abu Naçr Behadirchan, and consists of two divisions, the first treating of precious stones and the second of metals. It is interesting to note in this treatise the recognition of the essential likeness of the Oriental ruby, sapphire, topaz, etc.; these varieties of corundum are all grouped under the single designation "*yakut.*" Ben Mansur writes: [32]

> The yakut is six-fold: 1, the red; 2, the yellow; 3, the black; 4, the white; 5, the green or peacock-hued; 6, the blue or smoky-hued. Some divide the yakut into four classes: red, yellow, dark, and white, reckoning the peacock-hued and the blue among the dark. The yakut cuts all stones except carnelian and diamond.

Although the Oriental carnelian is hard and difficult to cut or polish only popular prejudice accounts for this statement, as it falls far short of the diamond in hardness.

Pseudo-Aristotle, writing some time from the seventh to the ninth century A.D., was the first to define clearly the three leading varieties of the corundum gems (yakut) as the same mineral substance, and differing only in color. These are the ruby, the Oriental topaz (jacinthus citrinus) and the sapphire. Instead of according different medicinal or talismanic virtues to these three precious stones, this writer states that each and all of them, when set in rings or worn

---

[30] Leopold Claremont, " Singhalese Gems," in The Jeweler and Metalworker, pp. 1936a–1936g, December 15, 1913.

[31] Abridgment by Von Hammer in the " Fundgruben des Orients," Wien, 1818, vol. vi.

[32] Ibid., p. 129.

suspended from the neck, protected the wearer from danger in epidemics, gave him the honor and good-will of his fellow-men, and also the privilege of having his petitions accorded.[33]

The great Athenian comic poet, Aristophanes (c. 448–c. 385), makes Strepsiades, one of his characters in the "Clouds," assert to Socrates that he knows of a stone having the virtue of saving him from the payment of a claim of five talents, for which suit has been brought against him. This stone, called ὕαλος in Greek, was to be found in the stock of those who dealt in medicines; it was transparent and with it fire could be kindled. The philosopher, although he knows the stone well enough, fails to see how it could be made to help the defendant in a suit at law, and asks Streposiades what he proposes to do with it. The latter is not at a loss for an answer and declares that when the clerk proceeds to write down the charge on his waxen tablet, he, Streposiades, will hold the stone in the sun's rays so that its beam of light will fall upon the tablet and melt the wax, thus quite literally "wiping out the charge." [34]

Rock-crystal was so highly prized in Roman times that one of the greatest treasures preserved in the Capitol was a mass of this stone, weighing fifty pounds, that had been dedicated by Livia, wife of Augustus Cæsar. Vessels of great size were also made from this material, one of the largest being a bowl owned by Lucius Verus, the colleague of Marcus Aurelius, the dimensions of which were so great that the stoutest toper of the time could not empty it at a single draught. If we can trust a statement of Mohammed Ben Mansur, the Arabs and Persians of a later age must have far surpassed the Romans in the size of their crystal vessels,

---

[33] Rose, "Aristoteles de lapidibus und Arnoldus Saxo," in Zeitschr. für Deutsches Altertum, New Series, vol. vi, p. 386.

[34] Aristophanes, "Clouds," lines 768 sqq.

for he says that a Mauritanian merchant owned a basin of rock-crystal within which four men could seat themselves at the same time. It is true that this basin was composed of two pieces of the material.[35]

The Chinese word for crystal, *ching*, was originally represented by the symbol ⊙⊙⊙; that is, three suns, an attempt to figure the refraction and dispersion of light by the crystal.[36] The *soui che* stone of the Chinese which is said to quench thirst if it be placed in the mouth, is almost certainly rock-crystal, for the Chinese, in common with the ancient Greeks and Romans, believed this substance to be a transformation of water, a kind of fossil ice. A similar power was attributed by Pliny to one of the varieties of agate.[37]

Labrets of quartz are used in Central Africa and we have a very interesting description by M. A. Lacroix regarding these ornaments as worn by the natives of a part of the French possessions. In the land of the Bandas the natives highly prize a piece of rock-crystal so shaped that it can be introduced into the lower lip. This usage is confined to the basins of the Ombella, the Kemo and the Tomi, affluents of the Oubanghi.

The following description of the labrets was communicated to M. Lacroix by M. Lucien Fourneau, Administrator of the Colonies:

These objects, called *baguérés*, consist of hyaline quartz, perfectly transparent; they are very regularly cut, and measure from four to seven cm. (two to three inches) in length. Some have the form of a very elongated and pointed cone, without any protuberances, the greatest diameter being about one cm. (about half an inch); the others, thinner and sharper, have at the base a rim destined to hold them in place; in all cases a pad of thread constituting a kind of permanent plug, assures and completes their stability. Some women wear as many as three of these singular ornaments, thrust, point downwards, into the same lip.

---

[35] A. R. Tutton, in Society of Arts, London.

[36] Chalfant, "Early Chinese Writing," Mem. of Carnegie Museum, vol. iv, No. 1, Pittsburgh, 1906, Pl. VI, No. 75.

[37] De Mély, "Les lapidaires chinois," Paris, 1896, p. lxiv.

The most regular quartz crystals are selected, and these are chipped off and roughly shaped by blows struck with a hard substance; the quartz is then set in a wooden handle, and the final shaping and polishing are accomplished by friction upon a round slab of quartzite or sandstone. These slabs show grooves along which the crystals have been rubbed. On an average the time required is four or five days of five hours. The completed ornament is valued at nine pounds of red wood worth about $1.20; sometimes one can be secured for three chickens, worth sixty cents.[38] Those who cannot afford quartz labrets substitute wood, glass, or pewter. M. Lacroix draws our attention to the fact that a study of the processes employed in shaping and polishing these pieces of quartz is of great importance for the elucidation of the methods in use during the Stone Age.[39]

A nose-jewel from the New Hebrides consists of a crystal of hyaline quartz reduced to a cylindrical form, one extremity having been pointed, while the other retains the natural faces of the crystal. This was passed through the septum of the nose, and was most likely worn as an amulet.[40]

Rock-crystal has been used extensively in the past year with ornaments of ribbon-like or plaque-like effects. Sometimes all the parts are made into the exact shape of a bowknot, with a bordering of platinum and diamonds, or of platinum and diamonds with a calibre-cut onyx; that is, the rock-crystal material is cut into minute square or oblong stones, which are run into double triangular edges that hold them. The crystals are dulled, and frequently have the appearance

---

[38] Lacroix, "Sur le travail de la pierre polie dans le Haut-Oubangi"; La Géographie, bulletin of the Société de Géographie, Paris, Oct. 15, 1909, pp. 201–206; figures.

[39] "Sur le travail de la pierre polie dans le Haut-Oubanghi," Comptes Rendus de l'Acad. d. Sc., vol. cxlviii, 1909, p. 1725.

[40] Giglioli, "Materiale per lo studio della Età della Pietra," Archivio per l'Antropologia e l'Etnologia, vol. xxxi, p. 85, Firenze, 1901.

of moonstones. At times, indeed, moonstones are used in their place. Sometimes these panels, or bits and pieces of rock-crystal, are drilled, diamonds set in platinum are inserted into the drill-holes, and the ornament is engraved in classic designs of Watteau-like effects.

The origin of Burmese rubies is thus explained in a Burmese legend current in the region of the Ruby Mines. According to this legend, in the first century of our era three eggs were laid by a female *naga,* or serpent; out of the first was born Pyusawti, a king of Pagan; out of the second came an Emperor of China, and out of the third were emitted the rubies of the Ruby Mines.[41]

Dealing in precious stones was by no means an unusual occupation in Europe more than four hundred years ago, as is shown by the fact that a certain Peter, one of the secret agents of Perkin Warbeck, a pretender to the throne of England in Henry VII's reign, was called in the secret correspondence of the conspirators, "The Merchant of the Ruby." Such dealers frequently travelled from place to place, and usually offered their wares to princes and nobles; hence the statement in a letter that the Merchant of the Ruby "was not able to sell his wares in Flaunders" might not seem suspicious if the letter were intercepted and read, although the meaning was that the emissary had been unable to obtain succor in Flanders for the cause of the pretender.[42] Probably this designation also contained a covert allusion to the Red Rose of York, for Perkin Warbeck gave himself out to be Richard, Duke of York.

A sixteenth-century traveller, the Portuguese Duarte Barbosa, after saying that "the rubies grow in India," proceeds to state that those of finest quality and greatest value were for the most part gathered in a river called Peygu and

[41] Communication from Taw Sein Ko.

[42] Archæologia, vol. xxvii, pp. 175, 207. London, 1838.

were named *nir puce* by the Malabars. As a test of their fineness, the Hindus would touch them with the tip of the tongue, the coldest (densest) being the best. When a superior ruby was thus picked out, the examiner would attach a little wax to its finest point, and so pick it up and look through it against a bright light; by this means any blemish would immediately become apparent. These rubies came not only from the river of Pegu but from other parts of the land of the same name, often being discovered in deep mountain clefts. However, they were not cut and polished in that country, but were merely cleaned and sent for cutting to "Palecote and the country of Narsynga." [43]

The balas-ruby (originally a spinel from Badakshan) was one of the most admired precious stones in medieval times, before the diamond was helped to its proud preëminence by having its beauties revealed through the exercise of the diamond-cutters' skill. Almost all the large "rubies" of which we read, those of Europe at least, were balas-rubies, as were also by far the greater part of the so-called rubies in Oriental royal collections of that and later times. The great Italian poet Dante uses this stone (*balascio*) as a symbol of the glowing radiance of divine joy in the following lines from the Divina Commedia (Paradiso, ix, 67–69):

> L'altra letizia, che m'era già nota
> Preclara cosa, mi si fece in vista
> Qual fin balascio in che lo sol percota.

In very ancient times as well as at the present day (if we admit that the *anthrax* of Theophrastus really was ruby and not a pyrope garnet), the ruby was the most valuable of all precious stones, the Greek writer stating that at the time he wrote, about 260 B.C., an exceedingly small speci-

[43] "A Description of the Coasts of East Africa and Malabar in the Beginning of the Sixteenth Century, by Duarte Barbosa, a Portuguese," trans. by Henry E. Staney, London, 1866, p. 208; Hakluyt Soc. Pub., vol. xxxv.

men would sell for as much as forty gold pieces. His statement that these stones came from Carthage and Marseilles should not induce us to prejudge the question as to their real character, as many articles of Asiatic commerce were distributed from these parts, more especially from the great Carthaginian seaport.[44]

A variety of sapphire, having, to a certain extent, the coloration of the ruby, was called by natives of Ceylon in the sixteenth century *nilacandi;*[45] this might be rendered sapphire-ruby. These stones are purple-red by daylight, but artificial light kills the blue and they appear red. They are frequently called phenomenal sapphires or alexandrite sapphires.

Indian poetic fancy has connected the creation of sapphires in Ceylon with the fair maidens of that island.[46]

> When the young Cingalese maidens sway, with the tips of their fingers, the stems of the lavali blossoms, then do the two dark blue eyes of the Daitya fall, eyes with a sheen like that of the lotus in full bloom.
>
> Hence it is that this island, with its long sea-coast and its interminable forests of ketskas, abounds in magnificent sapphires, which are its glory.

The following pretty bit of Oriental imagery occurs in a Cinghalese poem on the deeds of Constantino de Sá, a Portuguese Captain-General. Here the poet, writing of a river that flowed through the island, calls it "that lovely stream, the Kaluganga, which meandered as a sapphire chain over the shoulders of the maiden Lanka."[47] Lanka is a Cingalese name for Ceylon.

The depth of the coloration of sapphires and other stones

---

[44] Theophrasti, "De lapidibus (Peri lithôn)," ed. by John Hill, London, 1746; cap. 31.

[45] Garcias ab Orta, "Aromatum historia" (Lat. version by Clusius), Antverpiæ, 1579, lib. i, p. 175.

[46] Finot, "Les lapidaires indiens," Paris, 1896, p. 39, from the "Ratnaparikha" of Buddhabhatta.

[47] Ribeiro's "History of Ceylon," tr. by P. E. Pieris, Galle, n. d., Pt. II, p. 317.

was believed to indicate their degree of "ripeness," the pale stones being "unripe." As an illustration of this, Cardano instances a sapphire he had examined, a small part of which was blue, while the rest resembled a diamond. Specimens of this kind exist in several collections.[48] The writer has seen many that are dark blue when viewed from above, and almost white when viewed through the back. The Cinghalese lapidaries had very cleverly cut a crystal that was white, with a thin coating of blue, so that the blue was at the back, fully realizing the wonderful dispersive power of the sapphire, and that it would appear dark blue if viewed from above. The value was naturally only trifling compared with that of a perfectly even-colored gem.

Al-Berûnî (973–1048 A.D.) gives as the hues of the "red *yakut*" (ruby), pomegranate-colored safran (henna), purple, flesh-colored, rose-colored, and of the shade of a pomegranate blossom. Other colors of the *yakut* (corundum crystals) were yellow (Oriental topaz), gray, green (Oriental emerald), white (white sapphire), and black. A henna-colored *yakut*, if weighing one mitqal (about 24 carats), was valued at 5000 dinars ($12,500), if its weight was half as much, or about 12 carats, it was esteemed to be worth 2000 dinars ($4500), but for one weighing as much as 2 mitqals (48 carats) no definite price could be given, probably because of its great rarity and costliness.[49]

The Sanskrit name for the topaz, *pita,* signifies "the yellow stone." This Sanskrit word is thought by many to be the original of the Hebrew *pitdah,* a stone of the high priest's breastplate. Another Sanskrit name is pushparaga, "flower-colored."[50] It must be borne in mind, however,

[48] Cardani, "Philosophi opera quædam lectu digna," Basileæ, 1585, p. 329.

[49] Eilhard Wiedmann, "Ueber den Wert von Edelsteinen bei den Muslimen," in "Der Islam," vol. ii, 1911, pp. 347 sqq.

[50] Garbe, "Die indische Mineralien; Naharari's Rajanighaṇṭu, Varga XIII," Leipzig, 1882, p. 79.

that these names refer not to our topaz but to yellow corundum, or Oriental topaz, as it has often been called.

A topaz of exceptional size is that known as the "Maxwell-Stuart Topaz"[51] from the name of the owner. It was brought from Ceylon to England with a lot of inferior rubies and sapphires for use in watchmaking, and was believed to be simply a piece of quartz. So little was it appreciated that when sold at auction it only brought £3 10s. ($17.50). When on closer examination its true quality became apparent, the owner decided to have it cut in brilliant form. The operation required twenty-eight days' consecutive work, the diamond-wheel being used, and resulted in the production of a fine cut stone of a pure white hue, weighing 368 $^{31}/_{32}$ carats. When the cutting was partially completed, a "feather" became apparent that would have spoiled the table, but as it was still possible to reverse the position of table and culet, this was done, and the "feather" removed. At this time, in 1879, this topaz could lay claim to being the largest cut stone in existence, although its size is considerably surpassed now by that of the largest Cullinan diamond, 516½ carats.

The same exceptional position taken by jade among the Chinese is occupied by turquoise among the Tibetans; these are so emphatically primates among gem-minerals that the very name "stone" seems a designation unworthy of them, and as a Chinese would say, "it is *jade*, not a stone," so would a loyal Tibetan exclaim of his favorite gem, "it is a *turquoise*, not a stone." Another indication of the exceptional rank of turquoise in Tibet is that, as with the famous Oriental and European diamonds and also with some celebrated balas-rubies, certain of the first turquoises of Tibet have received individual names, such, for example, as "the

[51] J. H. Collins, "The History of a Remarkable Gem. The Maxwell-Stuart Topaz." Mineralogical Magazine No. 13, 1879.

resplendent turquoise of the gods" and "the white turquoise of the gods." A tradition relates that the largest turquoise found up to that time was discovered in the eighth century A.D. by King Du-srong Mang-po on the summit of a mountain near the sacred Tibetan city of Lhasa.[52]

In 1613, Shah Abbas of Persia sent to Jehangir six bags of "turquoise-dust," weighing in all some 23½ pounds Troy. However, the material proved to be of very inferior quality, for the jewellers searched in vain through the whole mass for a single stone fit for setting in a ring. Jehangir consoles himself with the reflection that "probably in these days turquoise-dust is not procurable such as it was in the time of Shah Tahmasp." [53]

When the Syrian monarch Antiochus XIII visited Syracuse during the prætorship of Caius Verres, he bore with him many richly adorned vessels, some of them being of gold set with gems after the Syrian fashion. However, the finest of all was a wine-cup carved out of a single piece of precious-stone material. When this had once met the gaze of the greedy Verres, he did not rest until he had got it into his possession. To attain his end he resorted to a most ignoble stratagem. Professing his ardent admiration of this as well as of the other richly-adorned and finely-wrought vessels, Verres requested that they might be left with him for a short time so that he might contemplate them at his leisure, and might also have an opportunity to submit them to examination by his goldsmiths with a view to having some copies executed. Antiochus readily acceded to this request, but when after the lapse of a few days he wished to regain possession of his things, Verres put him off from day to day, on

[52] Berthold Laufer, "Notes on Turquois in the East," Field Museum of Natural History, Anthropological Series, vol. xiii, No. 1, Chicago, July, 1913, pp. 5, 8.

[53] The Tûzuk-i-Jâhangîrî, or memoirs of Jahangir, trans. by Alexander Rogers, London, 1909, p. 238; Orient. Trans. Fund, N. S., vol. xix.

one pretext or another. Finally, as Antiochus refused to take the more than broad hints that the precious objects should be bestowed as gifts, Verres spread the rumor that a piratical fleet was on its way from Syria to attack Sicily, and forced Antiochus to leave the island that very day, retaining the borrowed vessels in spite of all remonstrances.[54]

That precious stones should be used to decorate the teeth seems a rather queer development of art, although the practice is not altogether unknown at the present day, when we hear now and again of diamonds being set in teeth to satisfy the vanity of some eccentric individual. In pre-Colombian times, however, there is abundant evidence that this strange form of personal adornment was by no means rare, several examples having been unearthed from burials in Ecuador, and evidence of the usage being offered by remains from Mexico and also from Central America. Among the Mayans here jadeite seems to have been the stone principally favored for this purpose, while in Mexico hematite has been met with in Oaxaca, turquoise in Vera Cruz, and at other places in the land, rock-crystal and obsidian.[55] For the insertion of the stones, the primitive dental artists carefully and skilfully cut or rubbed away the enamel from a section of the front part of the tooth to be decorated, and then applied the precious stone, cut to the required shape, as an inlay. The way in which this was done gives evidence of a remarkably high degree of skill in this line of work; in many cases an inlay of gold was used, instead of a precious stone, and it has even been conjectured that some of these gold inlays represent a kind of gold filling for the protection of the tooth. While this is open to question, the undoubted fact that new teeth were occasionally inserted to take the place of those which

[54] M. Tullii Ciceronis, "In Verrem," lib. iv, Oratio nona, cap. 27.

[55] Marshall H. Saville in the American Anthropologist, vol. xv, No. 3, July–September, 1913.

had fallen out or decayed, as shown in several specimens, might be regarded as corroborative of the broader assumption. The expert workmanship of these pre-Colombian "dental surgeons" is clearly manifested in the good condition of the teeth whence so much of the enamel had been removed, showing that the inlays must have been so closely adjusted that the tooth was effectively protected from the introduction of moisture.

One of the latest fashionable fads, suggested by the great variety of bright-colored costumes worn by the *mondaines* (and others) at the present day, is the selection and wear of jewelry set with stones of the same color as the striking gown. Thus with a costume of glowing red, the ruddy ruby would be chosen, a sky-blue costume would insure the wearing of the justly popular sapphire, dress of a golden-yellow hue would call for one of the shades of topazes, while the "new brown," now so much in vogue, finds its complementary stone in topaz of a slightly darker shade. The grass-green costume would suggest one of the many beautiful shades of the tourmaline, and jewelry of the pink tourmaline would be appropriate to garments of this color. With their wonderful play of color, opals would accord with all varieties of hue in costume and might thus be worn with either of the other more especially matched stones.

An old account of the London trades and guilds, in writing of the jewellers' art, makes the following statement regarding the qualifications of a jeweller, as appropriate to our own times as to any other.[56]

> He ought to be an elegant Designer, and have a quick Invention for new Patterns, not only to range the stones in such manner as to give Lustre to one another, but to create Trade; for a new Fashion takes as much with the Ladies in Jewels as in anything else; he that can furnish them oftenest with the newest Whim has the best Chance for their Custom.

---

[56] R. Campbell, "The London Tradesman," London, 1747, p. 143.

Index

B

C

N

A CATALOG OF SELECTED

DOVER BOOKS

IN ALL FIELDS OF INTEREST

A CATALOG OF SELECTED DOVER BOOKS IN ALL FIELDS OF INTEREST

BRASS INSTRUMENTS: Their History and Development, Anthony Baines. Authoritative, updated survey of the evolution of trumpets, trombones, bugles, cornets, French horns, tubas and other brass wind instruments. Over 140 illustrations and 48 music examples. Corrected and updated by author. New preface. Bibliography. 320pp. 5⅜ x 8½. 27574-4 Pa. $9.95

HOLLYWOOD GLAMOR PORTRAITS, John Kobal (ed.). 145 photos from 1926-49. Harlow, Gable, Bogart, Bacall; 94 stars in all. Full background on photographers, technical aspects. 160pp. 8⅜ x 11¼. 23352-9 Pa. $11.95

MAX AND MORITZ, Wilhelm Busch. Great humor classic in both German and English. Also 10 other works: "Cat and Mouse," "Plisch and Plumm," etc. 216pp. 5⅜ x 8½. 20181-3 Pa. $6.95

THE RAVEN AND OTHER FAVORITE POEMS, Edgar Allan Poe. Over 40 of the author's most memorable poems: "The Bells," "Ulalume," "Israfel," "To Helen," "The Conqueror Worm," "Eldorado," "Annabel Lee," many more. Alphabetic lists of titles and first lines. 64pp. 5$\frac{3}{16}$ x 8¼. 26685-0 Pa. $1.00

PERSONAL MEMOIRS OF U. S. GRANT, Ulysses Simpson Grant. Intelligent, deeply moving firsthand account of Civil War campaigns, considered by many the finest military memoirs ever written. Includes letters, historic photographs, maps and more. 528pp. 6⅛ x 9¼. 28587-1 Pa. $11.95

AMULETS AND SUPERSTITIONS, E. A. Wallis Budge. Comprehensive discourse on origin, powers of amulets in many ancient cultures: Arab, Persian Babylonian, Assyrian, Egyptian, Gnostic, Hebrew, Phoenician, Syriac, etc. Covers cross, swastika, crucifix, seals, rings, stones, etc. 584pp. 5⅜ x 8½. 23573-4 Pa. $12.95

RUSSIAN STORIES/PYCCKNE PACCKA3bl: A Dual-Language Book, edited by Gleb Struve. Twelve tales by such masters as Chekhov, Tolstoy, Dostoevsky, Pushkin, others. Excellent word-for-word English translations on facing pages, plus teaching and study aids, Russian/English vocabulary, biographical/critical introductions, more. 416pp. 5⅜ x 8½. 26244-8 Pa. $8.95

PHILADELPHIA THEN AND NOW: 60 Sites Photographed in the Past and Present, Kenneth Finkel and Susan Oyama. Rare photographs of City Hall, Logan Square, Independence Hall, Betsy Ross House, other landmarks juxtaposed with contemporary views. Captures changing face of historic city. Introduction. Captions. 128pp. 8¼ x 11. 25790-8 Pa. $9.95

AIA ARCHITECTURAL GUIDE TO NASSAU AND SUFFOLK COUNTIES, LONG ISLAND, The American Institute of Architects, Long Island Chapter, and the Society for the Preservation of Long Island Antiquities. Comprehensive, well-researched and generously illustrated volume brings to life over three centuries of Long Island's great architectural heritage. More than 240 photographs with authoritative, extensively detailed captions. 176pp. 8¼ x 11. 26946-9 Pa. $14.95

NORTH AMERICAN INDIAN LIFE: Customs and Traditions of 23 Tribes, Elsie Clews Parsons (ed.). 27 fictionalized essays by noted anthropologists examine religion, customs, government, additional facets of life among the Winnebago, Crow, Zuni, Eskimo, other tribes. 480pp. 6⅛ x 9¼. 27377-6 Pa. $10.95

FRANK LLOYD WRIGHT'S HOLLYHOCK HOUSE, Donald Hoffmann. Lavishly illustrated, carefully documented study of one of Wright's most controversial residential designs. Over 120 photographs, floor plans, elevations, etc. Detailed perceptive text by noted Wright scholar. Index. 128pp. 9¼ x 10¾. 27133-1 Pa. $11.95

THE MALE AND FEMALE FIGURE IN MOTION: 60 Classic Photographic Sequences, Eadweard Muybridge. 60 true-action photographs of men and women walking, running, climbing, bending, turning, etc., reproduced from rare 19th-century masterpiece. vi + 121pp. 9 x 12. 24745-7 Pa. $10.95

1001 QUESTIONS ANSWERED ABOUT THE SEASHORE, N. J. Berrill and Jacquelyn Berrill. Queries answered about dolphins, sea snails, sponges, starfish, fishes, shore birds, many others. Covers appearance, breeding, growth, feeding, much more. 305pp. 5¼ x 8¼. 23366-9 Pa. $8.95

GUIDE TO OWL WATCHING IN NORTH AMERICA, Donald S. Heintzelman. Superb guide offers complete data and descriptions of 19 species: barn owl, screech owl, snowy owl, many more. Expert coverage of owl-watching equipment, conservation, migrations and invasions, etc. Guide to observing sites. 84 illustrations. xiii + 193pp. 5⅜ x 8½. 27344-X Pa. $8.95

MEDICINAL AND OTHER USES OF NORTH AMERICAN PLANTS: A Historical Survey with Special Reference to the Eastern Indian Tribes, Charlotte Erichsen-Brown. Chronological historical citations document 500 years of usage of plants, trees, shrubs native to eastern Canada, northeastern U.S. Also complete identifying information. 343 illustrations. 544pp. 6½ x 9¼. 25951-X Pa. $12.95

STORYBOOK MAZES, Dave Phillips. 23 stories and mazes on two-page spreads: Wizard of Oz, Treasure Island, Robin Hood, etc. Solutions. 64pp. 8¼ x 11. 23628-5 Pa. $2.95

NEGRO FOLK MUSIC, U.S.A., Harold Courlander. Noted folklorist's scholarly yet readable analysis of rich and varied musical tradition. Includes authentic versions of over 40 folk songs. Valuable bibliography and discography. xi + 324pp. 5⅜ x 8½. 27350-4 Pa. $7.95

MOVIE-STAR PORTRAITS OF THE FORTIES, John Kobal (ed.). 163 glamor, studio photos of 106 stars of the 1940s: Rita Hayworth, Ava Gardner, Marlon Brando, Clark Gable, many more. 176pp. 8⅜ x 11¼. 23546-7 Pa. $12.95

BENCHLEY LOST AND FOUND, Robert Benchley. Finest humor from early 30s, about pet peeves, child psychologists, post office and others. Mostly unavailable elsewhere. 73 illustrations by Peter Arno and others. 183pp. 5⅜ x 8½. 22410-4 Pa. $6.95

YEKL and THE IMPORTED BRIDEGROOM AND OTHER STORIES OF YIDDISH NEW YORK, Abraham Cahan. Film Hester Street based on Yekl (1896). Novel, other stories among first about Jewish immigrants on N.Y.'s East Side. 240pp. 5⅜ x 8½. 22427-9 Pa. $6.95

SELECTED POEMS, Walt Whitman. Generous sampling from *Leaves of Grass*. Twenty-four poems include "I Hear America Singing," "Song of the Open Road," "I Sing the Body Electric," "When Lilacs Last in the Dooryard Bloom'd," "O Captain! My Captain!"–all reprinted from an authoritative edition. Lists of titles and first lines. 128pp. 5$\frac{5}{16}$ x 8¼. 26878-0 Pa. $1.00

THE BEST TALES OF HOFFMANN, E. T. A. Hoffmann. 10 of Hoffmann's most important stories: "Nutcracker and the King of Mice," "The Golden Flowerpot," etc. 458pp. 5⅜ x 8½. 21793-0 Pa. $9.95

FROM FETISH TO GOD IN ANCIENT EGYPT, E. A. Wallis Budge. Rich detailed survey of Egyptian conception of "God" and gods, magic, cult of animals, Osiris, more. Also, superb English translations of hymns and legends. 240 illustrations. 545pp. 5⅜ x 8½. 25803-3 Pa. $11.95

FRENCH STORIES/CONTES FRANÇAIS: A Dual-Language Book, Wallace Fowlie. Ten stories by French masters, Voltaire to Camus: "Micromegas" by Voltaire; "The Atheist's Mass" by Balzac; "Minuet" by de Maupassant; "The Guest" by Camus, six more. Excellent English translations on facing pages. Also French-English vocabulary list, exercises, more. 352pp. 5⅜ x 8½. 26443-2 Pa. $8.95

CHICAGO AT THE TURN OF THE CENTURY IN PHOTOGRAPHS: 122 Historic Views from the Collections of the Chicago Historical Society, Larry A. Viskochil. Rare large-format prints offer detailed views of City Hall, State Street, the Loop, Hull House, Union Station, many other landmarks, circa 1904-1913. Introduction. Captions. Maps. 144pp. 9⅜ x 12¼. 24656-6 Pa. $12.95

OLD BROOKLYN IN EARLY PHOTOGRAPHS, 1865-1929, William Lee Younger. Luna Park, Gravesend race track, construction of Grand Army Plaza, moving of Hotel Brighton, etc. 157 previously unpublished photographs. 165pp. 8⅞ x 11¾. 23587-4 Pa. $13.95

THE MYTHS OF THE NORTH AMERICAN INDIANS, Lewis Spence. Rich anthology of the myths and legends of the Algonquins, Iroquois, Pawnees and Sioux, prefaced by an extensive historical and ethnological commentary. 36 illustrations. 480pp. 5⅜ x 8½. 25967-6 Pa. $8.95

AN ENCYCLOPEDIA OF BATTLES: Accounts of Over 1,560 Battles from 1479 B.C. to the Present, David Eggenberger. Essential details of every major battle in recorded history from the first battle of Megiddo in 1479 B.C. to Grenada in 1984. List of Battle Maps. New Appendix covering the years 1967-1984. Index. 99 illustrations. 544pp. 6½ x 9¼. 24913-1 Pa. $14.95

SAILING ALONE AROUND THE WORLD, Captain Joshua Slocum. First man to sail around the world, alone, in small boat. One of great feats of seamanship told in delightful manner. 67 illustrations. 294pp. 5⅜ x 8½. 20326-3 Pa. $5.95

ANARCHISM AND OTHER ESSAYS, Emma Goldman. Powerful, penetrating, prophetic essays on direct action, role of minorities, prison reform, puritan hypocrisy, violence, etc. 271pp. 5⅜ x 8½. 22484-8 Pa. $6.95

MYTHS OF THE HINDUS AND BUDDHISTS, Ananda K. Coomaraswamy and Sister Nivedita. Great stories of the epics; deeds of Krishna, Shiva, taken from puranas, Vedas, folk tales; etc. 32 illustrations. 400pp. 5⅜ x 8½. 21759-0 Pa. $10.95

BEYOND PSYCHOLOGY, Otto Rank. Fear of death, desire of immortality, nature of sexuality, social organization, creativity, according to Rankian system. 291pp. 5⅜ x 8½. 20485-5 Pa. $8.95

A THEOLOGICO-POLITICAL TREATISE, Benedict Spinoza. Also contains unfinished Political Treatise. Great classic on religious liberty, theory of government on common consent. R. Elwes translation. Total of 421pp. 5⅜ x 8½. 20249-6 Pa. $9.95

MY BONDAGE AND MY FREEDOM, Frederick Douglass. Born a slave, Douglass became outspoken force in antislavery movement. The best of Douglass' autobiographies. Graphic description of slave life. 464pp. 5⅜ x 8½. 22457-0 Pa. $8.95

FOLLOWING THE EQUATOR: A Journey Around the World, Mark Twain. Fascinating humorous account of 1897 voyage to Hawaii, Australia, India, New Zealand, etc. Ironic, bemused reports on peoples, customs, climate, flora and fauna, politics, much more. 197 illustrations. 720pp. 5⅜ x 8½. 26113-1 Pa. $15.95

THE PEOPLE CALLED SHAKERS, Edward D. Andrews. Definitive study of Shakers: origins, beliefs, practices, dances, social organization, furniture and crafts, etc. 33 illustrations. 351pp. 5⅜ x 8½. 21081-2 Pa. $8.95

THE MYTHS OF GREECE AND ROME, H. A. Guerber. A classic of mythology, generously illustrated, long prized for its simple, graphic, accurate retelling of the principal myths of Greece and Rome, and for its commentary on their origins and significance. With 64 illustrations by Michelangelo, Raphael, Titian, Rubens, Canova, Bernini and others. 480pp. 5⅜ x 8½. 27584-1 Pa. $9.95

PSYCHOLOGY OF MUSIC, Carl E. Seashore. Classic work discusses music as a medium from psychological viewpoint. Clear treatment of physical acoustics, auditory apparatus, sound perception, development of musical skills, nature of musical feeling, host of other topics. 88 figures. 408pp. 5⅜ x 8½. 21851-1 Pa. $10.95

THE PHILOSOPHY OF HISTORY, Georg W. Hegel. Great classic of Western thought develops concept that history is not chance but rational process, the evolution of freedom. 457pp. 5⅜ x 8½. 20112-0 Pa. $9.95

THE BOOK OF TEA, Kakuzo Okakura. Minor classic of the Orient: entertaining, charming explanation, interpretation of traditional Japanese culture in terms of tea ceremony. 94pp. 5⅜ x 8½. 20070-1 Pa. $3.95

LIFE IN ANCIENT EGYPT, Adolf Erman. Fullest, most thorough, detailed older account with much not in more recent books, domestic life, religion, magic, medicine, commerce, much more. Many illustrations reproduce tomb paintings, carvings, hieroglyphs, etc. 597pp. 5⅜ x 8½. 22632-8 Pa. $11.95

SUNDIALS, Their Theory and Construction, Albert Waugh. Far and away the best, most thorough coverage of ideas, mathematics concerned, types, construction, adjusting anywhere. Simple, nontechnical treatment allows even children to build several of these dials. Over 100 illustrations. 230pp. 5⅜ x 8½. 22947-5 Pa. $7.95

DYNAMICS OF FLUIDS IN POROUS MEDIA, Jacob Bear. For advanced students of ground water hydrology, soil mechanics and physics, drainage and irrigation engineering, and more. 335 illustrations. Exercises, with answers. 784pp. 6⅛ x 9¼. 65675-6 Pa. $19.95

SONGS OF EXPERIENCE: Facsimile Reproduction with 26 Plates in Full Color, William Blake. 26 full-color plates from a rare 1826 edition. Includes "The Tyger," "London," "Holy Thursday," and other poems. Printed text of poems. 48pp. 5¼ x 7. 24636-1 Pa. $4.95

OLD-TIME VIGNETTES IN FULL COLOR, Carol Belanger Grafton (ed.). Over 390 charming, often sentimental illustrations, selected from archives of Victorian graphics–pretty women posing, children playing, food, flowers, kittens and puppies, smiling cherubs, birds and butterflies, much more. All copyright-free. 48pp. 9¼ x 12¼. 27269-9 Pa. $5.95

PERSPECTIVE FOR ARTISTS, Rex Vicat Cole. Depth, perspective of sky and sea, shadows, much more, not usually covered. 391 diagrams, 81 reproductions of drawings and paintings. 279pp. 5⅜ x 8½. 22487-2 Pa. $6.95

DRAWING THE LIVING FIGURE, Joseph Sheppard. Innovative approach to artistic anatomy focuses on specifics of surface anatomy, rather than muscles and bones. Over 170 drawings of live models in front, back and side views, and in widely varying poses. Accompanying diagrams. 177 illustrations. Introduction. Index. 144pp. 8⅜ x11¼. 26723-7 Pa. $8.95

GOTHIC AND OLD ENGLISH ALPHABETS: 100 Complete Fonts, Dan X. Solo. Add power, elegance to posters, signs, other graphics with 100 stunning copyright-free alphabets: Blackstone, Dolbey, Germania, 97 more–including many lower-case, numerals, punctuation marks. 104pp. 8⅛ x 11. 24695-7 Pa. $8.95

HOW TO DO BEADWORK, Mary White. Fundamental book on craft from simple projects to five-bead chains and woven works. 106 illustrations. 142pp. 5⅜ x 8. 20697-1 Pa. $4.95

THE BOOK OF WOOD CARVING, Charles Marshall Sayers. Finest book for beginners discusses fundamentals and offers 34 designs. "Absolutely first rate . . . well thought out and well executed."–E. J. Tangerman. 118pp. 7¾ x 10⅝. 23654-4 Pa. $6.95

ILLUSTRATED CATALOG OF CIVIL WAR MILITARY GOODS: Union Army Weapons, Insignia, Uniform Accessories, and Other Equipment, Schuyler, Hartley, and Graham. Rare, profusely illustrated 1846 catalog includes Union Army uniform and dress regulations, arms and ammunition, coats, insignia, flags, swords, rifles, etc. 226 illustrations. 160pp. 9 x 12. 24939-5 Pa. $10.95

WOMEN'S FASHIONS OF THE EARLY 1900s: An Unabridged Republication of "New York Fashions, 1909," National Cloak & Suit Co. Rare catalog of mail-order fashions documents women's and children's clothing styles shortly after the turn of the century. Captions offer full descriptions, prices. Invaluable resource for fashion, costume historians. Approximately 725 illustrations. 128pp. 8⅜ x 11¼. 27276-1 Pa. $11.95

THE 1912 AND 1915 GUSTAV STICKLEY FURNITURE CATALOGS, Gustav Stickley. With over 200 detailed illustrations and descriptions, these two catalogs are essential reading and reference materials and identification guides for Stickley furniture. Captions cite materials, dimensions and prices. 112pp. 6½ x 9¼. 26676-1 Pa. $9.95

EARLY AMERICAN LOCOMOTIVES, John H. White, Jr. Finest locomotive engravings from early 19th century: historical (1804–74), main-line (after 1870), special, foreign, etc. 147 plates. 142pp. 11⅜ x 8¼. 22772-3 Pa. $10.95

THE TALL SHIPS OF TODAY IN PHOTOGRAPHS, Frank O. Braynard. Lavishly illustrated tribute to nearly 100 majestic contemporary sailing vessels: Amerigo Vespucci, Clearwater, Constitution, Eagle, Mayflower, Sea Cloud, Victory, many more. Authoritative captions provide statistics, background on each ship. 190 black-and-white photographs and illustrations. Introduction. 128pp. 8⅞ x 11¾. 27163-3 Pa. $13.95

EARLY NINETEENTH-CENTURY CRAFTS AND TRADES, Peter Stockham (ed.). Extremely rare 1807 volume describes to youngsters the crafts and trades of the day: brickmaker, weaver, dressmaker, bookbinder, ropemaker, saddler, many more. Quaint prose, charming illustrations for each craft. 20 black-and-white line illustrations. 192pp. 4⅝ x 6. 27293-1 Pa. $4.95

VICTORIAN FASHIONS AND COSTUMES FROM HARPER'S BAZAR, 1867–1898, Stella Blum (ed.). Day costumes, evening wear, sports clothes, shoes, hats, other accessories in over 1,000 detailed engravings. 320pp. 9⅜ x 12¼. 22990-4 Pa. $14.95

GUSTAV STICKLEY, THE CRAFTSMAN, Mary Ann Smith. Superb study surveys broad scope of Stickley's achievement, especially in architecture. Design philosophy, rise and fall of the Craftsman empire, descriptions and floor plans for many Craftsman houses, more. 86 black-and-white halftones. 31 line illustrations. Introduction 208pp. 6½ x 9¼. 27210-9 Pa. $9.95

THE LONG ISLAND RAIL ROAD IN EARLY PHOTOGRAPHS, Ron Ziel. Over 220 rare photos, informative text document origin (1844) and development of rail service on Long Island. Vintage views of early trains, locomotives, stations, passengers, crews, much more. Captions. 8⅞ x 11¾. 26301-0 Pa. $13.95

THE BOOK OF OLD SHIPS: From Egyptian Galleys to Clipper Ships, Henry B. Culver. Superb, authoritative history of sailing vessels, with 80 magnificent line illustrations. Galley, bark, caravel, longship, whaler, many more. Detailed, informative text on each vessel by noted naval historian. Introduction. 256pp. 5⅜ x 8½. 27332-6 Pa. $7.95

TEN BOOKS ON ARCHITECTURE, Vitruvius. The most important book ever written on architecture. Early Roman aesthetics, technology, classical orders, site selection, all other aspects. Morgan translation. 331pp. 5⅜ x 8½. 20645-9 Pa. $8.95

THE HUMAN FIGURE IN MOTION, Eadweard Muybridge. More than 4,500 stopped-action photos, in action series, showing undraped men, women, children jumping, lying down, throwing, sitting, wrestling, carrying, etc. 390pp. 7⅞ x 10⅝. 20204-6 Clothbd. $25.95

TREES OF THE EASTERN AND CENTRAL UNITED STATES AND CANADA, William M. Harlow. Best one-volume guide to 140 trees. Full descriptions, woodlore, range, etc. Over 600 illustrations. Handy size. 288pp. 4½ x 6⅜. 20395-6 Pa. $5.95

SONGS OF WESTERN BIRDS, Dr. Donald J. Borror. Complete song and call repertoire of 60 western species, including flycatchers, juncoes, cactus wrens, many more–includes fully illustrated booklet. Cassette and manual 99913-0 $8.95

GROWING AND USING HERBS AND SPICES, Milo Miloradovich. Versatile handbook provides all the information needed for cultivation and use of all the herbs and spices available in North America. 4 illustrations. Index. Glossary. 236pp. 5⅜ x 8½. 25058-X Pa. $6.95

BIG BOOK OF MAZES AND LABYRINTHS, Walter Shepherd. 50 mazes and labyrinths in all–classical, solid, ripple, and more–in one great volume. Perfect inexpensive puzzler for clever youngsters. Full solutions. 112pp. 8⅛ x 11. 22951-3 Pa. $4.95

PIANO TUNING, J. Cree Fischer. Clearest, best book for beginner, amateur. Simple repairs, raising dropped notes, tuning by easy method of flattened fifths. No previous skills needed. 4 illustrations. 201pp. 5⅜ x 8½. 23267-0 Pa. $6.95

A SOURCE BOOK IN THEATRICAL HISTORY, A. M. Nagler. Contemporary observers on acting, directing, make-up, costuming, stage props, machinery, scene design, from Ancient Greece to Chekhov. 611pp. 5⅜ x 8½. 20515-0 Pa. $12.95

THE COMPLETE NONSENSE OF EDWARD LEAR, Edward Lear. All nonsense limericks, zany alphabets, Owl and Pussycat, songs, nonsense botany, etc., illustrated by Lear. Total of 320pp. 5⅜ x 8½. (USO) 20167-8 Pa. $6.95

VICTORIAN PARLOUR POETRY: An Annotated Anthology, Michael R. Turner. 117 gems by Longfellow, Tennyson, Browning, many lesser-known poets. "The Village Blacksmith," "Curfew Must Not Ring Tonight," "Only a Baby Small," dozens more, often difficult to find elsewhere. Index of poets, titles, first lines. xxiii + 325pp. 5⅜ x 8¼. 27044-0 Pa. $8.95

DUBLINERS, James Joyce. Fifteen stories offer vivid, tightly focused observations of the lives of Dublin's poorer classes. At least one, "The Dead," is considered a masterpiece. Reprinted complete and unabridged from standard edition. 160pp. 5³⁄₁₆ x 8¼. 26870-5 Pa. $1.00

THE HAUNTED MONASTERY and THE CHINESE MAZE MURDERS, Robert van Gulik. Two full novels by van Gulik, set in 7th-century China, continue adventures of Judge Dee and his companions. An evil Taoist monastery, seemingly supernatural events; overgrown topiary maze hides strange crimes. 27 illustrations. 328pp. 5⅜ x 8½. 23502-5 Pa. $8.95

THE BOOK OF THE SACRED MAGIC OF ABRAMELIN THE MAGE, translated by S. MacGregor Mathers. Medieval manuscript of ceremonial magic. Basic document in Aleister Crowley, Golden Dawn groups. 268pp. 5⅜ x 8½. 23211-5 Pa. $8.95

NEW RUSSIAN-ENGLISH AND ENGLISH-RUSSIAN DICTIONARY, M. A. O'Brien. This is a remarkably handy Russian dictionary, containing a surprising amount of information, including over 70,000 entries. 366pp. 4½ x 6⅛. 20208-9 Pa. $9.95

HISTORIC HOMES OF THE AMERICAN PRESIDENTS, Second, Revised Edition, Irvin Haas. A traveler's guide to American Presidential homes, most open to the public, depicting and describing homes occupied by every American President from George Washington to George Bush. With visiting hours, admission charges, travel routes. 175 photographs. Index. 160pp. 8¼ x 11. 26751-2 Pa. $11.95

NEW YORK IN THE FORTIES, Andreas Feininger. 162 brilliant photographs by the well-known photographer, formerly with *Life* magazine. Commuters, shoppers, Times Square at night, much else from city at its peak. Captions by John von Hartz. 181pp. 9¼ x 10¾. 23585-8 Pa. $12.95

INDIAN SIGN LANGUAGE, William Tomkins. Over 525 signs developed by Sioux and other tribes. Written instructions and diagrams. Also 290 pictographs. 111pp. 6⅛ x 9¼. 22029-X Pa. $3.95

AUTOBIOGRAPHY: The Story of My Experiments with Truth, Mohandas K. Gandhi. Boyhood, legal studies, purification, the growth of the Satyagraha (nonviolent protest) movement. Critical, inspiring work of the man responsible for the freedom of India. 480pp. 5⅜ x 8½. (USO) 24593-4 Pa. $8.95

CELTIC MYTHS AND LEGENDS, T. W. Rolleston. Masterful retelling of Irish and Welsh stories and tales. Cuchulain, King Arthur, Deirdre, the Grail, many more. First paperback edition. 58 full-page illustrations. 512pp. 5⅜ x 8½. 26507-2 Pa. $9.95

THE PRINCIPLES OF PSYCHOLOGY, William James. Famous long course complete, unabridged. Stream of thought, time perception, memory, experimental methods; great work decades ahead of its time. 94 figures. 1,391pp. 5⅜ x 8½. 2-vol. set.
Vol. I: 20381-6 Pa. $12.95
Vol. II: 20382-4 Pa. $12.95

THE WORLD AS WILL AND REPRESENTATION, Arthur Schopenhauer. Definitive English translation of Schopenhauer's life work, correcting more than 1,000 errors, omissions in earlier translations. Translated by E. F. J. Payne. Total of 1,269pp. 5⅜ x 8½. 2-vol. set. Vol. 1: 21761-2 Pa. $11.95
Vol. 2: 21762-0 Pa. $11.95

MAGIC AND MYSTERY IN TIBET, Madame Alexandra David-Neel. Experiences among lamas, magicians, sages, sorcerers, Bonpa wizards. A true psychic discovery. 32 illustrations. 321pp. 5⅜ x 8½. (USO) 22682-4 Pa. $8.95

THE EGYPTIAN BOOK OF THE DEAD, E. A. Wallis Budge. Complete reproduction of Ani's papyrus, finest ever found. Full hieroglyphic text, interlinear transliteration, word-for-word translation, smooth translation. 533pp. 6½ x 9¼.
21866-X Pa. $10.95

MATHEMATICS FOR THE NONMATHEMATICIAN, Morris Kline. Detailed, college-level treatment of mathematics in cultural and historical context, with numerous exercises. Recommended Reading Lists. Tables. Numerous figures. 641pp. 5⅜ x 8½.
24823-2 Pa. $11.95

THEORY OF WING SECTIONS: Including a Summary of Airfoil Data, Ira H. Abbott and A. E. von Doenhoff. Concise compilation of subsonic aerodynamic characteristics of NACA wing sections, plus description of theory. 350pp. of tables. 693pp. 5⅜ x 8½. 60586-8 Pa. $14.95

THE RIME OF THE ANCIENT MARINER, Gustave Doré, S. T. Coleridge. Doré's finest work; 34 plates capture moods, subtleties of poem. Flawless full-size reproductions printed on facing pages with authoritative text of poem. "Beautiful. Simply beautiful."–*Publisher's Weekly.* 77pp. 9¼ x 12. 22305-1 Pa. $6.95

NORTH AMERICAN INDIAN DESIGNS FOR ARTISTS AND CRAFTSPEOPLE, Eva Wilson. Over 360 authentic copyright-free designs adapted from Navajo blankets, Hopi pottery, Sioux buffalo hides, more. Geometrics, symbolic figures, plant and animal motifs, etc. 128pp. 8⅜ x 11. (EUK) 25341-4 Pa. $8.95

SCULPTURE: Principles and Practice, Louis Slobodkin. Step-by-step approach to clay, plaster, metals, stone; classical and modern. 253 drawings, photos. 255pp. 8⅛ x 11.
22960-2 Pa. $10.95

CATALOG OF DOVER BOOKS

PHOTOGRAPHIC SKETCHBOOK OF THE CIVIL WAR, Alexander Gardner. 100 photos taken on field during the Civil War. Famous shots of Manassas Harper's Ferry, Lincoln, Richmond, slave pens, etc. 244pp. 10⅝ x 8¼. 22731-6 Pa. $9.95

FIVE ACRES AND INDEPENDENCE, Maurice G. Kains. Great back-to-the-land classic explains basics of self-sufficient farming. The one book to get. 95 illustrations. 397pp. 5⅜ x 8½. 20974-1 Pa. $7.95

SONGS OF EASTERN BIRDS, Dr. Donald J. Borror. Songs and calls of 60 species most common to eastern U.S.: warblers, woodpeckers, flycatchers, thrushes, larks, many more in high-quality recording. Cassette and manual 99912-2 $8.95

A MODERN HERBAL, Margaret Grieve. Much the fullest, most exact, most useful compilation of herbal material. Gigantic alphabetical encyclopedia, from aconite to zedoary, gives botanical information, medical properties, folklore, economic uses, much else. Indispensable to serious reader. 161 illustrations. 888pp. 6½ x 9¼. 2-vol. set. (USO) Vol. I: 22798-7 Pa. $9.95
Vol. II: 22799-5 Pa. $9.95

HIDDEN TREASURE MAZE BOOK, Dave Phillips. Solve 34 challenging mazes accompanied by heroic tales of adventure. Evil dragons, people-eating plants, blood-thirsty giants, many more dangerous adversaries lurk at every twist and turn. 34 mazes, stories, solutions. 48pp. 8¼ x 11. 24566-7 Pa. $2.95

LETTERS OF W. A. MOZART, Wolfgang A. Mozart. Remarkable letters show bawdy wit, humor, imagination, musical insights, contemporary musical world; includes some letters from Leopold Mozart. 276pp. 5⅜ x 8½. 22859-2 Pa. $7.95

BASIC PRINCIPLES OF CLASSICAL BALLET, Agrippina Vaganova. Great Russian theoretician, teacher explains methods for teaching classical ballet. 118 illustrations. 175pp. 5⅜ x 8½. 22036-2 Pa. $5.95

THE JUMPING FROG, Mark Twain. Revenge edition. The original story of The Celebrated Jumping Frog of Calaveras County, a hapless French translation, and Twain's hilarious "retranslation" from the French. 12 illustrations. 66pp. 5⅜ x 8½.
22686-7 Pa. $3.95

BEST REMEMBERED POEMS, Martin Gardner (ed.). The 126 poems in this superb collection of 19th- and 20th-century British and American verse range from Shelley's "To a Skylark" to the impassioned "Renascence" of Edna St. Vincent Millay and to Edward Lear's whimsical "The Owl and the Pussycat." 224pp. 5⅜ x 8½.
27165-X Pa. $4.95

COMPLETE SONNETS, William Shakespeare. Over 150 exquisite poems deal with love, friendship, the tyranny of time, beauty's evanescence, death and other themes in language of remarkable power, precision and beauty. Glossary of archaic terms. 80pp. 5 3/16 x 8¼. 26686-9 Pa. $1.00

BODIES IN A BOOKSHOP, R. T. Campbell. Challenging mystery of blackmail and murder with ingenious plot and superbly drawn characters. In the best tradition of British suspense fiction. 192pp. 5⅜ x 8½. 24720-1 Pa. $6.95

THE WIT AND HUMOR OF OSCAR WILDE, Alvin Redman (ed.). More than 1,000 ripostes, paradoxes, wisecracks: Work is the curse of the drinking classes; I can resist everything except temptation; etc. 258pp. 5⅜ x 8½. 20602-5 Pa. $5.95

SHAKESPEARE LEXICON AND QUOTATION DICTIONARY, Alexander Schmidt. Full definitions, locations, shades of meaning in every word in plays and poems. More than 50,000 exact quotations. 1,485pp. 6½ x 9¼. 2-vol. set.
Vol. 1: 22726-X Pa. $16.95
Vol. 2: 22727-8 Pa. $16.95

SELECTED POEMS, Emily Dickinson. Over 100 best-known, best-loved poems by one of America's foremost poets, reprinted from authoritative early editions. No comparable edition at this price. Index of first lines. 64pp. 5$^{3}/_{16}$ x 8¼.
26466-1 Pa. $1.00

CELEBRATED CASES OF JUDGE DEE (DEE GOONG AN), translated by Robert van Gulik. Authentic 18th-century Chinese detective novel; Dee and associates solve three interlocked cases. Led to van Gulik's own stories with same characters. Extensive introduction. 9 illustrations. 237pp. 5⅜ x 8½. 23337-5 Pa. $6.95

THE MALLEUS MALEFICARUM OF KRAMER AND SPRENGER, translated by Montague Summers. Full text of most important witchhunter's "bible," used by both Catholics and Protestants. 278pp. 6⅝ x 10. 22802-9 Pa. $12.95

SPANISH STORIES/CUENTOS ESPAÑOLES: A Dual-Language Book, Angel Flores (ed.). Unique format offers 13 great stories in Spanish by Cervantes, Borges, others. Faithful English translations on facing pages. 352pp. 5⅜ x 8½.
25399-6 Pa. $8.95

THE CHICAGO WORLD'S FAIR OF 1893: A Photographic Record, Stanley Appelbaum (ed.). 128 rare photos show 200 buildings, Beaux-Arts architecture, Midway, original Ferris Wheel, Edison's kinetoscope, more. Architectural emphasis; full text. 116pp. 8¼ x 11. 23990-X Pa. $9.95

OLD QUEENS, N.Y., IN EARLY PHOTOGRAPHS, Vincent F. Seyfried and William Asadorian. Over 160 rare photographs of Maspeth, Jamaica, Jackson Heights, and other areas. Vintage views of DeWitt Clinton mansion, 1939 World's Fair and more. Captions. 192pp. 8⅞ x 11. 26358-4 Pa. $12.95

CAPTURED BY THE INDIANS: 15 Firsthand Accounts, 1750-1870, Frederick Drimmer. Astounding true historical accounts of grisly torture, bloody conflicts, relentless pursuits, miraculous escapes and more, by people who lived to tell the tale. 384pp. 5⅜ x 8½. 24901-8 Pa. $8.95

THE WORLD'S GREAT SPEECHES, Lewis Copeland and Lawrence W. Lamm (eds.). Vast collection of 278 speeches of Greeks to 1970. Powerful and effective models; unique look at history. 842pp. 5⅜ x 8½. 20468-5 Pa. $14.95

THE BOOK OF THE SWORD, Sir Richard F. Burton. Great Victorian scholar/adventurer's eloquent, erudite history of the "queen of weapons"–from prehistory to early Roman Empire. Evolution and development of early swords, variations (sabre, broadsword, cutlass, scimitar, etc.), much more. 336pp. 6⅛ x 9¼.
25434-8 Pa. $9.95